NEW HAMPSHIRE

Weddings

*Three Women's Stories
of Longing for Something More*

RACHEL HAUCK

BARBOUR
PUBLISHING

ISBN 978-1-59789-629-0

Published by Barbour Publishing, Inc., P.O. Box 719, Uhrichsville, Ohio 44683, www.barbourbooks.com

Our mission is to publish and distribute inspirational products offering exceptional value and biblical encouragement to the masses.

 Member of the
Evangelical Christian
Publishers Association

Printed in the United States of America.

Dear Reader,

I hope you enjoy this book, a compilation of stories about the Lambert family. The idea for this series came from talking with author Lynn Coleman, and we enjoyed brainstorming the characters and plot lines together.

Each story focuses on letting God take control of some area of the characters' lives and how sometimes ambitions or fears get in the way of God's blessings.

As you read these stories, my heart hopes you find some new truth of God's love to apply to your own life. May you always feel His embrace.

Blessings,
Rachel Hauck

Lambert's Pride

Dedication

From Lynn:
To my granddaughter, Kayla, and the love she's brought to our lives
and who has a bit of Elizabeth Lambert inside of her.

From Rachel:
Thanks to Lynn for calling me one July afternoon
with an invitation and an idea.
Thanks to my husband, Tony, ACRWCrit7,
and my fireman brother, Pete, for his contribution and advice.
And to Dad and Mom who always said I could.
Dedicated to Jesus, my Beloved and my Friend.

Chapter 1

Elizabeth Lambert rushed through the kitchen door and hustled up the back stairs to her room, taking them two at a time.

"Dinner's on the table, Beth," her grandma said when she scurried past.

"No time," Elizabeth called over her shoulder. "Sinclair's wants me to come in as soon as I can."

In her room, she shoved the door partially closed and slipped from the slacks and blouse she'd worn to Lambert's Furniture into her uniform for Sinclair's, the department store where she worked several evenings a week.

From the bottom of the stairs, Grandma admonished her, "You can't work seventy hours a week without taking time to eat a healthy meal."

"I'll get a burger on the way," Elizabeth replied in a clear, loud voice.

With quick, short strokes, she ran a comb through her hair and pulled it back with a red ribbon. A subtle knock caused her to turn toward the door. "Enter," she said.

Grandma pushed the door open and stood in the doorway, her hands on her ample hips. "A fast-food burger is not a healthy meal."

Elizabeth laughed and started to hang up the clothes she'd worn to the office. "I'm used to it."

Grandma settled on the edge of the bed. "Why don't you take a break from all this work? There's no need—"

"You know I didn't want to come to White Birch in the first place," Elizabeth interrupted, tossing her low-heeled pumps onto the closet floor in exchange for a pair of white sneakers. "But if Dad insists I take a break from school to learn the value of money and good, hard work, then *work* is what I'm going to do."

She plopped onto the floor and stuffed her feet into her white leather sneakers. "Besides, I've been living at this pace since my freshman year at college. Grabbing a burger on the run is nothing new."

"Doesn't mean I have to like it."

Elizabeth looked at her grandmother's wise, gentle face. "I appreciate your concern, but right now, eating a well-balanced meal is the least of my concerns."

Grandma stood and smiled. "You better run along, or you'll be late."

Elizabeth hopped up, then grabbed her backpack and car keys. In a soft tone, she admitted, "I know I don't seem grateful, Grandma, but I do appreciate all you and Grandpa have done for me."

"We know life in White Birch is a far cry from the life you can live in Boston, but we love having you here."

Elizabeth leaned over and kissed her grandma on the cheek. "Well, if I have to be someplace other than Boston, being with you and Grandpa is a pretty cool alternative."

Grandma beamed. "Well, hurry, or you won't even have time for a quick burger." She made a shuffling motion with her arms and feet.

Elizabeth chuckled and darted down the stairs with a quick glance at the large hall clock. She would barely make it on time even if she *didn't* stop for a burger.

Her father's classic 1973 Volkswagen Super Beetle sat on the edge of the driveway; its candy apple red paint glistened in the evening light. Tossing her backpack into the passenger seat, Elizabeth slipped in behind the wheel.

The restored car, a graduation present from her parents, came with a condition: Spend a season working in the family business in White Birch, New Hampshire. When she balked at the idea, they sweetened the deal, offering to pay all of her graduate school tuition if she agreed to their proposal.

Shifting into fourth gear, Elizabeth zipped through the center of White Birch. The quaint New England town looked to her as though it'd grown from a Norman Rockwell painting.

Remembering the discussion with her parents set her on edge. After all, at twenty-three, she had the right to make her own decisions about life. But in the whole vast scheme of things, she decided a summer in the quaint town was a small price to pay for an all-expense-paid ride to grad school—plus the title to the red classic car. She'd wanted to go to grad school for about as long as she wanted to inherit her father's vintage car.

To her surprise, Elizabeth enjoyed the few weeks she'd spent living with her grandparents, though their devotion to the Lord exposed her unrequited faith. The senior Lamberts sought God at every turn, over every issue. Even the decision to let Elizabeth live with them came after several days of prayer.

How could anyone depend on God so much? Elizabeth preferred to chart her own course in life, depending on reason instead of the ethereal world of prayer.

All at once, a loud bang resonated in her ears, and the little car swerved hard to the right. Elizabeth gripped the steering wheel tighter, and with one foot on the brake and the other on the clutch, she slowed the car and forced it safely to the shoulder.

Trembling, she got out of the car and examined the outside. "Great," she mumbled, the flat right tire testifying to her problems. She knelt to inspect the damage. Pieces of shredded tire littered the road.

I'm going to be really late. She sighed, making her way to the front of the car. She popped the VW's round trunk and peered inside. *Figures. No spare.* She let the trunk close with a bang.

Propping herself against the trunk lid, Elizabeth contemplated her next move. She had her cell phone in her backpack, so she knew she could call one of her cousins for help. But calling on a Lambert meant the whole family would somehow become involved in this minor incident. During her short time in White Birch, Elizabeth had quickly learned that nothing seemed sacred or private among the Lambert clan.

I'll handle the problem myself. She stepped around to the passenger side, fetched her backpack, locked the doors, and started jogging toward Sinclair's.

Kavan Donovan focused his binoculars and scanned a local camping area from the top of the run-down White Birch fire tower.

Aerial surveillance replaced most of the forest ranger's manual chores, but Kavan still climbed the tower to survey the area. Something about the ancient tower enchanted him. In fact, he'd persuaded the forestry division to invest money in its renovation.

A light June breeze tickled the treetops and scattered the thin trails of smoke rising from campfires. The hushed wind stirred his spirit. "God, You're so good." His gaze surveyed the beautiful peaks of the White Mountains.

A couple of young men hiked into his magnified view, and Kavan watched as they made their way along the mountain path.

Setting the binoculars aside, he checked the sky overhead. Clear and blue, no sign of rain. *When did it rain last? Six weeks, maybe,* he thought. It was a little too dry for his liking.

A flash of light nabbed his attention, and with calculated motion, he reached for the binoculars.

A flare. Kavan zeroed in on the area with the binoculars. The white smoky trail led to the general location of the hikers. He grabbed his radio.

"White Birch, this is Donovan. We've got hikers in trouble on the south ridge, 150-foot line. Clear."

The voice of Rick Weber crackled over the radio. "They climbed that high? Go ahead." He sounded dubious.

"Yes. Go ahead."

"I'll send out the chopper. Weber clear."

"Donovan clear." Kavan searched the mountainside for a glimpse of the hikers.

"Kavan," Rick called back in a low voice. "Switch to channel eight five."

Kavan clicked the dial on his radio. "What's up?" he asked.

"When you come in, be ready to rescue yourself from Travis. Rumor has it he's on the warpath over the expenses you submitted."

Kavan exhaled and lowered his arm, letting the binoculars dangle from his right hand while gripping the radio in his left. With a shake of his head, he said, "Thanks. I'm on my way in now."

He took one last glance around the venerable tower before starting for the steps.

Ever since he'd started working on the fire tower refurbishment, his boss, Travis Knight, had scrutinized all his expense reports with a critical eye.

Driving down the mountainside, Kavan recalled the debate he had had with

Travis. "You've barely started the project and already I'm getting heat from the division about the expense."

"Travis, I've ordered several hundred board feet of pine and a few large-cell batteries for energy."

"Large-cell batteries? You're wasting division money."

"I planned for the energy cells in the refurbishment budget. Otherwise, we'd have to run power lines to the tower."

Travis shook his head. "I won't have it look as if my office is frivolous with expenses."

"Frivolous? Pine board and batteries are not frivolous." Kavan tried to reason with him, but Travis turned a deaf ear and ordered him to hold off on any more expenses.

Kavan hated the memory of that day. Now, arriving at the office, he dreaded a second confrontation. He addressed Travis's secretary when he entered.

"Hi, Kavan," Cheryl said sweetly, winking at him with mascara-laden lashes.

"Evening, Cheryl. Travis around?"

She tipped her head toward the office door. "Careful, he's in a mood."

"So I've heard." Kavan knocked lightly on the director's door.

"Come in," a deep voice bellowed.

"Evening, Travis," Kavan said, shutting the door behind him.

Travis Knight looked up, the skin under his chin jiggling like jelly. His dark eyes glared at Kavan, and he tossed some papers on the edge of the desk. "What's the meaning of this?"

❧❧

Elizabeth jogged toward Sinclair's, determined to make it on time. When the short, loud blip of a siren sounded behind her, she jumped off the road with a yelp.

The passenger-side window of a White Birch police car slid down. The officer leaned over and peered up at her. "What are you doing?"

Elizabeth scowled at yet another member of the Lambert family. "Going to work," she said, then added with a thump of her fist on the car door. "What's the big idea of scaring me half to death?"

Her cousin Jeff Simmons gave his wide, teasing grin. "Sorry, Beth, just messing with you."

"You about gave me a heart attack."

"Get in." Jeff pulled the handle and pushed the door open. Elizabeth tossed her backpack inside.

"Why are you jogging to work?" he asked, starting in the direction of the Sinclair's super department store.

Elizabeth hesitated to answer. She loved her cousin Jeff, but if she told him about the tire, he'd do the Lambert family thing and fix it for her. She gave him the first excuse that came to mind. "I need the exercise."

He laughed. "Yeah, right. I saw your car on the side of the road back there."

Elizabeth looked over at her cousin and confessed. "The right front tire blew."

"Ah," he said.

They rode in silence for a minute before she said softly, "Thanks for the lift."

"Lamberts stick together."

"So I've noticed." A wry smile touched her lips.

"A little overwhelming, is it?" Jeff asked, his tone understanding.

"Just a tad. Everywhere I turn, there's a Lambert family member, or worse a family friend, watching me. It's like living in a fishbowl."

"No one's watching you, Beth. The folks in White Birch are just friendly and interested."

"You mean nosy," Elizabeth retorted.

"No, I don't mean nosy." Jeff gave her a sidelong glance. "You like your privacy, don't you?"

Elizabeth laughed and shook her head. "Just a little."

Jeff continued. "I was the opposite when I went to college. Didn't know anyone, struggled with that alone-in-a-crowd feeling. I hated those first few months on campus. I never told anyone, but I think Grandma always knew."

A picture of bighearted Jeff wandering the campus alone caused a wave of mercy to splash Elizabeth's heart. But his situation didn't compare to hers. "I'm the opposite. Grad school can't come soon enough."

Jeff shook his head with a chuckle. "It's the next hill to conquer, is it?"

She twisted her lips to hide a wry grin. "I wouldn't put it like that. . .exactly."

Jeff laughed. "I hope you get the school you want."

"There's no doubt I will," Elizabeth said, confidence rising within her.

"How do you like working for Lambert's Furniture?" Jeff asked, slowing to turn into Sinclair's giant parking lot.

Elizabeth shrugged and looked out the passenger window. "It's a job."

Actually, she enjoyed working at the family business, though she would never admit it. Seeing the business from the inside, she gained a new respect for Lambert ingenuity and vision.

He stopped near the front entrance of Sinclair's. "Here you go."

Elizabeth grabbed her backpack and hopped out of the car. "Thanks, Jeff."

"Anytime, cousin. Would you like a ride home?"

"No, thanks." She hurried inside and ran past the store's café-style grill. Breathless, she paused long enough to order a grilled ham and cheese. The sandwich waited for her when she came down from the employee locker room.

She ate as she walked toward the front. The evening manager, Joann Floyd, met her in the main aisle. "Take over the customer service desk."

"All right." Elizabeth swallowed the last of the sandwich.

"And can you stay and help me close? MaryAnn called in sick again." Joann fell into step with Elizabeth.

"Sure," she replied, stepping behind the counter and signing into the register. In the past few weeks, the twenty-nine-year-old Joann had become more of a friend than a boss. Elizabeth hated to refuse her request, knowing the extra work would fall to the dedicated manager.

A smile of relief lit Joann's oval face. "Thank you."

Elizabeth shrugged. "What else is there to do in this dinky town?"

Joann answered without preamble. "Meet a nice man, fall in love, get married, have a few kids."

Elizabeth groaned. "You've gone crazy from too much work, Jo. When have you *ever* heard me talk about love, marriage, and kids?" She shook with an exaggerated shudder.

Joann laughed. "Well, I've never heard you talk about it, but it's got to be more fun than grad school."

"You'd rather I stay in White Birch and forget about my plans," Elizabeth said, picking through the basket of returned items.

"Oh no, I don't want you to forget about your plans. I want you to change them."

Elizabeth chuckled at Joann's forthright confession. "Nothing doing. I'm getting my master's in nuclear engineering, maybe a Ph.D."

"And then what?"

Elizabeth shrugged. "I don't know," she said as Joann headed off to check on a price for a register customer. "I'll cross that bridge when I come to it," she muttered to herself.

For the next hour, the grad-school-bound Lambert handled refunds and sorted the return items. Occasionally Joann walked by, whispering words about love or romance in her ear.

"There are other things in life besides romance," Elizabeth whispered in response.

"I need to return these." A smooth, baritone voice rose from the other side of the counter.

Elizabeth looked up into the chocolate brown eyes of a handsome, uniformed forest ranger. The sparkle in his eyes caused her heartbeat to quicken. Her voice wobbled when she asked, "Do you have a receipt?"

"Right here." He reached into his shirt pocket and pulled out the thin register tape. "After you do the refund, I need to purchase these items again."

Elizabeth peered over the counter and into his cart. It was loaded with all kinds of kids' crafts: poster boards, paints, colored paper, balloons, and sparkles. With an upward glance, she asked, "Whatever for?"

Chapter 2

For a moment, Kavan felt lost in her large blue eyes. Sapphires set against pure white silk. Realizing he stared, he shifted his gaze and said, "I'm sorry, what did you say?"

She laughed. "You said you wanted to return these items and then purchase them again?"

"Right." Kavan's gaze met hers, and he smiled. "Seems the New Hampshire Division of Forests and Lands can't afford a few balloons and poster board."

Surprise sparked in her eyes. "So you're buying them with your own money?"

"Fun tools make it easy for me to teach the kids about fire safety."

"And our tax dollars don't pay for it?" she asked, incredulous.

Kavan shook his head and said woefully, "Politics."

The lovely brunette behind the service desk recoiled. "Politics? Over kids, crafts, and a few balloons?"

"No reasoning for the whims of the politically minded."

"Oh," she said, her lips forming a perfect O.

A distinct desire to get to know the woman behind Sinclair's service counter stirred in Kavan. Casually, he read her name tag: Elizabeth.

About that time, a lighthearted male voice said from over his shoulder, "Here, Beth." A brown paper bag slid across the counter.

"What's this?" she asked, looking past Kavan to the man behind him.

"Dinner. Grandma sent it over."

Kavan watched Elizabeth flare, her face reddening. "I told her that I would. . ."

"Kavan! Hello." A hand clapped on his shoulder.

He turned to the familiar voice. "Jeff." He extended his hand.

"How are you?" Jeff greeted him with a hearty handshake.

"Good. It's been awhile."

"Too long," Jeff said. "I see you've met my cousin Beth."

"No, I haven't had the pleasure." Kavan peered again into her jewel-like eyes.

"Well, let me do the honors. Beth Lambert, meet my old friend, Kavan Donovan. Beth is my cousin from Boston."

Her silky hand slipped into his. "Nice to meet you, Kavan."

The melodic sound of her voice speaking his name stunned his heart. "The pleasure is all mine, Beth."

"Elizabeth," she said, pointing to her name tag. "It's Elizabeth."

"Ah yes," Jeff said, a lilt in his voice, "she prefers not to use her country-cousin name."

She eyed him with ire. "Isn't there a crime in town you need to solve?"

Kavan stifled a grin, but Jeff chuckled heartily. "Calm down, Beth; I'm going."

"Here, take this with you." She held out the brown paper bag. "I told Grandma I'd get something to eat, and I did."

"She's just watching out for you," Jeff stated. "When I stopped by Grandpa and Grandma's to see what Gran made for dessert, I told her about your car. She thought maybe you didn't have time to grab that burger you mentioned."

Kavan listened, letting his thoughts linger over the picture of family love and care Jeff's explanation painted. His family life had been very different from that of the Lamberts. Too many lonely nights eating frozen dinners, sitcom reruns his only company.

Moving his thoughts out of the shadowy past, Kavan tuned in to Jeff's monologue. "I got some good news and some bad news about your car."

"My car?" Elizabeth asked while ringing up Kavan's refund.

"The good news is I had your car towed to the garage."

Elizabeth stopped working. "Jeff, you shouldn't have. I can take care of my car."

Jeff held up his hands in surrender. "I know, but I'm family, and I'm helping whether you like it or not."

Elizabeth smiled in defeat. Kavan felt captivated by her beauty. But her precious attention centered on Jeff, not him. "What's the bad news?"

"You need to replace all your tires. Besides the flat right front, the tread is thin on two more, and the fourth one has a nail."

Disappointment etched the elegant planes of her face. "You're kidding, Jeff. How much is that going to cost?"

"Don't worry about it. We'll take care of it."

Elizabeth slammed her hand on the counter, startling Kavan and Jeff. "No you won't." She leaned toward her cousin, waving her index finger in his face. "Don't even try to pull one of your family strings to get me some deal and leave me feeling eternally indebted."

Amused, Kavan watched. He liked the woman's resolve and determination. She didn't think twice about facing down the brawny police officer. Cousin or not, it showed guts.

"All right, all right." Jeff held up his hands. "You're looking at about two hundred dollars."

With a flurry, Elizabeth finished the forestry refund. Kavan engaged Jeff in casual conversation, keeping one eye on the White Birch police officer and one on Elizabeth. He'd been to Sinclair's a thousand times and never saw her before.

When the conversation with Jeff lulled, he heard himself ask the curly-haired brunette, "How long have you worked here?"

"Two weeks." She handed him a credit slip and a pen. "Sign here, and give a reason for the return."

"She's up here from Boston, fresh out of MIT." Jeff spouted more detail.

"Came to spend some time with the family. She works for Will over at Lambert's Furniture during the day."

Kavan whistled low and contemplated Elizabeth in a new light. "MIT, I'm impressed."

Jeff's radio suddenly squawked, demanding his attention. "Gotta go. Beth, what time do you get off? I'll come by and pick you up."

"I already told you; I don't need a ride."

"How are you going to get home? Jog? What time do you get off?" Jeff demanded.

"One," she blurted out as if it were a final confession.

Jeff glanced at Kavan with a smirk, then back at his cousin. "I'll see you at one." Jeff headed for the door. Suddenly he stopped and pointed at Kavan. "Have Kavan tell you about the time he saved my life."

Elizabeth raised a brow at the broad-shouldered redhead, charmed by his gentle manners and ruddy cheeks. She wondered how he'd saved her cousin's life and why the mere mention of the fact caused a crimson hue to wash over his face.

"You saved Jeff's life?"

"He likes to embarrass me." Kavan fussed with the balloons and construction paper. "I need to buy some other items for the kids, so I'll just check out at one of the registers."

"Have a good night." She studied his straight back as he walked away, disappointed that he no longer stood at the service desk. She liked the ranger, drawn by the kindness and sincerity that emanated from his deep-set eyes.

Elizabeth's musings froze at the sudden realization that Kavan intrigued her. She did not have time for romance or a summer love. Graduate school loomed on her horizon, and she was determined to see her goal to completion.

I'm not stopping five yards short of the goal line. With determination, she shoved her curiosity and attraction for the man aside.

When Joann returned to the service desk from roaming the store, Elizabeth blurted out, "I forbid you to talk about love or romance, Jo."

"Forbid?" Joann echoed, arching a brow. "What sparked that comment?"

"Never mind." Elizabeth exchanged money from one of the cashiers standing in front of the service desk and gave her several rolls of change.

Joann stared at her, one hand on her hip. "I make no promises."

Elizabeth started to reply, but at that moment, eighteen-year-old Millie hurled herself against the counter and asked in a breathless murmur, "Joann, can I please go on break? Mark is meeting me—"

Joann leaned forward and asked in the same breathless whisper, "You two still an item?"

Millie blushed. Elizabeth rolled her eyes.

"Sure, go on," Joann said with flare. "Who am I to stand in the way of true love?"

Elizabeth laughed at the melodrama. "You're ridiculous, you know that?"

"Never," Joann countered with a flip of her hair.

"You take the cake on romance."

"Never mind the cake," Joann said, picking up the clipboard and reading the schedule. "Open register ten so Millie can go on break."

"For you, yes. For love, no," Elizabeth answered with a light laugh and headed for the register.

"So, we meet again." Kavan steered his cart between the magazine rack and the register. He smiled and winked.

A breezy feeling fluttered across her stomach. "I think you are following me, sir. I'll have you know my cousin is a White Birch police officer." Elizabeth scanned Kavan's items and dropped them into plastic bags.

"Well then, me lady." Kavan bowed with a large sweep of his arm, an Irish lilt to his words. "I'll be minding me manners."

His accent and exaggerated movements made her laugh. "You never told me how you saved Jeff's life."

Kavan swiped his debit card through the checkout terminal to pay for his purchase. "Well, if I told you everything about me, you'd be bored and less inclined to join me for dinner."

Bold. Clever. But as much as the ranger fascinated her, dinner for two might spawn romantic notions, and Elizabeth refused to let her heart, or anyone else's, dictate to her head.

Nevertheless, she didn't want to hurt or embarrass Kavan. Thankfully, she had a legitimate excuse for turning down his offer. "I work most nights." She cashed out his purchase and passed over his receipt.

Slowly, he slipped his debit card into his wallet and reached for the bags. "I see." He paused. "Maybe some night when you're free."

"Maybe." She shrugged, knowing the chances were slim.

"Good night, Elizabeth."

"Good night, Kavan."

On his back porch, Kavan popped the top from a cold bottle of soda. He eased down into a polished oak rocker and set it into motion. Two German shepherds, Fred and Ginger, lay at his feet.

In the distance, a glow of light from the town center burned above the tree-tops. And on Kavan's kitchen windowsills, oil lamps burned against the darkness.

Overhead, the night sky glistened with starlight, and the songs of crickets filled the air.

Peaceful and reflective, Kavan relived the evening's events. It had been good to see Jeff Simmons. Hard to imagine that they'd once been best friends. Strange how time and life's pursuits changed relationships. He grinned thinking of Jeff's claim that he'd saved his life. Truth of the matter, it'd been the other way around.

Jeff saved his life, though it had nothing to do with life *or* death.

An image of Elizabeth crept into his mind and painted warm colors over his thoughts. Growing up in White Birch, the Lambert clan was the closest thing Kavan had to a real family. But somehow, he'd never had the pleasure of meeting Elizabeth. If he had, he was sure he would have remembered.

Standing behind Sinclair's counter, she appeared young and innocent. Jeff's announcement that she graduated from MIT added a whole new dimension to the resolute, blue-eyed woman. He could still hear the slap of her hand on the counter, warning Jeff not to pull any favors to get new tires for her car.

Independent, he thought, *a good attribute for a ranger's wife.*

Just then Fred picked up his head and bayed at the moon. Ginger echoed. Kavan stopped rocking and looked down at them with a furrowed brow. "What? It's okay for you two to have a companion, but not your old master?"

The shepherds tilted their heads, as if trying to understand. Kavan chuckled and scratched Fred behind the ears. Setting the rocker into motion again, he took a swig of the cola and addressed his Lord in a low, intimate voice. "Only You know what kind of wife I need. I trust You to help me find her."

The shrill ring of the kitchen telephone ignited a barking frenzy. "Settle," Kavan commanded the dogs. "I hear it." He hurried through the back door and reached for the receiver on the third ring.

"Hello." He glanced at the clock. *12:45 a.m.*

"Kavan, it's Jeff. Sorry to call so late."

Kavan grinned. "Seems like old times."

"Well, it'll really seem like old times when I ask you to do me a favor."

Kavan's deep laugh reverberated through the kitchen. "A favor after all these years? It'll cost you."

"Wait till you hear the favor." Merriment laced Jeff's words.

"Proceed with caution," Kavan retorted.

"Pick up Beth from Sinclair's for me and take her home. She's living with Grandpa and Grandma."

Kavan slid the mouthpiece away from his mouth and drew a deep breath. His heart thumped in his chest. His reaction to hearing Elizabeth's name surprised him.

"You there?" Jeff asked.

Kavan breathed out slowly. "You're really taking us back to high school days now, old buddy. I thought you were picking her up."

"I'm processing a domestic violence case and won't get out of here on time. The wife is pressing charges."

"Sad," Kavan managed to say.

"Very. Kids involved. Makes me want to—well, never mind. You going to pick her up or not?"

"With all the Lamberts in this town, you call me?"

"I've never seen any of the Lamberts look at her the way you did tonight.

17

I thought maybe the two of you—"

Kavan blurted out, "Your imagination causes you to see things that aren't there."

Jeff's bass laugh rumbled through the line. "Don't kid a kidder. Can you pick her up?"

Kavan checked the clock again. *Twelve fifty*. If he agreed, he needed to do so quickly. "All right, I'll do it, but you owe me, Simmons. You owe me."

"Thanks, buddy."

Hanging up, Kavan grabbed his keys and headed for his truck. He regretted not taking the time to clean it out. The seats were covered with dust and dog hair from Fred and Ginger's last ride. Quickly he wiped them with an old but clean rag and started the engine.

Driving to Sinclair's, he imagined what he would say to her. His invitation to dinner met with resistance and little hope for a future date. A nervous twitch ran through him. What if she refused his offer to drive her home? Surely Jeff called and warned her.

Too late now, he thought, turning into the store's parking lot. He spied Elizabeth just inside the doors, leaning against the wall, arms folded, peering out.

"Hi," Kavan said, slowly approaching.

Her eyes showed surprise. "Hi. Kavan, right?"

"Right." He shuffled his feet, feeling awkward. Seven years out of high school and the sight of a pretty lady still made him feel like a clumsy ox.

"Did you forget something? Glue perhaps?" She grinned a saucy grin, exposing white, even teeth.

Kavan laughed. "No, got all the glue I need. Actually, I'm here for you."

Elizabeth stood up straight, though her arms still crossed her petite frame. "For me? Where's Jeff?"

"Tied up with a case. He called and asked if I'd pick you up."

Kavan saw the muscles of her face tighten. And her eyes narrowed. "What is it with this family of mine? They hover and watch. . ." Elizabeth paused, wriggling her fingers in the air as if kneading dough. "I'm sorry Jeff brought you out here at one o'clock in the morning for nothing." With that, she turned and walked back into the store.

Kavan followed her. A tall blond woman behind the counter glanced at him, then at Elizabeth. A mischievous grin spread across her face.

"Joann, can you give me a ride home?" Elizabeth asked.

"Ah, honey, I live all the way across town. What about your friend here? Hi, I'm Joann Floyd."

"Kavan Donovan." He shook her hand.

Elizabeth protested, motioning to Kavan. "He's a stranger."

Joann winked at him. "But I have plans."

Elizabeth cocked her head to one side and narrowed her eyes. "Sure you do. At one in the morning?"

"My husband rented a movie. Besides, you don't want to make Kavan come all the way out here for nothing."

"I didn't ask him to come out here."

Joann answered with a shrug. She picked up the cash drawer she'd been counting and ducked into the back office.

Elizabeth stared at Kavan, one hand on her hip. With resignation, she said, "Guess you're my ride."

"Jeff should have called to tell you." Certain he saw a sparkle in her blue eyes, he continued. "My truck is right outside. Curbside service."

They walked in silence. Kavan held the passenger door open for her. As she climbed in, she said, "I overreacted. Seeing you here on Jeff's behalf, well, embarrassed me."

Kavan paused, his hand on the door. "Embarrassed you?"

"Yes, where I come from, one doesn't pick up a stranger from work in the wee hours of the morning."

Kavan pushed the door shut and peered through the open window. "Well," he said, "in White Birch, we do."

Chapter 3

Elizabeth stretched, stifling a yawn. Flopping against the customer service counter, she faced another mindless night at Sinclair's. Working days at Lambert's Furniture, then evenings and weekends at the superstore left her exhausted. And the summer had barely begun.

She glanced up to see Kavan Donovan standing at the service counter, off to one side, watching her. He flashed his lopsided, yet rakish smile.

Instantly, she shot upright and smoothed her hands over her wrinkled smock. Was it her imagination, or were her hands trembling?

Over the past two weeks, Kavan dropped by the store almost every evening. If he didn't, Elizabeth noted his absence with a sharp pang of longing.

"Hi," he said, moving closer.

Elizabeth smiled easily. "What did you forget this time?"

He held up a slender, narrow package, and Elizabeth recognized the familiar toothbrush casing.

"Fred ate mine," Kavan explained.

She gaped at him. "Who's Fred?"

With a deadpan expression, he said, "My dog."

Elizabeth laughed. "Is that anything like 'my dog ate my homework'?" The warmth of his presence wrapped around her heart.

"No, completely different. Not even in the same 'dog eating my stuff' category." Kavan whipped a mangled toothbrush from the pocket of his green khakis.

She inspected the damaged toothbrush. "Hmm."

"Hmm? What's that supposed to mean?" he asked, raising one eyebrow. He placed the new toothbrush on the counter for Elizabeth to scan. "You doubt my story."

"Oh no." She stifled a chuckle. "Sounds perfectly plausible to me. That'll be two fifty-six."

Kavan handed over three ones. "Are you busy tomorrow night?"

"Working again."

"No rest for the weary, eh? Don't they ever give you a night off?"

"Yes, but people call me to work for them, so I do."

"What are you doing with all the money you're making?"

"Spending it on new tires," Elizabeth said with a quick wink, referencing the night they met.

Kavan nodded with a grin.

"Other than that, I'm saving it for my parents," she added.

He furrowed his brow. "You're giving money to your parents?"

"No, I'm proving to them I know the value of a hard-earned dollar. It was my dad's idea, mainly. Send his overachieving daughter back to the family roots, work hard, and take a break from school. I think Dad's afraid I'll turn into an academic with no grasp of day-to-day life. So, I'm. . ." Elizabeth stopped midsentence. She said too much. How did the forthright yet humble ranger rouse her to speak her inner thoughts?

"Working is a worthwhile endeavor," Kavan said in polite response.

"That's what I've been told," Elizabeth said with an edge, handing Kavan his change and toothbrush.

Kavan reached for his purchase and dropped the loose change into a charity basket by the register. "If you have a day off soon, give me a call. Jeff has my number. We could go for pizza."

Elizabeth struggled against the desire to say yes. She was leery of getting close to the man who made her wonder about romantic love for the first time since she was a giggly preteen.

"Have a nice night, Kavan." The ranger turned and walked away. As she watched him leave, a distinguished-looking woman with silver hair and perfect makeup approached the service counter. The customer caught Elizabeth staring.

"He's a handsome one, isn't he?"

Startled, Elizabeth gasped, "Oh, hello, um, may I help you?"

"Kavan Donovan, right?" the woman asked.

Elizabeth stared at the older woman. "He's a friend of my cousin's." Once more, she asked how she could serve the woman.

Instead of announcing what she needed, the woman persisted with the subject of Kavan. "Perhaps a friend of yours, too? A special friend?"

"No!" The word resounded around the service counter like a trumpet blast.

"Too bad," the woman said, moving on to her Sinclair's business.

Elizabeth succinctly finished the transaction, hoping for no more personal prying.

Joann passed by the service area as the woman left with her refund in hand. "Why is it that people are so intrigued with romance?" Elizabeth asked, tossing the woman's returned items into a waiting cart with unusual force.

Her boss stopped. "What are you talking about? What people?"

"Never mind." Elizabeth dismissed the question with a slight wave of her hand. "I'm just tired."

"No, out with it." Joann propped one elbow on the counter. "You got me curious now. Since I'm Queen of Romance—"

Joann's moniker jolted a light laugh out of Elizabeth. She broke down and explained. "Some lady came to the counter as Kavan was leaving and—"

"Ah," Joann interrupted. "This is about Kavan."

"No, it's about why the whole world thinks a young, single female must have a man."

Joann chuckled. "The whole world?"

Elizabeth wrinkled her nose. "You know what I mean."

"Let me ask you a question," Joann started, resting her hand lightly on Elizabeth's arm. "Why are you so adamant against falling in love?"

"I'm not against falling in love. It's fine for most people."

"Just not for you," Joann responded with a shake of her head. "You, my friend, are missing out on one of the best wonders of life. I can't imagine life without David."

Elizabeth didn't know what to say. Since high school, she'd been so busy with academic achievement that love seemed more like a nuisance than a wonder.

When her friends lost all sense of themselves over a cute boy, she plowed ahead with school, making the grade and winning awards. While her friends crumbled with broken hearts, she soared.

During those days, Elizabeth determined never to become one of romance's walking wounded, foiled by the illusions of lasting love.

"You're one of the lucky ones, Joann."

"No luck, Elizabeth. Love. David is a gift from God. And you better be watching, 'cause God just might grace you with the same amazing gift."

Elizabeth sighed. "I'm going on break, Jo."

"Good idea."

The golden day faded to twilight blue as Kavan drove down County Road toward home. A New Hampshire summer breeze passed through his open window, and he rested his tanned arm along the door of the truck.

He'd not made his routine stop by Sinclair's to see Elizabeth, though he longed for an excuse to go by the superstore. Yet, he needed nothing. His pantry shelves were starting to overflow with superfluous stuff he'd purchased on routine stops by the store to see her and say hello.

Careful, Kavan coached himself. *She'll get wise to you.*

During the past week, he'd run into more Lamberts than he had in the past year. Each one thanked him for helping Jeff a few weeks ago by fetching Elizabeth.

Grandma Betty seemed especially pleased about his acquaintance with her granddaughter. He talked with her one afternoon when she brought several of the great-grandchildren to the state park.

She whispered in his ear, "If that granddaughter of mine would get her head out of the academia clouds for a moment, she'd see what a great catch you are, Kavan Donovan."

Kavan appreciated Grandma Betty's encouragement, but pushing Elizabeth would do the exact opposite of what he wanted. Already she resisted his attempts to get together outside of Sinclair's main aisle. It frustrated him to think she might never surrender to his overtures, though he admired her decisiveness.

No, a clan of Lamberts wouldn't bring Elizabeth into his arms. Only the hand of God could move her heart in his direction.

The blast of a gunshot pealed through the evening air. Kavan slammed on his brakes and stuck his head out the window. He quickly scanned the area.

What's going on?

Another shot cut through the silence. Two white-tailed deer darted across the road followed by two young hunters.

The boys stopped in the road and fired a third time in the direction of the fleeing deer.

Poachers. "Stop!" Kavan jumped out of the truck, incensed.

The poachers swerved at the sound of his voice.

Kavan flashed his forestry badge. "Hunting season starts in November, boys. Put your guns down." He started walking toward them.

The hunters appeared to be in their late teens. They stared at him for a moment, then raced away toward a dark cluster of trees.

"Drop your guns," he hollered, chasing them into the growing shadows. He hurdled rocks and fallen limbs and waded through the thick green forest floor.

As he gained on the poachers, their rusty red pickup came into view.

"Let's go. Let's go," one of the boys yelled, tumbling into the bed of the truck while the other fumbled with the driver's side door. The engine roared to life.

"You're in violation of New Hampshire hunting ordinances," Kavan bellowed.

The truck accelerated, and the driver aimed it toward a dirt road. Kavan leapt toward the fleeing vehicle, counting on his authority as a ranger to intimidate the young men. "Stop!"

The driver jerked the wheel, grazing Kavan's side with the right front fender. He twisted and turned, trying to maneuver out of the truck's path. He tumbled headfirst down a steep ravine.

Bouncing head over heels toward the bottom, Kavan's knee smacked the ground over and over. Finally, he slid to a stop. The walls of the narrow chasm claimed him like a fortress.

Every part of his body burned and ached. He struggled to stand, but a fiery pain shot through his knee and forced him down again.

"Lord, rescue me," Kavan whispered and slumped to the forest floor. He hoped someone would drive by and see his truck, but few traveled along the side of County Road.

Falling back against the mossy growth covering the forest floor, he set his hand over his head and whispered prayers to Jesus.

❧❧

Elizabeth woke the next morning, weary. Feeling in a fog, she moved through her morning routine, grateful for her first Sunday off in a long time.

She hated to admit it, but perhaps she did need a break in her schedule. She'd gone straight from studying for finals to working day and night at Lambert's Furniture and Sinclair's.

"Good morning, Beth," Grandma said, catching Elizabeth after she'd showered and dressed. The older woman peered around the door casing of Elizabeth's room.

"Morning, Grandma."

"You look tired, Beth."

"I'm fine, really."

Grandma remained in the doorway. "You can't keep up this pace."

"I've endured worse."

"Perhaps, but even in school you had breaks between terms. A night or two off during the week." Grandma moved to the antique rocker by the bay window.

Elizabeth ran a comb though her wet curls. "I can't remember that far back."

"It's only been a little over a month since you graduated," Grandma chortled.

"Feels like years."

"Well, this old woman here"—Grandma paused and tapped her chest with her finger for emphasis—"takes one day a week to literally rest. No cooking, cleaning, or running errands. You should consider doing the same."

"That idea sounds foreign to me, Grandma. I'm used to being on the go, studying or working on projects. Sitting around seems like a waste of time."

"It's good for the heart and the soul to slow down one day a week, rest, and ponder. I always hear the voice of the Lord so much clearer after a day of no activity." Grandma got up, patted Elizabeth on the arm, and started to leave. She paused at the door. "Your grandpa and I would love for you to come to church with us this morning. Ponder it, and let me know."

Ponder. What a choice word for Grandma to use.

Now that the demand of school was over, Elizabeth had time to ponder things she never had before. During nights at Sinclair's, when the hustle and bustle died down and a hush fell over the store, she allowed her thoughts to dance with images of Kavan and her heart to awaken with love for Jesus. She reveled in childhood memories of Sunday school, comforted by the notion that the Lord loved her.

But ever since high school, her commitment to the Lord remained casual. Instead, she believed more in personal destiny and triumph over the idea of a personal, intimate God.

Elizabeth decided she thought of the handsome Ranger Donovan far too often. She spent most of her shift on Saturday wishing he'd stop by for a purchase and maybe hang around for a while. But he never showed.

Grandma stepped into the room again. "Did you decide to join us?"

Elizabeth faced the pretty, plump Lambert matriarch and said, "I'd love to."

"Good," Grandma said with a quick clap of her hands. "Cereal and bread for toast is out on the kitchen counter. Help yourself." She left to get ready.

Elizabeth dressed for church and went downstairs. She poured a small bowl of wheat cereal and sat at the polished cherry table her grandpa made just after the Second World War. Nervous twitters mixed with flashes of excitement about going to church for the first time in a while.

She took a bite of cold cereal. Grandpa entered the kitchen through the back door.

"Where have you been?" Elizabeth asked, winking.

Grandpa looked at her seriously. "They found Kavan Donovan's truck by the side of the road yesterday afternoon. No one had heard from him in almost twenty-four hours. The Division of Forests and Lands sent out a search-and-rescue team."

Elizabeth dropped her spoon in the cereal bowl. Her heart thumped wildly in her chest. "Did they find him?"

Grandpa nodded. "He climbed out of an eighty-foot ravine on his backside, pulling along a busted knee."

"Is he all right?"

Grandpa reached for a coffee cup and poured. "A little cold and hungry, but he'll live." He sported a saucy grin as he sat down at the table.

"So, you were out helping to rescue him?" Elizabeth asked, spooning another bit of cereal, squirming under her grandpa's stare.

"Me? No, I was taking my morning constitutional. I think it might rain today."

Elizabeth sat back and stared at him. "Then why'd you make it sound as if he was still missing when you came in the door?"

"I just wanted to see the look on your face. They rescued Kavan last night."

"Har, har. You're a regular riot, Grandpa. A regular riot."

"You looked pretty flustered."

"Well, of course. You come in here somberly announcing that a man is missing."

"Oh, I beg to differ. Not just any man. Kavan Donovan."

Elizabeth rapped her knuckles lightly on the table. "You haven't gone senile on me, have you, Grandpa? Why would Kavan Donovan be more important to me than anyone else?" she bantered.

"You tell me? Handsome forest ranger, single, loves the Lord. . . Has a nice home up off I-89. . ."

Elizabeth sighed. Gazing into her grandpa's twinkling eyes, she shook her spoon under his nose. "I have two words for you, Grandpa: graduate school. Can you say 'graduate school'?"

"Oh sure," he said, shifting sideways in his chair and slinging one arm over the back. "Grad-u-ate school. But can you say 'true love'? 'Kavan'?"

"Honestly! What is with this town and romance? It's like reliving junior high school."

"What are you two going on about?" Grandma asked as she entered the large, airy kitchen.

"I hate to tell you, Grandma, but Grandpa has finally gone senile."

Grandma laughed and played along. "Well, then, guess we'd better get going to church so the preaching can give your grandpa the sound mind of Christ. Matt, hurry and change."

He pushed away from the table. "Two words, Bethy, two words: 'Kavan Donovan.' "

Laughing, Elizabeth tossed a wadded-up paper napkin after the older man. "How do you put up with him, Grandma?"

"Love. More than sixty years' worth."

The word sank into Elizabeth's soul like a pebble in the sand. *Love.* How could one simple, four-letter word pack so much power?

A verse from her Sunday school days flashed across her mind. *"For God so loved the world. . ."*

Elizabeth studied her grandparents for a moment, realizing how much a part of each other they'd become. The lines of their individuality blurred so that it had become hard to define where one stopped and the other began. The two had become one.

She shook her head, trying to loosen the hold her thoughts were taking on her soul. A love like her grandparents', no matter how beautiful, was too much for her. She preferred the independent life of a single woman. It was heart-safe.

On the drive to church, Grandma serenaded her with hymns. Grandpa sang along, his bass harmony supporting Grandma's clear, wispy melody.

Inside the sanctuary, Grandpa led them to a pew already filled with Lambert children and grandchildren. Feeling a bit overwhelmed, Elizabeth opted to sit in the back alone.

As the pastor stood to call the congregation to worship, a warm masculine voice whispered over her shoulder. "Is this seat taken?"

Chapter 4

Kavan slipped in beside Elizabeth before she had a chance to respond. Stiff and sore, he slowly sat down and settled his crutches in the aisle alongside the pew.

"What are you doing here?" Elizabeth whispered. Her blue eyes focused on his bandaged knee as she scooted over an inch or two.

"It's Sunday," he whispered back. "Time to worship the Lord with the rest of the saints."

"You're hurt!"

Kavan slipped his arm along the back of the pew and leaned in toward Elizabeth. "Hurt, not dead."

"How did you get here? You didn't drive, did you?"

"Got a ride from a good Samaritan."

The three children sitting in front of Kavan and Elizabeth stole a peek at them. Their mother motioned for them to face forward with a fast flick of her wrist, then gave Kavan and Elizabeth a stern, you-should-know-better glance.

Elizabeth hid a laugh behind her slender hand.

"Shh," Kavan said softly into her ear, "you're setting a bad example for the children."

Elizabeth answered him with a dark blue-eyed wink. The urge to envelop the delicate woman in an embrace almost overwhelmed him.

Elizabeth Lambert, someday you'll be mine. Before God and man. Someday.

From the front of the sanctuary, the worship leader strummed the first chords of the opening song on his guitar. "Let's stand and worship the Lord," he said.

Awkwardly, Kavan tried to rise. His damaged knee throbbed with pain. To his surprise, Elizabeth slipped her hand into his and aided him to his feet.

"You don't have to stand, you know. I think people will understand."

Kavan leaned on the forward pew for support. "Feels good to stretch," he said in a low voice. He kept a light grip on Elizabeth's hand, loving the touch of her soft skin against his. He didn't want her to feel obligated to hold on to him, so he relaxed his fingers a little more so she could let go anytime she wanted.

Yet, her hand remained in his, eyes fixed forward, her smooth contralto voice rising in worship.

Smiling, Kavan offered thanks to his Lord and King, his Friend. Last night in the ravine was a reminder of the Lord's love and protection. His injuries could have been severe. Worse, the poachers might have returned, realizing he could identify them.

What an awesome God You are, he thought.

Elizabeth's hand still clung to his even after worship and the offering, until Pastor Marlow stood at the pulpit, his Bible open. "Glad to see Kavan Donovan with us this morning," he said first thing, motioning to the back where Kavan sat with Elizabeth. "For those of you who don't know—"

Kavan listened as the pastor shared the details of his ordeal. With a sidelong gaze, he watched Elizabeth. A crimson hue spread across her pretty face. All eyes were on them. She moved her hand out of his and nestled it in her lap.

Across the way, Jeff Simmons smiled broadly and waved. *I'll never hear the end of this one.* He hoped none of the Lamberts had seen him holding Elizabeth's hand. He'd rather take a ribbing about being bested by a couple of poachers than have Elizabeth scared off by good-natured teasing.

"Today's text is John, chapter three," Pastor Marlow said after concluding Kavan's story.

Throughout the congregation, pages rustled. Kavan opened his Bible to the Gospel of John.

"Here," he said to Elizabeth, sharing the open book with her.

She smiled shyly, glancing first at him, then at his Bible. Kavan longed to know the thoughts running through the private, independent Lambert granddaughter's mind. Did she enjoy worship? Sitting next to him? Did the pastor's focus on him embarrass her? Would she ever hold his hand again?

Kavan leaned back against the pew and tried to control his rambling thoughts. But the violet scent of Elizabeth's perfume filled his nostrils like the aroma of a cool spring morning just after a rain.

Suddenly, he realized this was the first time he'd seen Elizabeth outside of Sinclair's. The first time he'd seen her in anything other than a green smock and black khakis. He yearned to spend time with her outside the walls of Sinclair's store.

But how?

"'For God so loved the world,'" Pastor Marlow read from John 3:16. *Concentrate on the preaching, Donovan. This is the Lord's time.*

After the sermon, Kavan turned to Elizabeth. "Thanks for helping me stand earlier."

She smiled but averted her gaze. "No problem. I'm glad you're okay."

"I was thinking maybe we could have lunch—"

"Kavan," Jeff called over his shoulder. "You're looking none the worse for wear."

Kavan turned awkwardly to face his friend, disappointed at the interruption. "I'm banged up, but I'll live." He watched Elizabeth out of the corner of his eye.

"Listen, come to the station tomorrow and give us some details on the guys you were chasing. We'll round them up and—"

Elizabeth's lovely, low voice interrupted. "Grandpa is motioning for me. I'd better go. Bye, Kavan. See you later, Jeff."

Leaning on his crutch, Kavan waved good-bye, then gave Jeff a light pop on the shoulder with his fist. "Thanks, man. Thanks for nothing."

Jeff stared at him wide-eyed. "What? What'd I do?"

Chuckling, Kavan eased down the aisle toward the door. "Ruined my lunch."

There she stood holding his hand. Unbelievable.

Why didn't you move your hand, Elizabeth? she chided herself.

She couldn't get the picture out of her head. Standing next to Kavan with her hand in his—and in the middle of a church service!

All morning while logging purchase orders at Lambert's Furniture, the image of her hand in Kavan's flashed past her mind's eye over and over until she thought she could actually feel the strong, warm curve of his palm enfolding hers.

It felt divine, like a soft pair of kid gloves she once tried on during a Manhattan shopping spree with her mother.

Truth be told, she didn't know how her hand got into his. He attempted to stand for worship, and without much thought, she reached to help him. Simple as that.

She wondered if anyone saw them. Well, if anyone she knew saw them. The whole town knew her anyway, so what did it matter?

How humiliating. Elizabeth plopped her head onto the desk.

"Beth? You okay?"

She jerked her head up, smoothing her hair with her hand. "I'm fine, Will. Fine. Just thinking."

Her cousin and boss chuckled. "Try not to think so hard."

Elizabeth wrinkled her nose. "I'll try."

Will started to walk away, but stopped short. "See you up at the homestead this Friday for the barbecue?"

"What? Oh, Grandpa and Grandma's barbecue. I'm working at Sinclair's that night."

Leaning against the door frame, his hands in his pockets, Will shook his head. "No you don't. Take the night off. Have some fun with the family."

The look in his dark blue eyes persuaded her. "I'll see what I can do."

"Good."

Once again, Elizabeth faced the pile of work, determined to focus on the task at hand. She clicked the left mouse button to open the next account, New Hampshire Division of Forests and Lands.

Ranger Kavan Donovan's face popped into her thoughts again. Beneath the bruises and scrapes, his brown eyes laughed and his smile possessed the world.

I've got to think of something besides him! Elizabeth pushed away from her desk and snatched up her coffee cup. She started for the door, but changed her mind. Diet soda. *Umm, sounds good.*

She opened her bottom desk drawer and fished her wallet from her purse. *Fifty cents, can of soda. Oh, and a candy bar. Midmorning snack is what I need—anything to get my mind off of Kavan Donovan.*

Elizabeth dug out another quarter, two dimes, and a nickel. Dropping her wallet back into her purse, she glanced at her computer to check the time.

Her eye caught the next purchase order on the stack. Kavan Donovan's name was scrawled across the bottom of the order in bold letters. Elizabeth sank into her chair.

She scanned the order that totaled one thousand eight hundred thirty-seven dollars. "Hmm, five hundred twenty-five board feet of. . ." Elizabeth scanned the page, then checked the invoice on the computer, muttering to herself. "Cherry?"

No wonder Kavan's boss took issue over a few paints and balloons for a kids' display. What was he doing buying expensive lumber for the forestry division?

Elizabeth sat back, the change for the soda and candy machine sticking to her palm. After a moment, she reached for the phone and dialed Grant Hansen, the production floor manager.

"Hi, Mr. Hansen, it's Elizabeth."

"Beth, what can I do for you?"

Elizabeth liked the deep resonance of the older man's voice. "Do we fill lumber orders for people? You know, order the wood without making it into furniture?"

Grant laughed. "I see you've run across our little company secret. We have customers from the old lumberyard days that we still service."

"Do we fulfill orders for the forestry division?"

"On occasion. Maybe for a special repair or construction project."

"Cherry?"

With a chuckle, Grant answered, "No, no. Not for the forestry division. Cherry's very pricey. We use it here for fine furniture."

"I see," Elizabeth said, fighting a rise of disappointment. Why would Kavan order expensive lumber for the forestry division?

"Everything okay, Beth?"

She hesitated. "Yes, Mr. Hansen. Thanks for your help."

◆━▶

For Kavan, turning into Matt and Betty Lambert's driveway Friday night felt like a homecoming. How many nights and weekends had he spent at the Lamberts' home on the hill, as he called it, during his childhood and teen years? He and Jeff had pitched their tent on the crest of the hill many a summer night. Remembering, he smiled.

He parked his truck and stepped out.

"Kavan!" Ethan Lambert greeted him with a hearty hug before calling to his wife. "Julie, come say hi to Kavan."

Jeff beckoned to him from across the lawn, waving large barbecue tongs. The smell of roasting meat rose up from the wide barbecue pit and wafted on the wind across the lawn. Kavan's mouth watered.

"You're just in time, my friend," Jeff hollered.

Kavan scanned the grounds for signs of Elizabeth, his heart beating slightly faster at the idea of seeing her.

Suddenly, a soft voice greeted him. Turning, he looked into the delicate green eyes of Jeff's sister, Heather Simmons. "Well, Heather. Hello." He gave her a light hug. "It's been a long time."

Heather agreed that it'd been too long since they'd seen one another. Then, she introduced her husband, Thom. "It's Heather Barrett now, by the way."

Kavan positioned himself on his crutches so he could shake Thom's hand. "A pleasure to meet you."

"And this is Baby Barrett," Heather said, patting her round belly.

"Congratulations," Kavan said, kissing Heather's cheek tenderly. He'd never been particularly close to Heather, but on several occasions during high school, they found themselves in deep, heart-to-heart conversations. She would always be special to him for that reason.

Betty Lambert came alongside him and rested her hand gently on his arm. "Why don't you sit down? I'll get you a plate." She winked at him like she knew a deep secret.

"Grandma Betty, I don't need you waiting on me. I can manage."

"Oh, now, I see you hobbling around. I won't have my good barbecue falling on the ground and going to waste."

Kavan laughed. "Well, then I accept your offer."

He made his way over to one of the long picnic tables and eased down to the plank bench, searching again for Elizabeth. Surely she had to be here. It appeared to him that every Lambert in White Birch was in attendance.

"I didn't know you were invited."

Kavan did an about-face at the sound of Elizabeth's voice. The sight of her took his breath away. The setting sun laced her brown curls with golden ribbons. The blue sparkle in her eyes made him feel both hot and cold. She smiled at him as if she knew what she was doing to him.

He said the first thing that came to mind. "So, Sinclair's gave you the night off?"

"I had no choice." She picked up his crutches and rested her underarms on the padded tops. "Between Will and Grandma, I couldn't say no to this family event."

"You look lovely," he said in a low tone.

"Will said he'd fire me from Lambert's Furniture if I didn't come tonight," Elizabeth continued. She put the crutches back and settled against the edge of the picnic table.

"Good for him."

"Thank you."

Kavan smiled. "You've lost me. 'Thank you' for what?"

"The compliment."

"Anytime," he said, locking his gaze with hers.

She let it linger, but only for a second. "I heard Jeff tell Grandpa that they may have found the poachers who knocked you down the ravine."

"Turns out a detective knew one of the boys from my description."

"Ah, the woes of a small town. Can't commit a decent crime. Everyone knows you."

Kavan's smile faded. "Don't be fooled," he warned. "People get away with stuff around here all the time. Problem is they pat you on the back in church on Sunday, then steal from you on Monday."

Elizabeth's posture seemed to stiffen. "Is that so?"

He nodded. "Unfortunately. But let's not talk about poachers and White Birch crime." Kavan paused, studying her face, trying to read her expression. "Let's talk about going for pizza."

"I don't date." Elizabeth stooped to pick a yellow dandelion and twirled the green stem between her thumb and forefinger.

"What? Pizza with a friend is not a date."

"It's the classic date," she said with a harrumph. "Boy meets girl. Boy hounds girl at her place of employment. Boy asks her to go for pizza and a soda."

"Hound you? Come on, Elizabeth, give me a break. Besides, I never said anything about a soda."

She made a face at him.

He laughed.

"Here you go." Grandma Betty passed between the two of them, placing a heaping plate of food in front of Kavan. She stepped back, surveying the two of them. "Having fun?" she asked, buoyancy in her voice.

"Tons," Elizabeth droned.

"We were enjoying ourselves until I asked her to go for pizza," Kavan admitted without preamble.

In a way that only Grandma Betty could, she encouraged Elizabeth. "Go for pizza. You might surprise yourself and have a good time."

Kavan held his breath for a moment. Elizabeth sighed. When she turned toward him, a whirlwind of butterflies seemed to explode in his stomach.

"How's Monday night?"

"I'll pick you up at six."

"Six thirty," she countered.

Kavan chuckled. "Six thirty it is."

"My job here is done," Grandma Betty said, brushing her hands together as she started back up the hill toward the food tables.

Chapter 5

All day Monday, the pizza date with Kavan proved to be an utter distraction to Elizabeth.

She set an empty coffeepot on the burner and scorched the bottom. Will asked her for the week's receivables, and she delivered last year's. When the phone rang, she answered, "Sinclair's," and at lunch she noticed she had on one black pump and one navy.

"What's up with you today?" Will wondered, leaning against the doorjamb.

She smirked. "Marauding Monday."

Will stepped into her office and dropped into an empty chair. "Anything bothering you?"

Part of her wanted to come clean and cry, "Oh, Will, I have a *date* tonight!" But the words crumbled in her mind. How could she have ever agreed to have pizza with Kavan? But it wasn't a date, right? Kavan said as much, just pizza and a cola.

"Nervous about tonight?" His hushed voice conveyed his tenderness.

"Tonight?" Elizabeth echoed. Shifting in her seat, she pretended to read e-mail though her inbox was empty.

"Pizza with Kavan?"

"What is with this family?" She slapped the desk. "Everyone knows everyone else's business."

Will raised his hands in defense. "We look out for each other, support each other, and cheer each other on."

Elizabeth shuffled papers around, keeping her gaze averted. Will's piercing gaze made her feel vulnerable as if he could read her sacred thoughts. "I'm not used to it. Mom and Dad raised Jonathan and me to be independent and self-reliant." She forced herself to look up at him.

"Don't kid yourself, Beth. Grandpa and Grandma raised all the Lambert kids to be independent and self-reliant. Where do you think your parents got the idea?"

"Some things in life are just meant to be personal, that's all, Will."

He got up to leave. "Some things in life are meant to be celebrated."

❧

Kavan hit a wall of tension Monday morning.

"He's in a mood," Cheryl warned.

Kavan sighed. He didn't want Travis Knight's state of mind to spoil his day. The pizza date with Elizabeth was foremost in his own mind. During his morning workout, he'd barely been able to keep his mind focused on lifting the weights properly without overworking his knee. Now that he was using a cane instead of crutches, he wanted to keep it that way.

Taking in a deep breath, Kavan entered his boss's office.

"Morning. Is there a problem, Travis?" Kavan settled in the chair across from Travis's desk.

The large man jerked with irritation. "The refurbishment money. What are you buying, Donovan, gold-plated screws and platinum nails?"

The refurbishment budget again? He hadn't done anything with the project since Travis had ordered him to stop spending. "I don't understand."

Travis leaned toward Kavan, his mud-brown eyes narrow with indignation. "I'm getting heat from accounting. This is government money you're spending, Donovan."

Kavan stood carefully, leaning heavily on the cane. "Heat for what?"

"Outrageous charges to the refurbishment account." Travis rattled a report under Kavan's nose.

"I've barely spent any money." Kavan hated being on the defensive.

"Not according to accounting's records." Travis rose to his feet and settled his plump hand on his plump hip.

Kavan circled the chair, running his free hand over his hair. "I don't like what you are inferring, Travis."

"Then stop spending money that isn't yours." Travis pounded the desk.

"What are you talking about?" Kavan turned toward the man. "Are you accusing me of stealing?"

Travis shook his head, his fleshy cheeks red with heat. "I'm not accusing you of anything." He paused, then added with force, "Yet."

Hearing all he could bear to hear, Kavan looked his superior in the eye. "I'm not stealing, and you know it."

"Then explain these reports indicating that we are over budget on lumber and supplies. That's your department, Kavan."

Kavan picked up the report and scanned pages. After a moment, he tossed it back onto the desk. "Those are just department numbers and totals, Travis. It reveals nothing."

"All the red numbers are under your department, Kavan."

Kavan pursed his lips, holding his answer. When his anger subsided, he said, "I'm not spending the money."

"I won't have my career toppled by your carelessness. I'm up for promotion, and this doesn't look good for me."

Whether Travis Knight dismissed him or Kavan walked out, he couldn't remember. He sat at his desk feeling as if he'd been sucker punched.

Cheryl sashayed by. "I told you he was in a mood."

Lord, what's going on? Kavan pushed away from his desk, grabbed his keys, and headed for his truck. He needed a quiet place to pray.

Driving out of town, Kavan wrestled with anger and disappointment. His solid relationship with Travis had been the reason he returned to the New Hampshire Division of Forests and Lands. Now the man challenged his integrity. Kavan prayed with purpose until peace settled over his soul.

Ahead, the White Birch covered bridge came into view. Rays of morning sunlight scattered diamonds of light across the surface of the White Birch River.

Kavan parked and slowly walked under the bridge's cover, letting the tension of the morning ease out of his mind. His thoughts wandered to his evening plans with Elizabeth.

A picture of her shiny curls and intense gaze made him smile for the first time all morning.

🙠🙡

Will's words echoed in Elizabeth's mind. *Some things are meant to be celebrated.*

I'll tell you what's to be celebrated, she thought with scorn. *Achievement. Certainly not a pizza date. What did an old bachelor like Will Adams know anyway?*

Elizabeth pounded the keyboard, entering new invoices for faxed purchase orders. How could this family get so excited over two people sharing a large pie of tomato sauce and cheese?

She liked Kavan all right. In fact, she might like him more if the family didn't meddle. Then there was Joann. Her Sinclair's boss called on Sunday to see if she could fill in Monday night. When Elizabeth said no, Joann insisted on a reason.

"I see." Joann's tone turned serious when Elizabeth caved and told her about her plans with Kavan. But she hardly fooled Elizabeth, who could hear the smile in the woman's reply.

"I don't even know why I'm doing this," Elizabeth muttered under her breath, getting up to file a stack of invoices. The idea of canceling appealed to her. Hadn't she always promised herself she'd avoid romantic entanglements until the end of grad school, maybe longer?

She regretted the agreement with her parents to live and work in White Birch. She felt as if she were losing momentum on the education front. All would be lost if she let her heart fall in love.

She picked up several invoices and slipped them into a folder and shut the file drawer. Back at her desk, she found the phone book in a cubicle on the credenza and looked up Kavan's number. She dialed and listened as his answering machine picked up.

"Hi, Kavan, it's me, Elizabeth." She paused to steady her voice. "I, um, well, I can't make it tonight. I'm really sorry. I appreciate you asking and all. See you around."

She hung up.

Some things in life are not to be celebrated.

🙠🙡

After resting in God's peace, Kavan left the covered bridge and headed up I-89 toward the White Mountains and the old White Birch fire tower. Parking at the base of the fire tower, he left his truck and headed over to the tower steps. Carefully he eased his steps around the old rotting boards, placing his feet firmly on the bright clean pine steps.

He examined the tower structure, climbing slowly, leaning heavily on the cane. A lot of work remained to be done. Kavan knew there was no way for this refurbishment project to be over budget.

At the top of the tower, he pulled out the binoculars and scanned the area.

The panoramic view before him deepened his sense of peace. Nevertheless, something about the ordeal with Travis bugged him. "I don't know how to fix this, Father. I need Your wisdom." He continued to release his concerned thoughts to the Lord. After a few minutes, Kavan understood the need to surrender his reputation to the Lord, trusting Him to guard it.

A warm breeze whistled through the broken boards of the fire tower roof. Kavan faced the wind and sighed with contentment. He thought of Elizabeth and reached for his cell phone, dialing the main number for Lambert's Furniture.

"Elizabeth Lambert, please," he spoke to the receptionist.

When she answered, his heart thumped.

"Elizabeth, it's Kavan."

Sinking into her chair, Elizabeth took a deep breath. "Hi."

"Pepperoni or cheese?"

"Where are you?"

"Up at the old fire tower."

"I see."

"So, what kind of pizza do you like? Pepperoni, cheese, veggie. . . ?"

Absently, she reached for a pencil and doodled on the edge of a piece of paper. "Cheese, I guess."

"Sounds good. Six thirty?"

She swallowed. "Six thirty."

Why didn't I just tell him? Now I'll have to explain my message. A knot tied Elizabeth's stomach. She was giving this whole event entirely too much mental and emotional energy.

Getting ready that evening, Elizabeth heard her grandma fussing around in the hallway, singing the same tune over and over.

"It's no big deal, Grandma. Just pizza," she called.

Grandma peered around the door frame. "Did you say something?"

Elizabeth's laugh filled the room. "I know you're hanging around in the hall, waiting for me to come out."

The older woman stepped into the room, her face lit with a smile. "You look very nice."

"Thank you."

"Can I give you some advice?"

Elizabeth pursed her lips and tipped her head to one side. "And if I say no, will that stop you?" She couldn't keep her serious expression and smiled.

"Doubtful." Grandma pulled out the desk chair and sat down. "Have fun, Bethy."

Elizabeth reached for a pair of small, blue diamond earrings. "I just wish everyone wouldn't make such a big deal about this."

"Everyone?"

"Everyone," Elizabeth repeated. "You, Grandpa, Jeff. . . Even Will knows."

"I mentioned it to him. Sorry." Grandma got up and stood behind Elizabeth, brushing her hair from her shoulder. "You've been so intent in your studies. It's okay to let go a little and see how the other half lives."

"Perhaps celebrate?" Elizabeth asked, using Will's word. She turned and faced Grandma. She was so beautiful with her carefully combed silver hair and steady blue gaze.

"Yes, celebrate."

"I'll try not to be too stoical and serious," Elizabeth consented with a smile.

"That's my girl," Grandma said with a hug.

Elizabeth glanced at the clock. She had a few minutes before Kavan would arrive. She checked her e-mail. A half dozen junk e-mails, which she deleted, a couple science e-newsletters, and one personal note from a friend filled her inbox.

Elizabeth, good news! I've decided on Ohio State's nuke engineering program. Have you heard yet? Let me know. It would be great if we ended up in the same program.

Hope you're having fun in New Hampshire.

Jenna

Despair sank into the pit of Elizabeth's stomach like a lead weight. No, she hadn't heard from any schools. Surely, she should have heard something by now. What was it Jenna wrote? Elizabeth reread the e-mail.

I've decided on Ohio State's nuke engineering program.

"She must have had several schools to choose from," Elizabeth whispered. "But not one school has contacted me."

Slipping on a pair of black, low-heeled ankle boots, she mentally reviewed the application process, sure she'd met every requirement. She'd carefully prepared for grad school submissions, not wanting to get rejected due to a technicality.

"Beth, what are you doing?" Grandma's voice startled Elizabeth. "Kavan is waiting."

Consumed in thought and fighting worry, Elizabeth missed the tenor sound of the doorbell ringing.

Elizabeth buried her head in her hands. "I can't go!"

Chapter 6

Kavan stood in the Lamberts' sunny living room, angled to one side, propped up by his cane.

Grandpa Matt made small talk and asked about his knee.

"It's a little sore, but healing nicely. Cane works well."

"That's wonderful." Matt Lambert leaned back in his chair.

Elizabeth seemed to be taking a long time to come down, and he wondered if she'd changed her mind.

"Hi, Kavan. Sorry to keep you waiting."

He turned at the sound of her voice, unable to suppress his smile. Dressed in a faded pair of jeans and a pullover, he thought she looked perfect.

"No problem." He hobbled over to her and whispered, "You look absolutely beautiful."

"Thank you," she whispered back. "Night, Grandpa. Night, Grandma."

"Good night, folks." Kavan waved back as he opened the door.

On the drive to Giuseppe's Pizza, he attempted to start a conversation with Elizabeth, but all his topics fell flat. He could see worry in her blue eyes. The couple remained silent for the rest of the drive and to the front door of the restaurant.

"Table for two," he told the hostess who greeted them.

Once they were seated and their drink order was taken, he studied Elizabeth's face for a second, then took the plunge. "What's bothering you, Elizabeth?"

She sat up a little straighter and her brow furrowed. A slight smile molded her lips. "Didn't know I was wearing my heart on my sleeve."

Kavan laughed. "It's right out there, about to fall off." He motioned to her arm.

The waitress set two tall glasses of fizzing soda before them. "What'll you have?" She glanced between Kavan and Elizabeth.

"I think we need a few more minutes," Kavan said after making eye contact with Elizabeth. He felt certain that she had not considered what she wanted to eat.

"I'm sorry, Kavan. I. . .uh—"

"Hey, Elizabeth," Kavan interrupted, "let's order, then we can talk about it over pizza."

The way she smiled made his insides shiver. They agreed to order a large supreme pizza with no olives. The waitress chewed a big wad of gum and blew a giant bubble before asking, "Is that all?"

As she walked away, cracking her gum, Kavan and Elizabeth shared a laugh.

"I'll be sure to leave her a big tip." Kavan sipped his soda.

"Do that. I needed a good laugh." Elizabeth swirled her straw in her glass.

"What's on your mind, Lambert?" Kavan settled back, prepared to listen.

"I read an e-mail from a friend just before you came to pick me up. She's already decided on a grad program, and I have yet to hear from any of the five schools I applied to."

"It's really important to you, isn't it?"

Elizabeth nodded, and her chin jutted out in determination. "Very. It's what I've planned to do since I was a teenager. The nuclear engineering field is wide open right now, especially for women."

"A lot of money in engineering."

Elizabeth agreed. "Most of my friends are satisfied with their bachelor's and are not going for their master's. I, however, refuse to go the traditional route because some biological clock tells me it's time for marriage and kids. I'm not falling for that old routine."

Kavan didn't miss the edge in her voice, her unspoken resolution to go against the grain. He idly fiddled with his fork and said, "Sounds like you have your life planned out."

Elizabeth gazed out of the window by their booth, a grin accenting her pretty face. "My dad used to tell me I could do anything I set my mind to. He helped me set goals. So far, I've achieved them all."

No goals for marriage and family, Kavan noted. He repositioned himself in the seat, poised to ask her about her future family plans when the waitress returned to refill their drinks. She plopped a basket of garlic knots onto the table. "Your pizza will be out in a few minutes."

Elizabeth reached for a knot and placed it on her plate. "Obtaining my master's degree is my next major achievement." She looked up at him. "Can't ruin my perfect record."

"No, I guess not." Kavan reached for a garlic knot. Funny how the thing he admired most about Elizabeth was the very thing that would keep them apart. "I remember waiting to find out about grad school—"

"You went to grad school?" Elizabeth's eyes were wide with surprise.

"Uh-huh. University of Maine."

"I didn't know one could get an advanced degree in your field."

Kavan looked at her, astounded. "Well, forestry is—"

Her soft laugh interrupted him. "I'm just kidding, Kavan."

He laughed. "You had me there for a minute." He took another swig of his soda.

"I should warn you about my weird sense of humor."

The waitress returned with a large pizza. "Here ya go." She set down two white plates and slipped a large slice onto each one.

Kavan thanked her and returned his attention to Elizabeth. "I actually got my master's degree in math." He bit into his slice of pizza.

Across the table, Elizabeth gaped at him. "Really?"

Kavan reached for his napkin and wiped his mouth. "I like math and actually thought teaching would be a good backup career."

"Name your favorite math course." Elizabeth propped one elbow on the table and reached for her pizza slice.

"Diffy Q."

Elizabeth made a face. "Differential equations? No way! I hated Diffy Q. Give me advanced dynamics or any physics course over Diffy Q or calc three."

"Advanced dynamics! Are you kidding me?" Kavan countered. "I attempted some of those courses as an undergrad and realized life was just too short."

Like alto chimes, Elizabeth's laugh filled the air. "I love anything to do with physics, figuring out how things work and why. I actually love robotics. The math, for me, is a means to an end."

Kavan responded, arguing the beauties of mathematics and with almost no effort, their conversation took flight, gliding gently on the wind of words.

Elizabeth picked up a third big slice of pizza. "Giuseppe's has the best pie."

Kavan agreed. "I loved coming here as a kid."

"You did?" Elizabeth regarded him. The news of his mathematics master's degree put him in a new light. She didn't deny it—she was impressed. With little effort, she found she liked him and appreciated his comfortable company. "What's your favorite childhood memory?"

Kavan paused. The glimmer in his eyes seemed to dim. "Probably coming here. Or winter Sundays at your grandparents' house."

"I see."

Clearing his throat, Kavan confessed, "I came along a little later in life than my parents anticipated."

Elizabeth leaned over her plate, poised for another bite of pizza. "Is that a bad thing?" She pulled a melted strand of cheese from her chin.

Kavan hesitated before answering. "Not necessarily." He took a long, slow sip of soda.

"Listen, Kavan, you don't have to talk about it if it's too personal."

He played with his fork again, tapping it on the table. "I don't mind, really. Most people in town know about my parents. They are good people, but they liked to travel."

"They didn't take you with them?"

"No. Every woman in town over the age of sixteen babysat me at one time or another." Kavan made a comical face, causing Elizabeth to chuckle.

"That's amazing."

"Your grandparents' place was my favorite. They always made me feel like a part of the family."

"That's how you and Jeff became friends?"

"Yep."

"In the course of things, he saved your life?"

Kavan jabbed his straw into the melting ice of his empty glass, a sly grin spreading across his face. "I'm not sure I remember all the details."

"Ah, don't keep me in suspense." Elizabeth moaned, tipping her head to one side. "Don't you know curiosity killed that cat? Think what it will do to an inquisitive electrical engineer like me."

A laugh rumbled from the ranger. "I'm telling you, I can't remember."

"Oh sure." She put on her best pout.

"Tell you what, give me a few days, and I'll see if I can remember."

"Deal."

Silence dropped over them like a thin veil. Elizabeth relaxed and thought the lull necessary. Like exhaling after holding her breath.

"Didn't I hear you had a brother?" she said absently.

Kavan nodded. "He's twelve years older than me."

"So you were like an only child."

Kavan nodded. "Only and lonely."

The inflection in his voice moved Elizabeth. It resonated with a sad, yet resolute tone. Obvious to her, Kavan did not crave sympathy. It seemed he'd come to terms with the condition of his childhood.

"Where are your parents now?"

"Europe. Paris in spring is my mother's favorite. They'll return to the States sometime this summer. They go to Florida a lot." He smiled.

To herself, Elizabeth resolved to appreciate her family more. She'd spent most of her teen years running here and there, desperate to grow up, hungry for independence.

"What about your family?" Kavan's rich voice interrupted her thoughts.

She grinned. "I was just thinking of them and how I didn't appreciate them enough."

"I see. Take it from me, appreciate them."

Resting her folded arms on the table, Elizabeth looked Kavan in the eyes and confessed, "White Birch is a difficult place for me. There's a Lambert, or so it seems, under every rock, around every corner."

Kavan laughed outright.

Elizabeth slapped her hand lightly on the table. "It's not funny."

He chided her. "Oh, come on. It is funny. You can't seriously be offended at your caring, giving family."

"They're meddlers, getting in everyone's business."

"Like Jeff trying to help you with your car."

"Exactly." She pointed her finger at him.

He raised his hands in surrender. "All I can say is, learn to love it. There's no greater feeling in the world than family."

The waitress returned, still snapping her gum. "Refill on your drinks?"

"Please," Kavan answered for both of them. He leaned toward Elizabeth, cocked his head to one side, and raised his right eyebrow. "Dessert? They make a great torte."

Before Elizabeth could answer, the waitress said, "I'll bring a dessert menu." Popping her gum, she turned away.

The two laughed again. "Really, Kavan, big tip for her. She's hilarious."

He grew serious. "I'm having a good time."

Elizabeth stared at her empty plate, somewhat unnerved by his forthright confession. "This place is great," she said after a moment, forcing herself to look up and into his eyes.

The waitress returned, and they ordered dessert: one chocolate torte with two forks. After that, the conversation drifted back to family matters. Kavan took another stab at trying to get her to see the value of a close family. She understood, but argued that too much closeness can turn into interference.

"I guess we have to agree to disagree," he finally said, shoving the dessert plate toward Elizabeth. "You have the last bite."

"It's a matter of perspective, Kavan," Elizabeth started, spearing the last morsel of torte. "You want what you never had: a close family. I want to be on my own, living my own life. Grad school is the last key to unlocking that door."

"Can't argue with you there, Elizabeth. But I don't think God meant us to do it all on our own. Independence can be a dangerous thing."

Elizabeth wiped her mouth with the edge of her napkin. "I'll keep that in mind."

The waitress brought the check, and Kavan signed. Elizabeth had already noted he was a southpaw and watched as he signed his name on the debit card receipt with a flurry and a flare.

"Nice signature, Kavan," she said, peering over the pile of plates and used napkins. "Think your *K* is big enough?" She glanced up at him, winked, and laughed. "It's unique, I'll give you that!"

"Do you want to pay for dinner?" He raised a brow at her.

"I might." She lifted her chin to accept the challenge.

He chuckled and reached for his cane, anchored in the corner of the booth. "That's it. We're out of here."

To her surprise, Elizabeth let him take her by the arm and lead her toward the door.

❧❧

Driving toward the Lamberts' home on the hill, Kavan tried not to process the events of the evening too much. But unless he missed his guess, Elizabeth was having a good time. She gripped his heart each time he was with her.

"Sorry I started out the evening so moody," she said.

He reached over and touched her arm tenderly. "Don't worry. I understand. Hang in there; you'll hear from those grad schools."

"I know, but time is passing and I'm getting anxious."

"I bet you'll hear something by the end of the week."

She smiled at him. He wanted to capture her light and bottle it. On bad days, he could pour himself a cup.

"Your optimism is infectious. And you're right; I'll hear soon."

The White Birch covered bridge came into view. Kavan pulled off and asked Elizabeth if she'd like to go for a walk.

"I'd love to if your knee isn't too sore."

"It's fine. Let's go."

She stepped out of the passenger side of the truck into the full light of the moon.

Kavan fished his flashlight out of the glove box and came alongside Elizabeth. He tucked the flashlight under his arm, leaning on his cane as they walked. Without contemplation, he reached for Elizabeth's hand, glancing sideways at her to catch her reaction. She walked steadily forward, her hand resting in his.

They walked in silence, the night resonating with the sound of their heels and the tap of his cane against the broad boards of the bridge floor.

"It's so peaceful here." A contented sigh escaped Elizabeth's lips.

"Great place to pray because it's so peaceful," Kavan added. He released Elizabeth's hand and moved to the middle of the bridge. Moonlight streamed through the small side windows, but he clicked on his flashlight nevertheless. "When we were kids, we liked to climb into the rafters." He moved the light beam up along the heavy support planks.

"Look at all the initials." Elizabeth stared up, turning in a slow circle. "There must be hundreds of them."

"Your grandparents' initials are in here somewhere." Kavan stepped toward the left end of the bridge. "Your grandpa showed me once, but I can't. . . Ah, here it is."

Elizabeth hurried over to where Kavan stood. At the end of his light she read, "ML loves BC 1940."

"Used to be all the engaged couples came here and carved their initials." Kavan took a step back and bumped right into Elizabeth. When he turned to apologize, her face was only inches from his. His heart thundered, and he swallowed hard, finding it difficult to breathe. *Kiss her,* his heart shouted. She was gazing at him.

"Well, it's late," he choked out after a moment. "I'd better get you home." He took one giant step back. *Kiss her?* he argued internally. *How can I kiss her? This isn't even supposed to be a date.*

"Right," she answered in a hushed tone. "I have to work tomorrow."

"Me, too."

His legs trembled slightly as he escorted Elizabeth to the truck, a passionate tension wafting in the air between them. The debate over whether he should have kissed her raged on in his mind.

At the Lamberts' door, he grasped her hand and shook it good night. "I had a great time. You're a fun pizza partner."

She stepped toward him. "I had a great time, too."

The moment lingered, and Kavan could feel a light sweat beading on his forehead. "Good night, Elizabeth."

He stepped back so quickly, he stumbled down the front porch steps.

"Kavan!"

"I'm all right, I'm all right," he shouted, getting his balance and hustling to his truck.

"Are you sure?" she called.

The melodious sound of her voice lingered in his ears as he headed toward home.

❦

Inside, Elizabeth leaned against the front door. Grandma called from the family room. "That you, Bethy?"

"Yes, it's me."

"Did you have a nice time?"

Lovely. "Yes."

Suddenly feeling self-conscious, Elizabeth hurried quietly up the front stairs. In her room, she shut the door and flopped onto her bed.

He almost kissed me!

Chapter 7

The next morning, Elizabeth hurried down to breakfast. She'd overslept, forgetting to set her alarm the night before. The smell of eggs, bacon, and coffee teased her senses before she entered the kitchen.

Grandpa peered at her over the top of his paper. "Must have been some date..."

Elizabeth halted him with a flash of her palm. "It was *not* a date, Grandpa."

"I see." He snapped the paper open again and retreated behind the front page.

"Grandpa," she started with a sigh, "I didn't mean to be sharp with you. I forgot to set my alarm, so I'm running late."

He set the paper aside. "Bethy, did you have a nice time?"

She fumbled around the kitchen, looking for her favorite glass. "Yes."

Grandma came into the kitchen. "Your glass is in the dishwasher. I ran it last night."

"Thank you." Elizabeth retrieved the tall, wide-mouth glass, filled it with ice, and popped open a diet soda.

"That's all I wanted to know," Grandpa said. "Having a good time is half the battle for you."

"I know how to have a good time." Elizabeth pulled out a chair and sat down at the kitchen table.

Grandpa chuckled and sat back, scratching his head. "I suppose you do. You just seem so opposed to it."

Grandma set a plate of eggs and toast in front of her. "Oh, Grandma, I'm not hungry."

"Eat," the older woman ordered. "You're not leaving my kitchen with diet soda as your breakfast."

The smell of hot buttered toast stirred Elizabeth's appetite. Her stomach grumbled. She reached for her fork and knife. Grandpa passed her the black raspberry jelly.

"I'm not opposed to a good time, Grandpa," Elizabeth said after swallowing a bite of her eggs. "I am merely cautious of my emotional energy."

Grandpa uttered a low harrumph. "I suppose the Allied forces of World War II couldn't stop that stubborn pride of yours."

Elizabeth spread an even layer of jelly on her second piece of toast. "Stubborn pride? And where do you suppose I get it?" There was a tender admiration in her question.

Before Grandpa could answer, Grandma brought her own plate to the table and interrupted. "All right, you two. Stop. Matt, leave the girl be." She turned to her granddaughter. "You know we're both very proud of you. You're a joy to us."

"Thank you, Grandma."

Grandpa sat back and crossed his arms over his chest. "She's right, kitten. I just hate to see you all wound up with this grad school notion."

Elizabeth smiled at him, deciding more debate was pointless. She may resist the Lamberts' constant intrusion, but she couldn't ask for more love and support than her grandparents gave her. They tolerated what they didn't understand, loved amid difficulty.

"Why don't you tell us about your dinner with Kavan," Grandma prompted.

"No comments from you, Grandpa."

He held up his hands in surrender. "Not a word. Not a word. The floor is yours, Bethy."

She glanced at her watch. "Okay, here's the five-minute version." Quickly, Elizabeth recapped her evening, giving them the details, devoid of any emotion. She omitted the intimate moment on the bridge entirely. Unsure of what really transpired between them in that instant when they were face-to-face and eye-to-eye, she was sure she could not describe it to her grandparents. Besides, the moment felt private, only for her.

"Well, good," Grandpa said when she finished. He picked up the morning paper again.

"Sounds lovely," Grandma chimed in.

On her way to Lambert's Furniture, Elizabeth's thoughts remained caught on the covered bridge moment with Kavan. Did he want to kiss her? Did she want him to kiss her? She shuddered with realization.

As she pulled into the parking lot and made her way to her office, Elizabeth resolved to stop thinking of Kavan Donovan and his possible kisses.

Focus, Elizabeth, focus. Your goal is grad school. Not to marry the first guy who comes along.

◆◆

Kavan sat on his back porch, sipping coffee and watching the summer mist dissipate over the White Mountains. Fred and Ginger lay at his feet. Content and peaceful, he conversed with his heavenly Father.

He woke up thinking of Elizabeth, and it concerned him some. "Lord, I don't want to get ahead of You. Clearly, Elizabeth is not ready for a serious relationship, let alone marriage. If she is not for me, let me know."

He paused, listening, waiting for the Lord to respond. He did, but not about Elizabeth. Instead, he sensed the Lord warning him about the workday ahead.

More trouble.

Kavan spent the next twenty minutes praying for his boss and the situation between them. He went to work with a sense of God's favor and justice but with no clue as to what events would unfold during the day.

"Morning, Kavan," Cheryl said, batting her heavy black lashes. She smiled at him in a way that made him uncomfortable and wonder what she was thinking.

"Travis wants to see you."

Kavan sighed and dropped his canvas bag onto his desk. Taking a deep breath, he limped toward Travis's office.

"Come in," the director bellowed at Kavan's light knock.

Kavan planted a smile on his face and stepped inside. "Good morning."

The large man stood. "We have to figure out how to solve this problem."

Exasperated, Kavan asked, "What problem, Travis?" He eased into a chair.

"Since our last discussion, nothing's changed. Your fire tower renovation is still way over budget."

Kavan clenched his jaw and consciously tried not to grind his teeth. "Travis, I haven't been working on the renovation. There are no expenses."

Travis tossed the accounting notice to him. "Can you explain this?"

Kavan picked up the paper. "This report has no details. It's just a summary. I can tell you my accounting shows the project in the black." He tossed the paper back onto the desk.

"The State of New Hampshire shows you're in the red." His tone challenged Kavan.

Kavan folded his hands on the curved head of the cane and leaned forward, extending his own challenge. "How long have you known me?"

Travis shrugged. "Since you were a kid."

"Do you really think I would steal from the division?"

"People change, Kavan."

"I haven't changed, Travis. I am not the reason the refurbishment budget is overdrawn."

For a moment, Kavan believed he could actually cut the tension with a knife. *Lord, give me wisdom.* "You're free to look at my records, Travis."

The man shook his head. "Won't do any good. Accounting can just say you doctored your records."

"I have copies of orders and receipts." Kavan held his tongue from declaring this whole thing an outrage.

"Whatever it is you're doing, end it now, Donovan. I don't want to see you in trouble."

Kavan left the office without being dismissed. Anger brewed in his chest. How could Travis believe he was stealing?

He booted up his computer and launched the fire tower refurbishment accounting program. To his anguish, the program came up with an application error. He double-clicked on the program shortcut to launch it again, but it crashed.

He pursed his lips and pounded the palm of his hand against his desk. *Backups. . . I have a backup at home.*

He grabbed his gear and started for the door.

"See ya, Kavan," Cheryl called after him.

At home, Kavan found his records were several months behind, but in order, showing his project to be in the black. A few purchases were not logged in the spreadsheet, but all copies of the project's orders and receipts were saved in a file at the office.

For a few moments, Kavan sat mulling over his next action. Fred and Ginger whined at the door, asking to be let in. Still lost in thought, Kavan got up and opened the door for them.

How do I handle this, Lord?

Oddly, Kavan sensed he wasn't to do anything. He had to let the Lord defend him. For a moment, the idea went against every instinct in his body, but the Lord would handle the situation righteously and justly.

"My reputation is on the line, Father," Kavan prayed. "But I trust You." He'd keep his records in order and updated. When Travis called for them, he'd be ready.

Driving back to the office, Kavan finally rested in the peace of the Lord. Thoughts of Elizabeth drifted across his mind for the first time since the confrontation with Travis.

Ironic, he thought. This morning, she was the first person he thought of when he woke up. Now, after the ordeal with Travis, their pizza dinner and walk on the bridge felt like a distant memory.

❧

"You're crazy not to fall for him," Joann told her over a large garden salad at the diner.

"Why do I have to fall for him? For anyone?" Elizabeth stabbed a large tomato wedge with her fork.

"I'm not saying you do, but Kavan Donovan is not one to let go."

For the rest of lunch, Elizabeth steered the conversation away from the topic of love and Kavan. She whispered a prayer of thanks when Joann let the subject drop.

After lunch, a pile of invoices and corresponding purchase orders covered Elizabeth's desk. She'd managed to put Kavan out of her mind during her morning routine—but not since her impromptu lunch with Joann. Facing an afternoon of mundane work, she found herself daydreaming about the handsome ranger. Joann was right. He was a great guy: kind and caring, funny, smart, and good-looking.

He would be a wonderful husband and, I bet, a good father. But I'm not looking for a husband or a father for my children! She scooted up to her desk and reached for the invoices.

After updating several accounts, Elizabeth came across another expensive purchase order from the Division of Forests and Lands for one hundred board feet of teak.

Kavan's name sat boldly across the header of the invoice. On the purchase order, his signature graced the bottom line.

She reached for the phone and called Grant Hansen again. "Hi, Mr. Hansen, it's me."

"What can I do for you, Bethy?"

"Would the forestry division order teak?"

He chuckled softly. "No, no."

Elizabeth scanned the order. "It says it's for the fire tower refurbishment."

"Oh no, honey. The fire tower would be finished with pine or oak."

Elizabeth could feel her heart sinking. What was Kavan doing buying teak? "Thank you, Mr. Hansen," she said low and unsure.

Driving to Sinclair's that night, Elizabeth could not stop thinking about the order in Kavan's name. *Could he be a fraud? Perhaps he's not the man everyone believes him to be.*

Joann caught her as she entered the store. "Hey, your man is in here."

Elizabeth froze. "What?"

"I said your man is in the store." Joann linked her arm through Elizabeth's and steered her toward the time clock. "Clock in. I need you at the front desk."

"No, I can't see him."

"Who? Your man?"

With force, Elizabeth said, "Would you stop saying that? He's *not* my man."

Joann reared back. "Don't get testy. So he's not your man."

Elizabeth clocked in, then grabbed her friend by the arms. "Joann, I don't want to see Kavan right now. This whole ordeal is ridiculous. I'm not becoming involved. I'm going to school in two months."

Resolve pursed Joann's lips. "All right, Elizabeth. I hear you."

"No more Kavan. No more love talk. No more romance."

Joann reached out and smoothed Elizabeth's curls. "Why don't you work back in stock for a while. Millie can help at the front desk."

With a sigh of relief, Elizabeth hugged her boss. "Call me when he's gone."

From over her shoulder, Kavan's mellow baritone filled her ears. "Hi, Elizabeth."

Chapter 8

Elizabeth whipped around. "Hi...Kavan."

"I'll see you later." Joann retreated.

"Long workday?" Kavan asked, pushing his cart out of the way so another customer could get by.

"I'm used to it." She avoided direct eye contact.

"Elizabeth, what's wrong?" Kavan's eyes searched her face.

She leaned her shoulder against the wall and fidgeted with the pen dangling from a string by the time clock. In the distance, she heard the cry of a small child. Finally, she looked at Kavan. "I don't want last night to mean more than it should." There, she said it.

"Pizza and a walk on the covered bridge. Don't see how any deep thing could be derived from that experience."

"Oh, you know this town, my family... Romance is all they think about."

Kavan shook his head. "Believe me, not everyone in this town is fascinated with romance. You can ask your police officer cousin about that."

"All right, but where I'm concerned, everyone is fascinated with romance. Trying to marry me off."

Kavan took a step back. "Have you been asked?"

Elizabeth stood straight and stared into Kavan's eyes. "What?"

"Who's asked you to marry him?" His eyes sparked with merriment.

"Well, I haven't been asked." She started to laugh.

"Then stop worrying about it. I've known you only a short time, but you are clearly the most goal-oriented, determined woman I've ever met. A little teasing about romance is not going to drive you off the road of educational success."

"You're right!" Elizabeth threw her arms around him. "Oh, Kavan, thank you!"

Sunday morning, Kavan found Elizabeth sitting by herself in the back of the sanctuary. He slipped into the pew beside her, hooking his cane over the seat in front of them.

"Good morning," he whispered.

She faced him, her eyes clear and bright. "Morning, Kavan."

He hesitated, then asked, "Do you mind if I sit here?"

"Of course not." She flashed her wide, white grin.

Kavan eased back against the pew, waving and greeting people as they passed. He glanced at Elizabeth from time to time, watching her expression, looking for signs of being uncomfortable. She appeared relaxed and at ease.

Five days had passed since the night she threw her arms around him in Sinclair's. But he could still feel the warmth of her skin touching his neck and smell the fragrance of her perfume.

He'd deliberately left her alone the rest of the week. If they were going to have any sort of relationship, Elizabeth had to feel safe.

The worship leader took the platform and called the congregation to worship. For a brief second, Kavan still wished he had his crutches so Elizabeth could help him stand. He rather enjoyed holding her hand.

"Need me to help you stand?" she whispered.

"I think I can manage." He grinned. *Ah, she remembered.*

His voice mingled with hers as they sang praises to the King.

During the offering, Kavan got an inspiration.

"Hey, Elizabeth," he whispered.

She shushed him, but a smile edged her lips.

He reached for the pen in his coat pocket and wrote on the bulletin, "Lunch? My place?"

He passed the paper to her.

She read it and wrote one word: "Okay."

~ ~

Sitting next to Kavan and among the members of White Birch Community Church, Elizabeth felt oddly at home. After that first Sunday she agreed to attend with her grandparents, she knew spiritual strength was missing in her life.

"Let's open our Bibles to John 15," Pastor Marlow said.

Elizabeth reached for her Bible and thumbed to the passage. She could hear the rustling pages of Kavan's Bible.

"Book of John," he muttered. "One of my favorites."

"Apparently, the pastor's, too."

Forty-five minutes later when the pastor closed with prayer, the words of Jesus danced through her head. *"'I have called you friends.'"*

Could she be Jesus' friend? Lately, He seemed more like a faraway entity that watched the world with vague indifference. Maybe He intervened in times of war or disaster, but did He really care and intimately watch over individuals like her?

In that instant, her soul yearned to know the Lord deeper. Tears stung in her eyes. "Jesus," she whispered so low she could barely hear her own words, "I'd like to be Your friend."

Her shoulders hunched forward as gentle sobs took control. Without a word, Kavan slipped his arm around her shoulders and stuffed a tissue between her fingers.

~ ~

The Lambert family gathered at the door after the service. Grandpa chased the youngest grandchildren in a game of tag, and Grandma organized lunch out.

"Where to?" she asked in a strong but caring voice.

Ethan and Julie said they preferred lunch at home. Will said he was up for pizza or a hamburger plate at the diner.

"Ah, no way," someone shouted. "Typical bachelor fare."

"What about you, Beth?" Jeff asked.

"I have lunch plans." Her heart pounded an extra beat. *Please don't ask with whom.*

"Beth's out," Grandma said, "so how many are going on this adventure?"

A chorus of young voices cried, "Me!"

The adults laughed. Grandma made a command decision. "Pizza it is. Let's go."

While everyone scurried to their cars, Elizabeth shook her head with wonder. She had a wonderful family, a little wacky at times and nosy, but so loving and kind.

In the distance, she saw Kavan waiting by his truck. He waved. For the first time, she saw him as a true friend. He didn't push or pry. His comment to her the other night in Sinclair's practically revolutionized her White Birch world. Who cared what everyone else thought?

"Let's go; I'm starving," he called, still leaning against the truck, his arms folded over his chest. The rust color of his tie brought out the ruddy hues of his complexion.

"I'll pull around behind you so I can follow," Elizabeth hollered to him, starting for her car on the other side of the parking lot. Slipping in behind the wheel, she realized she had two new friends today: Jesus and Kavan.

❧❧

"Oh, Kavan, your place is beautiful." Elizabeth walked through the main room toward the kitchen. Thick open beams crisscrossed over her head, supporting a large open loft that looked into the living area and kitchen. A white stone fireplace sat in the south wall, framed by large-paned windows.

"Thank you. It's taken awhile, but I'm finally getting it finished."

Elizabeth turned with a start. "You built this yourself?"

"Yes." Kavan opened the porch door. "Fred, Ginger. Come." Two large German shepherds bolted through the door.

Kavan joined Elizabeth in the middle of the room. The dogs followed, sniffing Elizabeth, their tails wagging. "The big one with the black face is Fred. And this lovely lady is his mate, Ginger."

With a sideways glance and a smirk, Elizabeth said, "Clever names! Do they dance as well as Fred Astaire and Ginger Rogers?"

Kavan laughed and scratched behind Fred's ears. "Nah; I just watched a lot of old movies growing up. Anyway, most of this room has been done for several years. But I'm finishing the loft and the porch."

Before Elizabeth could comment, Kavan slapped his hands together and said, "I'm hungry. How about you?"

She rested her hand on her stomach. "Starved."

"Couple of rib eyes cooked on the grill and a salad suit your appetite?" Kavan pulled the meat and salad fixings out of the refrigerator.

"Sounds perfect. How 'bout I make the salad while you cook the steaks."

He grinned. She liked his lopsided smile. It reminded her of a young 1950s movie star.

"We make a good team, Lambert," he said.

She nodded. "Good friends are hard to find."

He looked up at her, paused in midmotion. "Yes," he said. "Good friends are hard to find."

Chapter 9

"Two letters came for you today," Grandma said when Elizabeth came in after a Saturday shift at Sinclair's.

"Really?" A nervous shudder ran over her. " 'Letter' letters or grad school letters?"

"Official-looking letters," Grandma said. "I put them on your desk."

Elizabeth took the stairs to her room two at a time. In the fading light from the window, she saw two long white envelopes on the desk. She clicked on the desk light. With anticipation, she reached for the top letter.

She mumbled to herself as she read. "We regret to inform you that your application has been denied."

She reread the line. *Denied.* Slowly she sat in the desk chair.

Trembling fingers reached for the next letter.

Denied again.

"I can't believe it. I've been turned down by Michigan and South Carolina."

Fighting tears, she paced her room, trying to console herself. *It's only two schools.* She'd applied to five and only one needed to accept. Surely one of the remaining schools would respond positively.

Grandma appeared in the doorway. "Beth?"

"I got turned down."

"I see."

"I, uh. . ." Elizabeth's voice broke. She rushed past her grandmother and down the stairs.

"Hey there, kitten," Grandpa called from the family room.

Without responding, Elizabeth opened the front door and ran across the lawn. By the time she reached the covered bridge, she was out of breath. Beads of sweat trickled down her cheek and neck. She walked the length of the bridge, contemplating her situation. A June breeze whistled through the eaves.

Denied. She visualized the word over and over. Tears stung in her eyes, but she sniffed them back, refusing to give in. "I won't cry. I know I'll get accepted at another school."

She exited the bridge on the other side and stood along the riverbank, listening to the soothing sound of the water. Jesus' words from Sunday's sermon whispered through her. " '*I have called you friends.*' "

In the fading light of the setting sun, Elizabeth eased to the ground. "Jesus, I could use a friend right now."

Finally, she let the tears spill over and slip down her cheeks. "I know this is not the end of the world, but it sure feels like it. My plans are not working out."

She wiped her cheeks with the back of her hand, wondering how the Lord would respond to her. As a little girl, she pictured herself running up to Jesus like the children in the Bible. But now she felt old and stale, unable to run to her Savior.

Suddenly, a burst of anger riveted her. How could she *not* be accepted? Her credentials were stellar. If anyone qualified for a nuclear engineering graduate program, she did.

Yet, the anger faded as rapidly as it'd flared and disappointment surged again. She longed to shake the heavy burden that wrapped up her heart. "Lord," she said after a few minutes, "I want to be Your friend. Be my friend, please. Show me what to do in this situation."

Twilight settled over White Birch and grace over Elizabeth Lambert.

❧❧

"She worked during the day," Joann Floyd told Kavan.

He rapped his knuckles against Sinclair's customer service counter. "Thanks." He turned to leave.

"Hey, Kavan," Joann called after him. "Don't give up on her."

He paused, looking at Joann over his shoulder. "She doesn't make it easy."

Joann nodded. Kavan could tell she understood Elizabeth quite well. "She knows what she wants," the Sinclair's manager said.

"I can't fault her. I know what I want, too."

Joann came out from behind the counter and walked toward Kavan. "Elizabeth Lambert?"

He stepped away from her. "That's for me to know and you to find out."

Joann's laughter followed him out of the store.

He drove toward the Lamberts' home on the hill. He wasn't sure what he would do once he got there, but he headed there anyway. Normally, he'd knock on the door, confident of a warm welcome by Grandpa Matt and Grandma Betty. But now that Elizabeth lived there, he wondered if his impromptu visit would make her uncomfortable.

His Sunday lunch with her had gone well. Better than he'd hoped. But Elizabeth Lambert held strictly to the business of being friends. Only friends.

Steering around the bend in the road, the White Birch covered bridge came into view. In the fading twilight, Kavan thought the truck's headlights flashed across someone sitting on the riverbank. He slowed as he approached the bridge and leaned over the steering wheel. Peering out the windshield, he saw her. *Elizabeth.*

He popped his head out the open window. "You fishing?"

She jumped up, flicking leaves and dirt from her jeans. "Kavan. Hi," she said with a quick wave.

"I don't see a pole or a line." It was nearly dark, but in the remaining light he could see she'd been crying.

He parked in a gravel spot at the side of the road just before the opening of the bridge, cut the truck engine, and grabbed the flashlight. "Hey, hey," Kavan said tenderly, slipping out of the driver's seat and meeting Elizabeth by the bridge. "Everything okay?"

In one smooth motion, he wrapped his arms around her and pulled her to him. She cried while he stroked her hair and murmured to her that everything was going to be okay.

"Elizabeth, tell me what's going on." He inclined his head to look at her. "Why all the tears?" He reached for his handkerchief and gave it to her.

She wiped her face and blew her nose. With a steady voice, she confessed, "I received two letters from universities today."

Kavan stood straight. *News from grad schools. . .here goes.*

"What'd they say?" He smiled to encourage her.

"I was denied admittance."

For a split second, Kavan wanted to rejoice. But he knew better than to give way to his own selfish desires. Elizabeth needed his friendship and support right now. "Who turned you down?"

"What does it matter, Kavan?" she asked, stepping out of his embrace. "That's two less chances I have." She started toward the covered bridge.

"You have all the credentials, Elizabeth. You know you do."

"Apparently not enough for Michigan or South Carolina."

"Why don't you inquire?"

"No, I'm not going to go crawling to them. I have three other applications out there. I'll get accepted at one of those schools."

Kavan gave her a sly smile. Her attitude reflected the Elizabeth Lambert he was getting to know. He walked up behind her and touched her shoulder. "I'm sure you will."

"I've never had to deal with this before. I usually get what I want, when I want."

"Anything I can do to help?"

She faced him. He could see her lower lip tremble. "No, there's nothing you can do, really." Her weak tone told him otherwise.

He stepped closer and wrapped her in his embrace again. She rested her head against his chest. For the longest time, they just stood under the peaceful cover of the bridge.

At last Kavan prayed, "Lord, You know all things. You have Elizabeth's welfare on Your heart. You have plans for her good and not to harm her. Give her Your grace during this time and bless her."

Elizabeth whispered, "Amen," then tilted her head to look at him, still snuggled against his chest. "He's my Friend, you know."

"Jesus?"

"Yes, Jesus. And He sent you to me tonight."

At that moment, emotion for her almost overwhelmed him. He longed to whisper in her ear that he loved her. Slow and determined, he tipped his head toward her, intent on kissing her this time.

But just as his lips were about to touch hers, flashing red and blue lights illuminated the bridge and the loud bleep of a siren reverberated.

"Beth, is that you?"

Elizabeth jumped out of his arms. Kavan squinted in the light.

"Jeff?" he called.

"Kavan? Sorry to disturb you, man. I was looking for my cousin Beth."

"Here I am," Elizabeth said, her voice cracking.

From where he stood, Kavan couldn't see Jeff's face, but he knew the man was grinning from ear to ear when he said, "Oh, really now."

Suspended between emotions, Elizabeth didn't know whether to laugh or cry. She rubbed her forehead with her fingers. "What are you doing here, Jeff?"

"Grandma called. Asked me to look for you."

A wave of guilt washed over her. "Oh, Jeff, please tell her I'm fine, and I'm sorry."

His deep laugh echoed down the bridge. "I will. Kavan, you see she gets home safely, huh?" Jeff ducked back into the squad car.

"Oh, great. Now the whole family is going to wonder what I was doing out here with you."

"You worry too much about what they think," Kavan said matter-of-factly.

She rested her hands on her hips. "Don't hassle me, Donovan; it's been a hard night."

"I know. I'm sorry."

Elizabeth peered up at him. The white glow from his flashlight illuminated the area where they stood. What a wonderful friend he'd become. His comfort tonight was just what she needed.

Thank You, Jesus, for being my Friend and for sending Kavan to be Your arms and voice.

Kavan tapped her on the arm. "Here, use my cell phone to call Grandma Betty so she doesn't worry."

Reaching for the phone, Elizabeth thanked him. She dialed home and waited for an answer. "Hi, Grandma. . . . Yes, I'm fine. . . . I'm sorry I made you worry. . . . Uh-huh, Jeff found us. Kavan is here."

She listened to her grandma's soft, caring voice. "I've been praying for you. I think Jesus just wants you to know He's there for you to lean upon."

The words moved over Elizabeth's heart and invoked a fresh batch of tears. "Thank you, Grandma. I think you are right."

She pressed the END button and handed the phone back to Kavan. He enveloped her again and settled his arm on her shoulders. "You know, whatever doesn't kill you will only make you stronger."

She laughed. "Well, those are comforting words."

"I just mean—"

"I know what you mean, and you're right." She chuckled low.

"Hey, did you notice I'm sans cane?" Kavan said, pointing to his healing knee.

Elizabeth clapped her hands softly. "Yea, good for you!"

Kavan did a jig around the bridge floor. Elizabeth laughed, and it felt good. The wind whipped through the bridge, stirring up dirt and leaves.

"Kavan," she said suddenly, "let me see your handkerchief again. Something's in my eye."

Her eye stung and watered as she slid the white cotton cloth under her eye, hoping to mop up any remaining mascara or dirt. The edge of the fabric touched the inside of her right eye, and the sting worsened. "Oh, this hurts!" She stooped over and covered her watering eye with her hand. Debris rubbed against her contact lens.

Kavan knelt next to her. "Elizabeth, what's wrong?"

"My contact lens." She tried to open her eye, but the lens had repositioned and stuck to her eyelid, making it impossible to open.

"What can I do to help?"

"Nothing. Just a sec. . ." Elizabeth massaged her eye with her fingertips, trying to move the circular plastic piece. "I wear gas permeable lenses. And if it moves off the pupil, it really hurts."

She tried one more time to move the lens, just wanting it out of her eye. Suddenly the lens slipped into place, and Elizabeth popped it out of her eye with a quick blink. *Ah, relief.* Just as the lens hit the palm of her hand, the evening breeze gusted through the covered bridge.

Kavan laughed. "It's like a wind tunnel."

"Don't move!" Elizabeth commanded. "My lens dropped out of my hand."

"You've got to be kidding," Kavan said, frozen in place, shining his flashlight around their feet.

"I thought I heard it hit."

They looked for over half an hour before realizing the lens must have slipped through one of the cracks on the bridge floor.

"I'm sorry," Kavan said, making one last sweep with his light.

Elizabeth looked at him, one eye pushed shut. "I appreciate your help."

He ran his forefinger tenderly over her lensless eye. "Do you have a spare set?"

She shook her head. "One of the things I didn't get to between graduation and coming up here."

"How are you going to see to drive or work?"

"I have a good pair of glasses here. I'll have to go to Boston to get new contacts."

"Come on, I'll drive you home."

Elizabeth walked with Kavan to his truck. He opened the passenger door, and she paused before climbing in.

"Thank you for being so patient and kind." Without contemplating the implications, she rose up on her tiptoes and kissed him tenderly on the cheek.

Chapter 10

After church the next day, Elizabeth started for Boston. She rolled the window down and propped her elbow on the door. The sun burned warm on her bare arm. She beeped the VW's horn good-bye to her grandparents, who stood in the driveway, waving. Grandma's apron billowed in the breeze.

On the passenger seat, a fresh-baked loaf of banana bread filled the entire car with the sweet smell of all that is good in life.

At the bottom of the drive, she turned left, heading for the bridge and the road toward Boston. Just as she crossed the covered bridge, she saw Kavan's truck parked in the shade.

She steered her little car next to his big truck. Kavan still wore his Sunday shirt and tie, but the tie hung loose about his neck. He propped his hand on the steering wheel and leaned out the open window.

Her heart fluttered. "Surprised to see you here." She ignored the excitement stirring within her.

"I wanted to say good-bye again."

His tone caused a funny feeling to bubble up in her middle, and she squirmed under his intense stare. "I'll only be gone a few days."

He shrugged. "I know, but I'll miss you."

Miss me? She didn't know what to say. While growing to appreciate and value Kavan's friendship, it hadn't occurred to her that he would miss her. She pushed her glasses up on her nose and said the first thing that came to mind. "We can go to Giuseppe's when I get back."

"You're on."

She shifted the tiny car into gear. "Bye, Donovan."

"Bye, Lambert." He grinned, flashing white, even teeth.

Driving away, a strange sensation crept over Elizabeth, a picture of Kavan fresh in her mind.

❧❧

"Mom? Dad? Anybody here?" Elizabeth hollered a few hours later, walking through the front door of her parents' house. She tossed her overnight bag on the bottom step of the front staircase.

"Welcome home," her mother called, approaching from her office, arms wide.

"Hi, Mom." Elizabeth fell into her embrace and breathed in a scent like spring roses.

"Dinner's waiting in the oven. Your dad and Jonathan are washing up."

In the next instant, her brother bounded down the stairs and grabbed her in a big hug. " 'Lizbeth, you're home."

She laughed as he swung her around. "Put me down, you big lug."

"Good to see you, kiddo." Her dad greeted her with a kiss.

"Good to be home, Daddy."

Dinner was a lively event with Chinese takeout. "I was too swamped at work this week to do the grocery shopping," Elizabeth's mom explained.

Her dad added, "We've been eating out every night, and it's costing us a fortune." He reached over to pinch his wife's cheek.

Jonathan regaled them with a lifeguard story from his summer job at the pool and announced to his sister his plans to be All-State after next year's football season.

Their father looked at him sideways, pointing his fork in Jonathan's direction. "Any plans to keep those grades up, son?"

Elizabeth took a sip of water to hide her merriment. Her father's mock concern didn't fool her.

"Ah, Pop, 'Lizbeth is the brain in the family. I'm the brawn." He pushed up his shirtsleeve and flexed his muscles. Everyone laughed.

The conversation switched focus to Elizabeth when her dad asked, "How's grad school looking?"

Elizabeth felt like the sun had suddenly burned out. For a split second, she considered fabricating a story about her grad school status. But she knew it would be wrong and only prolong the agony of telling them the truth. "I've gotten two rejections."

"What?" they all said at once.

"Michigan and South Carolina."

Paul Lambert sat back in his chair, his hand propped on his leg. "Are you sure, kiddo?"

"Hard to miss the word 'denied,' Dad. It's in black and white."

"Did you apply late?" Mom asked.

"Mom, please," Elizabeth replied.

"Well, of course not. I'm sorry, Elizabeth," her mother apologized.

A heavy silence hung over the dinner table. Elizabeth pushed the remains of an egg roll around on her plate. Finally she said, "There are three more schools. . . ."

"You'll get into one of them, surely." Vicki Lambert clicked her long fingernails and smiled. "God has a place for you."

The resounding ring of the phone pierced the gloom and sparked the family into motion. Jonathan bounded from the table like he was going for the goal line.

He smirked and handed the phone to Elizabeth. "It's for you."

She reached for the phone. "Hello."

A familiar squeal pierced her ear. "You're home! How long?"

Elizabeth smiled at the sound of her friend's voice. "Hi, Bailey. I'll be here until Wednesday."

"Let's do dinner."

Elizabeth agreed to meet Bailey and several other friends for dinner on Tuesday.

Later, in the kitchen, Elizabeth helped her dad clean up while her mother read to her from her electronic data assistant.

"You see Dr. Roth first thing in the morning. His office manager thinks they can get you new contacts by the late afternoon."

"Perfect!" Elizabeth stored the leftovers on the bottom shelf of the refrigerator.

"It was good of Conrad to squeeze you in." Dad rinsed the dishcloth, wrung out the excess water, and wiped down the table.

"I set you up with Dr. Geller on Tuesday for a dental cleaning," Mom said.

"Tuesday? How'd you get me in so fast?"

"Told them you were only home a few days."

Elizabeth shook her head. If anyone could work a deal, it was her mom. She bundled up a full trash bag and set it by the door to the garage. Behind her, Jonathan dropped a fresh bag into the kitchen garbage can.

"Don't forget to take out the trash, son." Dad stood propped against the counter, legs crossed at the ankles, hands in his pockets. He regarded Elizabeth. "Grandpa tells me you have a *friend*."

Elizabeth sat at the kitchen table with a cold diet soda and glass of ice. "Grandpa is practically delusional, Dad. You should really consider checking him into a padded room."

Jonathan laughed. "Not Grandpa. He's too cool."

"I don't see you having time for romance, darling," Mom said, still focused on her electronic data assistant. Elizabeth glanced over to see her entering a list of to-dos.

"Exactly, Mom," she agreed. "I think all of White Birch has gone berserk with romantic notions. Every time I turn around, someone is trying to link me with Kavan Donovan.

"By the way, Dad, you never told me your family was so nosy."

Her mother laughed. "I told you, Paul."

"They aren't nosy, just interested, caring. . . ," he defended.

Elizabeth sipped her drink and sat cross-legged in the cushioned chair. "Don't get me wrong. I like White Birch. I'm actually having fun, which surprises me. But this whole 'get the granddaughter married off' has got to stop."

Her father walked over and kissed the top of her head. "You'll be in grad school in less than two months. White Birch and all the talk of romance and Kavan will be a pleasant but fading memory."

Lying in her own bed that night, the silver moonlight illuminating her room, her dad's words echoed in her head. *A pleasant but fading memory.*

Tears stung in her eyes. She actually missed White Birch and Kavan. Did she really want it to end in two months?

She rolled over onto her side. Truth be told, Elizabeth didn't want Kavan Donovan to be a fading memory.

"Okay, Rick, stop. We'll unload the lumber here." Kavan unlatched the tailgate on his pickup and hopped into the bed. Rick joined him, hauling boards to the Division of Forests and Lands' Fourth of July exhibition site in the center of town.

Kavan paused to look around. The town square buzzed with holiday preparations. He rubbed his hands together and faced his lanky partner.

"Let's get this booth built," he said, pulling plans from his shirt pocket.

"What's Travis Knight on your case about?" Rick asked, taking the plans from Kavan.

"He claims my refurbishment budget for the White Birch tower is *way* overdrawn."

Rick shook his head. "Interesting."

"Yeah, I bought this stuff with my own money just to avoid the hassle."

"Doesn't seem right," Rick muttered.

"No, it doesn't." Kavan smoothed out the construction plans on the ground. "It's a simple frame booth, Rick."

For the next hour or so, the two worked on the fire safety booth for the Fourth of July celebration.

"Whatever happened to those poachers you chased down?" Rick asked, wiping the sweat from his brow with the back of his hand. "Never heard the end of that story."

"They got caught, did a few hours of community service."

Rick dropped his hammer in the toolbox. "They'll do it again."

"Or worse," Kavan concluded.

"Afternoon, gentlemen." Matt Lambert walked up to the display.

Rick and Kavan each shook his hand.

"Need some help? Woodworking is my specialty."

Kavan nodded in recognition. Indeed, Matt Lambert's craftsmanship bordered on legendary. "We're about done, sir," he said. "Besides, we're just tapping together a few boards. Nothing fancy."

"Nevertheless, I should have strolled by sooner."

Kavan saw Rick peek at his watch. Dinnertime neared, and Rick had a new baby at home. "Why don't you go on, Rick. Grandpa Matt can help me finish up."

Rick thanked Kavan and dashed off toward his truck. Grandpa took up a hammer. "Elizabeth comes home tomorrow."

Kavan stretched the canvas across the back of the booth and grinned. "Is it tomorrow?"

"Yes, tomorrow." Grandpa tacked a nail into the canvas.

"Hmm," Kavan muttered.

Grandpa chuckled. "She won't be easy to catch, but it's possible."

Kavan moved to the side and held up the canvas. "Elizabeth doesn't want to be caught."

"Oh, she's caught all right," Grandpa said, nailing up the canvas for Kavan again. "She just doesn't know it."

Kavan shook his head. "I don't know, Grandpa."

Grandpa placed his hand on Kavan's shoulder. "Her whole life, she's set a goal and achieved it. Falling in love wasn't on the list. She's a lot like her sweet mother. Vicki is a very practical businesswoman. She wouldn't marry my son until he finished grad school and saved up several thousand dollars. That was a lot of money in the seventies."

Kavan gave a low whistle. He moved to the front of the booth and covered the bottom half with more of the canvas.

Grandpa continued. "Elizabeth has this notion that falling in love is trivial, a waste of time. She's seen her friends lose focus on their careers and education because men tell them they are beautiful."

"Can't see Elizabeth doing that," Kavan said.

"No, she won't let herself."

Kavan stopped working and faced the older man. "Elizabeth has a lot of pride in her pursuits."

Grandpa nodded. "Won't deny it."

"I can't see her giving it all up for me or anyone."

"Maybe not now, but someday, my boy, someday. Be patient. Be her friend."

Kavan resumed work. "That's the plan, Gramps. That *is* the plan."

On his back porch, Kavan sat in his rocker, gently swaying back and forth, the light of day evanescing. He sipped a cold bottle of soda and listened to the song of the breeze.

Talking to Grandpa Matt about Elizabeth stirred his longing for her. Though he confessed he would miss her, he'd tried to focus on other things while she was away.

Between his growing feelings for Elizabeth and the turmoil at work, Kavan made sure he took extra time each day to sit before the Father. Fortunately, Travis had taken the week off as vacation so the brewing trouble over the refurbishment budget was on the back burner.

Tipping his head back, Kavan took a deep breath. He loved the peaceful sounds of night and the abiding comfort of the Lord.

Now that his mind's eye was picturing the curly-haired brunette, he wanted to see her. He wondered what time she would be home and if he would see her soon. He imagined she'd have a full schedule between Lambert's Furniture and Sinclair's.

He reached for his cell phone. *Lord, should I call her?* He hesitated, punched in Elizabeth's cell number, but pressed the END button instead of TALK.

Grandpa Matt was right, he thought. *Elizabeth would be a hard one to catch.*

He punched in the number again and hit SEND before he could change his mind. He stood and leaned against the rail. *Friends, we're just friends.*

"Hello," she said, rather loud.

"Hi, it's Kavan." High-pitched voices and laughter filled his ear.

"Hello?" she repeated, louder.

"Elizabeth, it's Kavan."

"Just a second."

He could hear her shuffling around. The background noise faded.

"Wow, it's so noisy in the restaurant. I had to step outside."

He wanted to ask what she was doing, who she was with, but decided to keep his question neutral. "Having a good time?"

"Awesome." Her voice rose with excitement.

He smiled, picturing her face and the pink hue excitement always colored on her cheeks. "Sounds like a fun crowd."

"Bunch of engineering nerds." She laughed. "We've been talking shop."

Disappointment stabbed him, but he removed it from his voice when he said, "Good for you. Keep your eye on the goal."

"No doubt. These guys would never let me hear the end of it if I didn't go to grad school. Never."

"I'll let you go."

She suddenly asked, as if realizing Kavan Donovan was on the other end of the line, "Why did you call?"

"No reason."

"No reason?" She sounded suspicious.

"Yes. Drive home safely," he said, ready to hang up.

She snickered. "Is there any other way?"

"Guess not."

"Night, Kavan."

"Night, Elizabeth."

On the Fourth of July, Elizabeth strolled the White Birch square with Ethan and Julie. While Ethan greeted practically everyone they passed, Julie and Elizabeth carried on an intimate discussion of graduate school.

"Don't get discouraged," Julie said. "You have the right stuff to get into the best schools. But I remember the anxiety of waiting."

"Anxiety is putting it lightly," Elizabeth said with a chuckle. "It's just weird that I've been turned down and haven't heard from the remaining three schools."

"Come this way, ladies." Ethan motioned with his arm.

They followed. Julie gave a final word of advice. "If you don't hear from more schools, or if you get another rejection, call MIT's transcript office and have a copy of your transcript sent to you. It could have a clerical error."

Elizabeth opened her mouth in surprise. "I never thought of that."

Julie laughed. "You're a true linear thinking engineer, Beth. Gotta think outside the box sometimes."

Elizabeth spread out her arms and lifted her hands. "What can I say? Guilty as charged."

Laughing, they stopped beside Ethan and the fire safety booth. Kavan came around the corner with a passel of kids. He handed them balloons and candy, reminding them they could prevent forest fires.

"Hello." He glanced their way after sending the kids off.

"Nice display," Ethan commented as he scanned the booth.

Seeing Kavan made Elizabeth's heart dance, and she feared her feelings showed in her face. *Why does he affect me this way?*

"Hi, Elizabeth." He stepped toward her and kissed her cheek in greeting. "Welcome back."

"Good to be back," she said, his touch sparking a shiver.

Ethan started up a conversation, and the four of them chatted for a few minutes until another group of kids came strolling up, linked together by their hands. Some of them recognized Julie from school and called to her with a sweet chorus of "Hi, Mrs. Lambert."

While Julie hugged them and Ethan talked to more townsfolk, Elizabeth watched Kavan. He walked down the line of children, ruffling their hair, telling them they were going to learn how *not* to start a fire.

"Hey." He jogged over to her. "Want to help me with the kids?"

"Sure." For a split second, she was unable to imagine anything she'd want to do more.

"Great." He turned to walk away, hesitated, then faced her again. He pulled her into his embrace. "I'm really glad you're back."

She rested her head on his shoulder, breathing in the subtle scent of his cologne. "Me, too. Me, too."

Chapter 11

As dusk settled over White Birch, Kavan put away the last of the coloring pens and construction paper. "Looks like everyone is settling in for dinner before the fireworks." He stepped around to the front of the booth and closed the distance between them.

Her eyes shimmered with excitement. "That was fun."

He smiled. "Yeah, the kids are great."

She stretched and then rested her hands in the hip pockets of her jean shorts. "What now?"

"Dinner. Everyone will picnic or go to one of the restaurants before the fireworks."

He watched Elizabeth survey the area. Large groups of people were already gathering by the lake, picking premium spots for the pyrotechnic show. Some stood eating hot dogs from street vendors; others unpacked picnic baskets.

"I'd better find Ethan and Julie."

Kavan reached for his toolbox. "Or," he started, "you can help me tear this down, and I'll treat you to pizza at Giuseppe's."

"Oh no, Kavan, you don't have to do that. I'll help, but you don't have to buy my dinner." She reached for a hammer.

"Consider it a payback. The kids loved you. Besides, before you left for Boston, we agreed to a pizza date."

Elizabeth stiffened. "Not a date. A, um, get-together."

He shook his head at her insistence. "You know, even friends can use the word *date*. It doesn't have to imply anything romantic."

"Well, in this town, one cannot be too careful."

Grandpa Matt's words echoed through Kavan's head. *She won't be easy to catch, but it's possible.* Tearing apart the booth frame, Kavan wondered if he really wanted to catch Elizabeth Lambert. There were a lot of other lovely and gracious women to choose from; he just. . .

He stopped in midthought. Who was he kidding? He had yet to meet a woman who captured his heart like Elizabeth had. Pride and all, he'd ask her to marry him in a heartbeat if he thought she'd say yes.

"What are you thinking about so intently, Donovan?" she asked, walking up behind him.

He turned toward her with a start. "Lost in thought."

She propped her hands on her hips. "I guess so. I called for you twice."

"Sorry, what did you need?"

"I folded the canvases and put them over there." She pointed to a spot beyond the booth. " 'Cause I didn't know where you parked your truck."

He faced the last two boards of the booth and hammered them apart. "The truck is down the street."

"I'm going to find Ethan and Julie so they know I'm having pizza with you. Do you want me to get your truck?"

"Yes, please." Kavan pulled his keys out of his pocket. Their fingers touched when he handed them to her. A tingle raced from the tip of his fingers to the top of his arm.

She glanced down at her hand holding the keys, then looked into his eyes. For a moment, he thought she was going to say she felt a tingle, too. "Wh–" She cleared her throat. "Where did you park the truck?"

He motioned over his shoulder. "On the other side of the post office."

He watched her hurry away.

Lord, if she's not the one for me, You'd better send a bolt of lightning. . . . He gazed up at the twilight sky. *Not a cloud in sight.* He smiled.

❧❧

During dinner, Elizabeth studied him, trying to understand why the sound of his voice made her heart flip-flop. She focused on the strange feeling that came over her when she was in his presence, analyzing her thoughts and emotions. It couldn't merely be his striking face or lean, muscular frame. She knew lots of handsome men in college. In fact, one of her best buddies won a best-looking coeds contest. But Mark Wilder never made her feel the way Kavan Donovan made her feel.

During her short trip home to Boston, she renewed her commitment to grad school. How could she not complete the journey she'd begun?

Her mother's statement still echoed in her head. *I don't see you having time for romance, darling.*

She's right, she's right. I don't have time for a serious relationship. School is my destiny. Elizabeth twirled the ends of her hair.

"I don't know what's going on with the budget," Elizabeth heard Kavan say as she brought her thoughts into the moment.

She propped her elbows on the table and gazed into his eyes. "I'm sorry, what? A budget?"

Kavan chuckled and fell back against his chair. "Earth to Elizabeth."

She grinned and hid her eyes behind her arm. "I'm sorry." She lowered her arm so she could see him and confessed, "Distracted by my own thoughts."

Kavan waved off her excuse. "I understand."

"So, tell me about this budget." Elizabeth picked up another slice of pizza. She took a bite and glanced at Kavan, waiting.

"Just boring work stuff." He took a drink from his soda.

"What's wrong with the budgets?"

"Not budgets. Bud*get.* Just one."

A flicker of concern reflected in his brown eyes, and compassion moved

Elizabeth. She reached across the table and tapped his hand lightly. "Tell me what's wrong."

"Nothing's wrong, really." He shifted in his seat. "I am in charge of refurbishing the old White Birch fire tower, and it seems my budget is out of whack."

"What do you mean, 'out of whack'?" Elizabeth put her pizza slice down and pushed her plate away.

"Accounting claims I'm in the red, overdrawn. I can't seem to figure out what's going on. All they give us is a summary report."

She crossed her arms and leaned on the table. "Do you have records on your computer?"

He chewed a bite of pizza and nodded. The waitress came to the table and offered to refill their drinks.

"It's plugged into a spreadsheet. But the program I used for my spreadsheet keeps crashing. I can't get at the data. I have backups at home, but they're about a month behind. I've been too busy. . . ." He sighed and ran his hand across his forehead.

Elizabeth didn't know what to say, seeing his frustration and his uneasiness. "I'll pray for the Lord to bring you an answer."

He leaned forward. "Thank you. I appreciate it."

The subject changed, and by the time the waitress brought the bill, he had Elizabeth laughing over one of her cousin Jeff's high school antics.

She reached for the bill, but Kavan snatched the check out of her fingers. "Nothing doing. You helped me this afternoon, and I appreciate it."

She let the bill go. "Guess you can write it off as department expense."

Kavan feigned a laugh and pulled out his debit card. In a sardonic tone, he said, "I don't think so."

The waitress came over to pick up the bill with the card. Elizabeth excused herself to go to the ladies' room. She returned to the table just as Kavan signed the receipt.

"Ready?" he said, scribbling his name with a flourish.

Placing her hand on his shoulder, Elizabeth leaned over, squinting at the paper. "Again with that signature?" She laughed.

Kavan stood, a saucy grin on his lips. "I was premed for one quarter."

Elizabeth let go a robust chuckle and followed him to the door.

❧❧

"Your chariot, milady." Kavan opened the truck door for Elizabeth, bowing low.

"Thank you, my lord." She hopped inside.

Kavan shut the door and walked around to the driver's side. He'd enjoyed dinner but felt like he spent too much time rehashing his work problems.

Ask Elizabeth about herself. He tried to think of something to ask her.

"I have a blanket in the back. Care to share it with me and watch the fireworks?" He started the engine with a quick turn of the ignition.

"Sounds like fun."

Kavan shifted the truck into gear and pulled out of the parking lot.

"Thanks for dinner," Elizabeth said softly.

He looked over at her. She was lovely to him, so very lovely. "Can't think of a better way to spend the Fourth of July."

They drove in silence to the lake. The quietness came with peace and comfort. Kavan held back from taking it as a sign of blessing from the Lord.

Parking close proved impossible, so Kavan found a spot at the end of Main Street. Casually, he slipped his hand into Elizabeth's as they walked toward the crowd.

"Any more news from grad schools?" he asked, determined to let her talk for awhile.

"No." Her voice rang flat in the night air.

"You will, don't worry."

"That's what I keep hearing."

He didn't miss the irritation in her voice.

"What's your focus again? Nuclear physics?"

"Engineering," she emphasized.

"Ah right. Here's a spot over here."

She followed, but slipped her hand out of his. He glanced over his shoulder at her, gazing down on the top of her head. He couldn't see her face, but he sensed a change in her demeanor.

"What do you want to do with a master's in nuclear engineering?" He spread the blanket on the ground. "Here we go." He sat down, legs crossed at the ankle.

She stood, putting her hands on her hips. "What kind of question is that?"

He snapped his head up. Was she angry? In the fading light, he couldn't see her eyes. "What's the purpose of the degree? What field do you want to focus on? What kind of job are you thinking of getting?"

"Energy." She sat down on the edge of the blanket. "I'd like to work at a nuclear energy plant or do research."

"You've got to be kidding," he said. "Nuclear plants will be the death of us all if we don't—"

She cut him off. "Death of us all?"

"Ever hear of Chernobyl?" He fell back against the blanket, landing on his elbows.

"The safety of those reactors was ignored." Her voice warbled in a high pitch.

Across the lake, the first fireworks boomed and splashed fiery color in the night sky.

"Sure, and look at the devastation."

"You can't lump all nuclear reactors into the Chernobyl class. New energy standards are being generated every day."

"Yeah, like the standard of natural energy resources. We'd all be a lot better off—"

She hopped up again and peered down at him, hands on her hips. "Kavan, there are not enough natural resources to heat, cool, and feed the world. As it is now, most Third World countries are stripped of natural resources. Nuclear energy could provide relief for millions."

"And put them at risk." Kavan stood, not sure why he continued to banter with her. Clearly, the subject touched a nerve.

Another fireworks display exploded overhead. It popped open like an umbrella and sparks floated down. The crowd around them *oohed* and *aahed*.

She opened her arms. "Typical *naturalist*. The environment is all you care about. Yet you want to deprive millions the luxury of affordable energy. Meanwhile, the earth is drained of natural resources. All the while, your crowd insists nuclear energy will be the death of us all. You can't have it both ways, Kavan."

What is she saying? He reached for her arm and asked in a low tone. "Elizabeth, are you sure you're still talking about energy resources?"

Boom! Phosphorus light splashed against the darkness, and for a split second, he could see the hard lines drawn on her face.

"What else would I be talking about?" she snapped, turning on her heel. "I'll see you later, Kavan. Julie and Ethan are probably wondering where I am." She walked away, and in only a few steps, Kavan lost sight of her in the crowd and shadows.

Chapter 12

Elizabeth rode in silence to Grandpa and Grandma's house in the backseat of Ethan and Julie's car. She listened to their intimate conversation about the day's events that touched them. Julie enjoyed seeing the children and the fireworks, and Ethan rather liked socializing with White Birch's citizens.

"What'd you like most about the day?" Julie asked, adjusting to face Elizabeth. The lights from the dash showed her pretty smile.

Elizabeth gave a generic, safe answer. "The fireworks."

What she wanted to say was the entire day: Kavan and the fire safety booth, Kavan and dinner, Kavan and the fireworks. Yet, the entire situation conflicted her. How could she have feelings for him? Emotional attachments could devastate her future plans.

When he asked her about school, panic gripped her. She had not thought about higher education since she laid eyes on him at the fire safety booth. Not once!

She was going to let her dream go all because she allowed a summer crush to weave its way into her heart. So she picked a fight. Thinking about it now, she felt guilty. But she had to get away from him, put some distance between them.

She sighed and dropped her head against the window. *My friends would never let me hear the end of it. I gave them such a hard time when each of them fell in love.*

Suddenly, she sat up straight and stared out the front window. She clenched her jaw in resolution. *I won't lose sight of school. I won't fall for Kavan.*

Ethan turned into the driveway and started up the hill toward the house.

"Thanks for the ride home." Elizabeth leaned forward between the front seats.

Ethan smiled at her. "We had fun. Thanks for hanging with us."

Julie objected with a wink. "I think she spent more time with a handsome ranger than us, babe."

Ethan chuckled as he pulled around by the kitchen door. Elizabeth fell back against her seat. "He's a friend, you two. A *friend.*"

"They make the best partners." Julie glanced over her shoulder at her cousin-in-law.

Elizabeth stared straight into her eyes. "I'm going to grad school."

"I married Ethan right out of high school, and I still earned my master's." Julie's statement caused another wave of panic to splash over Elizabeth.

"Good for you." She reached for the door handle. "Marriage is not for me."

"Will it ever be?" Julie asked.

Elizabeth yanked the handle and opened the door slightly. "What is with this family and marriage?"

"We find it rather pleasant and safe and wonderful," Julie said.

Ethan added, "Beth, marriage isn't the issue; your ardent opposition to marriage is the issue."

"Oh right, Ethan. I'm the bad guy 'cause I'd rather finish school than be a giggly, lovesick house frau." She shoved the door the rest of the way open and stepped out. Her irritation showed and she knew it. "I'm sorry, you guys, I'm tired."

"Don't worry about it, Beth," Julie said. "Call me later if you need to talk."

"Thanks. Good night." Elizabeth watched them drive away, and instead of going inside, she slipped down the side of the hill toward the covered bridge. Her emotions felt raw and exposed. As she moved under the cover of the bridge, tears spilled down her cheeks. She fought for control.

"Lord, I know I haven't been close to You lately, but since You are my Friend, can I talk to You?" More tears came. For the longest time, Elizabeth walked the length of the bridge, unburdening her heart to the Lord. No cars drove past, and it seemed that the Lord arranged a private audience just for her, His friend.

🙢🙢

Kavan woke feeling as if he'd never been asleep. He slapped the snooze button on his alarm and buried his head under the pillow. He'd tossed and turned most of the night, his dreams invaded by fireworks and Elizabeth's sharp, sarcastic words, followed by Travis Knight's accusations and mistrust.

Last night, he sat on the porch, praying until midnight, asking the Lord to search him. The recent refurbishment fiasco and Travis's subtle imputations, coupled with Elizabeth's erratic behavior, caused him to wonder if the Lord was trying to tell him something.

He dozed for a few more minutes before the alarm sounded a second time. He sat up slowly and dangled his legs over the side of the bed. With a yawn, he headed for the shower. Morning light filtered through the bathroom window. Kavan hovered over the sink, splashing his face with cold water. *Gotta wake up.*

He brushed his teeth, shaved, and showered. Dressed in a freshly laundered uniform, he headed to the kitchen to make some coffee. Fred and Ginger waited by the back door, tails wagging.

"Morning, Fred. Morning, Ginger." He stroked them each on the head before turning the knob. They bolted out into the fresh morning air. Kavan left the door ajar and popped a couple pieces of bread into the toaster. When the coffee finished brewing, he poured a cup and took it to the porch along with the toast.

Sipping his coffee and munching his breakfast, he meditated on the Lord. A verse from the book of Psalms flowed through his head. *"Search me, O God. . . test me. . . See if there is any offensive way in me."*

Nothing came to mind. "Lord, I trust You to take care of me. My reputation is in Your hands. You will accomplish what concerns me."

He went inside after a few more minutes and set his dishes in the sink. He picked up the floppy with the refurbishment data on it and headed for work. First thing on his morning agenda was to get his office computer installed with a new spreadsheet program and load his backup records. With Travis on vacation, he had time to figure out what was going on.

"Morning, Rick." Kavan walked over to his desk.

Rick looked up. "Oh—um, Kavan. Good morning."

Kavan furrowed his brow and gave his coworker a second glance. He pulled up to his desk and booted up the computer. Reaching in his top desk drawer, Kavan retrieved the new software CD. "You okay, Rick?"

"Sure. Fine." He smiled. "Seems the fire safety booth was a success."

Kavan nodded. "The kids loved it. And. . ." He leaned back and arched his brow at Rick. "I had the prettiest assistant in White Birch."

Rick chuckled and consented with a nod. "Anything going on between you two?"

He didn't mean to, but Kavan sighed. "Just friends."

On his way home that night, Kavan took a detour to the fire tower. He wanted to resume the refurbishment project, but as long as the matter of the budget remained unresolved, he felt shackled. Climbing the old stairs to the top, Kavan gazed out over the White Mountains. He took the steps near the top two at a time.

He pushed open the trapdoor of the tower floor and climbed inside. He leaned out the tower window, and with a loud voice he hollered, "Good evening, Lord! Evening, White Mountains!"

He closed his eyes and breathed in the night mountain air. *Fresh and clean. . .* He stopped. His eyes popped open and scanned the horizon. Kavan took another deep breath.

He smelled smoke.

In one quick motion, he found the tower's stored binoculars and lifted them to his eyes. To the west, along the ridge, dark smoke billowed above the trees.

His heartbeat quickened.

Fire!

Closing the kitchen door, Elizabeth turned and kissed Grandma on the cheek, then snatched a warm cookie from the cooling rack.

"How was your day?" Grandma asked.

"Wonderful." Elizabeth dashed to the stairs. "Gotta change for Sinclair's. Be down in a minute."

She hummed as she changed her clothes and wrapped her long curls into a ponytail. She grabbed a makeup brush and touched up her foundation and cheek color before heading back downstairs.

Since her unburdening with Jesus last night, she felt renewed. If coming to White Birch for the summer produced nothing more than reconnecting with her friend Jesus, it was well worth it. She regretted her time in college where she dismissed the tugging of the Holy Spirit on her heart. She wouldn't make the same mistake in graduate school.

In the kitchen, Grandpa sat at the table with a stack of cookies and a tall glass of milk in front of him. He reached for the first cookie from the stack.

Elizabeth stopped and stared at him. "You can't be serious."

"I am." He winked at his wife.

"Your cholesterol must be ridiculous."

Grandma waved her spatula in the air. "He's healthier than men half his age. Got a hollow leg, that one. Never could seem to fill him up."

Elizabeth opened the fridge door and pulled out a packet of turkey and a slice of cheese. Grabbing the mayonnaise and mustard, she went to the counter to make a sandwich.

"While you're making that sandwich, Bethy, mind if I talk to you?" Grandpa asked. He picked up another cookie.

"Sure, Grandpa." Elizabeth peeked at him over her shoulder. She took two pieces of bread from the wrapper and set them on a paper towel.

"I got some of those lunch-size chips for you today," Grandma interjected. "They're in the pantry."

"Yum. . . Thanks, Grandma."

"I want to talk about grad-u-ate school." He reclined comfortably in his chair at the kitchen table.

Elizabeth laughed at his inflection. "What about grad-u-ate school?"

"Why are you going?"

A cold chill ran down her spine. At the same time, she felt a hot flash burn her cheeks. *He sounds like Kavan.*

"It's my destiny, Grandpa. You know that. Dad, Mom, and I have talked about it since I was twelve."

Grandpa motioned for her to sit by him. Grandma finished making her sandwich.

"I've been praying for you, Bethy. I'm not sure this is the time for you to go to graduate school. You have a fine degree in electrical engineering. I happen to know that Creager Electronics is hiring electrical engineers."

Why is he bringing this up? Her insides trembled as if she were cold. "Don't tell me you pulled a string for me at Creager, Grandpa. I'm going to grad school."

"Did you know I went to Harvard after the war?"

Elizabeth's eyes widened. "Harvard? No, you didn't."

"I did." Grandpa confirmed with a slight nod, picking up a third cookie.

"You are full of surprises." Elizabeth smiled.

"But you know, Bethy, I had no business being at Harvard. I didn't have any scholarly interest. I was just doing it because my pride wanted a Harvard diploma hanging on my wall. After all, I'd been to war. I was a man." Grandpa tapped his fist on his chest. "But deep down I knew I wanted to take over your great-grandpa's business here in White Birch."

Grandma said in a small voice, "My father promised us his mill business, which your grandpa grew into Lambert's Furniture."

Elizabeth turned to her grandpa. "What happened?"

He swallowed a bite of cookie, gazed toward his wife, and recounted. "We had no car, very little money. One snowy morning, I skipped classes, pretending to be sick. I told Betty I'd study at home." He paused, shifting his gaze to Elizabeth.

"Your grandma was pregnant with your aunt Barbara and had to go to work while I slept until noon. That evening I looked out the window to see my pregnant wife walking home from work in the falling snow, carrying a sack of groceries. She slipped on the ice and nearly fell. A passerby caught her arm and steadied her."

"How come I never heard this story before?" Elizabeth wanted to know. She glanced from her grandpa to her grandma and back again.

Grandpa shrugged and finished his story. "That night, the Lord spoke to me out of 1 Peter 5." Grandpa quoted the verse. " 'Young men, in the same way be submissive to those who are older. All of you, clothe yourselves with humility toward one another, because, "God opposes the proud but gives grace to the humble." ' "

A flush warmed Elizabeth's neck and face. "What's your point, Grandpa?" She peeked at her watch.

"I love you, Beth. But I believe your pride is causing you to pursue the advanced degree. Do you really want to study nuclear engineering?"

She pushed back her chair and stood. "It's a prestigious, lucrative field, Grandpa. And it's very open to women."

"Electrical engineering is a lucrative career, too. Also open to women."

"I'm going to grad school," Elizabeth said between clenched teeth.

"You sound like me sixty years ago when I wanted to go to Harvard. No advice of my father's or Betty's would change my mind. Then I see my wife, carrying my child, working harder than I was at keeping us together." Grandpa bowed his head and softened his voice. "It humbles me still."

Elizabeth rested her hands on the back of the chair. "You make my point. That's why I'm not about to get into a relationship until I'm finished with school."

"Wise decision," Grandpa countered. "However, my challenge to you, Beth, is not about Kavan or marriage, but your purpose in going to grad school. Pray; ask the Lord to reveal the secrets of your heart."

Elizabeth regarded him without saying a word. She loved and respected him too much to ignore his words. "I have to go to work."

"Pray about what I said," Grandpa said.

She grabbed her purse and started for the door. "I'll pray, but I promise you, I'm going to grad school."

❧❧

On the drive to Sinclair's, Elizabeth replayed the kitchen conversation, churning over Grandpa's words, searching for any truth to his challenge.

"Lord, is he right? I've planned on going to grad school for so long, I can't imagine *not* going. Everyone expects me to go. Mom, Dad, and Jonathan. . .my friends. But what is Your plan for my life?"

Before she resolved the issue in her mind and with the Lord, she arrived at Sinclair's. Elizabeth zipped into the large parking lot and dashed inside.

"Sorry I'm late, Joann."

Her boss followed her to the time clock. "No problem. Just relieve Molly at the service desk. Everything okay?"

Elizabeth paused, then looked her boss in the eyes. "I'm not sure. Grandpa thinks I don't really know why I'm going to grad school. That I have no purpose for going."

"Ha, I've been saying that since the moment I met you."

Elizabeth held up her hand and rolled her eyes. "Don't start."

She headed toward the front counter. Joann followed, reminding her to count down the afternoon tills and refill the candy racks by the cash register. Suddenly a blaring siren filled Elizabeth's ears. "What *is* that?" she asked, halting in the middle of the aisle.

Concern covered Joann's face. "Fire siren, calling all the volunteers."

Several men rushed past them out of the store.

From her post at the service desk, Elizabeth watched as men and women rushed in and out. Finally, she asked one of them, "Where is the fire?"

"Up on Pine Knoll Mountain. The rangers are fighting it now, but volunteers are being called in." He paid for his purchase and hurried away.

Kavan!

Throughout the night, news trickled into the store about the fire. Many believed it had been contained, but none of the rangers or volunteer firefighters had emerged.

Elizabeth could not stop thinking about Kavan. She called his house and cell phone. No answer. She prayed for the Lord to protect him, but her heartbeat pounded with concern for him like the ticking of the clock.

"Go," Joann finally said an hour before Elizabeth's shift ended.

"Go?"

"Go to the command center. See if he's okay."

Elizabeth hustled around the counter and darted toward the time clock.

"Keep me posted," Joann called after her.

"I will. I will."

She ran to clock out and grab her backpack.

❧❧

Somehow, in the chaos, she found Jeff. With his help, Elizabeth made her way to the fire's command center. She parked her VW out of the way and stood on the perimeter of the activity. In the distance, she could see the fire burning along the ridge, trees flaming like matchsticks.

The mountainside was engulfed in flames. Fire billowed up from the surface and danced across the treetops.

"Kavan!" a uniformed ranger communicated with the firefighters over a large, handheld radio.

From her vantage point, Elizabeth tried to spot Kavan among the men at the command center, hoping to see him safe in the crowd. But there was no sign of him. *He's on that ridge; I just know it.* Her heart hurt with anxiety.

Chapter 13

Kavan trailed the firefighters working along the ridge, flanking the fading fire, beating out hot spots. A chain saw dangled from one hand. He anchored a pickax with the other. Grateful for the cool night air and the valiant efforts of the firefighters, he believed the blaze to be contained. The knot in his stomach loosened slightly.

The radio strapped to his side crackled and clicked. Kavan tilted his ear toward the sound. "The wind is picking up, Kavan," the operations officer, Steve Mayer, warned over the radio.

Kavan peered over his shoulder, scanning the area he and the other firefighters had just covered. From the service road where they'd been dropped off to the point where they now stood, the embers burned low. "Steve, what does it look like from down there?"

"Fire is burning along the bottom of the ridge, but it's dying down."

"We're still fighting hot spots," Kavan reported.

"Watch the wind," Steve warned again.

The knot in Kavan's middle tightened. "Copy. I'll keep an eye out. Over."

The radio fell silent. Kavan hiked up the ridge, picking at hot spots, watching the progress of the other eight firefighters as they climbed higher. He could feel the wind gusting through the trees.

"Lord, calm the wind." He watched Rick beat out another burning patch.

Ash fluttered in the air, and the smell of smoke permeated Kavan's nostrils. The wind knocked against him.

Up ahead, hot spots still ignited. Behind him, the burned area smoldered with dying embers. So far there existed no threat of the fire igniting again. Vigilant, Kavan stepped forward.

"What's the word, Kavan?" Chet, one of the firefighters asked, pausing to wait for his leader.

"Strong wind gusts. Stay alert."

The firefighter nodded and went back to work. Several of the others beat out a spot fire.

Kavan worked the draw between the two ridges, climbing upward while swinging his pickax. The labor made the muscles in his shoulders ache, and the knee he'd injured chasing the poachers throbbed with pain.

More than seven hours had passed since he'd first spotted the smoke. He and his crew had worked tirelessly since the initial fire siren, breaking briefly just after dark to eat and rest. Kavan aimed his flashlight at his watch.

Midnight.

A picture of Elizabeth flashed through his weary thoughts. It seemed like forever since he'd seen her.

Kavan peered over his shoulder again, down the ridge. The smell of smoke intensified. Embers floated in the wind, and it alarmed him. Kavan made a quick assessment of the area, plotting an escape route, just in case those embers landed on fresh kindling. The men on the ridge were in his charge.

In the next minute, Steve called over the radio. "Team three, be advised the wind is picking up. Teams one and two are coming in. Over."

Kavan didn't like the eerie feel of the wind, either. "Ten-four. Send the pickup. We'll work our way down to the service road. Over."

"Truck is on its way. Over."

Relief popped inside of him when Steve radioed that the truck was on its way. Kavan instructed his team to sweep the area and head for the pick-up location.

The firefighters beat out hot spots while traversing toward the meeting point. Kavan's stomach rumbled with hunger. One of the men told a joke and had them all laughing just as Steve radioed again.

"Team three! Kavan!" Steve sounded panicked. "The access road is blocked. The wind ignited the fire. It's jumped to the trees. Get out of there! Over."

Kavan whipped around and ran to the top of the crevasse. The orange glow of fire and swirling smoke filled the horizon. Wind gusts funneled up the ridge. It was only a matter of time before the entire area would be consumed by fire.

"Crown fire! Run!" Kavan shouted, adrenaline driving him toward the top of the ridge.

Elizabeth hustled with the other volunteers at the command post, serving sandwiches and water to tired firefighters. A friend of her grandmother's had spotted her and enlisted her aid. Elizabeth welcomed the distraction. Concern for Kavan had her insides twisted into nervous knots.

She watched the men in charge from the edge of activity, listening as the man referred to as the operations officer directed the firefighting teams.

She lifted her head when she heard him bellow Kavan's name into the small black radio. Her heartbeat seemed to stop for a moment. Making herself small, she inched along the perimeter of the command post, yearning to hear more.

"Kavan, are you there?"

Elizabeth waited for the buzz of Kavan's voice over the radio, but no response came.

"Team three, come in! Kavan," the man shouted.

When the radio remained silent, she heard him whisper, "Come on, man, where are you?"

Elizabeth's knees buckled, but she caught herself. *Kavan, oh, Kavan, be all right. Please! Jesus, Jesus...*

The hair on her arms stood up, and a prickly feeling ran down her back.

"Get the helicopter up," the commander ordered.

Yes, do that, Elizabeth thought. *Find them. Please.*

She closed her eyes to pray, but a jolt caused her to open them. The operations officer stood before her.

"Can I help you?"

She swallowed and said in a shallow tone, "I'm a volunteer and, um, a friend of Kavan Donovan's."

He looked into her eyes. "He'll be all right. Smart one, that Kavan."

"Yes, I know." She slipped back into the shadows, using every ounce of faith to fuel the power of her prayers. "Jesus, my Friend, hear my prayer. Protect Your friends up on that ridge. Kavan loves You. Let him know You are with him now. You are good, and I trust You."

Hours passed. Elizabeth continued to pray as she worked along with the other volunteers. She could hear the dialogue between the man who spoke to her and the helicopter pilot.

"Any sign of them? Over."

"None," the pilot answered.

Glancing overhead, Elizabeth watched the helicopter circle the ridge, the enormous spotlight floating over the fading flames as two other teams fought the fire.

"Scan the bottom of the ridge. Surely they ran down the other side."

"Ten-four."

Biting the inside of her lip, Elizabeth strained to hear the pilot's response. It felt like an eternity passed before he came back over the radio.

"No sign."

When the commander sighed and dropped his head, despair snapped at Elizabeth. Tears blurred her vision. She remembered stories about wildfires and how their intense heat and fast-moving blaze could easily overtake a man.

From behind, a strong hand gripped her shoulders. "How are you holding up?" a familiar voice asked.

Elizabeth turned to meet the tender expression of her grandpa. "Not sure. Oh, Grandpa. . ." Her voice broke.

Grandpa embraced her. "The Lord knows what's going on. Let's keep praying. I believe it's going to be okay."

Elizabeth rested her head on his shoulder and prayed with him in silent unison. Finally, she stepped back and took a deep breath, smoothing her curls. Weary, but peaceful, she wondered aloud, "What time is it?"

"A little after midnight."

Gazing toward the ridge, she said, "He has to be okay, Grandpa. He has to be."

❦❦

Kavan's chest burned from breathing smoke as he ran uphill. His weak knee buckled several times when his foot landed on uneven terrain. Rick, Chet, and the other firefighters fell in behind him, single file. They could now see the glow of the fire a couple hundred yards behind them. The flames chased them up the hill. Treetops exploded into balls of fire.

Kavan reached for his radio, but it was not there. "I lost my radio," he shouted over his shoulder.

"Where are we going?" Rick asked, running on Kavan's flank.

"A cave!" Kavan directed.

Rick nodded.

Kavan led the troop several yards before the opening to the cave came into view. In one accord, the firefighters sprinted to safety as hot embers began to rain down on them. Inside the cave, they fell against the stone walls. Kavan tugged off his headgear and turned his face into a cool draft.

"There's an opening at the back of the cave. The draw from the fire is creating a breeze," he said, turning to Rick and the rest of the team. He smiled.

The others removed their headgear; laughter of relief echoed throughout the cave. Firefighter Liam Watson clicked on his lamp. The single glow filled the cave with low light.

The knot in Kavan's middle unraveled. With a quick scan, he counted to make sure each man had arrived to safety. *All here. Thank You, Lord.* He sighed a prayer.

"You did a good job out there," he said, letting his gaze fall on each man.

"We owe you," Liam said. "You were the only one who knew about this cave. We'd still be running."

A thin laugh escaped Kavan's lips. "I explored this cave as a kid. But I gotta tell you, I wasn't sure this was the right ridge." His body trembled as his nerves unwound and his taut emotions drained. "Rick, do you still have your radio?"

"Yeah." Rick clicked it on and tried to contact the command post. "Cave is blocking the signal."

Kavan dropped some of his gear to the cave floor and slid down against the rugged cave wall, favoring his bum knee. "When the fire burns through, we'll go back down the ridge through the burn area. Until then, have a seat."

The clamor of equipment releasing and hitting the ground echoed throughout the cave. No one spoke, each man left to his own reflection. Kavan used the last of his energy to pray. *Thank You, Lord, for hiding us in the cleft of this rock. Thank You.*

He closed his eyes and dreamed of Elizabeth.

❧❧

Exhausted, Elizabeth contemplated going home. But how could she when Kavan remained in harm's way? Grandpa had bid her good night a half hour ago, but he didn't try to convince her to leave.

I have to know he's all right.

With the blaze fading and contained, most of the volunteers had gone home. Wives of the firefighters remained, serving sandwiches and drinks to the returning teams. Blackened by smoke and exhausted, the firefighters collapsed on the ground around the command center. Silence hovered over them and, to Elizabeth, the ever-present knowledge that nine men had not returned.

"Lord, I know You are with them," she prayed, understanding that the peace she experienced was God's touch on her heart.

Suddenly, a strong, moist wind whipped through the camp, then a sweet, drizzling rain began to fall. Cheers erupted around the command center. Elizabeth joined them, laughing, clapping, cheering.

The operations officer shouted into the jubilation, "Team three is safe. They're on their way to the access road."

Elizabeth trembled with relief, and tears pooled in her eyes. "Thank You, Jesus. Thank You."

❧

In the distance, she watched the all-terrain vehicle bounce over charred ground toward them.

Kavan's safe. I can go home now, she resolved. But her feet refused to move. She stood planted by the food table, her gaze fixed in the distance. A load of soot-covered firefighters piled out of the all-terrain vehicle and walked toward the command center.

Amid cheering and applause, the firefighters entered the command center. With so many voices talking at once, Elizabeth could hardly make out the story they were trying to tell. Her gaze fell on Kavan. He looked absolutely wonderful, grime and all.

He dropped his gear to the ground and left the others for a drink of water. He downed a large bottle of water; then he spotted her. His gaze, intense and steady, locked onto hers. He set his water bottle on the table and strode toward her.

Trembling and overwhelmed, she started to cry.

Without a word, Kavan drew her to him. She lifted her face to his just as he bent toward her. With tender passion, his lips covered hers.

Chapter 14

Kavan woke late Wednesday morning. He was beginning to feel like his old self, having slept most of Tuesday and late this morning. He moved about slowly, feeling the ache in his knee as he showered and dressed, then tended the dogs. He decided to head into town for breakfast at the diner. He didn't have to work, and a late breakfast sounded just like what the doctor ordered.

He pulled into a slanted parking space along Main Street and shut off the truck engine.

"Welcome, Kavan, welcome!" the diner's proprietor, Sam Whitfield, greeted him, shuffling out from behind the counter. "Take this booth by the window. Best seat in the house."

Kavan stared at Sam, puzzled by his curious behavior. "Thanks, Sam." He slid into the booth.

"What'll ya have? It's on the house." The older gentleman hovered over him, exposing his big teeth.

"On the house?"

"On the house," Sam repeated.

"What for?"

"Ain't you seen the paper? You're a hero. Saved those boys up on the ridge."

Kavan stood, crashing his legs into the booth table. "What?"

"Maybel, bring Kavan some coffee and the morning paper."

Kavan eased back down into the booth seat.

"What'll you have, Kavan?"

He hesitated. *Hero?*

"Kavan?" Sam tapped his pen against the table.

Snapping to attention, Kavan answered, "The day's special with a side of pancakes."

"Coming up. Coming right up." Sam sauntered back to the kitchen.

Maybel brought the paper and poured coffee. "Nice picture of you," she said.

There on the front page of the *White Birch Record* was a picture of him and the eight men of team three. The headline read, "Ranger Kavan Donovan leads firefighters to safety."

"Nice work up there, Donovan," a diner patron commented on his way out.

Kavan looked up. Unsure of what else to say, he answered, "Thank you."

Other townsfolk stopped by his table, congratulating him and calling him a hero. He squirmed with embarrassment. When Sam brought his food, Kavan welcomed the distraction.

"Lord, what's going on?" he whispered in prayer, his head bowed over his plate.

I honor those who honor Me. The subtle impression surprised Kavan, but he could tell by the impact the words had on his heart that the Living Lord had just touched him.

Finishing his breakfast, he downed the last of his coffee. His cell phone rang.

"Good job up on that ridge, Donovan."

"Thank you, Travis." Kavan reclined against the back of the booth, dubious. "How was your vacation?"

"Too much family. I'm glad to be home."

Kavan smiled.

"Seems the town fathers want to honor you and the others in a little ceremony."

Kavan winced. "You don't say?" He didn't understand the big to-do. "We were just doing our job."

"Well, the townspeople just want to say thanks."

Rubbing his forehead with his fingers, Kavan asked, "When?"

"Friday night. Eight o'clock at the civic center."

"I'll be there."

"Kavan, don't think this gets you off the hook on your budget discrepancies."

He sighed. "I'll be in the office tomorrow."

Kavan went up to the counter to pay for breakfast.

"No siree, it's on the house." Sam pushed the money in Kavan's hand away.

"No, Sam, let me pay."

"Heroes eat for free in my place." He flashed his toothy grin. "Haven't had a hero around here in a while."

None of Kavan's arguments could convince him otherwise. He stepped outside into the warm July sun. Passersby honked and waved, calling out to him. He felt like Rip van Winkle. The world had drastically changed while he'd slept for two days.

Cruising slowly down Main Street, Kavan gathered his thoughts. Then, as if all the forces in his brain converged at once, he remembered! *I kissed Elizabeth.*

His heartbeat quickened with the memory of their first kiss. He glanced at his watch. He'd barely talked to her since that intimate moment. Right after the kiss, he had been called away to report on the fire to the operations officer. By the time he finished, she had disappeared.

Turning right at the next street, Kavan headed for Lambert's Furniture.

As his thoughts cleared, the postfire events flashed through his mind. He'd crawled into bed sometime early Tuesday, and except for a brief lunch Tuesday afternoon, he'd been sleeping ever since.

I've got to talk to her!

❧❧

"Hey, Elizabeth," Kavan said, peering around her office door.

She jumped to her feet. Papers fluttered to the floor. "Kavan."

"You got a minute?" Kavan stepped through the doorway.

Anticipation prevented her from speaking, so she simply pointed to the chair opposite her desk.

"I was wondering," he said slowly as he eased into the chair, his gaze fixed on her, "if you wanted to go for a cup of coffee or something."

She nodded, then managed an answer. "I was about to go to lunch."

"I just had breakfast, but do you mind if I tag along?"

Again, she nodded a response, unsure of her speech. Reaching for her purse, she glanced at Kavan and asked, "The diner okay?"

He grinned. "I'd rather avoid the diner if you don't mind. Giuseppe's?"

She relaxed and smiled. "Sounds good to me. I could eat their pizza every day."

They drove to Giuseppe's in Kavan's truck. He appeared to be deep in thought, so she rode quietly beside him. She wasn't too sure what to say anyway. "Why did you kiss me?" felt like an awkward way to start a conversation.

Kavan pulled into Giuseppe's lot and parked. His hand paused on the keys as he cut the engine; then he turned toward her and said, "I kissed you."

His pointed statement pierced the tension, and Elizabeth laughed out loud. "I know."

He chuckled. "The entire drive over here, I wondered how to bring it up, then bam, it just came out."

"I wondered how to bring it up, as well," she confessed. She loved his honesty and the sure way he regarded her.

He slid across the bench seat to grab her hand. "I'm sorry I didn't call you. I slept almost nonstop once I got home, and it wasn't until I finished breakfast this morning that I remembered what happened."

She broke her gaze and stared down at her fingers. "I understand."

He lifted her chin with the tender touch of his fingers and peered into her eyes. "Do you?"

She looked away. "Yes." How could she tell him?

"Elizabeth, what's wrong?" Kavan insisted. "I hope I didn't offend you by kissing you. It's just, well, when I saw you standing there. . . You were the last person I expected to see. Guess my heart overtook my head."

Tears slipped from her eyes. "I was so happy to see you walking out of that fire alive."

He chuckled. "I was happy to be walking out of the fire."

"I wanted to run up to you, but I couldn't." She wiped away the tears.

He waited, listening, smoothing her hair with his hand. She loved his touch. *Say it out loud, Elizabeth.*

"That was my first kiss." *There, I said it.*

His eyes popped wide open. "Ever?"

She laughed through the returning tears. "Well, since Jude McAllister kissed me in fourth grade on a dollar dare."

They stared at each other for a moment, then filled the cab of the truck with simultaneous laughter. "A dollar dare, huh?" Kavan repeated.

"Yep."

"Who made the dare?"

"Me!" Elizabeth pointed toward herself with her thumb. "I wanted to buy an ice cream bar and a soda after school."

Their laughter rose again. "My mother quickly gave me a lesson about girls who kiss for money."

Kavan guffawed and slapped his knee. "I can't picture it. I can't picture it."

She liked to hear him laugh. It made her feel light and free.

Suddenly, he grew serious. "I meant that kiss, Elizabeth."

Her insides quivered. "So did I."

◆◆

"So," Grandpa said after dinner, "I hear you ate at Giuseppe's this afternoon with our local hero."

Elizabeth set down the glass she pulled from the cupboard. "Is nothing sacred in this town?"

Grandpa looked up and rubbed his chin. "No, don't reckon so. Especially a pizza date."

"Date. . .it was lunch!"

"You thought any more about what I told you?"

"A little." She poured a glass of diet soda and joined Grandpa at the table. "And?"

"Kavan is wonderful. Funny how it took the fire to make me realize how much I care for him. But, Grandpa, this finding doesn't preclude my plans. I can't fall in love. Not now."

"Your pride is tougher than I thought. I'm going to double my prayers."

"You amaze me, you know that?"

Grandma entered the kitchen. "Bethy, I forgot to tell you. More university letters came today."

Elizabeth jumped up. She'd sat down to dinner right after work without bothering to go upstairs. "Thick or thin?"

"Thin."

Elizabeth dashed upstairs, struggling with the weight of looming disappointment.

In her room, she flipped on a light and booted her laptop. Sure enough, two thin letters sat on the desk. She sank onto the bed reading the first rejection letter, then the next.

She stared blankly, letting the letters slip from her fingers to the floor.

Lord, I don't understand. I don't understand. Elizabeth's confusion bubbled into frustration spiked with a little anger. She hopped off the bed and paced the room.

This is ridiculous. And not my plan! She moaned and covered her face with her hands. How could this be happening to her? She thought for a moment, deciding to check her e-mail. Perhaps she would discover a clue to this whole mystery.

A half dozen new e-mails displayed in the inbox. Two were from Jenna, asking if she had been accepted at Ohio State. She really wanted to room with Elizabeth.

Elizabeth clicked the REPLY button, started to type, and then cleared the message. *I can't tell her the truth, yet.*

The rest of the e-mails were from family—her mom and brother. He wrote more about his summer antics at the public swimming pool. She smiled. Jonathan had a way about him that deflected her frustrations. Kavan, she was discovering, had the same effect on her.

She started to reply to her brother, but a subtle nudge prompted her to respond to Jenna.

Humble yourself, Elizabeth. She squirmed, remembering her haughty attitude toward the family about her educational pursuits. Highlighting Jenna's e-mail, Elizabeth clicked the REPLY button. Fingers poised on the keys, she pondered what to say and how.

She whispered, "Lord, what should I say?"

The truth.

Elizabeth sighed. "The truth, eh?"

"Hi, Jenna," she typed, and the rest of the message flowed from her fingertips. A page or so later, Elizabeth typed her name and clicked SEND.

A nervous flutter caused doubt to rise, but only for a moment. After that, a confidence came, and Elizabeth knew her friend Jesus would handle the rest.

"Scary place to be, Lord, but I trust You."

Just then, Grandma called up the stairs. "Your grandpa and I are going out for ice cream. Since you're not working at Sinclair's tonight, thought you might like to join us."

She glanced back at the computer screen and smiled. "I'd love to, Grandma. Let me change, and I'll be right down."

Chapter 15

Kavan drove along the charred mountainside, surveying the damage. What was once lush and green from spring rains was now brittle, black, and broken. It would be next spring before life would bloom again.

He could still smell the smoke of the burning forest. Only a few days had gone by since he'd collapsed exhausted on his bed at home, the blaze finally stopped.

He smiled, remembering how he kissed Elizabeth. Her first kiss since Jude McAllister in the fourth grade and on a dollar dare. He chuckled softly. She still exuded some of that grade school innocence, and it charmed his heart.

The town bustled with preparations for the commendation ceremony Friday night. The whole thing made Kavan uneasy. All the attention embarrassed him. After all, he was just doing his job.

In the midst of his contemplation, Travis Knight's deep voice bellowed over the radio sitting on the dash. "Donovan, report in."

Kavan reached for the hand mike. "I'm on my way."

❧

Travis greeted Kavan cordially when he entered his office and sat in the chair across from his desk. But underneath his friendly exterior, Kavan sensed the same anger that had been brewing for weeks.

"How's it feel to be the town hero?" Travis settled in his wide desk chair, a subtle sarcasm laced his words.

Kavan breathed deep. "Uncomfortable, to be honest." From Travis's posture, he could tell the man really had no patience for small talk.

"I'm giving you room on this refurbishment budget deal, but let me tell you, Kavan. . ." Travis angled forward and pointed his fat finger at the ranger. "I'll turn your hero reputation into that of reprobate overnight if I figure out you've been pilfering the division's money."

Kavan jumped to his feet in one smooth motion. He placed his hands on Travis's desk and lowered his face toward his boss's. "I've told you before, and I'll tell you again, I am not stealing the division's money."

He trembled, using every ounce of self-control to keep himself in check. He wanted to explode at Travis, but he knew it would gain him nothing and only deepen Travis's suspicion of him.

"I don't see any records proving otherwise." Travis cocked his head sideways as if to challenge Kavan.

"My records are in order."

"What happened when your spreadsheet program crashed?"

"I lost my original records."

Travis leaned on the desk and folded his fingers together. "Rather convenient, don't you think?"

Kavan gritted his teeth. "I didn't purposefully crash a computer program, Travis. I had duplicate files at home. They are available for you to see anytime you want to see them."

"Did you doctor those files, Donovan?"

"Don't patronize me, Travis. I'm not a twelve-year-old kid lying his way out of trouble."

Travis stood and walked around the desk. "I've been patient, waiting for you to come clean while I can still help you. Sooner or later, this will be out of my hands. If this turns into an official investigation, you are on your own."

Kavan recognized Travis's intimidation tactics. Yet, he had nothing to confess, nothing to reveal. His records were in order. The whole implication that he would steal and commit forgery angered him. He thought his character and reputation were irrefutable.

He sensed the Spirit of the Lord whisper to him at the moment. *Humble yourself.*

Kavan paused, pondering what to say next.

"Well?" Travis said after a moment.

Taking a deep breath, Kavan said, "I can't confess something I did not do, Travis, but I will submit to whatever process you want me to go through."

Travis's hard exterior softened with surprise. Kavan saw the muscles in his face relax. "Well, uh, why don't you bring in your files from home, and we'll take a look at those. We'll get to the bottom of this, I'm sure."

Kavan turned to leave. "Thank you, sir."

❧

Elizabeth felt buried under a pile of papers. She'd spent most of the morning daydreaming between Kavan's kiss and heading off to grad school. She'd searched on the Internet for jobs in nuclear energy, and there were plenty available. New government initiatives would expand the field, and by the time she graduated with her master's, lucrative career opportunities would be waiting.

However, she ignored the churning in her stomach every time she thought about school. Dismissing it as nervous energy, she let her thoughts wander back to Kavan.

How sweet he'd been when they finally talked about their kiss. As far as she was concerned, it was about the best first kiss a girl could ever get—sincere, tender, and passionate.

Will peered around the doorway. "You got the quarterly report? We're meeting with the board of directors in a half hour."

Elizabeth snapped back to the present. "Yes. Yes, I do. I just need to call your secretary and ask her a quick question."

Will nodded. "Bring it to the board room when you're done."

Elizabeth dialed Rose's number. "Hi, Rose, it's Elizabeth. I have a question about the quarterly report."

Rose answered without hesitation, and within ten minutes, Elizabeth pulled the report together and rushed it down to Will.

"Thanks, Beth," he said.

Back in her office, Elizabeth took a deep breath and said a short prayer. "Lord, I need to focus. Stop daydreaming about Kavan and get on to my next goal—school."

The phone rang on the trail of her words. "Lambert's Furniture."

"Hi, it's Kavan."

"Hi." Elizabeth's resolve crumbled.

"How are you?"

"Fine. And you?"

"Tired of all this hero stuff."

Elizabeth laughed. "Typical White Birch, don't you think?"

"Yes. Guess that's why I love this town." He chuckled. "I just wish it wasn't focused on me."

"Well, if you ask me, you deserve it."

"The only way I can endure it is if you will accompany me to Friday night's ceremonies."

She answered without hesitation. "I'd love to, Kavan."

"Elizabeth," he started. She heard the seriousness in his tone. "This is a date."

She chewed her bottom lip and played with the pencils lined up on her desk. The whole town would see her with him. They'd assume. . .

"Well," she paused, "as long as you don't kiss me in front of everyone. . .'

Kavan's laughter floated over the line. "I promise."

"Okay, then." She felt like a schoolgirl.

"I'll pick you up at seven."

"Six thirty," she countered.

He chuckled. "Six thirty. I gotta go. Need to get some stuff for Travis. The refurbishment debacle won't go away."

"Really? I'm sure you'll figure it out."

"I'm praying so. I can only lean on the Lord on this one. It's a puzzler."

"See ya."

"Friday."

After she hung up, Elizabeth stared blankly at the wall. *What was I thinking, saying yes to him? The whole town will whisper about us. The family will tease me with "love and marriage" remarks.*

Hmm. . . For the first time, she realized she didn't care. The idea didn't petrify her, and she rather enjoyed the junior high jitters dancing in her middle.

Enough, Elizabeth. Back to work. Diving into accounts payable, Elizabeth worked steadily for several hours.

A collection of invoices surfaced from the Division of Forests and Lands. All of them like the ones she'd seen before. Cuts of expensive wood, all bearing Kavan's name.

She shook her head, withstanding the urge to assume. *What are you doing, Kavan?*

Elizabeth printed the invoices and placed them one by one on a worktable. She studied them, hands on her hips. After a moment, she moved to the filing cabinet and pulled the division's purchase orders. One by one, she matched purchase order and invoice. Hunching over, she examined each set.

Kavan's signature caught her attention. She smiled, liking the funny way he made his *K*s. That purchase order and invoice, dated in March, was for a load of pine. *Typical orders, according to Mr. Hansen.*

Her gaze moved to the next set of papers. "Oh, no," she whispered, picking up the purchase order for a closer examination. The order called for a load of teak, and while the bottom line carried Kavan's name, it was not his signature.

Swiftly, she found all the purchase orders that did not have Kavan's signature. She arranged them by date and moved to the copier.

Several minutes later, she dialed Kavan's cell phone. *No answer.* She read the Division of Forests and Lands' phone number from their account in the computer and dialed the office. "He's not here," a woman said, overly sweet.

Fumbling through the phone book, Elizabeth looked up his home phone number. *Kavan, be home, please.*

The busy signal beeped in her ear. *Busy.*

Elizabeth grabbed her purse, the copied stack of purchase orders and invoices, and dashed out the door.

❦

A low growl emanated from Fred. Kavan glanced up from the computer where he was copying his refurbishment report to a floppy. Ginger whined and scratched at the back door.

Kavan listened. "Lie down, Fred. Lie down, Ginger. No one is here." He clicked the printer icon above the spreadsheet. He thought it would be wise to have a hard copy of his spending. . .just in case.

A small knock on the back door sent the dogs into a barking frenzy. Startled, Kavan jumped from his chair.

"Pipe down, you two," he hollered, grabbing the doorknob.

"Elizabeth! Come in." He stepped aside to let her pass.

She came through the door grinning like the Cheshire cat. She plopped her big leather purse on the counter and beamed at Kavan, her sapphire eyes sparkling.

He joined her at the counter, resisting the subtle but sure urge to wrap her up in his arms and greet her with a kiss. He'd kissed her once, but kissing still felt like uncharted territory, and he wanted to proceed cautiously.

"Well, are you going to tell me why you're looking at me like I just won a million dollars, or do I have to guess?"

"I've discovered something," she blurted out.

"Fascinating. A new law of physics?" Kavan leaned as close to her as he could. She smelled like fresh flowers.

"Ha! No."

"Then what?" Kavan folded his arms and regarded her. He loved seeing a new side of Elizabeth.

She pulled a stack of papers out of her purse. Clearing the napkin holder and the salt and pepper shakers from the table, she systematically placed copies of Lambert's Furniture invoices and forestry division purchase orders in front of them.

"Purchase orders?" Kavan asked. "Invoices?"

"POs with your name on them."

Kavan examined the papers. "Two hundred board feet of cherry." He glanced at Elizabeth. "I never ordered cherry."

"Teak and cedar, too," she said, selecting another purchase order for him to review.

Kavan shook his head. "But that's not my signature."

"Exactly," Elizabeth said. "Kavan Donovan, I am afraid you're being framed."

His gaze met hers. "Come on, Elizabeth, who would do such a thing?"

"I don't know, but someone is charging expensive materials to the forestry division and signing your name. This must be the key to your budget problem." She paused, then added, "Your boss thinks you're embezzling, doesn't he?"

"It sure seems that way. How did you figure this out?" Kavan asked, picking up one of the forged orders. "Some of these date before I even started the refurbishment project."

"I noticed the cherry order one day. I called Grant Hansen to see why we cut several hundred board feet of cherry for the forestry division. He said we still provide millwork to some customers. Your name stood out to me because we'd just met a few days before at Sinclair's."

"Good eye, Lambert. Think I'll call you Eliz-a-sleuth from now on."

She narrowed her eyes at him. "Har, har. Don't even think about it. I'll take my evidence and leave you to your own measly devices."

Kavan cleared his throat, pretending to be threatened by her words. "How did you know it wasn't my signature?"

"Remember how I thought your *K*s were unusual? I noticed it when you signed the debit card receipt the first time we went to Giuseppe's."

Kavan looked at her and let his gaze linger on her face for a moment. "I can't thank you enough."

She reached out and tenderly touched his arm. "Anything for a friend."

Kavan pulled her to him and brushed her cheek lightly with the back of his fingers. Without a word, he kissed her.

After the kiss, she looked up at him, a spark in her blue eyes. "Are you always going to kiss me without warning?"

"Maybe." He winked.

"I'll be on guard, then." She gathered up the purchase orders and returned them to the folder. "Come on, let's go show your boss. I can't wait to see the look on his face."

Chapter 16

Kavan walked into the Division of Forests and Lands office like he owned the world, Elizabeth by his side.

"Cheryl, is Travis in?"

She nodded but narrowed her dark eyes at him. "Who's your friend?"

"Elizabeth, this is Cheryl."

The women greeted each other. Kavan stepped over to Travis's office and rapped his knuckles lightly on the heavy wooden door.

"Come in."

Kavan stepped through, motioning for Elizabeth to follow. The heavyset director studied him, waiting. He considered them with his hands clasped together on his round belly as if he expected a show.

Kavan dropped the signed purchase orders and invoices on Travis's desk.

"What's this?" Travis asked, reaching for one of the papers.

"That's not my signature, Travis."

Travis glanced at Kavan, indifference in his eyes.

"Someone is ordering teak, walnut, mahogany, and cherry from Lambert's Furniture and charging it to the fire tower account. They signed the POs with my name."

Travis moved to review the documentation, his brow raised. Kavan knew he finally had his attention.

"How did you come across this?" Travis examined each of the forms.

Kavan introduced Elizabeth and explained her discovery. "She recognized my signature. Look on those purchase orders." Kavan pointed to the ones with his legitimate signature. "The lumber is pine. That's all I've used on the fire tower."

"You're telling me somebody ordered lumber and charged it to your refurbishment account," Travis summarized.

"Yes," Kavan said without hesitation. "There are also some that were charged to the general department expenses before the fire tower project was even approved."

Travis picked through the orders again. Suddenly a shadow fell over his face. Quickly, he flipped through several of the pieces, then stacked them neatly together. He stood. "May I keep these, Miss Lambert?"

"Those are copies." Elizabeth glanced sideways at Kavan. "You can keep them." Kavan watched her trying to suppress her beautiful smile.

A heavy silence hung in the air. Travis remained focused on the forged purchase orders, his hands idly stacking them over and over. "Well, Donovan, looks like you've managed to clear your name."

Kavan nodded. "Yes, sir." He extended his hand to Travis.

It took a second, but the older man grasped his hand in a firm shake. "I'll take it from here. You keep working on that old White Birch fire tower."

"If you don't mind, I think I'll wait until the dust settles." Kavan eyed his boss. Travis had obviously seen something in those papers that bothered him. But Kavan knew better than to ask.

Outside, he laughed and grabbed Elizabeth in a swirling hug. "Thank you! I feel like I've lost a thousand pounds."

Once he landed her feet back on the ground, he kissed her again with enthusiasm.

Elizabeth stepped out of his embrace. "I can't believe you," she said, her tone sharp, her blue eyes sparking.

Kavan stared at her for a moment. "What? I told you I'd kiss you without warning."

"I can't believe you let Travis Knight off so easy. He all but accused you of stealing. Stealing, Kavan." She glared at him with her hands on her hips. "He questioned your integrity. And you let him off with a howdy-do handshake. He didn't even apologize!"

Her ire stirred his. "What'd you want me to do, slap him around?"

"Demand an apology. A written apology."

"What? Elizabeth, he was mistaken. Quite frankly, I can understand—"

"Your career and reputation are on the line, Kavan. Stick up for yourself." Elizabeth turned and marched toward the truck.

Kavan raced after her and grabbed her arm. He pulled her aside and peered into her face. "My reputation and career is not mine to defend. The Lord will look out for me. He's done so much already. How Christlike would it be if I sought revenge or retribution?"

"I could never let it go that easy."

"The Lord gives grace to the humble, Elizabeth."

To his surprise, tears glistened in her eyes. "Let's go," she whispered.

They drove in silence to his house. Slanted rays of late afternoon sunlight glanced over White Birch, and the serenading song of the crickets filled their ears. When Kavan pulled into the gravel drive, Fred and Ginger hailed them with a barking chorus.

"What's bothering you, Elizabeth?" Kavan stopped the truck, shifted into park, and shut off the engine.

She faced him and said with passion, "That you are just letting this go. You're letting it happen, not sticking up for yourself."

He glared at her. "Well, I don't see it that way. The Lord resolved the issue—"

"With my help. If I hadn't found those purchase orders and receipts, you'd still be suspect."

"Hold on there, Elizabeth. Yes, you were the key to this whole mystery, but the

Lord unlocked the door in the first place. He could have done it without you."

Elizabeth got out of the truck and slammed the door.

Kavan bounded out of the truck after her. "Where are you going?"

"To take command of my life." She jerked open the door to the VW and climbed in.

"Elizabeth, what's going on?" He looked through the open passenger side window. "Obviously this is about more than Travis Knight and the case of forged signatures."

She cocked her head to look at him. "You're right. It's about me, Elizabeth Lambert, taking charge of my life."

Kavan watched her drive away. He resisted the urge to chase after her, certain she would not welcome his prodding. "Lord, You speak to her. Comfort her."

❧❧

"Grandma, I'll be in my room," Elizabeth said as she entered the kitchen.

Grandma glanced up from the kitchen table where she read her Bible. "You're home early. Everything okay?"

"Any mail for me today?"

"Nooo," Grandma answered, drawing out the word.

Muttering to herself, Elizabeth entered her room. She pulled up the window shades to let in the day's remaining light and booted up her laptop.

"Let my relationship with Kavan distract me. . . And Grandpa's story about Harvard and a pregnant wife. . . Thinking I could live in this town. . . Who cares about school? Me. I'm going to find out what's going on with my applications."

Checking her e-mail, she found nothing new regarding her graduate school status.

Determined to find answers, she hopped onto the Internet and found Ohio State's admissions page. She clicked on the link for graduate students. Finding a telephone number, she reached for the phone.

A nervous trill came out of her throat as the phone rang and someone answered.

"Hi, my name is Elizabeth Lambert. I'd like to check on my graduate school application." She listened for a moment, then spelled her name and gave her social security number. "Yes, I'll hold."

You bet I'll hold. I'm going to find out what's going on.

She tapped her fingernails on the base of her laptop, staring out the window. Grandpa strolled up the drive with Will's dog, Harry. Elizabeth smiled.

"Miss Lambert?"

"Yes?" Elizabeth returned her focused to the call.

"Your application was denied."

Elizabeth resisted the urge to scream and asked through clenched teeth, "Yes, I know. But why?"

"I don't know." Irritation laced the woman's voice. "I—oh, wait. You didn't submit your transcripts from MIT."

Elizabeth stood so fast her desk chair tipped over. "What?"

"You didn't send us your undergraduate transcripts."

"I paid for the university to send them."

"Well, we didn't get them."

Elizabeth circled the room in small steps. "What do you mean you didn't get them?"

The woman answered slowly, tossing out her words one at a time, "We. . . did. . .not. . .get. . .them. They never arrived."

With a sigh, Elizabeth thanked the woman and hung up. After another quick search on the Internet, she found South Carolina's and Michigan's information. Quick calls to their admissions departments yielded the same result. MIT had not submitted her transcripts.

Stunned, Elizabeth sat on the edge of her bed, blinking back tears while her middle bubbled with a giggle. Denied admittance due to a clerical error.

How classic.

She took a second to mull the situation over, then got on the computer. A plan formed in her head while she fired off a few e-mails and checked all the universities' Web sites for application deadlines. Perhaps she still had time. . . .

The sunlight faded, and shadows appeared in the corners of her room. Grandpa appeared in the doorway. "Dinner's on, kitten."

Elizabeth glanced around at him with a smile. "MIT didn't send my transcripts."

"What?"

"MIT didn't send my transcripts. That's why my grad school applications have been denied."

Grandpa laughed. "Don't that beat all? How'd you find out?"

"I took command," she said. Linking her arm with his, Elizabeth walked with Grandpa to the kitchen, and during dinner, she regaled her grandparents with the events of the day.

Kavan rang the doorbell. Nervous, he mentally rehearsed what he wanted to say. He couldn't rest until he'd squared things with Elizabeth. He'd prayed and prayed about it, but still couldn't find resolve within himself. Funny, he didn't have the urge to make a defense before Travis and the New Hampshire Division of Forests and Lands, but, did want to explain his actions to Elizabeth. He couldn't bear the idea of her perceiving him as a coward or a weakling.

The door to the Lamberts' kitchen flew open, and a smiling, bubbly, all too beautiful Elizabeth stood there.

"Kavan," she gushed, throwing her arms around him. "You're just in time for dessert. Are you hungry?"

Shocked, yet amused, Kavan stepped inside. "I'd never turn down a Grandma Betty dessert."

Elizabeth led him to the table, his hand in hers. Grandpa Matt congratulated him on his forgery find while Grandma Betty slid a large slice of iced applesauce cake under his nose. Elizabeth chatted merrily about the strange signatures on the purchase orders and how they presented the material to Travis Knight.

"Our girl is full of discoveries today." Grandma handed Kavan a cup of coffee.

"Thank you." He took the cup, then fixed his gaze on Elizabeth. "What other discoveries have you made?"

Elizabeth related the story of the missing transcripts, the details punctuated with little points made by her grandparents. Finally, Elizabeth concluded, "Tomorrow, I'm calling MIT to straighten this thing out."

Kavan looked at her and thought she was actually beaming. He was proud of her, yet disappointed.

So this is what the Bible means when it says love does not seek its own. Kavan intuitively understood he had to let Elizabeth go.

Grandpa Matt and Grandma Betty excused themselves from the table and wandered arm in arm from the kitchen.

"Well, you're off." Kavan reached for Elizabeth's hand. He loved its velvety texture.

She placed her other hand on top of his. "You always knew that was the plan."

He nodded. "Yes, I did."

"I'm sorry I was so snippy earlier."

Kavan looked up and smiled. He caught her blue gaze with his own. "Don't worry about it. I am so grateful to be out of that mess, and I have you to thank."

"Glad to help, friend."

Kavan leaned forward, and with his fingertips, touched the side of her face. "Sure you want to leave?"

"I never planned to stay."

"And what does your Friend Jesus say?"

Elizabeth pulled her hand free and rested against the back of her chair. She focused on Kavan for a second before answering. "I don't know, but when I took command of my own situation, I found the answers. Maybe He helped me today like He did you."

"That's one way to look at it." At that moment, Kavan ached. Ached for Elizabeth, for a life with her. "I'm going to miss you."

"I'm going to miss you. But hey, I'm not gone yet. I'll be here another four to six weeks."

"And Friday night, you're my date to the big to-do-about-nothing ceremony."

"I can't wait." She smiled and kissed him lightly on the cheek.

Chapter 17

The White Birch Community Center hummed with excited voices. Elizabeth sat among the families and guests of the honored firefighters, watching as Kavan Donovan received a commendation for leadership and bravery.

Her cheeks ached from the constant smiling. When Kavan walked across the stage, the crowd in the auditorium cheered. His gaze fell on her, and he smiled with a wink. Elizabeth winked back and gave him two thumbs-up.

When he stopped at the podium to speak, Elizabeth imagined her heart might thump right out of her chest.

"Jesus said," Kavan began when the din died down, "that no greater love is there than this, that one would lay down his life for his friends."

The tranquil sound of his voice, combined with his opening statement, captivated Elizabeth.

"Up on that ridge, I did what any of these men would have done. I'm proud to be numbered among them. Mostly, I hope that in some small way I represented Jesus up there and honored His name with my actions. He is our greatest Friend." He paused and looked out over the crowd. "Thank you for honoring us today."

He returned to his seat, accompanied by a symphony of applause.

After the ceremony, Kavan wove through the crowd to Elizabeth. She hugged him with vigor. "I'm so proud! You are a gifted speaker."

"Thanks." He gently cupped her elbow with his hand and steered her through the throng. "I said five sentences. Can't mess that up, Elizabeth."

She laughed. "True, but you looked so calm and stately."

Kavan looked down at her, flashing his hooked grin. "Stately? Now that's a new one." He stopped to hug some ladies and shake hands with several men. As many as could reach him patted him on the back and belted out their congratulations.

Finally, they were outside, breathing in the warm July night air. Stars twinkled down at them.

"I'm hungry," Kavan said. "Let's eat."

"Giuseppe's?" Elizabeth asked, her hand in his as they trotted to his truck.

"Sounds great."

They laughed and talked the whole way to the pizza place, rehashing the tributary events. Kavan declared he never wanted to go through that again.

"The fire or the tribute?" Elizabeth asked, a lilt in her voice.

"Both," Kavan said.

She watched him watching her out the corner of his eye. *If I were ever going to get married, Kavan, it would be to a man like you.*

"You're quiet all of a sudden," Kavan said with a glance her way. He turned into Giuseppe's parking lot.

"Just thinking." Feeling caught by her own thoughts and sublime desire, she looked out the window and up at the mountain.

"About what?" Kavan cut off the engine and shifted his torso toward her.

About what? I can't tell him what I've been thinking. So she fudged a little. "About the future, school and all. MIT should have sent out my transcripts by now."

"Oh," he said, sounding sad. "I was wondering. . . ." He stopped and looked out the windshield.

Elizabeth's pulse quickened. "You were wondering?"

"Nothing. Let's eat," he said.

Nothing? What were you going to say? She waited for him to open her door. Sliding out of the truck, she slipped into his embrace. His kiss was warm, determined, and made Elizabeth's knees weak. The feel of his lips touching hers lingered for the rest of the night.

❧❧

Elizabeth hummed softly to herself as she readied for her Saturday afternoon shift at Sinclair's. Showered and dressed in her Sinclair's uniform, she curled up on her bed with one of Grandma's ham sandwiches on homemade bread.

Since last night, she could not forget the feel of Kavan's arms around her and the touch of his kiss.

She took a small bite of her sandwich, then set her plate on the corner of her desk. A picture of Kavan flashed across her mind, causing a giggle to erupt from deep inside. She covered her mouth with a swift move of her hand, shifting her eyes to peek around the room as if someone could have overheard.

So this is the feeling that moved the pens of the great poets. The emotion that stirred singers to sing and dancers to dance, she thought. Her heart felt light and airy. Peaceful. The feeling began to seem familiar, to become a part of her. And she liked it.

Suddenly, Elizabeth jumped to her feet and stood in the middle of her bed. Thrusting her arms wide, she belted out the first song that came to mind. "The hills are alive with the sound of music."

She crumpled to the bed, laughing.

Grandpa and Grandma appeared in the doorway. "And she tries to tell you *I'm* crazy," Grandpa said to Grandma.

"I'm sorry, you guys; I'm just feeling a little wacky today."

"Wacky? Is that what you kids call it these days? In my day, we called it being in love." Grandpa gazed at his granddaughter over the rim of his wire spectacles.

"In love? As in *falling* in love? Grandpa, you're certifiable. Grandma, watch him." Elizabeth reached over the edge of the bed for her shoes, unable to control the big grin sweeping across her face. "I'm excited that my life is finally moving forward. Grad school is on the horizon, the light at the end of the tunnel."

"Right," Grandpa said, propped against the door, his arms folded over his chest. "Studying physics and math, cramming for tests, working late nights, and getting up early always made me sing at the top of my lungs, too."

Elizabeth hopped up and yanked her purse from the hook on the wall. "No time for your delirium, Grandpa. Sinclair's awaits." She kissed her grandma on the cheek and hugged her grandpa on her way through the door.

"Beth, your sandwich. . . ," Grandma called after her.

"Save it for later. I'm not hungry," she called, waving from the bottom of the stairs with a flutter of her hand.

❧ ❧

Kavan strolled down Main Street toward the diner, his mind set on a late supper. He'd felt restless sitting at home, an unusual sensation for him. His cabinlike abode was his sanctuary, and he loved being there. But tonight. . .

He drove past Sinclair's, expecting to see Elizabeth's candy apple red Bug in the parking lot. He did but decided not to stop. As much as he wanted to see her, he needed time to think.

Last night's commendation ceremony—combined with an enchanting evening with Elizabeth—marked one of the best nights of his life. Despite his embarrassment over the hero hoopla, he couldn't help feeling honored by the town's expression of appreciation. Even his parents wired congratulations from Florida.

He smiled, recalling his father's words. *Congratulations, son. We are proud of you. Warm wishes, Dad and Mom*

They maintained their physical distance, but Kavan knew they loved him, and their hearts were close. He'd settled that in his mind a long time ago.

"Where to, Lord?" he asked absently after he parked the truck and started down Main Street.

Diner.

"Okay," Kavan said. "Dinner with You tonight, Jesus."

As he walked past the bookstore, mulling over the diner menu, a sparkle in the window of Earth-n-Treasures, Designs by Cindy Mae caught his attention.

Stop.

Kavan halted, then took a step toward the storefront. He studied the items in the display window, various pieces designed from gold and silver. All exquisite. He admired one gold filigree ring hosting a uniquely cut solitaire diamond.

"Hi, Kavan."

He looked up to see the owner of Earth-n-Treasures standing beside him.

"Hi, Cindy Mae. What are you doing in town on a Saturday evening?"

She grinned and shifted the weight of her large frame. "Brill took the kids to a movie, so I thought I'd come in and do a little work."

Kavan glanced up and down Main Street. "I forgot how dead this place is on the weekends."

"We roll up the sidewalks Friday at 5 p.m. until Monday at 8 a.m.," Cindy Mae said, twirling the ends of her thick blond braid between her fingers.

Kavan laughed outright. Cindy Mae painted a true picture of White Birch. "I came in for some dinner," he told her.

101

Cindy Mae nodded toward the diner. "Sam's the only one who does much business on the weekends."

Kavan agreed. "Can't beat his meat loaf." Next, he motioned to the piece behind the glass. "That's an unusual ring."

"Isn't it beautiful? It's one of the few pieces I didn't make myself." Cindy Mae invited him into the shop to take a closer look. "It's a century old, and that's the original one-karat diamond."

Kavan raised a brow and whistled.

Cindy Mae pointed to the intricate design of the ring's mount with the long tip of her pinky fingernail. "The ring is in classic Edwardian design. Thus, the filigree."

"It's amazing. I've never seen a diamond like this one."

"It's an Asscher cut. Very sought-after cut of diamond in its day," Cindy said, peering up at Kavan. "Still is."

In that instant, somehow Kavan knew he had to purchase the ring. It seemed to symbolize Elizabeth to him, a rare and beautiful find. She was valued by the Lord and valued by him.

"The ring comes with a story, too." Cindy Mae pulled up a stool and motioned for Kavan to sit.

He listened as Cindy Mae told her tale. "A relative, John Ashton, bought this ring for the woman he loved in 1904. She accepted the ring, but never wore it, telling Uncle John she wanted to consider his proposal for a while. A year passed without an answer, so Uncle John pressed his hopeful bride-to-be to set a date. She confessed that she loved another and returned the ring."

For a split second, Kavan imagined he felt the disappointment of John Ashton. "He must have been devastated."

Cindy Mae rested against a glass case and crossed her arms over her middle. "Heartbroken. Family lore has it that he buried himself in work. Made a million dollars, which for his day was a considerable amount. He never married and left the ring in a safety-deposit box he never bothered to tell anyone about."

"Guess he truly wanted to forget," Kavan offered.

Cindy Mae chuckled deeply. "I'm sure he did. He died in the late sixties. My father received the ring as part of his estate, but he was already engaged to my mother, who viewed the ring as bad luck and refused to ever wear it. Recently, Dad brought the ring to me and said to do what I wanted with it. After forty years, he's caved in to my mother's superstitions."

Kavan's heartbeat quickened. Surely someone else in Cindy Mae's family would want the ring. He said as much to his hostess.

She shook her head, disagreeing. "There's only my sister and me now. For some odd reason, we believe this ring belongs to someone besides us. Someone very special, we just don't know who."

Kavan blurted out, "Cindy Mae, how much?" His gaze darted between her face and the ring.

What am I doing?

She did not appear fazed by his question. "You have someone special in your life?"

Kavan chuckled and ran his hand over the top of his hair. "I'm working on it. She just doesn't know it yet."

"Is it the Lamberts' granddaughter?"

"You've seen her," Kavan said.

"She's a fine girl. Beautiful."

Shivers ran down Kavan's back, and his palms grew moist. With a jerky, forward motion, he placed the ring on the front counter. "How much, Cindy Mae?" He braced to hear thousands of dollars. He couldn't imagine how much an antique ring of this caliber would cost. The stone alone had to be worth. . . What? His head started spinning.

Cindy Mae picked up the rare jewel and walked behind the counter. Kavan hoped she wouldn't ring it up without telling him the price. As best he figured, he could spend about five thousand dollars. Even that would just about wipe out his savings.

He waited for Cindy Mae's answer while she worked on the ring, cleaning and polishing it. Then she placed it in a deep blue velvet box, the same color as Elizabeth's eyes.

"Here." She extended her hand, the box on the tip of her fingers. "I knew I didn't come into town tonight to balance the books."

Kavan gaped at her. He tried to answer, but no words would come. "Cindy Mae, I don't understand," he managed to say after a moment.

"Kavan, I don't know why, but I believe with all my heart, you and your girl are the couple for this ring."

"You must be joking. That ring must be worth—"

"Nothing without the right owner." She winked. "Otherwise, it's coal and metal."

"Cindy Mae, I—I don't know. . . I can't—"

"What's your girl's name? I'm drawing a blank."

"She's not my girl. We're good friends, but I don't think you could say she's my girl."

"What's her name?" Cindy Mae repeated.

Kavan stopped and stared at her. Gently he said, "Elizabeth. Elizabeth Lambert."

Cindy clapped her hands, tossed back her head, and laughed from the core of her belly. "Of course! Now I know this ring belongs to you! The woman my uncle bought the ring for was one Miss Elizabeth Clarke. This ring was purchased for an Elizabeth. Only a century too soon."

Kavan gripped the box. It felt hot in his hand. "Cindy Mae, I don't even know if I'm going to marry her. I mean, I've asked the Lord about it—"

"Well, there you go. The Lord your God knows." Cindy motioned toward the ceiling with her index finger.

"I can't take this," Kavan said with force and conviction. "Not if I don't know if I'll ever marry her!"

Cindy Mae walked around the shop, shutting off lights and covering her art with dustcovers. "Kavan, it's yours. You and God work out the rest."

In a few minutes, they were out of the shop, and Cindy Mae hugged him good-bye.

Dazed, Kavan walked into the diner, his appetite completely diminished. He picked a quiet corner and slid into the booth.

In his breast pocket, the weight of the little blue box burned against his heart.

Friday night, Elizabeth sat in the cozy living room, surrounded by Lamberts trying to decide which movie to watch.

"I brought a romantic comedy." Julie held up her DVD.

"Oh no," Will lamented. "Ethan, do something about your wife."

Ethan laughed and held up his movie. "I brought suspense."

A chorus of female voices erupted. "We watched suspense last time," Elle reminded the men.

Elizabeth turned around to see her cousin Bobby's wife. She'd always loved Elle, so elegant and sophisticated.

Twins Bobby and Will debated over watching an action movie or classic drama. Elizabeth smiled to herself. *How could two people who looked exactly alike be so different?*

For the first time since she came to White Birch and her grandparents' house, she felt at home and at peace. She didn't mind being an intricate part of the Lambert clan, answering their questions about her life and grad school. In fact, it made her feel treasured and special.

"I'm so excited for you." Julie flopped down on the couch next to her, cozying up to her like intimate sisters.

"Amazing, isn't it." Elizabeth leaned in close to Julie. "I never paid for the transcripts to be sent."

Ethan stooped down and said, "It's almost as if you didn't want them to be sent."

"Ethan!" Elizabeth said, incredulous.

"Hush, you." Julie said, giving his arm a loving tap.

"Get your snacks and drinks. I'm pushing PLAY in two minutes," Grandpa announced.

Everyone made a mad scramble to the kitchen and the bathroom.

Elizabeth remained put, Ethan's comment replaying through her head. *Did I subconsciously not want the transcripts to be sent?* She shifted her position on the couch and chewed her bottom lip.

"Ready, ladies and gentlemen?" Grandpa asked in his lighthearted master of ceremonies tone.

"Hit PLAY," Elizabeth said, grinning at him.

"Where's Kavan?" Grandpa asked.

"Home, I guess."

"Don't you want to invite him? I'll wait."

Elizabeth shook her head. She hadn't seen Kavan much this week, between his schedule and hers. She pictured his handsome face, alive with expressive eyes and his white, hooked smile.

Suddenly she missed him.

Grandpa started the movie. Elizabeth gave her seat to Ethan. "Sit by your wife."

"Where you going?" Julie asked, cuddling up next to Ethan.

"I'll sit by Grandma," Elizabeth answered.

Instead, she stood by the door and waited until the family became engrossed in the movie, a classic drama. She slipped out the front door and followed the silvery light of the moon to the covered bridge.

Once the transcript situation was straightened out, she'd finally felt relieved. She'd taken command and put her life into gear again.

Now she wondered. A subtle but sure uneasiness floated through her consciousness when she thought about leaving White Birch—when she thought about leaving Kavan.

The bubbling, excited feelings she felt a week ago for Kavan had settled into something solid at the core of her heart.

"Lord," she prayed, "grad school? How can I *not* go? I have to go."

For the first time since her talk with Grandpa, the verse he quoted out of 1 Peter came to mind. "Young men, in the same way be submissive to those who are older. All of you, clothe yourselves with humility toward one another, because, 'God opposes the proud but gives grace to the humble.'"

"Lord, give me grace." Elizabeth continued to pour out her heart, believing her Lord and Friend would direct her path.

Chapter 18

The ring sat on the kitchen counter. It seemed to Kavan that every fiber of his being was drawn to that velvet box every time he passed by, even in the dark of night.

Cindy Mae's gift still amazed him. "Lord, how did You move her to give so extravagantly?" he asked one night, sitting on the back porch, a cold soda bottle in his hand.

He sensed the Lord respond, *Because of My extravagant love for you.*

Kavan smiled at the remarkable working of his Lord, so kind and generous. Yet, he still did not know his next move. In his estimation, he had a ring, but no girl. Elizabeth never even remotely hinted that she would consent to marry him if he asked.

Kavan took a swig of his soda. How to win Elizabeth's heart remained a mystery to him.

He'd stopped by Sinclair's on his way home one evening after spotting her car in the parking lot. Her blue eyes twinkled with merriment when she saw him strolling across the front of the store.

"Hi ya, gorgeous." He leaned on the front counter.

"Hi ya." She grabbed his hands. "Guess what?"

Her enthusiasm engaged his heart. "Joann gave you a raise," he teased.

Joann stood within earshot. "Ha! Don't we all wish."

Elizabeth glanced at Joann. "Thank you, how kind." Then she aimed her sparkling smile at him. "MIT sent me an e-mail confirming that my transcripts have been sent."

Kavan stiffened, squeezing her hand a little. "Oh, really?"

"Did I tell you?"

"Tell me what?"

"That the reason they were never sent is because I never paid for them to be sent."

"Doesn't sound like you." Kavan's mouth felt as dry as a cotton ball.

"I guess with the pressure of finals and filing applications, I forgot."

"Are you sure it's not too late for admittance?" Kavan thought his tone sounded a little too hopeful.

She shook her head. "No, I checked, and I'm squeaking in under the deadline."

"Well, you'll be on your way soon." Kavan fought the desire to beg her to stay.

Elizabeth's eyes peered steadily into his. "Yep, on my way."

Sitting on his porch now, recalling that night, Kavan wondered about the tone in her voice. Did he hear an echo of doubt?

He stood and paced the length of the porch. Maybe he just imagined her doubt because that is what he wanted. And the whole ring thing. . . He sighed and propped himself against the porch rail. Fred whined and curled up by Kavan's feet.

None of it made sense to him. *Lord, why would You give me this ring? You've worked it out for Elizabeth to go to graduate school.*

The idea hit him that maybe the ring was for Elizabeth, just not now. Perhaps after she graduated.

He moaned. That would mean two more years. He'd only known her two months, but it felt like a lifetime. She fit with him. They belonged together.

Tell her.

The simple instruction sliced through his anxious thoughts.

Tell her what? Marry me? Don't follow your dreams? I can't do that. I love her too much.

Kavan didn't want to argue with the Lord, but he lacked courage. Fighting a fire up on the ridge paled in comparison to telling a beautiful, curly-haired brunette he wanted to spend the rest of his life with her. That idea terrified him.

What if she said no? How would he recover and keep their friendship?

"O Lord," he said with a quivering laugh, "I used to consider myself a man of faith, but this is a whole new terrain for me."

No tangible answer came from heaven except a sense of peace and the pleasure of God.

The sound of the phone's ring jolted him out of his deep thought and prayer.

Kavan dashed through the screen door, the sound of its slam following him into the kitchen.

The blue velvet box caught his attention once again.

"Kavan, Travis Knight here."

"Evening, Travis."

"I just came from a meeting down in Manchester. Your name's cleared. The division is investigating the embezzlement."

"Any clues so far?"

"Yes, but they aren't saying much. Possibility that it involves some higher-ups. Apparently, these things are dealt with quietly, and the person is dismissed without prosecution."

Kavan blew a shrill whistle. "Well, I'm glad I'm in the clear. I don't want to know what happens to the other guy."

"Well, you probably will eventually anyway. But, yep, you are in the clear, son. I'm sorry I doubted you."

"No problem, Travis."

"Have a good weekend."

"You, too." Kavan pressed the button to disconnect. He moved to place the cordless phone on its base, then paused. He had an idea.

He pressed TALK and dialed. Before the first ring, he hung up. He took a deep breath, pressed REDIAL, and set the phone to his ear. It rang once before he hung up again.

He laughed at himself. "This is worse than high school," he said to Fred, who peered at him through the screen door. The dog answered with one deep bark.

"Go for it? Is that what you're saying, boy? Be like you? Bold?"

Here goes. He sat on a stool at the kitchen counter, shoving the ring box out of sight.

He pressed REDIAL. She answered on the second ring.

"Elizabeth? Hi, it's Kavan."

The chime of Elizabeth's cell phone reverberated under the bridge's cover. The display flashed Kavan's home number. She finished the last of her prayer and answered.

"Hi," she said, a little too softly, a little too intimately. The sound of her own voice caused her to stand at attention. *What is it about girls that they turn to mush when a boy calls?* She steadied herself and lowered her tone. "How are you?"

"Doing well. Travis just called. I'm all cleared. Appears that some higher-ups in the division might be the source of the embezzlement."

"Really?" Excitement spiked her voice. "But your name is completely cleared?"

"According to Travis."

"Well, you know how well you can trust him."

"Elizabeth!" Kavan said, both shock and humor in his tone.

"Sorry, I just don't like when people I love. . ." She stopped, unable to believe the words that just flowed out of her mouth. "Well, when people I care about, you know, my friends and family, are falsely accused."

Kavan remained silent for a moment too long.

Why did I say that?

"That's understandable, Elizabeth. Anyway, that's not the main reason I called."

Her insides fluttered. "What's up?"

"I wondered if you, um, well, would you like to go to dinner?"

She wondered at his nervousness, all the while amused by her own jitters. The hand that held her cell phone to her ear trembled slightly. "You know I love Giuseppe's."

"Right, well, not Giuseppe's."

"Then where?"

"Italian Hills."

"That fancy restaurant up on the hill?" The romantic atmosphere of Italian Hills was legendary in the New England area.

"Yes, the fancy place on the hill."

The tone of his voice, the decisive way he spoke, told Elizabeth this was no ordinary dinner. She panicked. "Kavan, I'm going to school. In about a month."

"So I've heard. All the more reason to enjoy the days that are left."

"With romantic dinners?"

"Who said anything about romantic dinners?" Kavan's voice rose sharply. He sounded flustered.

Elizabeth walked out from under the bridge, into the light of the moon. "Italian Hills is synonymous with romance."

"I like their fettuccine. If you don't want to go, I'll go by myself."

"Oh now, that's ridiculous. When do you want to go?" She climbed the hill to the house.

"Tomorrow night. Saturday."

"What time?"

"Six."

"Six thirty."

His mellow chuckle tingled in her ear. "See you then."

"See you then."

Elizabeth was grateful for a day at Sinclair's. It kept her mind off her date with Kavan, or so she thought.

"Elizabeth," Joann called, coming out of the back office. "I recounted the cashiers' money bags and not one of them has the right starting bundle."

"What?" Elizabeth turned with a jerky motion. "How can that be? I counted those bags myself." She started for the back office. Joann followed.

"I think they're off 'cause your head is someplace else."

Elizabeth gaped at her boss while rubbing her hand along the top of her head. "Nope, my head is right here where I always keep it." She reached for one of the cashiers' bags and removed the cash bundle.

Joann gave her a sly smile. "Better check the clouds, girlfriend. I think your head is floating out there. You want to tell me what's going on?"

Elizabeth sighed and dropped the cash bag on the counter. "I'm going to dinner with Kavan. Italian Hills." She spilled her fears, confessing that she had feelings for him, but the timing couldn't be more wrong. The invitation to dinner at Italian Hills emanated with his desire for a deeper relationship—she just knew it.

Joann listened, her head bobbing in contemplation. When Elizabeth finished, Joann said, "When are you going to let go and let love?"

"Later. After grad school, you know that."

"But love is at your door now."

Elizabeth narrowed her eyes. "Joann, I'm not throwing away my future because a cute guy looks my way."

With chagrin, Joann retorted, "Lovely. You just let that pride of yours keep you from the best thing that ever happened to you." She stepped forward and grabbed Elizabeth gently by the shoulders. "Surrender, girl, surrender."

Joann's comments smarted. Only last night she'd cried out to the Lord for His grace in her life. But today, the same old feelings of control emerged. She looked at her boss.

"I'll admit," Elizabeth said, raising one hand, "that I've come to enjoy Kavan's attention and the schoolgirl feelings, but I won't let them govern me. I won't surrender."

"Fine, have it your way. But hear me now—" Joann paused, wagging her finger under Elizabeth's nose. "Before this time next year, I'll be dancing at your wedding."

❧❧

Waiting for Kavan to pick her up, Elizabeth paced the living room. Grandpa looked up at her from his chair where he sat reading. "Sit down, Beth. You're making me nervous."

Grandma set aside the book she was reading. "You are making more of this than you need to, Beth." She offered a simple, sincere prayer. "Father, give Beth grace and peace. Reveal Your will to her."

"Thank you, Grandma," Elizabeth said, bending to kiss her grandma's cheek. "How do you always know what I need and how to pray?"

❧❧

Kavan glanced at the clock. *Six fifteen! Where did the time go?* He reached for his black leather belt hanging on a hook in his closet. He slipped it through the loops of his dark gray slacks, while yanking a white mock turtleneck from a hanger. He pulled it over his head and quickly finished dressing.

Shoes, where are my shoes? He hunted around the closet floor and under the bed. *Where are my dress shoes?*

In stocking feet, he skidded along the polished wood floor of the living room, looking for his shoes under the sofa and chairs.

Aha. He spotted them in the corner by the bookshelf.

Finally ready, he raced out the door.

My keys!

He dashed back inside. Where were his keys? He looked under the papers on the kitchen counter. The blue velvet box still sat where he'd shoved it yesterday. In the bedroom, he checked his dresser and nightstand.

Of all the times to lose my keys. . . I never lose my keys.

He ducked into the laundry room and rummaged through the basket of dirty laundry. He heard a jingling sound coming from the previous day's work pants. He found his keys in the right front pocket.

Laughing at himself, he dashed for his truck. At 6:35 he pulled into the Lamberts' driveway.

Elizabeth opened the door and greeted him with a smile. "Come in; say hi to Grandpa and Grandma."

Kavan entered. He stooped to Elizabeth's ear as he passed her. "You look incredible."

A pink hue painted her cheeks. "Thank you. You're looking mighty dapper yourself."

He greeted the elder Lamberts, trying to appear relaxed, at ease, but he was sure they could hear the pounding of his heart.

The Italian Hills restaurant sat outside White Birch in the foothills of the White Mountains. As Elizabeth entered the elegant establishment, she felt like a queen on Kavan's arm. With confidence, he gave his name to the maître d' and gently guided her through the candlelit tables to a cozy window table in the corner of the restaurant.

"Kavan." Elizabeth allowed him to hold her chair as she sat down. "This is beautiful."

He sat across from her. "I know. I've only been here once, but this is better than I remember."

"Only once?" she teased. "You love their fettuccine?"

"Yes, it's the only thing I've eaten here."

She chortled, keeping her voice low. The sound of violins grew closer as a quartet strolled toward them. "You always make me laugh."

"Is that a bad thing?"

"No, actually. It's good. I used to laugh a lot, but the stress and competition of school kind of choked out my sense of humor."

Kavan nodded. She knew he understood. Perhaps it was her imagination, but he seemed to understand everything. He was always so patient and kind.

The waiter brought their menus. With polish, he recited the evening's specials. When he'd taken their drink order and gone, Elizabeth leaned toward Kavan and whispered, "I prefer the waitress with the bubble gum."

Kavan chuckled. "She did have a certain charm."

They ordered, and not long after, the waiter brought the plate of appetizers.

"Here, try one of these," Kavan said, dropping a stuffed mushroom onto Elizabeth's plate.

She took a bite, her blue gaze steady on Kavan. "Very good. Best stuffed mushroom I've ever had."

As they ate, their conversation fell into an easy, comfortable rhythm.

They found they had many ideals and desires in common. Despite their Fourth of July nuclear versus natural-energy debate, they found common ground in faith, love of life, and a fascination with science.

"Yeah, but you're a tree hugger," Elizabeth said, rolling her eyes.

"At least I can hug a tree. When was the last time you hugged a nuclear reactor?"

So the debate ensued again, but this time with gentleness and respect. When the main course arrived, they'd agreed to disagree.

"After my master's, I'll have more fuel for my fire." She swirled her fork through her fettuccine.

Kavan paused his fork in midair, then set it against his plate. "So, have you decided where you want to go?"

"Whoever asks me first, I'm going."

Suddenly, Kavan dropped his fork and stood to his feet. His napkin fluttered to the floor. Gazing down at her, serious and intent, he asked, "Elizabeth Lambert, will you marry me?"

Chapter 19

He heard the words come out of his mouth, but he couldn't believe his own ears. Jesus said that "out of the overflow of the heart the mouth speaks," and at that moment, Kavan understood the deep truth of those words.

Elizabeth stared up at him. Shock masked her face. "What?" she whispered.

Kavan hesitated, desperate to repeat his question while longing for eloquence. *The ring. Why didn't I bring the ring? I didn't know. . . .*

But the moment felt so right. A thrill shot through him as he dropped to one knee. "Elizabeth Lambert, will you marry me?"

"You can't be serious."

"Dead serious. You just said, whoever asked first. I'm asking."

She lowered her face to his. "We've never even said 'I love you.'"

Kavan rose from bended knee and sat in the seat next to Elizabeth. He took her hand in his. The food on their plates, shoved to one side, remained untouched. "I know we've never said it, but we feel it. At least I do. I love you, Elizabeth. I love you."

He could not read her emotions from the expression on her face. "Are you going to say anything?" he said after a long, hot pause.

"I don't know what to say. Kavan, I'm going to school. Why did you ask me to marry you?"

He dropped his gaze and studied the delicate lines of her petite, slender hands. "A wise man once said, 'He who finds a wife finds what is good and receives favor from the Lord.' You are a good thing, Elizabeth, and I want to share my life with you."

She would not look into his eyes. Quietly she said, "Please, can we go?"

❧❧

Midmorning Monday, Kavan drove to the fire tower, his refurbishment project under way again. He expected to meet with the carpenter later that day and finalize construction plans. The embezzlement accusations had soured Kavan on this project, but he wanted it complete before the winter snows.

He inspected the tower as he climbed to the top, making notes in his electronic data assistant. Yet, he paused every few steps, his thoughts trapped in the events of Saturday night.

Elizabeth, oh, Elizabeth, will you ever speak to me again?

He'd driven her home that evening in awkward silence. Neither knew what to say. Convinced he should not pressure her, he'd left her alone to process her emotions. However, he could not retract his question. Perhaps he'd let the romantic ambience of Italian Hills sweep him away momentarily. Perhaps his timing was all wrong, but in his heart of hearts, Kavan wanted to marry the blue-eyed electrical engineer.

He didn't regret the fact that his question would linger on the winds of time for all of eternity. His words still echoed in his mind, along with the story of Cindy Mae's uncle. Maybe his Elizabeth would not wear the ring, either. Kavan winced. He did not want to go the way of Uncle John.

With poise and grace, Elizabeth had avoided answering his question. She'd slipped out of his truck with a hushed "good night" and disappeared in the darkness. He waited until the porch light flashed before starting home.

Immediately, he went to prayer. *Lord, what have I done?*

For a split second, he imagined the Lord's kind smile over him. *Well, you told her.*

Kavan smiled as he drove home. *Oh yes, like a bull in a china shop.*

He had no idea what his next move should be. Sunday, he stayed home and fellowshipped with the Lord in the serenity of his own home. He thought it would be wise to give Elizabeth some space. Her relationship with the Lord was finally blossoming, and he didn't want to make her feel uncomfortable as she worshiped with the rest of the Lord's saints.

He enjoyed his Sabbath day, spending the morning in prayer and contemplation, then running Fred and Ginger through the foothills that afternoon.

Yet, truth be told, his mind never totally disengaged from his longing for Elizabeth. He imagined her sitting next to him in the empty rocker on the back porch, praying with him, talking with him, sharing life with him.

He imagined picnics with her in the shade of the oaks and maples.

Monday evening, Kavan's phone rang, shattering the silence of the house.

Kavan muted the television and reached for the phone.

"Hello."

"Kavan, it's Dad."

He sat forward and checked his surprise. "Dad. Hello. How are you?"

"Fine, son. July in Miami—can you imagine anything more insane?"

Kavan chuckled. "No, actually."

"Your mother loves it. She's as brown as a buckeye."

"I imagine you're staying cool in the condo with a pile of good books."

Ralph Donovan answered, "Naturally."

"So, what's up?" Momentary concern gripped him. Kavan loved hearing his father's voice, but the man did not call often. "Everything okay?"

"Yes. But I was going to ask you the same thing."

Kavan smiled into the phone, tears burning in his eyes. He stalled them by taking a deep breath. He steadied his voice and said, "Things are, um, good."

"You've been on my mind today." The brief expression communicated a mountain of words to Kavan. It was his father's unemotional way of telling him he missed him and cared for him. It was also an indication from his heavenly Father that He also loved him and watched over him.

"I talked with Alvin the other night," his father started.

Kavan pictured his father's former business partner. "How is he?"

"Fat and rich. He's making more money than ever. I left the business too soon."

"It happens."

"What's with you and the Lambert girl?" The question came in traditional Ralph Donovan style, without preamble.

"How'd you hear about her?"

"Alvin."

Elizabeth is right. This town is obsessed with romance.

"Nothing is up with the Lambert girl."

"Does she have a name?"

"Elizabeth." Knowing what questions would come next, Kavan recited her résumé. "MIT graduate, electrical engineering, 4.0, applying for graduate schools in nuclear engineering."

"Sounds like a stellar woman."

"She is pretty amazing."

"Well, are you marrying her?"

"No, Dad, I don't think so."

They talked for the better part of an hour, the conversation abating remnants of anxiety and concern over his Saturday actions.

"Bold move, son. Never regret a bold move," Ralph told him.

Later, as Kavan readied for bed, the sound of his dad's voice echoed in his head. How did his heavenly Father communicate His love so profoundly through his pragmatic, no-nonsense, earthly father? He considered it a mystery, but a beautiful one.

Just as he clicked off the light, the phone rang again.

"Hello?" Kavan said.

"Hi, it's me."

❧❧

Elizabeth sat on her bed, the light of her desk lamp illuminating the room in soft gold light, and debated with herself.

Should I call him? No, wait for him to call. He started this. Let him finish it. But he deserves an answer. He asked a sincere question.

Elizabeth glanced at the paper lying on the edge of her desk. Her résumé. Well, what could it hurt to pass it around? She'd heard wonderful things about Creager Electronics and their innovations with robotics.

"What you got there?" Grandpa appeared in the doorway.

Elizabeth looked up, setting aside the résumé. "Hi, Grandpa. I thought you and Grandma were playing bridge."

"We were, but Grant Hansen wasn't feeling well, so we cut the evening short."

"They're nice people, aren't they?" Elizabeth shifted position on her bed so Grandpa could sit on the edge.

"Fine folks." He surveyed the room while reaching for the résumé. Tipping his head upward, he read the neat black print through his bifocals. "Looking for work?"

Elizabeth grabbed a pillow and hugged it to her. "I enjoyed robotics at MIT. I spent a few terms in the artificial intelligence lab. Creager is a leading robotics company."

Grandpa stuck out his chin and scratched his head. "What a coincidence," he said, a lilt in his tone. "Sounds like you got a good plan, kitten."

Elizabeth couldn't hold it in any longer. "Kavan asked me to marry him."

As usual, Grandpa took the news in stride. "What did you say?"

Tears pooled in her eyes and slipped down her cheeks. She brushed them away with a quick swipe of her fingers. "I told him to take me home."

"Falling in love was not the plan for this summer, was it?"

She shook her head and reached for a tissue, trying to halt the tears. With her eyes fixed on the ceiling, she said, "I'm going to school, Grandpa. I am."

"I hate to sound preachy, Beth, but what is God saying to you? You think this transcript error might have been His doing?"

"No, it was clearly my doing. But I don't know what's what anymore except that I'm frustrated."

"Sometimes the Lord frustrates our plans to get our attention." He gently set the résumé back in its place. "I think Kavan is your *pregnant wife.*"

Despite the tears, Elizabeth laughed. "You can't smooth this over with a joke, Grandpa."

"I'm confident the Lord's plans for you are good. I'm confident they include Kavan."

"I wish I had your confidence. I'll feel like a failure if I don't go to grad school."

"I know the feeling. That's why I packed my bags and trotted off to Harvard. But it was my pride, Bethy. Your success is not in what you do, but in who you are in Jesus. His death on the cross, His resurrection life, and His righteousness define you."

"I hear you, Grandpa, and I'm trying to understand that truth more and more. But somehow Jesus dying on the cross doesn't seem to answer the question of school."

"If you are going to school to be considered a success, then you have already failed. Kitten, you are successful because you know Jesus. You realize only 10 percent of the world's population claims Him as their Lord and Savior. Look at you, you're in the top 10 percent of the world."

She laughed and tapped him on the arm. "You are making it too easy for mc to decide against school."

Grandpa nodded and patted Elizabeth's leg. "Only because I'm speaking what you already know in your heart."

Elizabeth bobbed her head in agreement, sighing. "Suddenly, school doesn't seem to be the right path, but I don't know what else to do."

"Marry Kavan."

She let go a wry chuckle. "The one thing I said I'd *never* do. . .let my heart rule my head."

"Well, that motto has merit," Grandpa conceded. "But either way you go, your heart is ruling your head. The prideful desire to go to grad school will win. Or the sincere desire to know true love. But sometimes the heart touched by love is privileged to make the choice."

"How did you get to be so wise?" Elizabeth asked. She scooted to the end of the bed and stood up. "I'm going down to the bridge to pray."

Grandpa stood and drew her into his embrace. "Good idea. Grandma and I will pray for you here."

Elizabeth slipped on her sneakers and grabbed her phone.

The serenity under the bridge always amazed her. It was as if God waited there for her. As soon as she walked under the cover, she sensed His presence.

Her thoughts and prayers wandered between school and Kavan. The issue did not seem to be a matter of choosing love over education; it seemed more about surrendering her will to God's.

Stubborn pride, she thought.

Leaning against the bridge's strong beam, Elizabeth uttered the words that finally unlocked her heart. "Lord, forgive my pride. I surrender my plans, my heart, to You."

Tears flowed, and doubt began to drain from her as if a big plug had been pulled. She didn't have to fight to be in control. Her Lord controlled her life, and He loved her. He was her Friend, and His plans for her were perfect.

Liberty rang through her. "I'm free to do God's will, not mine," she shouted.

Kavan. She reached for her phone and dialed.

Her heart throbbed at the sound of his hello.

"Hi, it's me."

❧❧

Kavan sat up in bed and clicked on the lamp. "How are you?"

He heard a rolling giggle. "I'm fine. Fine. Just fine."

He grinned. "Are you sure?"

"Uh-huh."

Kavan glanced at the alarm clock. "Where are you?"

"On the bridge."

"At eleven o'clock? Elizabeth, it's too late to be out alone." He ran his hand over his closely cropped hair and propped his arms on his knees.

"Grandpa knows I'm out here."

"Wait till I see him."

Her light chuckle floated from the phone, a melodic sound he loved.

"I never answered your question," she said.

Now his heart pounded like thundering horses, and he dropped the phone's mouthpiece below his chin, not wanting Elizabeth to hear his labored breathing.

"Look, Elizabeth," he said after a moment, his voice steady. "I'm sorry I surprised you with such a life-altering question, but I meant every word I said."

"I had no doubt. That didn't make it any easier."

Kavan stretched out his legs and leaned against a pile of bed pillows. "You can take your time answering."

"You know you have some nerve messing with a girl's heart and mind."

Kavan listened. He could tell Elizabeth needed to talk. Half of him dreaded the answer he felt sure would come at the end of her monologue, but he needed to know.

"I mean, I come up here to spend a quiet summer with Grandpa and Grandma, to work and prepare for grad school. Instead, you have to come waltzing into my life. A redheaded tree hugger!"

He guffawed. "You think I planned it just to annoy you?"

"If I didn't know you better, yes."

Low and steady, he responded, "I didn't intend on falling in love with a nuke advocate who happens to be so beautiful I see her eyes in the night sky instead of the stars."

"Oh, Kavan, you aren't making this any easier."

"I love you, Elizabeth. I love you. I hate saying that over the phone, but I love you."

The long pause on her end didn't reassure him.

Finally, she whispered, "I have an answer, I think."

He sat up again, so fast all the blood drained from his face and he saw spots. "Yes?"

"Can you meet me on the bridge?"

"When?"

"Friday night."

"That long, eh?"

"I'm sorry, I want to think and pray. Just to be sure."

"Ah, just like a scientist. Analyze everything to death."

"You'll appreciate it later in life."

He grinned, feeling as if she were throwing him a bone of hope. "Friday is fine, my friend."

"See you then."

"What time? Six thirty?"

She responded with a mock laugh. "Ha, ha. I have to work until ten. Eleven o'clock?"

"Sure."

"Good night."

She hung up before he could respond. But in an instant, Kavan was on his feet, bouncing on the bed, Fred and Ginger barking in time.

Chapter 20

Humming, Elizabeth got ready for work, letting her thoughts and feelings of love for Kavan sink in and take hold. What an amazing feeling, she decided. Amazing.

Imagine, Jesus feels the same way about me, only more. She giggled.

Brushing her long eyelashes with black mascara, she paused and spoke to her reflection in the mirror. "You are in love, Elizabeth Lambert. You! Of all people."

The summer's events astounded her still—meeting Kavan and falling in love. Reuniting with the love of her Lord, knowing Jesus as her Friend. Realizing it was selfish pride not purpose driving her desire to go to grad school.

It seemed as if the Father had this special summer all wrapped up like a present, waiting for her. But she'd refused to accept it.

How gracious and kind He is to wait for me to surrender. Me and my foolish pride. I should write a book about it, she concluded, dabbing on her lipstick and leaving the bathroom.

In her room, she slipped on her black pumps and suit jacket before picking up the attaché case that contained her résumé.

At five minutes of eight, Elizabeth climbed behind the wheel of her car. She slipped the key into the ignition, then fished her cell phone from the attaché's side pocket. She pressed the number to autodial Will's office.

"This is Will Adams."

"Hi, it's Elizabeth. I'll be a few minutes late."

"No problem." He sounded distracted. Elizabeth pictured him intent on his computer, running production reports. "Anything I can do for you?" he asked.

"No, thanks."

She pressed the END button and tossed the phone into the passenger seat. Steering the VW north of town, Elizabeth felt exhilaration, coupled with nervous jitters.

Her life had turned upside down with the declaration of four simple words: Will you marry me? Yet somehow, the world finally seemed right, as if missing pieces were found and snapped into place.

At the next light, she turned left into Creager Electronics' blacktopped parking lot. Slipping the compact car into a visitor's slot, Elizabeth grabbed the leather attaché case and checked her appearance in the rearview mirror.

An austere receptionist greeted her at the front desk.

"I'd like to speak to someone in human resources."

"Do you have an appointment?" the woman asked.

"No, but I'd like to submit my résumé to the personnel manager."

The woman pursed her lips and clicked through the appointment calendar on her flat computer screen.

Lord, open a door for me, please, Elizabeth prayed. *I'm at Your mercy.*

"Have a seat." The woman motioned to a curved couch situated on the right side of the sleek receptionist desk.

"Thank you."

Elizabeth waited only a few minutes before a tall, lanky gentleman appeared through a set of brass-handled double doors. She rose and shook his extended hand.

"Brad Johnston, Director of Human Resources."

"Elizabeth Lambert. I'd like to submit my résumé." She flipped open the flap of her attaché and pulled out a linen sheet, her credentials listed in dark print.

"We aren't hiring, Miss Lambert." Brad Johnston accepted the paper.

Mustering her courage, she said, "Please review my résumé before deciding. You'll find I have all the qualifications."

He chuckled. "New grad?"

She nodded.

"I can tell. New grads always come to us reciting from the 'How to Interview' textbook."

Elizabeth met his brown gaze. "How else do you expect us to get companies like yours to consider us?"

"Touché," he said, grinning at her bravado. He skimmed her résumé. "MIT. Impressive. Graduated with a 4.0 average." His eyes shifted between her face and the paper in his hands. "Three terms in the artificial intelligence lab."

His fingers fidgeted with the paper, tapping it slightly. The rhythm matched the twittering beat of Elizabeth's heart. Brad Johnston puckered his lips in contemplation.

Surely he knows this is nerve-racking, Elizabeth thought.

After a second, he said, "Come with me. There are a few people I think would like to meet you."

At one fifteen, Elizabeth dashed through the doors of Lambert's Furniture and scurried up the stairs to her office. Tossing the attaché onto the floor by her desk, she slipped into her chair and booted up her computer.

"A few minutes late, huh?"

Elizabeth turned, startled. Will stood in her doorway, his arms folded across his broad chest. He glanced at his watch.

"Will, I'm sorry. Really. I didn't know it would take so long. Bad timing with all the end-of-the month figures due."

He chuckled. "By the light in your eyes and the smile on your face, it must be good."

Elizabeth sighed. "Yes, it's all good. God is so good. I can't believe it."

He nodded. "You'll tell me when you're ready, then."

"Yes, I promise. Thanks for understanding."

At eleven o'clock Friday night, Kavan pulled up to the White Birch covered bridge. He cut the engine and reached for his flashlight. Stepping out of the truck, he saw a soft glow from the other side of the bridge, along the riverbank.

"Elizabeth?" he called, nerves causing his voice to pop and crack.

"Here," she answered.

The flashlight slipped in his perspiring palm as he fumbled with the light switch. "Hello." He stepped toward the sound of her voice. Thin ribbons of the half-moon's light filtered through the trees, dotting the path he walked.

Why did his mouth dry up like a desert in times like these? He tried to wet his dry lips with an even drier tongue. Kavan found Elizabeth perched on an old army blanket, the area lighted with several jar candles.

She patted the spot next to her.

"Hi." The golden glow of the candlelight fell on the soft curves of her face. Instinctively, he reached out and stroked the line along her jaw with his finger.

"Hi." She took his hand into hers and smiled.

Kavan's heart melted and pooled in his middle like warm syrup. "Elizabeth, you're. . ." He paused and drew a deep, shaky breath. With that came the sweet scent of her perfume. "You're killing me here. I don't know if my heart can take it."

She tenderly kissed the back of his hand. "I'm sorry, Kavan. I didn't mean to make this hard for you."

He settled next to her, wrapping his arms around his knees. Elizabeth leaned against him, and in that moment, it seemed as if all the pieces of his world came together. He kissed the top of her head. "I think I made this hard for myself, really. I knew you wanted to go to school."

"Me and my pride."

He lifted his arms to draw her into his embrace. She nestled her head against his shoulder, fitting perfectly there. "A woman has a right to her dreams."

"I judged girls who fell in love. I thought they were silly and stupid. Weak. I thought getting a bunch of degrees would declare me a success."

"Nothing wrong with a degree or two." He looked down at her, catching the image of a flickering flame in the blue hue of her eyes.

In one smooth motion, their faces drew close and their lips touched, a kiss warm with love and emotion.

He cupped her face in his hand. "I really do love you."

"I know, and that totally ruined my life this summer."

"Glad to be of service."

She turned to face him. "Kavan, when you asked me to marry you, I realized for the first time in my life that I even wanted to be married. Hearing a man declare his love and desire to spend the rest of his life with me changed me. I tried to hang on to my ideals about grad school, but suddenly I couldn't remember them anymore. I prayed and prayed about it, and the Lord gave me His answer."

He couldn't help it. He reached up, pulled her face to his, and kissed her again. After that, he asked, "What did He say?"

"Lots of things," she teased.

Kavan slapped his hand over his heart and fell back against the blanket. "I'm dying here."

"I got a senior engineering position at Creager Electronics." She delivered the news without warning.

"What?" Kavan said, unsure of what he'd heard.

"I start at Creager Electronics in two weeks."

"What about grad school?"

She shook her head and shrugged. "Maybe someday. But the desire is gone. Creager's work in robotics is another interest of mine. Kavan, they offered me an amazing salary." She laughed. "At that point, all notions of grad school vanished."

He gaped at her for a long time, trying to gather his thoughts. "I'm stunned. I don't know what to say."

Elizabeth moved to her knees. "Kavan, I'm choosing love. Will you ask me again?"

He sat up like a shot. "Ask you to marry me?"

She nodded.

He knelt before her and took her hands into his. "Elizabeth, will you. . . No wait. First, let me say I love you. You are the Lord's answer to my heart's desire for a wife."

She trembled, a sob escaping her lips. "I love you, too."

Feeling a little giddy at the sound of those words, he leveled his rising emotions with a quick breath. He reached into his breast pocket and pulled out the blue velvet box. He popped open the top and lifted out the ring. Slipping the polished gold onto her ring finger, he asked once more, "Elizabeth, will you marry me?"

She gasped, catching the glitter of the ring in the candlelight. "Oh, Kavan, it's beautiful." She brushed her forehead with her other hand. "Wow, I never imagined. . ."

"That ring has a story you would not believe."

She looked from the ring to his face. "Really?"

"Really," he repeated. "Are you going to answer the question?"

She smiled. With metered, determined words, Elizabeth gave her answer, "Yes, Kavan Donovan, I will marry you."

Laughing, crying, shouting, they embraced and sealed their promise with a kiss.

"You've made me a very happy man."

"You've made me a very loved woman."

For the next hour, they sat under the stars talking and dreaming. Kavan amazed her with the story of the ring, spurring tears. The love and pleasure of the Lord astounded them.

At midnight, Kavan grabbed her hand and said, "Come with me."

"Where are we going?" she asked, laughing, jumping up.

"You'll see." Kavan led her to the bridge, walking under the high roof. He flashed his light along the beams, looking up, turning in a small circle.

"What are you looking for?"

"A spot." He grinned down at her. "Let's finalize this deal by carving our initials into the tapestry of White Birch's lovers."

Elizabeth found the spot. Next to her grandparents' initials, there was just enough space.

Kavan pulled out his pocketknife and carved *KD loves EL.*

"You know, it should say 'EL loves KD.' " She tiptoed up to kiss Kavan. " 'Cause EL truly does love KD."

"I suppose I should speak to your father."

"He'd like that," Elizabeth said.

"For now, how about telling Grandpa Matt and Grandma Betty?"

They woke Grandpa and Grandma to give them the good news. The older couple whooped and hollered like youngsters, hugging Elizabeth, then Kavan.

"Grandma," Grandpa said, doing a little jig around room, "we're having a wedding! Our Bethy is getting married."

Epilogue

Elizabeth waited inside the bridal room of White Birch Community Church, the bright light of the October morning streaming through the window. Her father paced in a tight circle.

"Dad, sit down. You're making me nervous."

The man look back at his daughter with an accepting laugh. "Never thought I'd be so nervous giving away my baby girl. I figured you'd be in grad school for a while and I didn't have to worry about giving you to another man."

Elizabeth crossed the room and slipped her arms around her father's waist. "No one is more surprised than me, Dad, but I love Kavan."

Paul Lambert hugged his girl. "Your mom and I love him, too. We're proud of you."

A light knock sounded on the closed door. "Elizabeth?"

The bride glanced at her father. "Come in, Grandpa."

The senior Lambert's beaming face peered around the door. "Are you ready?"

Elizabeth sighed, glancing between her father and Grandpa. "I'm ready."

Grandpa jutted out his elbow. "Paul, thank you for sharing the honor of walking our girl down the aisle."

"You helped get her here, Dad."

Elizabeth linked arms with the two men. "Hopefully, the two of you won't scare Kavan off."

❧❧

Kavan stood at the end of the aisle, squinting toward the sanctuary door, his pulse thumping in his ears. The room was bright and beautiful, and crowded with friends and family. But all he wanted was to see his bride emerge from the other side of the sanctuary doors.

The doors open and Elizabeth glided down the aisle, her father on one arm, Grandpa Matt on the other. Through her veil, Kavan could see her smile.

Beautiful Elizabeth.

Kavan winked at her when the trio stopped at the top of the aisle. Life would never be boring with Elizabeth.

He listened as Pastor Marlow opened the ceremony with a word of prayer. And when Paul Lambert slipped his daughter's hand into Kavan's, tears surprised his eyes. He never imagined how much his life would change since the day he met Elizabeth in Sinclair's five months ago.

"You are beautiful," he said to her when she glanced up at him after the opening prayer. His voice was loud, echoing around the sanctuary. Kavan felt his cheeks burn.

She squeezed his hand. "So are you."

Kavan escorted her up the steps and with her hand in his, agreed to love and cherish Elizabeth Lambert the rest of his life.

He knew he would. Always.

Lambert's Code

Dedication

This story was written while enduring two hurricanes, Frances and Jeanne.
I'm grateful to my remarkable husband for
doing most of the cleanup after Jeanne so I could write.
He's my best friend, encourager, editor, and "babe."
What would I do without him?
Lambert's Code is dedicated to Tony.

Special thanks to Louise Gouge for her critique
and to my editor and friend, Susan Downs.

Chapter 1

Ethan breathed in the rich aroma of coffee wafting from the kitchen as he jogged downstairs and dropped his gym bag in the hall by the front door. "The league basketball championship is at five, Julie. You coming?" He kissed his wife on the cheek and broke off a piece of her muffin.

"No, my doctor's appointment is at four. Are you coming?" Julie raised a brow as she handed Ethan a cup of coffee. "Muffins are in the box." She sat down at the breakfast nook.

Taking the coffee, he paused. Her words echoed in his mind, *"Doctor's appointment." Am I supposed to be at this appointment?*

Pondering her question, he pulled a plate from the cupboard and picked a blueberry muffin from the box marked PERI'S PERK.

"I see Peri's coffee shop is making its mark here in White Birch, New Hampshire."

"She brought our cozy community into the twenty-first century." Julie sipped her coffee.

Ethan leaned against the counter, biting into his breakfast. He wished he'd whipped up a batch of eggs instead. He set his plate aside. "Am I supposed to go with you today?"

She picked at her muffin. "Only if you want to, Ethan."

He regarded her for a moment, thinking how tired she sounded. They were both weary of this medical process.

"Do you think you can handle this one by yourself? I have a lot of work to do today, and I need to be at the rec center by four thirty."

She regarded him with wide green eyes. Most of the time, they sparkled when she looked at him, but not this morning.

"Well, of course, the rec center is more important."

"Come on, Jules, you know that's not true."

"Do I?"

He sighed. "Julie, I've been to Dr. Patterson's OB-GYN office more than most of the women in this town."

She tipped her coffee cup and drank slowly. After a moment, she said, "Not lately. Besides, I thought we were in this together."

"We are. Why would you even say that? But today, can I have a pass?" He stooped to see her face. "Please, Mrs. Lambert, may I have a get-out-of-the-doctor's-appointment pass?" He flashed a cheesy grin and raised his left eyebrow.

She gazed into her coffee. "What if it's bad news?"

"It's not going to be bad news." He kissed her forehead. "Everything's going to be all right, babe. Don't spend the day worrying." He pulled her to her feet and wrapped her in his arms.

She dropped her face to his chest and held him like she didn't want to let go. "I won't."

But he knew she would. With a quick squeeze, he released her, his thoughts already on the day ahead.

Ducking into the pantry, he shoved food boxes around, hunting for pregame energy. "Do we have any protein bars?"

"Not unless you bought them."

"Babe, can we organize this pantry? Throw some of this out or give it away? I don't think we'll eat half this stuff."

"Have at it."

Ethan peered around the door. "Are you okay?" He tossed a couple of breakfast bars on the counter.

I wonder if Mark Benton will make tonight's game. He counted on big Mark for rebounds. If Mark couldn't play, he'd have to spend some of the afternoon finding a replacement center. White Birch didn't grow men over six-foot-five every day.

"I'm fine," Julie said, staring out the nook window. "But you can clean the pantry as well as I can. In fact, you're better—"

The phone's ring interrupted her rebuttal.

Ethan made eye contact with Julie as he answered. "Hello?" She gave him a quick glance and slight smile.

"What?" he said after a moment. "I'll be right there." He slapped the phone onto the wall cradle with a disgusted sigh.

"What's wrong?" Julie moved behind Ethan with her plate, setting it in the kitchen sink.

"The environmental inspectors are on their way to Lambert's Furniture again." He pointed to the plate in the sink. "You want to put that in the dishwasher?"

She stuck out her tongue. "Neat freak."

"Slob."

Julie tucked her plate away in the dishwasher and flipped off the kitchen light. "I need to get to school."

He captured her for a kiss, her oval face serious and beautiful, like the cello music she loved to play. "I need to get going, too. Are you sure you're okay?"

She smoothed her hand over his chest. "Nervous, I guess."

He handed Julie her navy peacoat from the front closet.

"Babe, it's going to be fine. Don't assume the worst."

"It's been three years, Ethan."

He hesitated. "I know." He slipped on his trench coat. Three years and thousands of dollars. They'd be in a house now, instead of the apartment, if only—

He shook the thought loose. No sense in rehashing the past, second-guessing their decisions. *What's done is done.*

Outside in the cold, clear morning, he fought a twinge of guilt, watching Julie walk to her car. *Should I go to the doctor's appointment?*

But what about the game? He felt sure he'd reminded Julie a month ago about the championship. The first game started at five. If they won, they'd play through the winner's bracket. He had every intention of winning the championship trophy.

If he met Julie at the doc's office, he'd never make it to the rec center in time to warm up.

If he gives us bad news, I'll miss the game altogether. He banished the thought from his mind. *It won't be bad news. It won't.*

Unlocking his Honda, Ethan tossed his gym bag into the backseat and glanced over the car's top as Julie pulled out of the apartment parking lot. She waved and tooted her horn good-bye.

Maybe I should call her. He reached for his cell and was about to dial her number when his phone rang.

He answered, "Ethan Lambert."

"Ethan, it's Mark Benton. I won't be able to make it to tonight's game."

<hr />

"Listen up, it's time to think about our spring concert." Julie passed out sheet music to the White Birch Elementary fifth-grade orchestra students. "Take these home. Practice them."

A collective groan filled the room. "It's only February, Mrs. Lambert."

"I know, I know. But let's start practicing now so you don't sound like a pack of hungry alley cats on a rainy night."

The girls giggled, the boys snickered, and when Cole Gunter started caterwauling, the whole class joined him.

"All right, all right." Julie held up her hands for silence, laughing. "If that noise doesn't frighten you into practicing, I don't know what will. Make sure you don't sound like that for the spring concert. And, Cole, let's get you signed up for chorus."

The ten- and eleven-year-olds laughed. Julie ruffled Cole's hair.

When the end-of-class bell rang, the kids scurried for the door, banging their instruments against the doorway on their way out. Julie cringed at the sound of the cases crashing against metal but called after them, "Don't forget, practice!"

She glanced at her watch. Three thirty. A nervous twitch made her feel lightheaded. In thirty minutes, she'd be in Dr. Patterson's office. The pizza plate she'd picked for lunch didn't seem like such a good idea right now. She pressed her hand on her abdomen. *Please, Lord, please let him have good news.*

Julie stared out the classroom window for a few minutes, waiting for a trickle of peace, fragments of the past few years flying through her thoughts. She'd been so hopeful when they sat in Dr. Patterson's office three years ago. He'd regaled them with success stories, explained the newest procedures and medications.

So far, none had worked for her.

"You still here, girl?" Sophia Caraballo strolled into Julie's classroom, hands on her hips.

Julie turned from the window. "Yeah, just thinking. I should grade these papers, though." She walked to her desk, motioning at the pile.

Sophia picked up the top sheet. " 'Why I Love Music.' "

"Come on, Sophia." Julie reached for the paper, but Sophia slapped her hand away. "I love music because it makes my mom smile after my dad yells at her." The svelte, overdone blond peered at Julie. "Now, *that* is sad."

Julie snatched the composition from her friend. "Yes, it is." She filed the stack of papers in her shoulder tote. "Now I've got to go or I'll be late."

"You nervous?"

"No." She regarded Sophia. "Yes. Well, more anxious than nervous. I'm trying to let go and let God have control of the situation, but it's hard." Julie walked to the door and flipped off the classroom light, picking up her coat from the wall hook.

"What do you think he'll say?" Sophia walked with Julie down the hall toward the front doors.

"That everything is all right. Give it more time." Julie gave Sophia a half-hearted smile. She ignored the fretful emotions that challenged her confidence.

"Is Ethan meeting you there?" Sophia asked.

Julie shook her head. "He's busy today."

"Busy? Are you kidding me?" Sophia grabbed her friend by the arm. "What a cad."

"He's not a cad, Sophia. He does have a lot on his plate, running production for Lambert's Furniture."

"So much he can't make this important appointment? His cousin is his boss, for crying out loud."

Julie sighed, not wanting to hash out her marriage issues with the school secretary. Despite her friendship, Sophia had a gossip's tongue.

"I'll talk to you later." Julie gave her a small hug and shoved open the glass door, cold air rushing past.

Sophia shivered. "Call me, okay?"

"Okay."

On the trip across town to Dr. Patterson's office, Julie's anxiety increased. She tried to pray with faith, but after the years of trying, failing, and trying again, her hope waned. "Lord, give me courage, please."

It bothered her that Ethan didn't want to come. She was as weary of the medical process as he was. Even more so. How could he leave her alone for this important appointment, the one that could make or break their hopes? He'd missed one or two before, but this one. . .

In the waiting room, Julie fidgeted in her chair and wondered why she'd bothered to press the speed limit to be on time. "Hurry up and wait," she muttered to herself.

She flipped through a parenting magazine before realizing what she was doing. She tossed it aside. Fishing her cell from her purse, Julie dialed Ethan. If she reminded him, he might come. Maybe. But he didn't answer his cell or office phone.

"Julie, you can go back now." The nurse behind the glass smiled and motioned to the inner-office door.

"Thanks, Amy."

"Good to see you."

"You, too."

In Dr. Patterson's wide, cluttered office, Julie lowered herself into the soft leather chair across from his desk.

"Well, young lady, how are you today?" Dr. Patterson came in after her, chipper and smiling. He sat with a thud in his worn leather chair.

Julie clasped her hands in her lap and leaned toward him, as if to draw on his gentle strength. "Fine, thank you."

He smiled. The lines of his weathered, kind face fanned out under his eyes, and his demeanor calmed her inner turmoil.

"Everything going okay?"

"You tell me," Julie said with a light laugh but winced thinking how glib she sounded.

Dr. Patterson chuckled. "Guess I am the doctor." He opened the file in front of him and reviewed information.

Julie shifted, straightening her skirt and adjusting her wedding ring. Corkboards, cluttered with pictures of Dr. Patterson holding naked newborns in his hands, lined the office walls.

Her heart palpitated at the idea of a child, her child, Ethan's child.

Dr. Patterson closed the folder. "Is Ethan joining us today?" He looked directly into her eyes, his expression molded with compassion.

Her eyes burned as she shook her head no.

"Should we call him?" Dr. Patterson placed his hand on the phone. "I can move a few things around in order to wait for him."

Julie swallowed the lump in her throat. "He's working; then he has a basketball game. I'll give him the news."

"A basketball game?" A flicker of concern flashed in Dr. Patterson's eyes.

"It's the league championship." Julie managed a smile. "You know how Ethan loves sports."

"Well, if you're sure, I'll go over the results with you. But if you and Ethan need to come in together, just give Amy a call. She'll get you right in. What you and Ethan have been through can put a strain on a marriage."

"Yes, I know. I appreciate your offer." Julie wrapped her arms around her waist and cuddled against the back of the chair. For a split second, she didn't think she could endure waiting for the news.

"I ran every test in the book, Julie. I even consulted with Dr. Llewellyn down in Manchester. He has a great deal of experience with infertility matters."

"Second opinions are always nice." She tried to sound confident.

The doctor slowly rose and walked around his desk, sitting in the chair next to her.

The chair that Ethan should be sitting in.

"You're scaring me." She trembled, and her tears spilled.

He took her hands in his. "I know how much you and Ethan want children."

Julie freed her hand to wipe her cheeks. Dr. Patterson leaned over his desk for the tissue box.

Taking the one he offered her, Julie blew her nose and balled the tissue in her hand. "This is not going to be good, is it?"

"Well, it depends on your definition of good."

She smiled despite her tears. "Grandchildren for my parents."

Dr. Patterson sighed. A chill slithered down Julie's spine.

"My dear, unless God intervenes, the test results show that you and Ethan have a very, very slim chance of conceiving and an even slimmer chance of carrying a child to term."

"No, please, Dr. Patterson." Julie shook her head, sobbing. "There must be something else we can do."

"We've done all we can do, Julie."

"But I've gotten pregnant before. Surely—"

"Yes, nine years ago, and you miscarried."

The words pierced Julie's heart as if the news of her miscarriage were fresh and current. She'd convinced herself it was the business of college, grad school, and Ethan's long days learning the production of Lambert's Furniture that prevented them from conceiving again.

"The endometriosis caused a lot of scarring." Dr. Patterson spoke with care. "Your womb can't support a pregnancy."

"What about a second surgery? Can't surgery correct it?"

Dr. Patterson shook his head and comforted Julie with a fatherly touch on her shoulder. "The last surgery didn't improve your situation. With a second, you risk more scarring. Perhaps God has other plans for you and Ethan."

Julie's shoulders slumped, and she buried her face in her hands. Dr. Patterson slipped his arm around her. She leaned against him and wept.

Chapter 2

Late in the afternoon, Ethan pressed SEND, e-mailing the last compliancy report to the environmental inspector's office. He felt spent, his day consumed by the tedious review of Lambert's Furniture's environmental practices.

He'd not planned to answer waste disposal questions for the second time in six months. His to-do list looked the same this afternoon as it did this morning. And he still needed a big man for tonight's game.

"Is the inspector's report done?" Will Adams, Ethan's cousin and president of Lambert's Furniture, came in and sat down.

Ethan nodded. "It's done, but, Will, those guys have to leave us alone. That's the second visit."

"I know, but we want to cooperate. Otherwise, they'll think we're hiding something."

Ethan leaned back, hands clasped behind his head. "Guess this is why you pay me the big bucks. I didn't get an industrial engineering degree for nothing."

Will laughed. "Big bucks? If that's what you want to call it, you're more than welcome. I wish I could pay you big bucks."

Ethan chuckled, shifting to work on his computer. "Well, when we get this new warehouse built, then we'll talk. I didn't have time to call the contractor, by the way."

Will checked his handheld personal data assistant. "Let's meet on that tomorrow morning. The new warehouse is key to our growth."

Ethan clicked on his computer calendar. "What time?"

"Nine is fine."

Ethan glanced at Will. "Bet Grandpa never imagined his little wood and whittle company would ever get this big."

Will tapped on his data assistant, nodding with a smile. In another second, he looked up and said, "Ethan, I drove past Milo Park on my way back from the town council meeting."

"Yeah?" Ethan typed in his reminder about tomorrow morning's meeting. *Meet with Will re: warehouse contractor.*

"Julie was there, sitting alone on one of the benches."

Ethan glanced at his watch for the first time all afternoon. Four thirty. Already? *Wow, I need to get to the rec center and start warming up.*

"It's snowing. She was sitting in the snow."

Ethan clicked icons on his computer, shutting it down for the day. "I'll ask her about it tonight."

Will stood. "Do. Something didn't feel right. I wish I'd stopped to check on her."

Packing up his laptop, Ethan glanced up just as Will exited his office. He was about to comment on his introspective wife when a brilliant thought flashed across his mind. *Will can play center. He's tall, athletic. He played some basketball in school.*

He dashed around his desk and bounded down the hall. "Will, buddy. What are you doing tonight?"

❧❧

Julie felt one with the snow, cold and frozen. Falling flakes powdered her head and shoulders while Dr. Patterson's words fluttered across the plains of her heart.

Unless God intervenes. . .a very, very slim chance of conceiving. In her whole life, she had never felt as hopeless as she did now. Not even when she miscarried the first year of their marriage.

"You're young. You'll have more children." Everyone said so, even Dr. Patterson.

But today his diagnosis bore an entirely different message. *Barren.* Julie thought. *At twenty-eight, I'm barren.*

Tears slipped down her chilled cheeks. She wiped them away with her gloved fingers, squelching the scream that pressed against her soul: *God, it's not fair!*

But she restrained the words from riding on the wind. What good would it do to yell out? What change could it bring?

A sharp wind brushed through the park, tugging at her hair and hat. Three years of trying for a child, and this was the end of their hopes and fears.

At least now she knew.

I should go home. But she didn't move. If ever she needed to pray, it was now. But her words felt shallow and inadequate. "Lord, I don't understand."

From her coat pocket, Julie's cell chirped. She hoped to see Ethan's number on the tiny screen. For the first time since she'd left the medical center, she longed for his comfort. But the caller ID flashed Sophia's name and number.

"Hi, Sophia." Julie tried to sound cheery and light.

"Well, what did the doctor say?"

Her vision blurred. Julie looked over the snow-covered park and pursed her lips, contemplating her answer. The news felt personal and private. She hadn't even told her husband yet. How could she broadcast the news to her friend, the gossip?

"Julie?" Sophia pressed.

"He said—" She hesitated before continuing. "It might be awhile."

"Aw, girl, are you kidding?"

Sophia's tone provoked more tears. Julie pressed her gloved fingers against her eyes. "It's no big deal."

"No big deal? Since I met you five years ago, you've wanted babies."

Julie lifted her face to the falling snow, drawing a deep breath. "It's okay, Sophia."

"What did Ethan say?"

Julie inhaled, the cold air numbing her emotions. "Nothing. I—"

"Nothing? The man said nothing?" Sophia's voice spiked with indignation.

"I haven't told him yet."

"Why not?"

"Listen, I'll talk to you tomorrow."

"Meet me for coffee at Peri's Perk in the morning."

Julie agreed, thinking how Peri Cortland's hip coffee shop had rejuvenated the town's morning routine. A cup of her freshly brewed coffee would cheer her day.

"See you in the morning."

"See you at Peri's."

Julie pressed END and stood, brushing the snow from her coat. She plowed through white drifts to her car and climbed behind the wheel. When she turned the key, the car responded with a clicking sound.

"Oh, come on. Not now." She clenched her jaw and tried again.

Nothing. The car's engine would not turn over. Julie dropped her head to the steering wheel and pounded the dashboard of her twelve-year-old economy car. "God, this is not fair!"

She'd have a new car if she hadn't convinced Ethan to try for one last round of fertility treatments. He'd wanted to wait another year, rebuild their savings, give their emotions a break, but she'd argued fervently against him.

In the end, what little money they'd set aside for a down payment was spent, and it still wasn't enough. Her parents, eager for grandchildren, loaned them the last of the money they needed. At the time, Julie felt so sure she would conceive. Now, looking back, all she could think was what a waste it had been. All that money spent with nothing to show for it.

When she didn't become pregnant, Dr. Patterson insisted on a thorough battery of tests.

I'm barren. Barren. The word echoed in her soul like the *tick, tick, tick* of a clock in an empty room. *Barren, barren, barren.*

Julie jerked her head up. *I've got to get moving.* She tried the key again, but the old engine refused to fire.

She yanked open the door, grabbed her purse and shoulder tote, and stepped out into a foot of snow.

❧❧

Sweaty but exhilarated, Ethan drove home from the rec center, the large championship trophy sitting in the seat next to him, the seat belt clicked around his treasure.

Don't want it bouncing all over the car, do I?

He grinned, turning down Main Street, cruising past Milo Park. The hue of the amber-colored streetlight reflected off the new fallen powder, and Ethan, well, he couldn't resist a sudden impulse.

He pulled into the park and bounded toward the winter wonderland. He flopped on his back, pumping his arms and legs to make the perfect snow angel.

With a hooting laugh, he hopped up without destroying his creation and flopped down in the snow for a second snow angel. Then with his bare finger he wrote "Ethan" under one and "Julie" under the other.

How long had it been that way? Ethan and Julie. Forever, it seemed to him. Since they were sixteen.

Chilled from his romp in the snow, Ethan jogged back to his car. Out of the corner of his eye, in the dim light of the streetlamp, he saw a little car buried under mounting snow.

Is that Julie's car? Ethan swerved right to investigate. He brushed the snow from the hood to see the chipped paint of her faded blue heap. *Yep, it's hers. What's it doing parked here?*

Suddenly he remembered. *Will.* What did he say about Julie sitting in the park? He'd forgotten all about calling her.

Returning to his car, he revved the engine and blasted the heater. Digging his cell phone from his sports bag, he autodialed home. Julie did not answer.

Next he called her cell. He let it ring until voice mail picked up. Then he dialed home again. Still no answer.

He drummed his fingers against the steering wheel. *Julie, where are you?* He called her cell one more time. She didn't pick up.

Come on, Jules, where are you? He took a deep breath and exhaled slowly. *She's not at home and apparently not with her cell. Yet her car is abandoned at Milo Park.*

Ethan tried to remember her weekly schedule. What night did she help the church youth choir? Lately their schedules took them in opposite directions. *Thursdays,* he concluded. *She works with them on Thursdays. Today is Monday.*

Ethan tapped his cell phone against his chin. After a few seconds, he dialed a different number. The crisp, aristocratic voice of Ralph Hanover answered. "Good evening, Hanover residence."

"Hi, Ralph. It's Ethan. Is Julie there?"

"No, son, she's not."

"Have you heard from her?" Frustration laced his words.

"Let me check with her mother."

Ethan waited, listening to the muffled tone of his father-in-law. "Sandy hasn't talked to her since Saturday."

"Thanks." Ethan started to press END, but Ralph continued.

"Did you two quarrel?"

"No, sir, we didn't. She's just not answering the home phone or her cell."

"I see. Don't forget Friday night. Sandy's planned a big party. She wants to cheer everyone from their midwinter doldrums."

Friday, right. "Yeah, I'll talk to Julie."

Ralph cleared his voice. "She's never missed one of Sandy's parties. Don't see why she should start now."

"It's been a tough week, Ralph."

"All the more reason to join us." His words sounded so final. No was not an option.

Ethan tossed his phone into the passenger seat. Ralph and Sandy Hanover never ceased to exert influence on their only child's life. When were they going to be grandparents? Shouldn't Julie try out for the New Hampshire symphony? Julie somehow managed to obtain a healthy amount of independence, but she also carried a certain level of obligation. Deep obligation.

"Wife, where are you?" Ethan squinted in the darkness. Surely she was safe. *Lord, help me out here. She's safe, right?*

Chapter 3

In the living room, Julie graded papers, her legs crossed Indian style, a carton of Chinese food on the floor beside her.

"Julie." Ethan charged through the front door, his voice like a foghorn.

"Ethan?"

"Why didn't you answer the phone?" He stood in the middle of the room, his coat askew, a trophy under one arm and a basketball under the other.

"I see you won." Julie motioned to the golden guerdon. She picked up the beef and broccoli carton.

"You didn't answer my question." Ethan didn't move.

Julie kept her eyes averted. If she looked at him, she'd burst into tears, and quite frankly, she didn't have the energy to go through it again. She'd tell him the news, but not tonight. Not now. *Where would I find the words?*

"I took a bath." She omitted that she was just about to sink into the sudsy water when he called the first time.

"Why didn't you call me back?"

"I knew you'd be home soon, and I needed to get these papers graded."

"Why is your car at Milo Park?" He walked past her to the spare bedroom they referred to as the den. "It's practically buried in snow."

Julie bit her lower lip and stared at her students' papers, not really seeing the words. She heard Ethan's movements in the study, the bounce of the basketball against the hardwood floor, the shuffle of items on the computer desk to make room for his prize.

"Jules? What happened to your car?" Ethan called from the den. "Gave me a good scare seeing it abandoned there and you not answering the phone. I called your parents to see if you were over there."

She chewed slowly on another bite of beef and broccoli. "I thought you were taking the trophy to work."

"I will." Ethan stood over her. "Why won't you answer my questions?"

Julie set the carton aside, stacked her students' papers on the end table, and strode toward the kitchen. "Do you want some dinner?"

"Yes." Ethan smiled. "The Chinese smells good."

Mechanically Julie retrieved a plate from the cupboard. Ethan hated to eat from the carton. While she served his plate, he filled his glass with ice and water from the refrigerator.

I can't tell him now. I can't. Tomorrow. She felt weary and frayed.

"Who did you play?" She handed him a plate of Wong Lee's finest, plastering a smile on her face. Though proud of her athletic husband's win, her heart could not rejoice.

"Creager Technologies. Beat the pants off of 'em. Will played center for us."

"Good for him."

Ethan sat at the table, laughing. "Ol' Jeff played for Creager." He slapped his knee. "He huffed and puffed up and down the court the whole time."

Ethan's merriment infected her a little. She leaned forward, elbows propped on the kitchen counter, picturing Ethan's police officer cousin, Jeff Simmons—burly like a grizzly bear—playing basketball.

"How'd he get roped into that job?"

Ethan scooped a mouthful of fried rice and teriyaki chicken with his chopsticks. "Ten bucks says Elizabeth got him into it. Since she started at Creager Technologies, she's enlisted several of the cousins into their league teams."

"It's dangerous to be a Lambert cousin in this town."

He gazed at her, serious. "Is it dangerous to be a Lambert wife?"

"What? Of course not."

"Okay, then tell me what happened to your car. Why is it at Milo Park? And by the way, Will said he saw you there this afternoon, sitting in the snow."

Feeling exposed, Julie went to the living room and reclined on the couch. "I went to the park to think. When I went to leave, the car wouldn't start."

"Babe, why didn't you call me?" Ethan twisted toward her.

She lifted her head. "Call you? You were too busy to—" She stopped short.

"Too busy to what?"

"You know what." She struggled to contain her anger. *But I should be angry.*

Ethan ate in silence. After a few moments, he asked in a low tone, "How did you get home?"

"Walked."

"All that way?"

"Yes, the exercise felt good."

He let loose a wry laugh. "You? Exercise? What's wrong?"

"Nothing."

He fell silent, then asked abruptly as if he suddenly remembered, "How was your doctor's appointment?"

"Fine." She stopped before her emotions betrayed her.

"Fine?" He regarded her, waiting for more.

"Just fine." She rested her arm over her closed eyes and breathed deeply.

Ethan walked to the kitchen with his plate. "See, I told you the news wouldn't be bad."

"Right." She swallowed hard.

"So why did you sit in the park under the falling snow?"

"Felt like it." Julie heard the water running from the sink and then the click of the dishwasher.

"But everything's fine?"

141

No, it's not. It will never be fine. "Sure."

Ethan's touch on her leg startled her. "What exactly did Doc Patterson say?"

"Ethan, my head is killing me. Can we talk about this later?" A thought flashed through her mind that changed Julie's weepiness to resolve. *I want a new car.*

Ethan squeezed her leg. "Sure. I'll call the tow truck in the morning." He disappeared down the hall.

She bolted upright. "Ethan, I want a new car." *Can't have a baby? I'll get a new car.*

His head popped around the corner. "What?"

"I want a new car."

"Babe, we're paying off debt. Medical bills, school bills, your parents."

She stood. With quick movements, she adjusted her baggy sweats. "I'm tired of that ol' jalopy. It's held together with duct tape. You said so yourself."

Ethan chuckled. "No, the mechanic said so."

Hands on her hips, she raised her chin. "Jesse knows what he's talking about."

With a shake of his head, Ethan answered, "I don't want to spend any more money, Julie. Think how great it will be to pay off our debt. And, for the first time in a year, our savings is above zero."

She bristled. "In the meantime, I drive around in a twelve-year-old piece of junk."

"That piece of junk has another good year or two left. Peter-John Roth drives the same make and model, and his car runs like a top. It has to be fifteen, sixteen years old."

"I want a new car, Ethan." She couldn't put her emotions into words, but suddenly the idea of driving a new car captivated her.

He sighed and drew her to him, kissing her softly. "Don't cry, Jules. Maybe we can look in the fall when the dealers have sales. It's not just spending money for a down payment; it's adding the monthly car payment I don't want right now."

She stiffened, tugging on the sleeves of her sweatshirt. "It's my money, too. I work, bring in an income."

"Right, and that's what goes to the debt."

They argued for several minutes over who could make the call on spending money for a new car. Julie thought since she worked, she should be able to use her money the way she wanted.

"Does that theory apply to my salary, too?" Ethan asked.

They went around until Ethan stopped the conversation.

"I don't understand your sudden urgency, but can we talk about this later? I need to go over some things for work tomorrow."

When he left for the den, Julie tiptoed upstairs to the bathroom, kicked the cabinet, then wept.

❧❧

Ethan stared at the open document on his laptop screen but didn't read it. The championship trophy stood guard over him. He clicked the page closed, the desire to work abated.

Falling back against the desk chair, he propped his hands on his legs. *What happened here tonight?* He came home, admittedly a little angry. He asked about her car, asked about the doctor's appointment. She said everything was fine. She listened to his championship game recap. Then suddenly the squabble over a new car ignited.

Something wasn't right, but he didn't know what. He wanted to press Julie for an explanation, but lately, if he pushed her, she went deeper within herself.

When did their communication become so hard? Since eleventh grade, she'd been his best friend. They talked about everything.

Ethan wandered out to the living room, his body stiff from the night of play. He collapsed in his chair and clicked on the television. Blankly he stared at the images on the screen.

The last few years had been difficult. As they waded through the waters of new careers, stress wove its way into their lives, even more so once they realized starting a family would not be easy. Dr. Patterson was hopeful in the beginning. Julie took a year off work while she completed grad school, hoping to conceive.

Then came the special treatments, medications, and one surgery. Their small savings depleted, her parents loaned them money. A gift, they said. But Ethan insisted on paying it back.

Meanwhile, Ethan worked his way up in the family business, starting on the production floor at the same pay rate as all the others on the crew. Those were lean years.

But by now, Ethan wanted to be more financially solvent. At the very least, buy a house. He'd never factored in the cost of conceiving a dream.

What sparked the idea in Julie to buy a car? She'd been more than happy with her old vehicle until tonight. She'd rather spend money on medical treatments. Last year, they'd had a whopper of an argument over money and the value of their unsuccessful fertility treatments. But tonight, she had a different look in her eyes.

He checked the mantel clock. Eleven thirty. He'd been home for over two hours, and as on most nights, he sat up in the living room while she read upstairs and fell asleep with the light on. They were in the same place but definitely apart.

The urge hit him to run up to his wife, his best friend, and wrap her in his arms, promising that everything would be all right. He'd done that after their first newly-wed arguments, though lately. . . He wondered when resisting became so simple.

Ethan pointed the remote control at the plasma screen and upped the volume. He felt exhausted from the emotional turmoil. Trying to have a baby was one thing, difficult and disappointing. But losing touch with his wife burdened him. He slumped down in his lounge chair, closed his eyes, and listened to the noise.

❧

Julie drew the down comforter up to her chin, the resonance of television laughter bouncing up the stairs. Emotionally drained, she tried to pray, knowing she needed

NEW HAMPSHIRE *Weddings*

the Lord's comfort. But her thoughts twisted around Ethan and how she wanted him to come to bed. She ached to snuggle next to him and bury her face in his chest. Her heart longed to hear him promise everything would be all right.

When did they stop talking face-to-face? Were they the same two people who sat up all night in her family's basement game room, talking? The two who bought cell phones with anytime minutes the moment they could afford them?

She should confess Dr. Patterson's conclusions. Yet if he wanted to know, if he cared, he would have made it to the medical center. Fifteen minutes. All he needed to surrender was fifteen minutes. Her disappointment over his lack of interest only made her barrenness more pronounced.

"Lord," Julie said in the darkness, "I can't go on like this."

Burrowing under the covers, she sobbed until her soul released its burden.

Sleep eluded her, and the longer Ethan stayed downstairs in front of the TV, the more her sorrow turned to anger.

She went to the bathroom to blow her nose. *All he cares about is sports and winning a basketball trophy.* She crawled back into bed with a burning in her middle.

"Lord, do something with him." Julie rolled over on her side, determined to think of something else—like a new car.

I need a new car. My old broken-down heap is on its last leg. She felt sure her parents would prefer she drove a reliable car over paying back their loan.

When Ethan tiptoed upstairs and slid into bed, Julie remained awake, her back to him.

The bed gave way to his long, lean frame as he adjusted the sheets and blankets to suit him. She wondered if he would reach for her, as so many times in the past when things weren't right between them.

When they first married, they agreed never to go to bed angry or discontent. Many a quarrel had been resolved on this very bed. Remembering caused familiar feelings to stir in her heart. When did they first bend the rule? Had they broken it completely?

To Julie, life itself felt broken.

Ethan, if you reach for me, I'll respond. Despite her anger, she yearned for his touch. She craved his kisses on her hair, her face, and her lips. She wanted to lose herself in his safe embrace.

Making up her mind, Julie inched toward the center of the bed and lightly touched her husband's back with her fingertips. He did not stir. The soft sound of his breathing filled the air around them.

Julie moved back to her side of the bed. *How can you fall asleep so fast, Ethan?*

She tried to sleep but couldn't. Images of her future loomed before her, blank and void, without the melody of children's laughter, without porcelain faces molded with her eyes and his nose.

Long into the night, Julie finally fell into a fitful sleep.

Chapter 4

In a sleepy stupor, Ethan slapped the alarm button and rolled out of bed. He showered and dressed, then checked his data assistant for the day's action items while slipping his keys and wallet into his pockets. He clipped on his cell phone and tied on his shoes.

"Julie," he called. He caught her made-up side of the bed in his peripheral vision. If he didn't know better, he'd wonder if she'd slept next to him at all.

But he remembered how warm the bed felt when he climbed in a little after midnight. He'd wanted to reach for her but didn't, considering her mood when she went to bed. Besides, she seemed to sleep so peacefully.

"Babe, I thought we'd grab a little breakfast on our way in this morning. I can drop you off at school afterwards." Ethan leaned out the bedroom door, fastening on his watch, his ear tuned to the sounds of the house. Silence. He sniffed. No coffee.

"Jules?" Ethan ambled downstairs. "Julie?" *Did she leave already?* Her carton of beef and broccoli from last night remained on the living room floor. But her school papers were gone.

With a shake of his head, Ethan tossed the leftovers in the garbage. Back in the den, he found a note from Julie tacked to his new trophy.

Ethan, Sophia came by for me. We'd planned to have coffee at Peri's anyway. Julie

Ethan crumpled the note, juxtaposed between ire and relief. He wished she'd told him she was leaving, but hopefully today would be better than yesterday.

He sat down in his desk chair. "Lord, we're in a rough patch, aren't we? Give us grace. Give *me* grace."

A thought flashed through his mind. What about a nice romantic dinner at Italian Hills? *Hmm? Good idea, Lord.*

Candlelight? Soft music? Julie would love it. She could forget about her cares in the peaceful ambience and enjoy fine cuisine. Ethan made a mental note to secure a reservation for six o'clock.

Snapping up his cell, he dialed the familiar number of his grandpa and grandma Lambert.

"Hello?" The soothing voice of the Lambert patriarch eased down the line.

"Grandpa, it's Ethan." He cradled the phone on his shoulder as he packed up his laptop.

"How's my favorite grandson?"

"Is it my week to be your favorite?"

Grandpa chuckled. "It is if you're inviting me to breakfast."

"How'd you know?"

"Why else would you be calling me so early?"

"All right, if you know so much, what's Sam's special today?" He hooked his laptop bag on his shoulder and reached for the trophy.

"All-you-can-eat pancakes with a side of bacon and eggs."

"Guess I'm buying then." With a chuckle, Ethan grabbed his coat from the closet.

"I'm the retired old guy. Of course you're buying."

"Deal," Ethan said, locking the front door behind him. "See you at the diner."

Hopping into his Honda sedan, Ethan shifted into gear and backed out of his parking slot, pausing to look through his cell phone contact list. If Julie liked driving a stick shift, he would trade cars with her. But she'd contended she liked her automatic, albeit dilapidated, car.

He pressed TALK when the screen flashed MEL BROTHERS' TOWING.

❧❧

"If you ask me, he's an insensitive clod," Sophia said with conviction before sipping from her grandé caramel coffee topped with whipped cream.

Julie tore at her napkin. "He didn't know."

As disappointed as she was in Ethan, Julie defended her husband. She blamed herself for Sophia's skewed perception. She'd painted a bad picture of him lately, and she resolved to change that image.

"You should have told him then." Sophia waved her long, manicured finger in the air.

Julie swirled her latte. "I couldn't form the words. Then, all of a sudden, I wanted a new car, so we argued over that."

"Girl, you need a new car."

"I know, but—" She stared out the coffee shop window and wished she was sitting with Ethan instead of her acerbic friend.

"If you ask me, he'd rather play sports than raise a child anyway."

"Sophia, stop. That's not true."

"Seems to me he's always finding some jock thing to do."

Julie pressed her fingers to her temples. "Can we please change the subject?"

"To what? My dateless life? There are no good men, I tell you, none."

Oh, but there are good men. Ethan. "You're just not looking in the right places."

"Where shall I look? Church?" Sophia rolled her eyes and shifted in her seat.

Julie jabbed her in the arm. "Don't knock it until you try it."

Sophia immediately changed the topic and launched into the latest politics of White Birch Elementary School and the status of the new building budget. "By this time next year, we should have a dozen new classrooms."

Julie sipped her coffee. "Do you think I'll get that new music room?"

"It's in the plan." Sophia winked with a nod.

"Wouldn't that be amazing?"

"Yes, but don't hold your breath. Until they hand you the classroom key, anything is possible."

Julie sighed. "So true."

"Speaking of teaching—" Sophia pointed to her watch. "We'd better get going."

Sitting in the passenger seat of Sophia's SUV, Julie watched the town of White Birch slide past her view. Her heart leaped when she saw Ethan step out of his silver Honda.

Ethan! Hi. He looked handsome. She loved the way his coat hung straight from his square shoulders and how his slightly gelled brown waves glistened in the morning light.

She jerked her purse onto her lap and dug for her cell phone. *Did he get my note? Did I miss his call?*

After a second, she tossed her cell back into her purse.

"He didn't call?" Sophia asked in a low tone.

"No."

"Clod."

"Stop, Sophia. He's not a clod."

"Okay, cad."

"Stop."

"So the inspectors are bothering you," Grandpa said, cutting his pancakes in long strips and loading them up with butter and syrup.

"Does Grandma know you eat like this?" Ethan motioned with his fork at the syrup and buttered pancakes.

Grandpa smirked. "What, you think I'd do this behind her back?"

Ethan laughed. "She'd find out for sure, knowing this town."

"I imagine you're right."

"If you had a coronary, I was worried I'd have to out you. But if she knows—"

Grandpa speared his first bite. "I told her on my way to meet you, 'I'm having Sam's pancakes.'"

Ethan squirted ketchup on his pile of scrambled eggs. "Those inspectors are about to give me a coronary."

"Just oblige them, son. It will make life easier."

"You'd think in this day and age a man would never hear the words 'in triplicate,' but it's standard op for those guys."

"Your dad struggled with them until he retired."

Ethan spread a thin coat of jam on his unbuttered wheat toast. "Yeah, when I asked him about it, he laughed."

"Might just be why he retired early."

"That or Mom getting on his case about working so hard." Growing up, Ethan often overheard his parents discussing his father's devotion to the business. Many times, his mother reasoned for more time at home and family vacations. His father talked about responsibility, loyalty, and hard work.

It was his father who masterminded the production process Ethan now managed. The implementation of his ideas rocketed Grandpa's small furniture business into a multimillion-dollar furniture factory.

Grandpa sipped his coffee. "He and your mom are having fun with their little tax business. Your dad always was good with numbers."

"It's a great second career for him. Keeps them busy in the winter so they can vacation the rest of the year."

The waitress came over with a coffeepot in each hand. "Heat up your coffee, Matt?"

Grandpa lifted his cup to her. "Janet, you've waited on me for over ten years. You know the answer."

"Sam makes me ask." She winked at the older man. "How about you, Ethan?"

"Decaf."

Janet poured from the orange-lipped pot in her left hand. "Can I get you anything else?"

Grandpa held up his fork. "I'll have another round of pancakes."

Ethan glanced up at Janet. "He tells me Grandma knows about his eating habits."

She laughed. "I'm sure she does. I'll put in the order."

Grandpa sat back and patted his flat belly. "Your grandma knows everything I do. It's our code."

Ethan furrowed his brow. "Your code?"

"Lambert's Code. I'll tell you about it some time. You're 'bout due, I think."

"I've never heard of Lambert's Code."

"It's one of the marriage rules your grandma and I live by. Just might help you and Julie along the way."

Ethan bent over his breakfast wondering if Grandpa could read the concern of his soul through his eyes. He'd never heard of Lambert's Code, but if it helped Grandpa's marriage to Grandma, he wanted to know.

"Want to tell me about it, Ethan?" grandpa interrupted his thoughts.

Ethan looked up. He regarded his grandpa's lean face, the one that had seen a great war, the one that had built a great business, and the one that knew great love. "Not sure I can put words to it."

"Work or home?"

"Home." The sole word spoke volumes.

Grandpa nodded, understanding without a word.

Ethan set his fork down and gazed out the diner window. The White Birch horizon promised sunshine. "We're snapping at each other, miscommunicating. We don't connect anymore."

"Consider the last few years, trying to start a family. Doctor visits, medical expenses, going to school, launching your careers. It's a lot to bear, Ethan."

Ethan's eyes burned for the first time in a long, long time. "I guess you're right. So tell me about this code you and Grandma invented."

"Well, I'll tell you—"

"Excuse me."

Ethan glanced up to see Dr. Patterson standing by the table, his hand extended.

"Dr. Patterson, good to see you." Ethan shook his hand.

The gentlemanly doctor greeted Grandpa Matt, then asked Ethan, "Could I speak to you for a moment?"

Grandpa scooted out of the booth. "I think I'll find Sam and compliment his pancakes."

Dr. Patterson slid into his place. "I just wanted to remind you, these things are always hard."

Ethan rubbed his chin. "What things?" He didn't like the way the light faded from the good doctor's face.

"Did you talk to your wife yesterday?"

"Yes." *Sort of.*

Dr. Patterson regarded Ethan for a second. He started to say something when Grandpa returned.

"Janet's about to bring out my cakes. Is it safe?"

Dr. Patterson laughed and gave Grandpa his seat back. "I never get between a man and his breakfast."

"You're a good man, Casey."

Ethan felt unnerved, unsure what had prompted this odd conversation.

Dr. Patterson rapped his knuckles on the tabletop. "Ethan, why don't you stop by my office at twelve thirty?"

He nodded. "Okay."

"Nice to see you, Matt. Give my best to Betty."

Grandpa shook his hand. "Will do."

Ethan watched him leave, a gnawing feeling in the pit of his stomach.

Chapter 5

"All right, class, settle down." Julie walked the breadth of the music room, passing out the graded short essays to her sixth graders. "Overall, very good work. May I suggest a review of your grammar rules?"

A collective moan filled the room. Julie laughed. *Groaners.* She taught a bunch of groaners. They groaned when she told them to practice, groaned when she gave them assignments. Yet despite the groans, she cared deeply for each of them.

She was about to move on to the day's music lesson when her classroom door opened and Ethan filled the doorway.

"Can I see you outside?" Only his lips moved; his jaw remained tight.

In the hall, Ethan did not greet her with a kiss or hello. "Were you planning on telling me that we can't have kids, or were you going to wait 'til we're fifty and say, 'Oh, by the by, Ethan, on that kid thing? Never gonna happen.'" He popped the wall with his fist.

A chill ran down Julie's back. "How did you find out?"

"Dr. Patterson, who else?"

"What? How?"

"I ran into him at the diner this morning. By the way, I wanted to take *you* to breakfast."

"How was I supposed to know?" Julie modulated her voice. Her words felt hard and brittle. "You could have told me you wanted to have breakfast."

Ethan stood right in front of her. "You could have told me, too, about the test results."

She focused on her shoes. "I couldn't find the words."

"Couldn't find the words? I'm your husband. Remember me, Jules, the man you vowed to cherish your whole life?"

She jerked her head up, eyes intent on Ethan. "Yes, and remember me, the woman you vowed to cherish your whole life?"

Ethan stood back, arms akimbo. "What are you saying? I don't cherish you?"

"I think I have stiff competition." There, she said it.

"Competition? With whom?" Ethan spread his arms, defensive, inviting conflict.

"Not whom. What." Julie counted off on her fingers. "Basketball, golf, football, racquetball, ice hockey. If it rolls, slides, bounces, or spirals, you give attention to it."

He huffed. "You're jealous of sports? I've always played sports. We *met* on the high school football field."

"Don't make me sound petty and stupid, Ethan. You know what I mean. You play or watch sports seven days a week. If it's not sports, it's work."

"And what about you? Music doesn't consume you?"

"No, not like sports consumes you."

"Having a child consumed—"

She gasped. He stopped, a contorted expression on his face.

"Is that what you think? Really?"

He regarded her with his hands buried in his pockets. "It got to be a little consuming, I guess, at times, to be honest."

"Why didn't you say something? I thought we were making the decisions together, Ethan." She trembled with the reality of their conversation.

"I couldn't stand to—"

Snickers billowed from the classroom. Julie whirled around to find the door wide open, her class of sixth graders absorbing every word.

Horrified, she commanded, "Back to your seats." She shut the door with a bang and whipped around to Ethan. "Now see what you've done?"

"Don't blame me. You're the one with all the secrets. I suppose Sophia knows."

"She does not." Julie crossed her arms. "Can we talk about this later?"

"Later? What time would be convenient for you?" Ethan walked away.

"Please, don't go away mad. I planned to tell you today." Julie stepped toward him, touching his sleeve with the tips of her fingers.

Ethan faced his wife. "I'm not mad. I'm hurt and confused, Julie. You had all night to tell me."

She felt her heart lock down and couldn't form an answer.

He continued, "All you needed to say was, 'Ethan, we need to talk about something serious.' Instead, you get me in an argument about buying a new car."

She let her gaze fall on him. "I couldn't make myself say the words, 'I'm barren.'"

Ethan sighed as he walked toward her and pulled her to him. "I'm sorry, babe. I'm so sorry."

Julie rested her chin on his shoulder and cried a little, but most of her tears had already been shed.

"I'd better get back to class." She backed away. "I'll see you tonight."

"I thought we could go out tonight, the Italian Hills." He brushed her hair away from her face.

"Oh, Eth, that place is—"

"Jules?" He tugged on her hand, his brown eyes pleading.

"No, I can't. I just can't."

***

Ethan shut the door to his office and whirled his desk chair around. He snatched up the production reports, his thoughts a million miles away.

Crash! Ethan peered over the desk's edge. *Perfect, just perfect.* His favorite coffee mug lay shattered on the hardwood floor.

As he swept up the last shard, Will rapped lightly on the door's glass window. Ethan motioned for him to come in.

"Everything okay in here?"

"In here, yes. With my wife, no." The residue of his conversation with Julie coated his emotions—frustration mingled with ire, compassion with sadness.

"Ah, I see." Will's voice contained the proper amount of understanding, but Ethan knew he would not probe further.

Lambert's Furniture was a place of business, not a counseling center. Will ran a family-oriented company, but he wouldn't take business time to untangle Ethan's marriage knots.

"Did you e-mail me those warehouse construction estimates?" Will asked.

Ethan meant to do that after their nine o'clock meeting, but the prospect of meeting with Dr. Patterson, and an issue with the new product line, distracted him.

"On their way right now." Ethan fished through his inbox for the contractor estimates.

"Okay, thanks." Will shut the door behind him as he exited. Ethan found the e-mails and forwarded them to Will's address.

Julie, what's happening to us?

He found it hard to concentrate on his afternoon tasks. Normally, the day-to-day routine calmed him, even on his worst days. He liked the feeling that some things never changed.

But the confrontation with Julie caused him to cringe. He shouldn't have infused the situation with his anger and embarrassed her in front of her students. He'd only added insult to injury.

"Lord, forgive me." With decisive motion, Ethan dialed his wife's cell. She would be in class, but he planned on leaving a humble message.

"Julie, I'm sorry I went to the school upset and angry. Please, let's go to the Italian Hills. We can have a nice romantic dinner and talk, okay? Bye, babe."

He hung up, feeling better but unable to escape his restlessness. He stared out the window for a minute, thinking, watching the narrow rays of the sun moving westward.

Then he knew what he wanted to do. He shot a quick e-mail to Will.

Gone for the rest of the day. Call my cell if you need me. See you in the morning.
Ethan

Ten minutes later, he walked under the shadows of the covered bridge, whispering prayers to his heavenly Father like the wind whispering under the eaves.

❧❧

Julie followed the Italian Hills maître d' to a candlelit table under the western window where snow powdered the windowsill.

Ethan held her chair as she sat down. "Isn't this great, babe? Fantastic food, romantic atmosphere, you and me."

Julie smiled at him, attempting to appreciate his efforts to smooth a healing balm over the wound of the day. *Think of something nice to say.* "They do have good food." She regarded her husband as he scanned the menu. He looked like a kid poring over a Christmas toy catalog.

She resolved to enjoy herself, or at least pretend to for Ethan's sake. He was trying to fix things between them after all.

But the Italian Hills' amorous atmosphere made her feel like an alien. How could she wander down the dreamy path of romance when her heart still lingered in the valley of the shadow of death?

Oh Lord...

"Are you having the usual?" Ethan peeked over his menu, the flame of the candle flickering in his brown eyes.

Julie glanced at the entrée section. Items that used to make her mouth water now made her stomach churn. "I'm not terribly hungry."

"Not hungry for portabella pasta?" He motioned at the waiter passing by. "Could we get some bread here?"

The young man answered with a slight bow. "I'll get your server."

"Mercy, Ethan. Are you that hungry? Wait for our server to come over."

"Yes, I'm that hungry," he retorted.

Silence lingered as they decided their order. When the server brought their bread and took their drink order, Ethan commented, "You look beautiful, Julie."

"Thank you." Ethan was charming yet sincere; Julie wondered how he managed to find the weakness in her emotional barriers time and time again.

He looked equally as handsome in his white mock turtleneck and navy slacks, but she couldn't form the words. He knew, didn't he, after all these years?

"So how're we doing tonight?" Ethan leaned over the table toward her.

"*We* are fine."

He took her hand in his. "I'm really sorry about today, babe. I was out of line."

She bowed her head. "I'm sorry, too, Ethan. I wanted to tell you, but just—"

"I understand. It's okay."

"Oh, Ethan, what are we going to do? All my life, I've—"

"Ethan. Julie. Hi." Julie swerved to see Ethan's cousin, Elizabeth Donovan, and her husband, Kavan, approaching.

"Good evening, you two." Ethan stood to greet them, glancing down at Julie with a what-do-we-do-now face.

"Would you like to join them?" the maître d' asked, a server already moving another two-top table over.

"That would be lovely. Do you mind?" Elizabeth smiled at them. "We've been wanting to get together with you two."

"Same here," Ethan said halfheartedly.

But not tonight, Julie thought. How could they chitchat with Elizabeth and Kavan when they had so much to discuss? Would it be rude to ask them to sit someplace else? Surely they would understand.

But the table was set, Elizabeth and Kavan were seated, and the server headed for the kitchen with their drink order.

Ethan touched her leg with his foot under the table to get her attention. His eyes pleaded with her. She smiled with a nod.

They never should have gone out to dinner. She hated the feeling of *I told you so*, but he'd insisted, forgetting that a Lambert in White Birch, New Hampshire, was like a magnet.

Everywhere a Lambert goes, another Lambert is sure to show.

So they had company for dinner. It took every ounce of Julie's energy to engage in small talk with Elizabeth while Kavan and Ethan discussed something she couldn't quite hear. Any other day, any other time, they would have treasured Elizabeth and Kavan's company, but tonight, oh, not tonight. The casual conversation only added to the heaviness of her soul.

In short order, their server set down a round of iced teas and a basket of hot bread. Ethan buttered a hot slice and asked Kavan, "So what brings you and Elizabeth here night?"

The young couple beamed at each other, holding back enormous grins, or so it seemed to Julie.

"Well, we're celebrating." Elizabeth's smile lit her face.

"We could ask the same of you," Kavan interjected, reaching for the butter plate. "What are you two doing here?"

Julie peered into Ethan's eyes as if to anchor her turbulent emotions.

Ethan coughed and stumbled over his words, but finally said, "Nothing special, just a nice dinner." He buttered another slice of bread, though the first one remained uneaten.

Julie ached to change the topic away from her and Ethan. Didn't Elizabeth say they were celebrating? Perhaps she got a raise or promotion at Creager.

"How's your job at Creager?" Julie asked Elizabeth with a hint of enthusiasm.

"Great, actually." Elizabeth sipped her tea. "I'm still in awe of how the Lord led me to that company. It's way more fun than grad school."

"We make our plans, but the Lord directs our steps," Ethan paraphrased from Proverbs.

"The pay is better than grad school." Kavan winked at his wife. "She makes a lot more than I do."

Elizabeth laughed. "That will all change soon, Kavan."

"I know, but let me relish having a rich wife for a moment."

Julie squirmed in her seat, feeling as if the world were closing in around her. She was about to excuse herself for the ladies' room when the server brought their salads.

Ethan prayed for the food, and when they echoed his amen, he asked, "So, Beth, what's going to change soon? You're not leaving your job, are you?"

In her peripheral vision, Julie saw Elizabeth catch her husband's gaze.

"Should we tell them?" she whispered.

Kavan grinned. "Some things are meant to be celebrated, honey." He tapped his fork against the side of his tea glass. "We have an announcement."

"Let's hear it, man." Ethan clapped his cousin-in-law on the back.

Julie's stomach knotted. *No, Ethan, let's not hear it.*

Kavan motioned for Elizabeth to do the honors. "Well, we weren't expecting this." She tucked a strand of her curly brown hair behind her ear. "But. . .we're *expecting.*"

Kavan burst with laughter. "Elizabeth, pregnant. Can you believe it?" He toasted her with his glass of iced tea.

Ethan coughed. "Congrat–congratulations." He wiped the edge of his lips with his napkin with a covert glance at Julie.

Elizabeth reached across the table for Kavan's hand. "My life has been all about change and hanging on to God this past year and a half, but this moves me to a whole new level."

"We weren't planning on it so soon." Kavan stopped as the server set down another round of iced teas.

Elizabeth shook her head. "Last month, the idea of being a mom freaked me out. But this month we decided, it's happening. Let's celebrate and tell people." She laughed. "A baby. Our very own baby."

"Julie?" Ethan nudged his wife. "Isn't this great?"

Julie shook all over and deep in her inner being. "Excuse me." She pushed away from the table and fled the restaurant.

Chapter 6

Well, what did you want me to say? 'Oh, that's terrible? We can't have kids, so why should you?'" Ethan paced the length of their bedroom, one hand on the back of his neck, the other on his hip.

"Of course not." Julie lifted her face from the pillow. Black mascara covered her high cheekbones, and her green eyes were swollen.

"Then what do you want from me?" Ethan faced her, his arms spread.

She opened her mouth but lost her words to a deep, gut-wrenching sob.

Ethan sighed. "Jules, you've got to stop crying. We'll never get anywhere otherwise." He sat on the edge of the bed, his hand on her leg.

She jerked away from his touch. Ethan fell back on the bed. "Don't be this way. We're in this together, aren't we?"

"I don't know; are we?" Julie slid off the bed, unzipped her dress, and dropped it to the floor.

Ethan could see her arms and hands trembling. All this, and they still had yet to discuss, heart to heart, the curveball life had just thrown them.

He decided to take a different approach. "Do you want to talk to Dr. Patterson together? He recommended meeting with him."

"Why? It's not going to change anything." Julie ducked into the bathroom. Ethan heard the water running in the sink.

"He's experienced, walked other couples through this. He understands the last few years have been difficult for us."

She leaned out the bathroom door, toothbrush in her hand. "So sorry to have been an inconvenience to you."

Ethan lowered his head. "Did I say that? I said us, Julie, us."

She shut the door.

This is going nowhere fast. Ethan got up and changed his clothes.

"Are you going to leave your dress and slip in the middle of the floor?" he asked his wife when she emerged from the bathroom.

Julie picked up her clothes and dropped them on the bedside rocking chair. "Happy?" She crawled into bed with one eye on Ethan.

"Julie, I'm not the bad guy here." Ethan draped his shirt over a hanger.

"Too bad you'll never pass on your neat-freak genes to some poor unsuspecting child."

"Too bad you won't be able to create another slob." As soon as he spoke the words, Ethan regretted them.

"Jules, I'm sorry." But it was too late. She'd burrowed under the covers.

Julie woke with a start, shivering. For a moment or two, she felt lost in the cold darkness, unable to discern her surroundings. Her head and eyes ached. Squinting, she read the time from the bedside clock.

Two o'clock in the morning.

Then, like waking up from a peaceful sleep into a nightmare, she remembered the night before. Dinner at Italian Hills. Elizabeth and Kavan having a baby. The horrid exchange with Ethan. And the tears, the river of tears. She was so weary of tears.

She scooted toward Ethan's side of the bed, her hand outstretched. But the sheets and pillow were cold and empty.

"Eth?"

No response.

She called again, louder. "Ethan?"

Tossing the blankets aside, Julie scurried to the bathroom for her robe. A wintry chill hovered in the room.

She eased down the stairs and made her way through the apartment by the dim glow of light that filtered through the drawn verticals. Pausing briefly, she peered out to see it snowing again.

"Ethan?" She peeked around the den door. Ethan lay curled and cold on the short sofa. "Oh, babe—"

Fumbling for the closet door, Julie patted around the shelves for a spare blanket. From its scent, she could tell it was the one they used for fall picnics in Milo Park.

She buried her face in the blanket and tried to remember the last time they'd actually picnicked together. Two years ago?

Spreading the cover over her husband now, Julie thought it odd, yet wonderful, that the old blanket still carried the fragrance of Saturday afternoons in the park.

Shivering, she wriggled onto the edge of the couch, fitting next to Ethan. He stirred and scooted over to make room for her. Curling his arm around her waist, he kissed her softly on the nape of her neck.

In a moment or two, Julie drifted to sleep, Ethan's warmth melting away the chill of the night.

Friday night, Ethan parked along the curb of Wiltshire Street beneath the bright lights of the Hanover home. He turned to Julie. "Let's miss this one."

"We'd never hear the end of it." She pulled on her door handle.

"A hundred of their soirees and you'd think we'd get a reprieve from one." Ethan caught her hand. "Say the word, and we leave."

"You say that every time." She cupped his cheek with the palm of her hand.

"I mean it every time."

Snow crunched under his feet as he stepped out of the car into the orange glow of the streetlights. Ethan followed the lights' hue to the edge of the driveway where Julie waited.

Without a word, she started up the steep drive, but Ethan stopped her with his touch on her coat sleeve. "Wait, Julie."

When she faced him, his heartbeat echoed in his ears. "You look amazing tonight."

Her smile challenged the moon's glow. "Thank you."

He brushed her coat sleeve with his hand. "Let's phone in our apology and go eat pizza. We can get a corner in the back, talk, kiss."

She smoothed her hand over his chest. "Give it a rest, Ethan. This routine is getting old."

"*This* routine is getting old." He motioned toward the Hanover's triple-story home, then drew her to him. Her scent made him think of beauty and kindness. "Think about it, Jules. Snobby society people, your mom suggesting you change your hair, your dad introducing you to violin players." He made a face.

She laughed. "Violin players do have their purpose, darling. Don't be a complete cello snob."

He kissed her. "Since Tuesday, we've been out every night this week: church on Wednesday, private lessons on Thursday."

"I'm used to it."

Ethan drew back. "Used to what?"

"You going one way, me the other."

"All the more reason to skip this shindig."

"Perhaps you could skip a ball game."

Ethan lifted his arms. He was out of words. "Yeah, whatever; that'll fix it."

Julie snapped, "You might as well tell me my opinion doesn't count, Ethan."

"Let's just go inside. I'm tired of debating."

"Fine with me."

The front door opened. Sandy Hanover graced the porch, elegant in a black dress and a string of pearls. "Come in, you two. You'll catch cold out here."

"We're coming." Julie waved like all was right with the world.

Ethan stepped in front of her. "Julie, sooner or later we have to talk about our life and what's next."

Julie peered into the dark shadows beyond the Hanovers' front yard. "Yes, I know." She started up the drive again.

Ethan fell in stride. "We can't keep diffusing the issue with frivolous arguments. Half the time we don't even know what we're arguing about."

With that, Julie stopped. "Do you want to talk about it? I'm barren. There, we've discussed it. End of the issue."

Ethan balked. "We haven't discussed it at all." He paused. "Julie," he said, firm and resolute, "pizza. Let's go for pizza."

Ralph Hanover came out this time. "Julie, Kit Merewether is inside. She's eager to talk with you."

Julie glanced at Ethan. "Can we do what I want for a change, without a big brouhaha?"

"Brouhaha? What brouhaha? I want an evening with my wife to discuss our future."

She sighed. "Ethan, I'm going inside. You can come if you want."

He rubbed his gloved hand over his head and followed.

⨾⨾

Music and laughter warmed the room. Julie maneuvered her way to the buffet, feeling like an ice cube among burning coals. She thanked her mother when she handed her a hot cup of tea.

"Are you well?" Mom asked, brushing her hand over Julie's forehead.

Julie pulled away. "Yes, I'm fine."

Kit Merewether joined them with a broad smile. "Julie, you're as lovely as ever."

"Thank you, Kit." Julie let the older woman link their arms and drag her away to meet the newest members of New Hampshire's elite orchestra.

Kit introduced Julie to a small circle with a great deal of enthusiasm. "She won the George Houston Musical Fellowship," Kit concluded, beaming as if she herself had given birth to Julie Hanover Lambert.

"Congratulations."

"What was the focus of your fellowship study?"

Julie told them, "Bringing the classics back into the elementary and secondary school level."

From another room, Julie heard a roar of *yeahs!*

"Golf," someone said.

Without looking, Julie figured Ethan was among that crowd. In fact, he probably inspired the idea of watching the game. No matter where or what, her husband found a home watching sports.

Kit shook her gray head, her expression one of amusement. "One would think it better than rocket science, or the melodies of Brahms, for a man to knock a small round ball into a small round hole."

A laugh rose from the circle. "One would think."

Kit inquired of Julie, "Will you battle Ethan over the value of music versus the value of sports for your children? Certainly you will."

The room faded to shades of gray. Kit didn't know, of course. But like a moth to the flame, Julie's mother flitted over at the mention of children.

"We were talking about Julie's children. Shall they learn to putt a tiny white ball or the fine art of playing the cello?"

Sandy Hanover brushed Julie's hair from her face. "Probably both." She smiled at Kit. "Julie and Ethan's children will be beautiful, talented, and take the world by storm."

Julie coughed. "Does it really matter?"

Mom rested her hand at the base of her throat. "Of course it matters." She moved her other hand to Kit's arm. "At the age of five, Julie lined up all of her dolls and taught them 'Jesus Loves Me,' and I don't know what all."

Turning to Julie, she asked, "Do you remember your little doll choir?"

Julie nodded. "But I don't think it means my children will be brilliant. I think it means my dolls couldn't protest."

Kit peered at Julie with a raised brow, but Julie looked away. Her probing gray eyes might unearth a bomb Julie did not want exposed.

"Her father and I wanted more children, but—"

Julie touched her mother's shoulder. "We all know, Mom."

A server with a tray of punch paused at their trio. Sandra Hanover picked up a cup. "Nevertheless, we expect to hear we are going to be grandparents any-time now."

Kit took a cup, but Julie declined, gripping her hands together at her waist.

"How long have you two been married?" Kit asked.

"Ten years this summer."

Sandra sipped her punch, then told Kit, "They virtually dragged both families to the church the summer after graduation."

"Young lovers, I see." Kit's words were simple and few, but Julie felt the rev-elation of them. Yes, they were young and in love.

"We met on the high school football field. A fourth and goal play knocked Ethan out, and when they called for smelling salts, I ran onto the field." Julie stuck her arm in the air. "Nurse Julie."

Kit's deep, pure laugh billowed around them.

Julie's mom laughed a little too heartily and finished the tale Sandra Hanover style, waving her hands. "Ethan came to, looked at his nurse, and got knocked out again."

"With love," Kit concluded. "The world's most powerful potion."

Sandy flipped her hand in the air as if it were no big deal. "So you see, Kit, we've been waiting to be grandparents for almost ten years."

"Well, well." Kit looked at Julie as if she could read all her secret thoughts. "Grandchildren are always a blessing."

"Ralph already set up a trust account, two of them, as a matter of fact. He didn't want to wait." Julie's mom chortled, pressing her hand on Kit's arm. "Julie and Ethan will have a time keeping us from spoiling them."

"Leave it to a finance lawyer to think ahead," Kit said.

Julie squirmed, Kit's piercing gaze bore right through her. She glanced around to avoid eye contact and caught the back of Ethan's head in the family room, where, sure enough, he hovered around the golf game.

"But you chose to get an education, Julie?" Kit tipped her head and raised a brow.

"Yes, she and Ethan both earned their degrees," Sandy Hanover answered for her.

My mother, the broadcaster. Julie squared her shoulders and said to Kit, "We wanted children right away, but I miscarried our first year of marriage. We took a long look at things and realized we weren't very well prepared, financially, emotionally—"

"Spiritually," Kit interjected.

"Yes, of course." Julie knew Kit to be a wise, godly woman. And tonight she seemed to have a direct line to her heart. "We decided to wait."

"Well, the waiting is over. I want to Christmas shop for my grandchildren." Mom said the words with an air of finality, as if saying them would make it true.

Julie's stomach knotted. "I hear you, Mom."

"Hasn't Dr. Patterson worked his wonders yet?"

Treading on tender ground, Mom. "God is the God of wonders, Mom. Dr. Patterson in limited to what man can do."

"I tell you, if such things had been available to your father and me—"

"Mom!"

She faced Julie with a sharp turn. "I don't appreciate your tone, Julie."

"Julie," Kit interjected. "I'm forming a quartet. Please say you'll join us. We need an outstanding cellist." Her comment diffused the moment.

"A quartet? I thought of auditioning for the symphony—"

Kit touched her arm. "Join our quartet. You'll have more fun, and it'll give you something to look forward to."

Chapter 7

Ethan liked Steve Tripleton, a friend of Julie's father, with his over-the-top confidence and successful businessman bravado. He could do without the designer slacks and Italian loafers, but otherwise Ethan found Steve engaging.

"We'll go down to Costa Rica mid-April. Heredia has a beautiful golf resort. Absolutely beautiful."

Ethan rubbed his hands together. Golfing in the Caribbean, sun on his back, warm breeze in his face. . . For the first time all night, he was glad to be at the Hanovers'. "Sounds like my kind of trip. How much, Steve?"

"For five days? Around fifteen hundred, give or take. That'd cover your flight, accommodations, greens fees. You'd need a little spending money for food and incidentals."

Very reasonable. Ethan mentally reviewed their finances—current savings balance plus whatever he could add in the next month after paying their monthly bills. *I can swing it, I think. Still have all summer to save a down payment for Julie's car.*

"I'm game," her father said. "Winter is wearing me down. I think the office can do without me for a few days."

Steve clapped him on the back, his smile exposing overly white teeth. "You have the Internet? We can get online and take a tour."

"Right this way." Ralph headed for his upstairs office.

Ethan followed, offering ideas and suggestions. "I think my cousin Will Adams might want to come along."

"Ethan."

He turned to see Julie at the bottom of the stairs. He leaned over the railing. "Yeah, babe, what's up?"

In a low voice, she said, "I'm ready to go."

He hesitated. "Okay, give me a minute. I'm checking on something with your dad and Steve."

Her father called down from the mezzanine. "Julie, Eliza set up a grand smorgasbord fit for a king. Did you try her shrimp puffs?"

Julie gave him a thin smile, her hands clasped at her waist. "I had my heart set on pizza."

At that, Ethan responded, "Finally saw it my way?"

"Whatever, Eth. Let's go."

"Five minutes." He dashed upstairs. He didn't want Steve to get too far ahead on the virtual tour.

A little while later, when Ethan strolled out of the office with Steve and Ralph, visions of blue-green seas and lush lawns danced in his head.

"I'll get my secretary on the arrangements. Ethan, speak to your cousin. A foursome would be nice."

"Done." Ethan flipped Steve his card. "Here are my numbers, cell, work, and home."

At the bottom of the stairs, he remembered Julie. A quick peek at his watch told him five minutes had turned to thirty.

"See you gentlemen later. I need to find my wife."

Ethan mingled among the crowd, searching for Julie. Sandy caught him and reminded him it was not too late to give her a grandchild by Christmas.

He blushed and said, "Sure, Sandy."

Eliza tried to entice him with a plate of food, but he wanted to save room for pizza, the one junk food he enjoyed.

He found Kit Merewether by the fireplace in a lively small-group discussion.

"Pardon me," he interrupted, popping into the group, addressing Kit. "Have you seen Julie?"

"No, I haven't, dear."

"She left," someone said.

Ethan turned around. "Do you know when?"

"Twenty minutes ago, maybe?"

Ethan jerked his coat from under the pile on the bed in the guest room. Without saying good-bye, he stepped into the cold night and strode with purpose toward his car.

But it was gone.

※ ※

At a booth in the back of Giuseppe's Pizza, Julie shoved aside the remains of a large house salad and sipped on a diet soda.

She twisted the paper straw wrapper between her fingers, wondering if Ethan would show.

"She's a-waiting for you. Back here." The sound of Giuseppe's voice neared.

Ethan slipped into the booth across from her with a quick thanks to the round-bellied proprietor. "Do you want to tell me why you left?" He shrugged off his coat, his face red from the cold.

"Did you walk here?" She swirled the ice in her soda glass and took a drink.

"Yes, I needed to cool off."

"You're mad then."

He leaned toward her. "I asked you to wait."

"I told you I wanted to leave."

"Five minutes. All I wanted was five minutes."

Julie tapped the face of her watch. "Yet here it is, an hour later."

He reclined against the padded booth. "I'm sorry. I got interested in something else."

"What? Sports? Why is that always more important than I am?"

"That's unfair. And not true. What happened anyway? Why did you want to leave?"

She leaned toward him. With a clipped tone, she said, "My mother."

He winced. " 'Nuff said. Sorry, babe."

"She went on and on to Kit Merewether about *her* grandchildren." She wiped her nose with the tip of a wadded-up napkin. "She told her about Dad's bank accounts for them."

"Yeah, she cornered me about giving them a grandchild by Christmas."

"Let's not tell them, Ethan. Please."

He shook his head, a wry grin on his lips. "We have to tell them eventually."

A skinny, squeaky-voiced teenager stopped and crouched at their table. He set his elbows on the table, his pen poised over the order pad. "Can I get you something to drink?"

"Coffee," Ethan said. "A big mug."

"I'll take a hot tea this time." Julie slid her empty soda glass across the table.

"Bring us a large cheese pie, too." Ethan ordered.

Julie looked into Ethan's eyes. "There's no little Ethan or little Julie in our future. Does it bother you?" To her surprise, verbalizing her thoughts comforted her heart.

He reached for her hand. "Yes, it bothers me."

With her head down, she confessed, "I can't stop thinking about it. The idea lives with me. I've let you down."

"Let me down? No, you haven't, babe."

"I feel betrayed by my own body. I've let you down, Mom and Dad. Your parents."

With his fingertips, Ethan lifted her chin so she faced him. "Don't carry this burden yourself, Julie. We are in this together. For better or worse."

"Then why do I feel so alone?"

"Because you exclude me. I had to hear the news from Dr. Patterson. Does that seem right to you?"

The waiter brought their drinks and a basket of garlic knots. Ethan reached for one.

"I don't know what seems right to me anymore."

"We're going to figure this out. We just need time to think, and talk."

"And pray. Ethan, what is God saying in all of this?"

He shrugged, his eyes fixed on some point beyond her. "I wish I knew. But He's faithful. He has a plan and a purpose, babe."

"I cling to that, or I'd give up completely," Julie said. She watched him for a moment and then asked, "What'd Jesse say about my car?"

"It was your starter. He fixed it, good as new."

"Good as new. Ha! I want a new car, Ethan."

Ethan swigged his coffee. "A new car isn't going to take away the pain, Julie."

"I didn't say it would." Julie chewed her lower lip, wondering what would make the pain go away.

"You know our financial situation. Adding a monthly car payment would really strap us."

When their large cheese pizza arrived, Julie took a plate and a large slice of pizza. "So it's my fault I don't have a new car?"

Ethan sighed. She understood he was frustrated, but she didn't care. So was she.

"Did I say that? We decided together to continue seeking medical help, didn't we?"

"You agreed after pressure from me and my parents."

He nodded. "Yes, but I wouldn't have agreed if I didn't think it was the right decision."

Julie wondered for the first time how much her parents' desire for a child had impacted her and Ethan's decisions.

"It's seems if I can't have a baby, I should at least get a new car."

"Jules, those two things are mutually exclusive." He reached across and squeezed her hand. "We'll get you a new car."

"Tomorrow."

"Not tomorrow, but soon. Next year."

Saturday morning, Ethan slept until eleven. He loved that about the weekend—sleeping in. Half awake, he rolled over to snuggle Julie.

But he found her side of the bed empty. "Jules?"

He waited a moment for her answer. "Julie?" When she didn't respond, he crawled out of bed.

Cold air permeated the apartment as he jogged downstairs. "Jules?"

"In here."

He found her in the den, curled in the recliner, Bible propped open in her lap, her expression somber. His heart yearned for her. "Hey, sweetie, what's going on?"

He scooped her up and sat down, cradling her in his lap. He kissed her softly when she dropped her head against his shoulder.

"I was just talking to the Lord about our situation."

He brushed her hair away from her face. "Did He say anything?"

Julie shook her head. "Why does He seem so silent when I need Him the most?"

Ethan wondered the same thing. He wished he knew the answer, but his own prayer life lacked luster these days. His list of excuses seemed more and more frivolous, but he had yet to adjust the situation. He knew they could trust Him, believe in Him, even when they didn't understand their life circumstance. "Remember what I said last night? He's faithful, Julie. He has a plan and a purpose."

"I know He works all things together for good. I just can't find the good here."

She cried, wiping her face with wadded tissues. "Will you pray with me?"

"Absolutely." He rested his cheek on the top of her head, regretting that she had to ask him to pray. He should have offered.

"Lord, we don't understand this situation, but You do. We can count on Your faithfulness, Your goodness, Your blessings. Give us grace to submit to Your will for our lives."

For the first time in a long time, Ethan sensed the presence and peace of God. They stirred a hunger in him and a resolve to seek the Lord's strength and stop depending on his own devices.

After a peaceful interlude, Julie pressed her lips against his cheek. "Thank you."

"Do you feel better? Do you sense the Lord's peace?"

She nodded slightly. "Yes. I know He loves me, but, Ethan, I don't know if I'll ever feel better."

He frowned at her. "That's my beautiful little pessimist."

She flicked him on the forehead, grinning.

"Ouch!" He slapped his hand over the sting.

"That's what you get for being sarcastic." She kissed the red spot and hopped off his lap. "Do you want some breakfast? Your Highness slept until lunch, but I think I can whip up something breakfastlike for you."

"Eggs, please."

"Eggs it is." She smiled at him. "Thanks for praying with me." She disappeared around the corner to the kitchen.

He followed her. "You're welcome. Sorry you had to ask for prayer. I guess I've been a little dense lately."

"Just lately?" She snickered and retrieved the skillet from the bottom cupboard and sprayed it with cooking oil. "Can you believe we have a whole day with nothing to do?"

He slipped his hands around her waist. "Not me. I've got to run by the plant to check on the equipment." He nuzzled her neck.

"Really?" She faced him and slipped her arms around his neck.

He kissed her with passion.

"Let me guess. The eggs can wait."

"Maybe?" He searched her eyes, hoping to see a reflection of what he felt.

She returned his kiss without a word, then clicked off the burner and led him by the hand upstairs.

Chapter 8

Praying with Ethan lifted Julie's countenance and strengthened her resolve. *Move on with life. No more tears.*

Nevertheless, the word *barren* floated aimlessly along the breezes of her mind like tumbleweed across the desert plains.

She understood now, in some small way, what the apostle Paul meant when he wrote, "But one thing I do, forgetting those things which are behind and reaching forward to those things which are ahead."

With her life plans now defunct, new plans awaited. She merely needed to pray, dream, and let the Lord paint a new picture on the canvas of her life.

At the breakfast nook, she stared out the window at the glistening snow. *Time to give Kit Merewether a call and take her up on the quartet invitation.*

Ethan clattered around in the kitchen, putting away the breakfast dishes. "Kitchen is tidy, ready for your inspection, Mrs. Lambert." He bent to kiss her cheek.

The scent of mountain-spring soap drifted under her nose. "If it meets your standards, it meets mine."

Ethan lifted his arms over his head in a victory stance. "Ethan Lambert, Neat Freak Champion of the World."

She laughed at him. "Neat Freak, where's the paper? I want to catch up on the news. I feel out of touch."

"Probably on the porch. I'll get it."

The phone rang as he opened the front door. Still smiling, Julie answered.

"Hi, Julie, it's Mark Benton. Is Ethan around?"

"Hi, Mark. Hold on, here he is."

Julie handed the phone to her husband. He tossed her the paper. Slowly she removed the plastic wrap, listening to Ethan's conversation.

He talked to Mark with animated movements—dribbling and shooting a pretend basketball. Julie perched on a nook stool and scouted out movies.

When he said good-bye to Mark, Ethan lobbed the phone to Julie. "Incoming. . ."

She caught it. "What's up?"

Ethan cupped her face in his hands and kissed her with enthusiasm. "A rematch. Mark ran into a couple of the guys from the Creager Technologies team, and they want a rematch of our championship game. Creager versus Lambert Furniture."

"Really. When?"

Ethan glanced at the stove clock. "Wow, is it that late? I've got to run by the plant, then get to this game." He dashed upstairs.

Julie trailed him. "What am I supposed to do?"

Ethan peeled off his sweater and jeans. "Come to the game." He folded the clothes and set them on top of his dresser.

"What about our free day?"

"Aw, babe, I have to check on the new CNC machines. I'm sorry I didn't tell you about that." He grabbed her and whirled her around. "But come to the game. It'll be fun." He disappeared in the closet for his basketball gear. "I can't believe those guys want to get beat again."

She flopped down on the bed. "I don't know. . ."

He slung his gym bag over his shoulder. "You can cheer me on."

She made a face and laughed. "You never hear me."

"It's the thought that counts." He ruffled her hair.

"And I lose my voice for nothing."

He looked at his watch. "Ooh, gotta go. Come on, Jules, come. Or, hey, call Elizabeth for a movie if you want."

"Well, I haven't talked to her since that night at the restaurant. I guess I could—" But he was gone.

Julie sat in the living room, acknowledging her sour attitude. She wanted to hang out at home with Ethan. He had to work and play basketball. So typical.

Work I understand, but basketball? She considered going to the game but didn't want to give Ethan the satisfaction.

When the phone rang a few minutes later, she answered, hoping to hear Ethan's voice.

"Do you want to catch a movie tonight?" Sophia sounded like an energetic teenager.

With a sigh, Julie leaned against the kitchen counter. "What a coincidence."

"Huh?"

"Never mind. Yeah, a movie sounds good."

"What do you want to see?" Sophia asked.

"I don't care as long as it's a comedy. The more inane, the better."

Sophia snickered. "That new place out by Sinclair's has eight theaters. I'm sure one of them is showing something inane."

"Great. Guess we could do dinner, too."

Julie scribbled Ethan a note. *Gone to dinner and the movies with Sophia.* She tucked it under his laptop and bounded upstairs for a shower.

❧❧

Ethan knocked lightly on his grandparents' kitchen door. "Hello. Anyone home?" He wandered through the kitchen, snatching a piece of chocolate cake.

"Who's there?" Grandma came in from the family room with her knitting in her hands. "Ethan, what brings you here?"

"Stopped by to see my two favorite people." He bent to kiss her cheek.

Grandma chortled. "Have you had dinner?"

"Actually, no."

"Sit, sit. Let me get you something." Grandma set the yarn and needles on the kitchen counter and hustled around the airy kitchen.

"Where's Grandpa?" Ethan glanced through the kitchen door to the family room.

"Ratting around in the basement, making something, I think." With a Tupperware bowl in hand, Grandma opened the basement door. "Matt, Ethan is here."

Ethan heard footfalls on the stairs. "Well, to what do we owe this pleasure? Where's your lovely bride?"

"At a movie with a friend." Ethan watched as his grandpa hugged his grandma.

"How's *my* bride?" Grandpa kissed her and picked up the cake plate.

Bride? It had been many years since Ethan thought of Julie as his bride. Wife? Yes. Friend? Certainly. But bride? The word painted a different image on his emotions—an image of zealous love, of intimacy.

Grandma regarded Grandpa, a large spoon in her hand. "She's fine as long as you don't die too soon from cholesterol poisoning. Don't eat that whole cake, Matt."

"Ah, Betty, you worry too much." He fished in the silverware drawer for a fork and joined Ethan at the table.

Ethan watched, amused. His grandparents' enduring love and affection were a Lambert family treasure. Their example, along with his parents', gave him the confidence to marry Julie after high school. He had been blissfully unaware that desert winds would blow.

"What have you been doing today?" Grandpa scooted up to the table, a large white napkin tucked into his collar.

"Slept until noon, stopped by the plant to check on the equipment, then met the guys at the rec center to beat Creager again in a championship rematch."

"Those fellows must love punishment."

Ethan grinned. "They must."

"A lovely March Saturday and you went to work, played basketball, and Julie went out with a friend." Grandpa shook his head. "Times have sure changed."

Ethan narrowed his eyes. "What are you implying?"

Grandma came around the table. "All I had was leftover steak and baked beans from the senior center cookout." She patted him on the back and winked.

"Well, if that's all you have. . ." Ethan cut a bite. "I'll have to endure."

Grandpa lifted his chin. "When's the last time you and Julie went out together?"

Ethan thought for a moment. "Um. . ."

"Um? That doesn't sound good."

"Wait, we went to Italian Hills the other night." Ethan pointed at Grandpa with his fork. "She'd had a bad day." He left it at that.

"A consolation date?"

"No, not exactly." Ethan flushed and took a long sip of his water. "What's wrong with a consolation date?" *Never mind how rotten it was.*

"Nothing, if that's the kind of relationship you want with your wife. Are you two living life from the same game book?"

Ethan felt invaded by his grandpa's words. The man saw too much. "Where'd you come up with that? Game book? Of course we're living life from the same game book." *I think.*

"Would Julie tell me the same? Does she still drive that old car?"

Ethan squirmed. Grandpa painted him into a corner. "Yes."

"Matt, leave the boy alone. He and Julie can manage their own affairs." Grandma hushed Grandpa with a pat on the head.

"I never told you about Lambert's Code, did I?"

"Just that there was some mysterious family code." Ethan speared a piece of meat, grateful for Grandma's defense, shoving aside any guilt about Julie's old car. Two weeks ago, she happily drove that old car. How did the baby news change all that?

Grandma answered, "No mystery to it, Ethan. Just submit to one another."

Ethan gave her a quizzical look. "That's it?"

Grandma assured him, "That's it."

"Submit to one another?" Ethan repeated with a slight shake of his head. "I have no idea what that means."

"Exactly." Grandpa speared the air with his fork. Cake crumbs littered the table.

"Matthew Lambert, you're worse than the great-grandchildren." Grandma got up for a wet cloth.

Ethan twisted his expression. "I'm supposed to live by a code that I don't understand?"

"You've watched spy movies, haven't you?" Grandpa asked.

"Sure."

"Don't they crack some kind of code? That's what you have to do. Crack the code."

Grandma gave him a clue. "Read Ephesians 5:21."

"I know Ephesians 5. Husbands, love your wives. Wives, respect your husbands." He didn't say, "Blah, blah, blah," but his tone did.

"That's a big part of it, sure, but rethink it. Go deep. Hold up your marriage to Julie against that verse. Hold up your relationship to the Lord in light of that verse."

Ethan swirled the last of the water in his glass. "What do I win when I figure it out?"

Grandma and Grandpa grinned. "When you figure it out, you win."

"Well, guess I'd better crack this code then. Does the rest of the family know this, or am I in on a rare secret?"

"If they need to know, they know."

Grandma brought over a small dessert plate and cut Ethan a piece of cake. "Good news about Elizabeth and Kavan, isn't it?"

Being reminded of the Donovan baby stabbed his heart a little and resurrected the dark memory of his fight with Julie. "Yes, good news."

Ethan imaged how his and Julie's news would hit the family. Everyone knew their journey. In fact, the decision to try infertility medications had sparked a family debate. Should they trust medical technology or wait to see what the Lord would do? Ethan decided it was up to the Lord no matter what path they chose.

Remembering caused a gnawing pain to work over his shoulders and neck.

"Are you and Julie going to join them anytime soon?" Grandpa asked.

"You're full of questions tonight, Grandpa." Ethan turned to his grandma. "Did you take away his gossip magazine again?"

How do I get out of this one? His cell phone chirped just in time. He grinned at Grandpa as he unclipped it from his belt.

"Saved by the bell." Grandpa scooted back his chair and mumbled something about a cold glass of milk.

"Hello?"

"Eth, it's me."

"Where are you?" Ethan flipped his wrist over so he could see his watch. He remembered the Celtics game and hoped to catch it.

"At the theater. My car died."

Ethan ignored the sting of guilt and asked, "Why did you even drive your car? Doesn't Sophia have a new SUV or something?"

"Forgive me. I thought you said my car was fixed up, good as new."

He rubbed his forehead. He did say that. *Stop being a jerk, Eth, and give her a break.* "What do you want me to do?"

"Come and get us in a couple of hours?"

"Can you call me when you're ready?"

"I will. Thanks, Ethan."

"No problem, babe." Ethan pressed END, muttering about missing the game and driving across town to pick up Julie and her friend.

Grandpa rapped on the table. "Lambert's Code." He took the empty cake plate and milk glass to the sink. "Get cracking."

Chapter 9

Sunday after church, Julie called Kit Merewether. "So tell me about this quartet."

"I thought I'd hear from you." Her laughter resonated like the notes of a violin. Julie wondered if her own laugh would sound like the cello in years to come.

"Have you already started practice?"

"No, I was praying for the right cello player. The Lord led me to you."

The Lord sent Kit a cello player but neglected to send me a child? "Monday nights are best for me."

"You met the other two at your parents' last Friday night, Cassie Ferguson and Mike Chason. I'll confirm their availability, and we'll get started. I live half-way between White Birch and Manchester. We'll practice at my place."

"Sounds fun." Julie manufactured a bit of enthusiasm. Joining the quartet kept with her resolve to move on with life, to allow the Lord to paint new colors on her heart.

While music was one of her life's treasures, she never anticipated it being a pacifier for her troubles.

After her conversation with Kit, Julie surveyed the apartment, contemplating her options. She could clean, but. . . She chuckled. *Why give Ethan a heart attack?*

Despite the lack of harmony in their relationship these days, she wasn't ready to arrange his funeral.

Standing in the middle of the living room, hands on her hips, she stared out the front window. Snow still blanketed the ground, and the forecast called for more. It was the first week of March, but spring felt light-years away.

Church had been good this morning. Pastor Marlow preached from the Gospel of John. She loved the image of John leaning on Jesus during the Last Supper. "I want to lean on You, Lord."

But she found it hard to rest in Him, hard to trust Him with every area of her life. Especially when life was not turning out as she had planned.

She and Ethan quarreled last night after he picked her up from the movies and dropped Sophia off at home. They argued about her car, his sporting appetite, and why her jeans remained on the bathroom floor.

Julie cringed, remembering her statement to Ethan as he got in bed and turned out the light.

"It's probably a good thing we're not having kids. They might be an inconvenience to you."

"Julie, how can you say that? I hurt over this situation, too."

"Really?" *It's so hard to tell, Eth.*

Recalling the conversation made her insides clench. *How do we get out of this cycle, Lord?*

After church and a quick lunch at home, Ethan took off to watch a NASCAR race with his cousins. She thought of going over to visit Bobby's wife, Elle, but remembered she visited her parents on Sunday afternoons.

Deep in thought, Julie jumped when the phone rang. "Hello?"

"Hi, Julie, it's Elizabeth."

"How are you?" Julie sank down on the couch. She loved hearing from her cousin-in-law, though it brought such a sharp reminder. "I missed you in church this morning."

"I missed being there. But ever since we saw you and Ethan at Italian Hills, I've had the worst morning sickness."

Julie smiled. "Oh, the joy." *A joy I'll miss.*

"Talk about paying the piper." Elizabeth laughed. "Kavan almost had to take me to the ER."

"I'll pray for you."

"Oh, please do."

Julie tugged a loose thread on the hem of her sweater. "I'm sorry about the other night—"

"Don't mention it, Julie. Ethan said you were having a bad day. Kavan's with the guys watching some car race, so I thought I'd give you a call."

Her eyes burned. "Ethan's there, too."

"How are you?"

She chewed her bottom lip. "Fine. Doing fine."

"Do you want to talk about the other night?"

Julie smiled, remembering when Elizabeth came to White Birch almost two years ago, driven and determined to go to grad school but falling in love with Kavan instead.

What was it I told her? Marriage is pleasant, safe, and wonderful. Now she's moving on, having children, living my life. "Nothing to say right now, Beth, but—" She lost control of her voice for a moment. "I'm sure we'll be talking later."

"You know my number."

Being keenly aware of Elizabeth's happiness only highlighted Julie's disappointment. Taking a deep breath, she cleared the frog from her throat and said, "I never told you congratulations."

"Thank you." Elizabeth's words bubbled. "We weren't planning on it. You know what they say. It happens when you least expect it."

That's what they say. "A child is a blessing at any time. Expected or not."

"It took awhile to get used to the idea, but now I can't imagine anything else."

Julie rode the wave of Elizabeth's jubilant emotion. "How wonderful."

"To think I wanted to be a nuclear engineer. This is way better. I mean, Julie,

I'm going to be a mom. Me." Elizabeth chortled.

For a split second, Julie contemplated telling her the news but decided against it. It would only make Elizabeth feel bad.

A long pause lingered between them. *Think of something to say, Julie.*

"We should have your baby shower at Grandma Betty's." The words popped out of her mouth before her brain had time to process them.

"Oh, wouldn't that be lovely?"

"Yes, it would." Julie rested her forehead in her hand.

"You are my closest girlfriend, Julie. You're family, too, but my best friend in White Birch."

Julie straightened and inhaled slowly. "Well, then we should plan a spring shower."

Elizabeth giggled. "That's funny. A spring shower."

"A spring shower?" Julie didn't understand. *Oh, a spring shower.* "Yes, that's funny."

"Hey, Julie, I have a little pun in the oven." Elizabeth laughed heartily at her joke.

Julie laughed with her. "May you and your pun do well. Meanwhile, I'll talk to Grandma. I'm sure Elle would like to help—and Ethan's mom."

They chatted about registering for gifts and compared baby showers they loved with the ones they hated.

When Julie finally said good-bye, she let the tears flow. "Lord, will it ever *not* hurt?"

She yanked a couple of tissues from the box on the breakfast nook, feeling as if the dark cloud over her would never dissipate. *I need some sunshine in my life.*

When she stooped to toss her tissues in the trash, a brightly colored newspaper ad caught her eye. Ethan had stacked Sunday's paper by the garbage, ready for recycling.

Wiping her eyes, she picked up the folded broadsheet and read. *Why not?* She thought for another second. *Should I? Ethan would be shocked.* She glanced at the color ad again. With a pound of her palm on the countertop, she decided. *I'm taking control of my life, at least where I can. I'm going to do it.*

Snatching up the phone, she thought for another second, then dialed Sophia. "Come pick me up." Her car sat dead in the cinema parking lot.

"Why? Where are we going?"

"You'll see."

❧❧

Ethan, Kavan, Will, and Bobby found a booth at the diner.

"I'm having one of Sam's cheeseburgers," Will said without reaching for the menu. "And a sundae for dessert."

"In my dreams." Bobby opened his menu. "Elle has me on a diet."

"I'll have a salad." Ethan glanced between Will and Bobby's identical faces, then at Kavan. "Don't tell me Elizabeth has you on a diet."

Kavan shook his head. "Gentlemen, my wife is pregnant. Right now, the sight of food makes her sick. I only eat when I'm not with her."

They were empathizing with Kavan when Jarred Hansen came for their order.

"Do you believe that's our production supervisor's grandson?" Ethan motioned toward the young man.

Bobby nodded. "They grow up fast."

"Speaking of growing up fast, aren't you and Julie ready to bless us with a Lambert baby?" Will asked.

Bobby added, "We thought you'd have two or three by now."

Will stacked the menus behind the salt and pepper rack. "I can't believe you let Elizabeth and Kavan beat you to it."

Kavan scoffed. "I didn't know there was a competition, but believe me, we didn't think we'd start a family so soon."

Ethan unrolled the napkin from his fork, spoon, and knife. The table talk pinged the deep recesses of his heart and returned a sad sensation. "Guess it's not our time."

Should I tell them? He glanced at their faces, thought of Julie, and decided against it. It didn't seem fair to take the focus from Elizabeth and Kavan. Besides, they had yet to tell each set of parents.

Not ready to break the news to his mother-in-law, Ethan knew Sandy meant well, but she set too many of her hopes in Julie.

"Forget babies." Bobby grinned at Ethan and Kavan and leaned against the back of the booth. "Will, when are you going to find a nice girl, settle down, get married?"

A crimson hue colored Will's cheeks, and it wasn't from the heat of the diner.

Ethan laughed. "Give him a break, Bobby. He's got to go on a date before he can get married."

Jarred interrupted with their order.

"Thank you, my man, just in time." Will reached for his soda and took a deep sip.

When Jarred left, Ethan asked, "Didn't you have a thing for his aunt? What was her name?"

"Taylor." Bobby shot out her name like he'd been thinking the same thing.

Ethan nodded. "That's right. Taylor. What ever happened with her, Will?"

"She got a life. Which I suggest both of you do."

Laughter rippled around the table, and the conversation turned to town happenings and Lambert's Furniture.

"Tomorrow I'll have the contract for the new warehouse construction signed," Ethan told Will, stabbing a forkful of salad.

Will waved a french fry at him. "Good. We need that warehouse to get under way the first of spring. The VP of sales tells me summer is going to be busy."

Ethan looked at Bobby. "Is that so, VP of sales?"

Bobby nodded. "If we land every deal we're working, it'll be a record sales year."

"Sounds like Grandpa's business is doing well," Kavan noted.

"Grandpa never dreamed his furniture ideas would turn to this," Will said.

Talk of Grandpa reminded Ethan. "Have any of you heard of Lambert's Code?"

Bobby creased his brow, thinking. "I've heard Grandpa mention it but don't know the definition."

Kavan shrugged. "I've been around the Lambert household most of my life, and I've heard Grandpa mention 'The Code,' but that's all I know."

"Same here," Will said. "Pass the ketchup."

Ethan slid the red bottle Will's way. "He and Grandma said something about submitting to one another?"

"You got me."

"Guess it's up to me to crack the code." Ethan looked at their faces.

"Ethan Lambert, 007," Bobby said in a deep voice.

The men laughed.

"All right, leave it to me." Ethan pointed at them with his fork. Most of the time, he thought he had a great relationship with Julie. Though these days, they did seem to live life from a different game book.

But they'd been busy. She completed grad school and started teaching. He took over the production department for the family business. She started teaching private lessons. He learned golf.

Lambert's Code, he thought. *Submit to one another. Lord, show me how.*

Jarred brought Will's sundae just as Ethan's cell rang. "Hello?"

"Ethan, Steve Tripleton. I'm putting the final plans together for Costa Rica. Are you still interested?"

"Absolutely." Ethan smiled. Five days of paradise. How could he say no?

"Excellent." Steve listed the April dates and told Ethan his travel agents would book the flight. "What about your cousin?"

Ethan rapped his knuckles on the table to get Will's attention. "Do you want to go on that Costa Rica golf excursion?"

Will nodded. "I'll leave Bobby in charge of Lambert's Furniture."

"Sure, leave me holding the bag."

Ethan grinned. "Yes, Steve, Will's in."

When he hung up, Bobby and Kavan quizzed him. "You're golfing in Costa Rica? Does Julie know?"

"Not yet."

"Not yet? You just committed." Bobby shook his head.

"Don't worry, Bob. She'll be fine with it."

"Elle would be livid if I planned a trip like that without talking to her first."

Kavan slapped him a high five. "I've only been married a year, but I know better than that."

Ethan scoffed. "Please, Julie understands. Besides, she's my wife, not my mom."

"I can't imagine Julie's going to pat you on the head and say, 'Have a nice time.'" Bobby eyed Ethan as he dropped a few bills on the table. "Dinner is on me today."

Kavan laughed, clapping Ethan on the back as they slid out of the booth. "That may be the last kind thing that happens to you today."

"Come on, you guys, you're overreacting." Ethan waved at Sam and Jarred as they exited, wrestling with the twinge of conviction.

Chapter 10

Julie stood back, hands on her hips, adrenaline pumping. "Should I do it, Sophie?"

The lithe blond puckered her lips. "Yes, you deserve a new car."

"I do, don't I?" Julie walked around the two-seater sports car. It was a little expensive, but not much more than the van Ethan considered buying if they had children.

But we aren't having children. In the past three years, they'd spent the price of the car trying to conceive. *Might as well have something to show for the money we spent.*

She looked at Sophia. "Do I do it?"

"Yes. It's last year's model, you're getting a great deal, and it's an incredible car." Sophia held up her fingers as she ticked off her reasons.

Julie shrugged with excitement and walked around the car. "It's a gorgeous car, but I think our niece's Barbie car is bigger than this one."

Sophia laughed.

The salesman clapped his hands together. "We can use your old car as a down payment. I can get you in this fine car within an hour. It's a great deal. Probably won't be here tomorrow."

Julie chewed her bottom lip. She'd brought the jalopy's title. The salesman said they'd happily tow it from the theater parking lot. Should she call Ethan? But that would ruin the surprise.

She liked the car. A lot. They were both making nice salaries now, especially since Ethan took over the production manager's job at Lambert's Furniture last year. And they wouldn't be spending any more money on medical procedures. *We can manage.* With one last look inside, she asked, "This is the only one? Do you have an automatic?"

The salesman muffled a chuckle. "All of these models come standard with manual transmission. They are made to be driven."

"Oh." Julie wrinkled her nose. She preferred an automatic, but for a car like this, she thought she could get used to shifting gears.

"It's a beaut."

"Yes, it is." Julie followed the salesman to his desk on the showroom floor, determined to make this the first day of the rest of her life. *I'm going to do it.*

Sophia leaned over her shoulder when the salesman took a phone call. "Pick me up for work tomorrow."

Julie grinned up at her. "Should I do this?"

"For crying out loud, yes."

Julie thought of Ethan with his quick wit and decisive actions. If he wanted something, he got it. Now it was her turn. Besides, she'd spent money before, not this much, but they were two successful, working people. And she didn't even count the money Kit estimated she'd make playing spring and summer engagements with the quartet.

Mental note: Tell Ethan about the quartet.

In less than an hour, Julie slipped into the driver's seat and turned the key. As she gripped the wheel, power vibrated up her arms. Grinning up at Sophia, she wondered for a moment if having a baby could ever feel as sensational as this.

A sad *no* resonated in her heart.

"Don't forget to pick me up." Sophia stepped back and waved.

Julie shifted into first and let out the clutch. "See you tomorrow, I hope." The car lurched forward and stalled. She peered up at the salesman. "I can do this."

She maneuvered slowly out of the parking lot under a twilight sky and gingerly shifted out of second gear. *Oh my. . .*

At once, buckets of doubt poured over her. *Did I really do this? Was it the right thing? Ethan's going to kill me. No, I needed a new car. And this was a great deal.* She gripped the wheel as if to ward off panic.

I got tired of waiting. She hugged the curve that led to the White Birch covered bridge. Lights glowed from the house on the hill, warm and inviting.

Grandma and Grandpa Lambert's. She jerked the wheel right and into their driveway, sending a spray of gravel into the air. She prayed she wouldn't stall the car before getting to the top of the hill. When she made it, she sighed with relief and parked by the kitchen door.

"Hello?" Julie called, knocking lightly on the door as she entered.

Grandma Betty welcomed her with a hug and kiss. "Julie, come in."

Julie breathed in her fresh, ironed-cotton scent. "Hi, Grandma."

She wriggled out of her coat and mittens. For as long as she could remember, Grandma Betty was her grandma as much as she was Ethan's.

Grandpa Matt got up from his easy chair. "Pretty Julie. Come on in. It seems the Ethan Lambert household is visiting one at a time this weekend." He propped his book on the end table.

Julie fell into his embrace. "Oh, Grandpa, I think I made a big mistake." She slowly sat on the sofa.

"What's wrong?" Grandpa sat next to her.

Julie opened her mouth to speak, but emotion choked her words. Grandma came in and lowered herself onto the couch next to Julie.

"I'll go make some hot tea," Grandpa said.

"That won't help," Julie mumbled.

Suddenly tears took over. She'd kept it in too long: the pain of barrenness, the strain between her and Ethan, buying a car with a price tag that challenged her annual salary.

Grandma passed her a tissue. "Tell me what's going on."

Julie wiped her face and tucked her hair behind her ears. "It's all wrong. Everything."

"Come now, it can't be all that bad." Grandma picked up her Bible perched on the edge of the coffee table.

"It can be and it is." Julie stared at the ceiling while wiping away tears.

"Here we go." Grandpa bent over Julie's shoulder with a steaming cup of tea in a china saucer. "Since this is an emergency, I microwaved the water to get it done faster."

Light laughter broke the burden of sorrow. "You even put cream in my tea." Julie looked at Grandpa through watery eyes.

"Of course." Grandpa Matt settled in his chair adjacent to the women.

Julie cried softly. She pondered the words she should use to tell her story. *Straightforward,* she decided. *Honest.*

Setting her tea saucer on the table, she propped her forearms on her knees, a ragged tissue between her hands. "Dr. Patterson told me last week I can't have children."

Grandma held her hand tightly.

Julie cleared her throat and continued. "After all we've been through, the trying and waiting, we find out it's almost impossible."

"So that's what Casey wanted," Grandpa muttered.

Julie stood, noticing for the first time the fire crackling in the fireplace. "Dr. Patterson thought Ethan knew, but he didn't. When he found out, he came by the school, angry. We argued and my class saw us. It seems all we do is growl or snap at each other. The last three years have been hard, trying to have a baby. But the doctor's news seemed to expose something we didn't know was there. We've drifted apart and lost our way with each other."

"That kind of news is devastating, Julie. You and Ethan need time to process." Grandma flipped her Bible open to Proverbs. "Here's one of my favorite verses: 'Trust in the Lord with all your heart, and lean not on your own understanding.' "

Julie's voice quivered. "I want to trust Him. I had so much faith as a child, but now He seems so far away."

Grandpa ambled across the room and stirred the fire. "You've let your adult thinking interfere with your faith, Julie. Even an old man like me has to lean on Jesus like a child. Our heavenly Father has good plans for you and Ethan. Learn to submit to His will and trust in Him."

"I know, Grandpa. I want to trust.. . . ." Julie sighed, burying her face in her hands. "There's one more thing."

"Can't be all that bad." Grandpa stirred the embers one last time before returning the fire poker to the holder.

"I bought a new car." Julie sat up straight. "A convertible sports car."

"I see." Grandma clasped her hands over her knees. "And you didn't talk to Ethan first?"

"No," Julie said, resolve replacing her sadness. "Life felt so out of control, I decided I'd do something about it. My old car broke down again, so I bought a new one."

Grandpa sat down in front of Julie, his chin jutted out. "Julie, you and Ethan have been through a lot these last few years. Like you said, focusing on starting a family took its toll on you both."

She met his gaze.

"But your marriage is about more than having children. You two need to work together, communicate, live by Lambert's Code."

Julie tossed her used tissue onto the table. "What's Lambert's Code?"

"Submitting to each another. Yielding. Considering each other's opinion and concerns."

She smirked and said halfheartedly, "Now you tell me."

"Never too late to start," Grandpa said.

"Julie, your identity in life is not in children or cars." Grandma closed her Bible but kept her finger between the pages. "It's about how much Jesus loves you. If all else fails, His love will not."

Julie winced. "I know it in my head; I'm just not confident in my heart."

Grandpa narrowed his eyes and tipped his head to one side. "Did you get a good deal on the car?"

With a half grin, she answered, "As a matter of fact, I did."

Grandma stood. "Julie, pray and ask for understanding on what it means to submit, to yield to one another. You and Ethan should row in unison, not in opposite directions."

She was right. So why did Julie find it so hard to grasp? Why did God's voice seem so far away, so small?

Grandma took Julie's hand and pulled her off the sofa. "It's late. Go home. Talk to your husband."

"All right. Thank you."

At the bottom of the long Lambert driveway, Julie turned right toward the covered bridge instead of left toward home.

She parked the crimson car under the shadows of the old landmark. Lovers' initials were etched in the bridge's wide rafters for all time. EB LOVES LJ. TOMMY LOVES CINDY 12–7–60.

Ethan had climbed to the top and carved their initials into the dark wood ten years ago. Julie wandered the length of the bridge and stood under the spot where she thought he'd made their mark.

With the slow trickle of the river in her ears, she prayed, asking the Lord for wisdom—and a yielded heart.

Chapter 11

Ethan sat in the dim light of the television, flicking through the channels, one after another, looking but not seeing.

The program guide channel told him it was ten thirty, and he grew more agitated with each second that ticked away.

Julie, where are you?

For the second time this month, she didn't answer her cell phone. She couldn't have gone too far with her car parked at the theater. He made a note to have it towed, again, tomorrow.

Out of desperation, he hunted down Sophia's number to see if Julie was with her. Sure enough, she'd seen Julie earlier but had no idea where she was now.

When he heard the small click of the front door, he leaped out of his seat. His emotions rumbled with anger and relief.

"Did you forget your cell phone?" He met her by the hall closet. He fired the question but kept his voice low and steady.

"It was in my purse." Julie eased the closet door shut, her movement stiff, her attitude guarded.

"Where were you? I almost called Jeff."

Julie walked past him with no more explanation. "Is he on duty tonight?" She flipped on the light over the stove and tugged open the refrigerator.

"Where *were* you?" Ethan stood in front of the open refrigerator door and peered into her face.

Julie's posture stiffened. "Excuse me, I want something to eat." She shoved him aside.

The last time she acted like this, she had just found out they couldn't have children. What happened this time?

He touched her arm. "Please tell me where you were. You scare me when you disappear and don't answer your phone."

Julie faced him, her chin high. Wisps of her sleek blond hair, freed from her ponytail, fluttered above her narrowed green eyes.

"I bought a car."

Ethan drew back. His jaw tightened as he held his tone in check. "You bought a car?"

"Yes, I got tired of driving that broken-down heap. Now you know." She brushed past him for the stairs.

Ethan went after her. "How can you buy a car without talking to me?"

"If you wanted something, you'd buy it." She kicked off her winter boots and slipped from her jeans.

"Not something that huge, Jules. Give me some credit. What did you buy?"

"A Honda S2000. They had one of last year's models on the lot. I got a good deal." She lifted her gaze for a split second to meet his, then disappeared into the bathroom and shut the door.

"A Honda S2000? Are you kidding?"

A muffled "No" came through the door.

Ethan balled his fists and took a deep breath. *Lord, help me out here. I want to understand her, but please. . .a Honda S2000?*

He slowly opened the door and propped himself against the door frame. "Julie, why?"

She faced him, wielding her toothbrush in the air. "Oh, I don't know. I can't have a baby, so how 'bout a car? I was tired of that broken-down heap." Julie snapped around to the sink and resumed brushing her teeth.

"Don't be mad at me; I'm trying to understand." Ethan stepped farther into the bathroom. "What are the monthly payments? What's the gas mileage, insurance, and maintenance? Did you make a down payment?"

He watched his wife through the mirror. "Julie?"

She rinsed and dropped her toothbrush into the holder. "They took my old car title as a down payment. Plus, I'll be playing in a quartet with Kit Merewether. That money will help cover the expenses."

"Quartet? What quartet?" Ethan sighed, his anger fading with the realization that his relationship with Julie was on shifting sand. "When will you be doing that?"

She sat on her side of the bed with her brush. "Not sure, but I told her Mondays were best for me."

"Were you going to talk to me about this?"

"Sure, but, Ethan, you're at the rec center most Mondays. What does it matter?" She brushed her thick hair with fast, strong strokes, then crawled into bed and set her alarm. "Were you going to talk to me about your next sports deal thing?"

As a matter of fact, yes. But he was too frustrated to bring up Costa Rica now. "Your clothes are still on the floor."

She sighed and climbed out of bed. She picked up her jeans and top and dropped them over the back of the rocker. She tossed her boots into the closet. "Happy?"

"Yes. Thank you. Where are the keys?"

She got back into bed. "In my purse."

"You knew you were buying a stick shift, right?"

"Yes." She held his gaze.

"You hate driving my—never mind." Ethan took the stairs down two at a time. He grabbed his coat and fished the keys from Julie's handbag.

Outside, snow fell again. *Ah, Lord, the winter of my discontent.* His breath hung in the air like miniclouds, and sure enough, there under the amber glow of the parking lot lights sat a brand-new sports car, the convertible top buried under winter's tears.

❧❧

Julie listened to Ethan's quick, decisive movements as he thundered down the stairs, found her keys, and opened the hall closet.

When the front door slammed, she slipped under the covers and tried not to think of anything, anything at all.

This is not how she meant the night to go. He had a right to know where she was, but Julie had struggled with feeling defensive and irritated during the ride home. When she walked into the apartment, Ethan's tone pushed her to the edge.

Awake in the dark, she tried to put her finger on when the rocky moments became more frequent and more devastating. Their pursuit of a pregnancy strained their marriage instead of bringing them closer. She saw now that they leaned on their own hopes and not the Lord. To deal with the letdowns, they retreated into their own private worlds.

All the time, money, and emotional energy spent trying to conceive seemed to haunt them now. How stressful life became when they lived month to month, year to year, hope giving way to hopelessness, only to hope again. In the end, barrenness was the final judgment.

Julie rolled onto her side, wiping her cheeks with the edge of the pillowcase. Worse than the barrenness of her body was the growing desert between her and Ethan.

"God," Julie whispered in the dark, "I'm sorry about my attitude and that I bought the car without talking to him first—or You."

She pictured Ethan driving the new car, and a wave of guilt splashed against the sandy slope of her emotions. Wasn't she taking charge of her life? Grandpa's code came to mind. *Submit to one another. Yield.* They hadn't lived by that standard in a long time, if ever.

Restless, Julie threw back the covers and crossed the cold hardwood floor to gather her robe and slippers.

Music. She needed music. In the spare bedroom where she practiced and taught her private students, she lifted the cello from its case and rosined her bow.

She played freely, dissonant chords reflecting the sadness of her heart. *This will never do. I need to worship.*

Julie padded to the living room where her Bible sat on the end table. Back in the bedroom, she opened it to the Psalms.

With precise, well-trained movements, she used music to verbalize the words on the page. *"I will lift up my eyes to the hills—from whence comes my help?"*

The cello's soft melodies engaged her heart, and Julie released her burdens as God's Word saturated her soul.

❧❧

Ethan searched the Internet for a weekend retreat in upper New Hampshire or Vermont. He and Julie needed an escape from work, music students, string quartets, bad doctor reports, and impulse car buying.

They needed to huddle up, talk, pray, and map out a new plan for their lives. Ethan regretted the Sundays they'd slept in, ate pancakes and bacon for breakfast, and read the paper instead of worshiping God at White Birch Community Church. Now that he needed God's strength and wisdom in his life, he realized the shallowness of his reserve.

A light knock on the office door drew his attention. "Grandpa. Come in." He stood, smiling.

Grandpa moved past his outstretched hand and embraced him. "Working hard?"

Ethan sighed. "Pretending to."

Grandpa sat in the adjacent chair. "How do you like your new car?"

Ethan rocked back in his desk chair. "You mean Julie's new car?"

Grandpa nodded once. "I saw her sporting around town in that thing. Very nice."

"Sure it's nice. It'll cost us a week of her salary every month."

It had been over a week since Julie came home with her new toy, and the atmosphere in the apartment was cordial but chilly.

Grandpa whistled. "I suppose you're keeping it."

Ethan stood and stretched, then perched on the edge of his desk. "We have to. She has no other means of transportation. Plus, with the depreciation of the car once the tires hit the streets, we'd lose money if we traded it in. It's not worth arguing over anymore."

"You figure out Lambert's Code yet?" Grandpa regarded Ethan as he asked the million-dollar question.

"Other than submit to one another?" Ethan searched his grandfather's face for the keys to his wisdom. "I have an idea, I think."

Grandpa gave Ethan another single nod. "What's on your computer screen?" The older Lambert got up and walked around the desk.

Ethan enlarged the view with a mouse click. "Looking for a weekend away for Julie and me. I thought we could ski."

Grandpa slapped him on the back. "Good thinking."

Ethan peered up at him. "Am I on track for cracking the code?"

Grandpa rocked back on his heels. "You're on your way. But it's more than a weekend ski trip."

Ethan grinned. "Good to know."

"Dig deeper, son. By the way, Will owns a cabin up north. Why don't you ask him if you can use it?"

Ethan brightened. "I forgot about Will's cabin. That'd be nice and inexpensive."

"Don't know about nice, but certainly inexpensive. If you ask me, you have other business to take care of with Julie besides skiing."

Ethan chuckled, but he didn't need a mirror to tell him a red hue crept across his cheeks.

Chapter 12

Julie lay in Ethan's arms, gazing at the glowing embers of the fire. The heat from the wide stone fireplace warmed her face and hands. The biggest log crackled and started to burn.

"This was a great idea, babe," she said, lifting her eyes to see his face.

He kissed the top of her head while weaving her hair through his fingers. "I imagined some place nicer, but—"

Julie snickered. "Will told you it was a hunting cabin."

"It's a dump." Ethan grinned at her.

"Come on, it has a fireplace and plenty of rustic character. What more do we need?"

Ethan drew her to him and kissed her cheek, then her lips. "All I need is right here, in my arms. Kings envy me."

"And the queens?" Julie tweaked the square end of his chin.

"Queens envy you. You're beautiful."

Julie loved the word *beautiful* coming from his lips. The word skipped across her mind and into her heart.

"Julie?"

"Hmm?" She felt so peaceful it was hard to stay awake.

"Want to talk about anything? Babies, cars?"

Julie's heart thumped. For a minute, she'd managed to forget.

"No." She sat up and drew her knees to her chin, staring at the fire. The large log burned steadily.

Ethan scooted closer to her. "I think we should."

Julie pondered the events of the past few weeks.

"How are you dealing with this new curve in our life? Really dealing."

She grinned. "Besides buying sports cars?"

He nuzzled her cheek. "Yes."

"How do you deal with a heartbreak this deep? With a dream that will never come true?"

"I wonder the same thing." Ethan rose from the pallet and ambled to the dented fridge situated in the corner of the room. "I feel disappointed and sad, not sure where to go from here."

Julie sensed his sadness. "That's how I feel." *Guilty, too.* No matter what Ethan said about them being in this together, it was her body that betrayed them.

"You never told me why you bought the car, especially *that* car." Ethan bent to look in the fridge. "Do you want something?"

"No, I'm fine."

"So why?" Ethan asked again, returning to their pallet with a soda in his hand.

Julie shrugged. "Life was changing, out of my control. I wanted to forget the past and press on to the future."

Ethan leaned against the couch cushions. "Oddly enough, Jules, that makes sense to me. I'm sorry I couldn't see it."

"I'm sorry I didn't tell you how I felt. It's hard to speak my heart sometimes." She grabbed his hand and kissed the back of it.

Ethan smoothed her fingers with his. "Your parents will take it hard."

Julie moved to lay her head on his chest. "Do you want to adopt?"

He curled his arm around her. "It's an option, but I. . .*we* have to have a heart to adopt, don't we? I don't want to adopt and say, 'Problem solved,' unless we know that's a right choice for us."

Julie tipped her head to see his face. By his tone and words, she could tell he'd pondered the situation.

"I agree," she said, almost in a whisper.

"I was so confident we'd get pregnant again. Now I realize the miscarriage the first year of marriage—"

"We didn't even realize I was pregnant." Julie lifted her head. "Do you think if we'd known, maybe I wouldn't have lost the baby?" The idea stirred her adrenaline.

"No, I don't. What could we have done differently?"

But the notion stuck in Julie's head. "I could have eaten better or taken vitamins. I think we averaged about six hours of sleep a night that summer." More guilt surfaced and clung to her soul like seaweed on the shore.

Ethan held up his hand. "Stop. Julie, there's nothing you could have done. We didn't know."

For a few seconds, Julie relived that one hot night nine years ago when she discovered she was pregnant and losing a baby at the same time. The joy was crushed by the heartache.

"I wonder how different our lives would be if that child had lived."

"Don't go there, sweetie. We can't know. Besides, God has plans for us, right?"

"I want to believe He does." Julie scooted over to the fireplace and wedged another log on the fire. She hated to see the hot embers die.

When she returned to Ethan, he pulled her down to him.

She laughed. "You have that look in your eye, Ethan Lambert."

He kissed her, brushing her hair from her face. "What look?"

"You know what look." Julie returned Ethan's kiss and let her worries melt away in the light of the fire.

❧❧

Ethan made a breakfast of pancakes, eggs, and bacon on a two-burner hot plate. Julie curled up in a chair to watch, amused, wrapped in a thick blanket.

"You're ready for your own cooking show, Eth."

He grabbed the handle of the griddle and let go with a yelp. "Hot!"

Julie guffawed and slapped her leg.

Ethan grimaced, puffing on his hand with quick, short breaths. "Can Your Highness get some snow for my poor hand?"

Julie hopped up and found Will's old tin bucket and filled it with snow. "Dunk your hand in this."

"Ah, that's better."

"I guess those cheap burners don't heat evenly."

Ethan gaped at her. "Ya think?"

She popped him on the arm. "Don't be smart."

When he leaned to kiss her, the bucket of snow slid off the short counter. Cold snow covered Julie's slippers.

"Watch it, Eth." She laughed and bumped into him, kicking off her slippers.

"Julie, watch out for—"

With a loud clatter, the skillets tumbled to the floor. Half-cooked eggs and pancake batter oozed across the rough-hewn wood and dripped between the cracks.

All they could do was laugh and laugh.

An hour later, after frying up what was left of the eggs and batter, they stepped outside into cold, crisp air.

Julie drew a deep breath, the bright sunlight illuminating her face. "I wish I'd brought my cello. I'd put this moment to music."

Ethan pulled on his gloves. "What would it sound like?"

Julie thought for a moment and hummed a few low, smooth notes. "Something like that."

"I like it." He motioned to where a white snowy thread snaked through the trees. "Will said this path goes down to a creek."

Julie took his hand. "Let's go see."

Snow crunched under their boots as they walked, resonating in the stillness. Contentment fortified Ethan. They needed this weekend away so they could talk without tension, without argument.

A sharp gust cut through the trees. The wind carried Julie's scent and made him think of summer flowers. She'd showered that morning in the closetlike room Will dared to call a bathroom, then dried her hair by the fire. Watching her, his heart beat with awakened love.

"I'm sorry about the car." Julie's green eyes shifted from the narrow path to him.

"Babe, it's over. I wanted to get us back on track financially before getting you out of that old heap."

"Whose financial track, Ethan?" Julie fell into him.

"Mine, I guess." He grabbed her around the waist.

"Should we sell the car?" She started the monkey walk.

Ethan fell in step with her. "No, we're upside down on the value right now.

We're going to be apartment dwellers a little longer than we planned." He stepped on her toes.

"Watch it, klutz." She laughed and tried to step on his booted foot.

"Okay, Bigfoot." He skipped out of her way.

She was silent for a moment, then said, "I really thought I was taking command of my life—" Her words trailed off.

"You took command all right." Deep down, he was sort of proud of her. This side of his wife rarely surfaced, and he liked it—only he wished it didn't cost them so much.

She faced him, chin jutted out. "All right, Eth, that's it."

"What? I—"

Before he knew it, she wrapped her arms around his waist and kicked his feet out from under him. He tumbled to the snowy ground, hollering, taking her with him. Suddenly cold snow slipped down his back.

"Hey, whoa, cold, very cold." Ethan scrambled away, molding a snowball on the run. He lobbed the white bomb at Julie.

"Missed me, missed me, now you gotta kiss me." She danced a jig, making faces at him.

"Oh really? Now you've done it." Ethan charged her, determined to take her challenge.

"Ack! Ethan, wait." Her laughter rang out like a thousand tiny bells as she tried to run.

Ethan lassoed her with his arms and kissed her with all the emotion his heart contained.

The creek turned out to be a trickle with not much to see. Ethan took a few pictures with the digital camera he'd stored in his coat pocket. He set the timer, propped the camera on a tree stump, and ran over to where Julie posed. Looking through the snapshots, the top of his head was missing in all of them.

"Hmm, I wonder if God is trying to tell you something." Julie jabbed at him with her fingers, chuckling.

"That I'm a bad photographer?" Ethan deleted the worst of the shots. One, he thought, was worth saving. He wanted a visual memory of this day.

"No, that you're losing your head." She bumped into him, laughing.

"Funny." He bumped her back.

The sun burned high overhead as they walked back to the cabin. Inside, the fire still crackled and warmed the small cabin.

"Come here." Ethan motioned for Julie to join him at the hearth. "Grandpa's been talking to me about Lambert's Code."

"Submitting to one another?"

Ethan raised a brow. "I see he's talked to you, too."

"Yes, right after I bought the car."

"I'm not sure I understand completely, but I want to try. I guess we could communicate better, stop living so independently, consider each other, and remember being married means we each give a hundred percent, not fifty-fifty."

Julie regarded him, serious. "No more surprise championship rematches or unplanned stops by the plant?"

"No surprising me with convertibles or string quartets. Don't hide the doctor's bad news from me."

"Please, what could possibly be worse than what we already heard?" Julie brushed his brown waves with her fingers.

"Something that could take you away from me." Ethan peered into her eyes. "I couldn't bear it."

She snuggled next to him. "Me neither."

He reclined on the blanket pallet, stretching his long legs before the fire.

Julie lay down beside him. "We need to fellowship with other Christians, too."

He nodded in agreement. "I admit I've missed a few too many Sundays and am a little overly sports-minded."

"A little? Ha!" Julie rested her hand on his thick chest. "Sometimes I think you love ESPN more than me."

"How can you say that? Don't you know, Julie?" Emotion choked his words. "There's no one like you, Ethan."

❧❧

Monday evening, Julie parked Ethan's car in front of Kit Merewether's home. He laughed at her when she packed her cello and kissed him good-bye.

"Where you going with that thing?"

"Practice at Kit's."

"How are you getting there?"

Julie made a face at him. "My car."

Ethan crossed his arms, waiting. Julie grimaced when realization dawned. Her little two-seater would never do. "Ethan, may I borrow your car?" How could she buy a car that was too small for her cello?

"Certainly." His wide grin remained on his face as he gave her the keys and helped wedge the cello case into the backseat.

Kit's home glowed with low lights and candles. Trays of finger foods waited on the dining room table.

"Good evening, all." Julie embraced Cassie Ferguson and Mike Chason.

"Good evening, Julie."

The first fifteen minutes, they snacked and talked, catching up on each other's lives. Kit briefed them on her plan for the group. She wanted to play weddings, receptions, parties, and festivals.

At last Kit picked up her viola and tapped her bow lightly on her music stand. "Let's get going, shall we?"

Julie patted her cello case. "Give me a second, Kit."

The quartet played together like seasoned musicians, as if they'd played together for years. They laughed at their blunders and complimented each other's musicianship.

Toward the end of the evening, while they finished the plate of cheese and crackers, Kit announced their first engagement opportunity.

"I wanted to hear how we sounded together, but, ladies and gentleman"—she nodded at Mike—"we've been invited to play at a wedding."

"Where?"

"When?"

Kit smiled. Her youthful face concealed her age. "Florida. Three weeks from now. Julie, I think it times perfectly with spring break. You may need to take an extra day off. Is that okay?"

"Yes, that would be fine." *Florida? Away from winter winds and mountains of snow?* Julie loved the idea. She'd lift her face to the sun and squish the soggy sand between her toes.

Kit explained. "My cousin is getting married for the umpteenth time. She booked a quartet that had to back out. I mentioned our little group, and she invited us down. It's a paying engagement."

Enough said. They agreed with one voice to go. To prepare, Kit planned an extra practice every week until they left.

"Thursdays? Does that work for everyone?"

Driving home after discussing the trip to Florida, Julie looked forward to telling Ethan about her evening and of the Merewether Quartet's first engagement. She'd have the new car paid off in no time.

Ever since their weekend retreat, their communication was better, though they still seemed to go about their own business.

The code was not so easy to crack, they decided.

How did we let ourselves get so far out of balance? Julie wondered. But deep down, she knew the answer. They grew older and matured but forgot to bring their marriage forward with them.

Then the focus became children. So much mental and emotional energy spent on talking about children, making medical decisions—which treatments to try, which ones to avoid. Did they have the money? Should they continue when the desired results eluded them?

They sifted through all the parental and family advice, heard her parents yearn for a grandchild. But that was behind them now, at least for a while, Julie thought, turning into the apartment complex. What did God have in store for them? She unlocked the front door. "Ethan?" She lugged her cello to the spare room. "Babe?" He wasn't in the den or upstairs.

She found a note in the kitchen.

Met Will at Sam's for dessert.

Love you.
E

Julie peered down into the parking lot. Sure enough, Ethan had taken her car.

His ferocious bark about the new car morphed quickly to halfhearted yips. He drove the sporty machine at every opportunity.

Grinning, Julie wandered into the den to check the answering machine. A single red light flashed. She pressed PLAY.

"Ethan, Steve Tripleton. Just checking to see if you got the itinerary for Costa Rica. I had my secretary e-mail you—"

Julie pressed STOP, her heart thumping. What itinerary? Costa Rica?

Chewing her bottom lip, she pulled open the top desk drawer. *Should I look in his stuff?* With the tips of her fingers, she pulled the drawer out farther.

There, on top of the neat pile, she spotted a colorful brochure and the itinerary. She picked it up and scanned for the date. April seventeenth.

Fuming, she slammed the drawer shut.

Chapter 13

Jules, I'm back." Ethan hung his coat in the closet and strolled toward the office to toss the spare S2000 keys in the desk. "Jules?"

She came downstairs with her hair wrapped in a towel and green goop on her face. Ethan snickered. "There's my beauty queen."

He maneuvered to slip his arms around her, but she stepped out of his embrace. "Ethan, do you have anything you need to tell me?" She took a bottle of water from the fridge and went to the living room.

Ethan watched her walk away. Even when she was angry, her body motion, fluid and coordinated, reminded him of a symphony. She'd have been a great athlete.

"Okay, what's up?" He reviewed the evening in his head. They had a nice dinner together before she went to quartet practice. He borrowed her car to meet Will for pie, but he didn't think she would be upset about that since she had his car. So why the cold shoulder?

She regarded him for a second, water bottle in her hand, then disappeared in the den. When she returned, she dropped his Costa Rica itinerary and the resort brochure on the kitchen counter.

He slapped his hand against his forehead. "The golf trip? That's what you're upset about?" He picked up the printed Web pages.

"Were you planning to tell me about this trip or just send me a postcard once you got down there? 'Sorry, babe, I won't be home for dinner.'"

"Funny. Of course I was going to tell you."

"When?"

He shrugged. "Soon, I guess." He really didn't have an answer. He'd forgotten about it. But the excuse sounded lame, even to him.

"Ethan, what was that speech up at the cabin? Let's communicate, submit to each other, and remember we're married. No more fifty-fifty, but a hundred percent. Here you are, going on vacation without me, your wife."

"It's not a vacation; it's a golf trip."

"Don't patronize me, Ethan."

"I'm not. Don't mother me."

"Mother you? I can't ask why you're going to Costa Rica with Steve Tripleton?"

"How did you find out?"

"He left you a message. Wanted to know if you got the itinerary." He could see her shaking. "How come you didn't tell me this last weekend?"

"I don't know." He shrugged without reason. "I was up to my eyeballs in snow.

I wasn't thinking about sunny golf trips."

"Do you expect me to believe you accidentally forgot to tell your wife you were going on a five-day golf vacation to Central America?"

"No, well, yes. I did forget. And I expect you to believe your husband was going to tell you, eventually." Ethan rubbed his hand over the back of his head. He didn't expect to come home to this.

"So was that big speech just for me? You can do whatever you want, spend whatever money you want, but I can't?"

"You know that's not it, Julie." He felt on the defensive and didn't like it.

"How are you paying for this?"

"Well, savings."

"Without asking me? What about getting on track financially?" She stood in the same place, the same position she did when she brought out the trip info. She had yet to take a sip of her water. "I bought a car; you bought fun."

"Do you really want to compare price tags?" Ethan picked up her water and downed half the bottle. "And I was going to tell you."

Hands on her hips, Julie asked, "Who are you going with? Besides Steve."

"Your dad, actually, and Will."

"You're ashamed of me." The words came out of nowhere.

Ethan regarded her, not sure he'd heard correctly. "I'm not ashamed of you. Where'd that come from?"

"There goes Miss Julie, barren and silly, buys fancy cars 'cause she won't ever have a baby. One day she'll be an old lady with a hundred cats." Julie moved from the living room into the kitchen and jerked another water from the refrigerator.

"That's ridiculous and you know it. Do you remember last weekend at all?" Ethan still smiled when pictures of their romantic escape popped into his head: cozy nights in front of the fire, the snowball fight, and trekking through the woods to see a trickle of water Will called a creek.

"Do I remember? The question is, do you remember? How is it possible that sometime during that weekend, our walks, our talks, the drive up to the cabin, it never occurred to you to tell me about the trip?"

"I get it, okay? I get it. I'm a cad, so sue me." Ethan flung his empty water bottle in the trash. "I forgot."

"Sophia was right. You are a cad."

"You talked to Sophia about this?"

"No, that's her general opinion."

"You have friends who think I'm a cad?"

"Get over yourself. You just admitted to being one." Julie unwrapped the towel from her head as she went toward the stairs. "You broke your word, Ethan." She bounded up and out of his sight.

❧❧

When Ethan came upstairs, Julie announced, "I'm going to Florida with Kit and the quartet."

She dropped a washcloth under warm water and hung her towel on the towel bar.

"Florida? When and what for?" Ethan stood behind her, hands on his hips.

"In three weeks. To play for her cousin's wedding." Julie wrung out the cloth and pressed it against her face.

"And there's no discussion. You're just doing it."

Wiping the green mask off her face, Julie patted her face dry with a hand towel. "Yes. Just like you and Costa Rica."

"When did you find out about this?"

"Tonight, as a matter of fact. Kit offered our services when the quartet her cousin hired canceled." Julie flipped her hair over her head and clicked on the hair dryer. *He makes me so mad. . . . Lambert's Code, indeed. I have to live up to it, but he doesn't.*

The hair dryer stopped. Julie bolted up to see Ethan with the plug in his hand.

"What are you doing?" She jerked the plug from him and stuck it back in the socket.

"I was talking to you."

She resisted the temptation to click the machine back on. With her jaw clenched, she set her brush and hair dryer down and walked into the bedroom.

"Talk." She flopped down on the bed.

"Right, like you're going to listen." Ethan stood tall, away from the bed.

Julie struggled against the tears. But her emotions, tender and weak, buckled under the stress. Would their struggle ever end? The chasm looming between them seemed irreparable. Just when things were going well, another issue surfaced, bringing past hurts with it. "You started this, Ethan."

"No, you started this with that car purchase."

"Which, I note, you don't mind driving every chance you get."

"That's not the point."

"Are you saying you scheduled the trip to Costa Rica because I bought the car?"

Ethan propped his elbow on the chest of drawers. "No. I scheduled it—" He stopped.

Julie slipped off the bed. "You scheduled it before the car?" Realization dawned. "That night at Mom and Dad's."

"I don't want you to go to Florida."

"Why not?" She stood in front of him, arms crossed.

"Because we're arguing and stressing. Stay here—work on our relationship."

"Okay, then don't go to Costa Rica." Seemed simple enough to her.

"I already put down money."

"Ah, I see. You can do what you want, but I can't."

"No, Julie. Don't put words in my mouth. I'm just saying I've already paid money."

She stared into his brown eyes for a long moment. Her bottom lip quivered, but she had a clear mind when she said, "We need a break, Ethan."

He sighed, running his hand through his dark waves. "You're right. Let's take a night together this week." He stepped toward her and gripped her hand with his hands.

"No, we need a break from each other." The words sank like heavy boulders into her heart.

He squeezed her fingers. "What do you mean?"

Clarity braced her. She knew what she had to do. "Ethan, since we've been married, all we planned for was our future children and buying an old farmhouse off Craven Hill Road. Now that we don't have that plan anymore, all we do is pick and fight with each other."

"So running off to Florida is going to solve that?"

"No, I'm not talking about just Florida. I'm going to ask Bobby and Elle if I can stay with them until I go."

"What?"

"You heard me."

"Until you go to Florida? That's three weeks away."

She weakened but kept to her decision. "Ethan, we, I, need to get away and think."

"Without me?"

"Without you."

❧❧

Ethan positioned his car next to the White Birch covered bridge. Flashlight in hand, he zipped up his jacket and wished he'd remembered a pair of gloves. But even fur-lined leather mitts wouldn't help against the cold he felt. No, his cold feelings came from the inside, not New Hampshire's winter night.

He strolled onto the bridge, the beam of the flashlight covering the ground in front of him. Inside the covered bridge, he ran the light along the length of the rafters, remembering the April evening he'd asked Julie to marry him and how he fell when he tried to carve their initials in the heavy crossbeams.

Why is it that I'm at odds with the woman I love more than anything?

An icy breeze cut its way under the bridge. Ethan hunched against the cold. It had been a long time since he leaned on his God for help, but he knew he had no place else to turn.

"Father, what do I do? I've really bungled things with Julie."

The image of his wife crying hit his heart as he prayed.

"How do we get out of this mess?" Ethan hung his head. The flashlight beam illuminated the ground around his feet. *Staying with Bobby and Elle. . .I need to get away and think.*

It seemed unreal. The events of the past few weeks eclipsed the years of happiness he shared with Julie. Ethan hated that.

He stayed on the bridge praying until the cold got to him. He fumbled for his keys as he hustled to the car, slipping on the bridge's edge where ice had formed.

A few minutes later, Ethan knocked on the front door of the Lamberts' home on the hill. He checked his watch and winced. Ten o'clock. *Is it too late?*

Grandma opened the door with a big smile. "Ethan, what a nice surprise. Come on in. It's cold."

"Who is it, Bet?" Grandpa made his way from the living room, book dangling from his hand. "Ethan, my boy, you're out late."

"Matt, put another log on the fire."

Ethan walked into the living room. His grandparents bustled about, moving in different directions yet seemingly synchronized. Grandpa tossed a log onto the fire, and Grandma worked in the kitchen making hot chocolate.

"Your dad and mom were over for dinner tonight," Grandpa said as he returned to his chair, slipping a bookmark into his book.

"Mom mentioned it." Ethan stood in the middle of the living room, lost.

"Are you going to stand all night?" Grandpa motioned toward the couch.

Ethan removed his coat and took a seat on the sofa.

"I'll bet you didn't come here to see what your grandma made for dinner, did you?"

Ethan grinned. "No, not really, but what did she make?"

"Her pot roast." Grandpa smacked his lips and patted his belly.

"Sorry I missed it." Normally the idea of feasting on one of Grandma's roast beef sandwiches would have Ethan dashing for the kitchen. But tonight, anxiety filled him.

For a few minutes, he and Grandpa talked Lambert's Furniture business. The new warehouse plans had been approved, and Will scheduled the groundbreaking for the spring.

"Will's doing a great job. I couldn't be more proud of you boys."

Ethan nodded, feeling more shame than pride at the moment. He could run the production department of Lambert's Furniture without a hitch—organized and efficient. But he couldn't do the same with his marriage.

"Here we are." Grandma rounded the corner with a tray of steaming mugs. "Hot chocolate and cookies."

Ethan reached for his mug, though he didn't feel like he could drink it.

"What's on your mind, Ethan?" Grandma perched on the edge of her chair.

What's not on my mind? "Not much."

" 'Not much' didn't bring you here at ten o'clock at night."

Ethan looked into his grandma's pretty face with her bow lips and sparkling blue eyes. He'd always wanted his daughter to have those features of Grandma Betty.

"Julie and I—" His voice broke.

Grandpa and Grandma waited patiently while he gathered his emotions. Ethan got up and paced in a circle. "I planned a golf trip to Costa Rica and didn't tell her."

Grandpa let out a whistle. "I see you still haven't figured out Lambert's Code."

Ethan regarded him. "Apparently not."

"Matt, let him finish." Grandma shushed Grandpa with a wave of her hand.

Ethan stopped in front of the fire, the weekend at Will's cabin breezing across his mind. "Then she tells me she's going to Florida with Kit Merewether's quartet. I told her I didn't want her to go, and she told me she wanted a break from me."

"What does that mean?" Grandma asked.

Ethan explained Julie's plan. "She's going to stay with Bobby and Elle until she leaves for Florida. I was so angry I came to the bridge to think and pray."

"Sit over here, Ethan." Grandma reached across and patted the sofa cushion. Ethan obeyed.

"Your grandpa and I went through a hard time early on in our marriage. We couldn't agree on anything." Grandma chuckled, with a look in her eye that told Ethan she was viewing images from her past.

Grandpa took up the story. "We'd just moved back from Boston. I felt pretty humble over not making it at Harvard, knowing Betty worked harder than I did to make a life for us there."

Ethan settled back, listening, letting his soul exhale.

Grandma nodded. "We lived with my parents. I thought since I'd worked so diligently in Boston, I could make decisions without your grandpa's input. My father employed both of us at his mill, and I often gave directions to the workers that directly opposed Matt's."

Grandpa laughed. "We charged one customer three different prices for the same cut of lumber."

"Oh, and at home, he'd help me with the dinner dishes, telling me I didn't wash them right."

"Didn't you have Aunt Barbara by then, Grandma?"

She sipped her cocoa and nodded. "Yes, my mother watched her so I could work. We were saving money for a house."

"Then I had an idea for making a piece of furniture," Grandpa said, winking at Betty. "I took our savings and bought new tools, figuring if I could produce a table fast enough and cheap enough, we could open a side business."

"Ah, the birth of Lambert's Furniture." Ethan had heard variations of this story many, many times over the years but never tired of hearing them.

"I became pregnant with your dad and pressed your grandpa to buy our dream house," Grandma added.

"What a face-off we had the night she found out we only had a fourth of our savings left."

Grandma recounted the rest of the story. Absently, her finger traced the rim of her mug. "It's funny now, but then, land-a-mercy. I asked where all the money went, and your grandpa takes me down to my parents' basement and shows me a couple slabs of wood, some shiny equipment, and tells me this stuff is going to buy me the best house in all of White Birch."

Ethan imagined the scene they described, two strong forces like Grandpa and Grandma colliding. He shook his head and said, "Couldn't have been pretty."

"Oh no." Grandma glanced at Grandpa. "I had Barbara in my arms, but before I said another word, I walked upstairs, handed her to my mother, and told her to leave the house."

Grandpa smiled. "She came back down with an invisible rolling pin in her hand and verbally beat me with it." He raised his mug to Grandma. "I bow to the master."

"Shush, Matt. It was a horrible, horrible argument."

Serious, Ethan asked, "How'd you work it out?"

"Well, we went our separate ways and barely spoke for about a week," Grandpa answered. "I had pride issues and thought I'd conquered them, but my soul still harbored that dark sin. Finally the Lord tapped my heart and said, 'Matt, are you loving your wife?' I said, 'No, Lord, I'm not.' I dropped to my knees and begged God to lead me out of that mess."

Ethan's ears tingled. Grandpa's words echoed his own heart's cry tonight on the bridge.

"That night, reading my devotions, I came across Ephesians 5, and verse 21 jumped off the page: 'Submitting to one another.' "

A light dawned for Ethan. "Lambert's Code."

Grandma nodded. "Lambert's Code. The Lord spoke the same thing to me. I had to do some repenting and submitting of my own."

"So what do Julie and I do?" Ethan had an idea but wasn't sure where to start.

"These things take time, son. Your grandma and I knew we had to submit one to another and walk in our respective husband and wife roles. It took a few years to live it out." Grandpa's narrow gaze told Ethan he spoke to him man-to-man.

Ethan paced again, wandering the length of the grand living room. "We had this plan, you know. Get married, have children, be like you and Grandma and like my mom and dad. Then she miscarried, and we decided to go to school, get established, thinking we had plenty of time for a family."

"That's not your issue, Ethan." Grandpa cut to the chase.

Ethan faced him. "What's our issue?"

"You two started with an idyllic perspective of married life. Getting to where your grandma and I are, where your parents are, takes work. It doesn't just happen. You and Julie just wanted it to happen. You can't live separate lives. How many times have you been over here in the last six months without Julie? A dozen, I bet. She has her music. You have sports. Add to that the strain of trying to conceive while rowing toward different shores. Why are you surprised at the wedges in your relationship?"

Ethan perched on the hearth. Grandpa didn't mince his words, and finding out Ethan wasn't the husband he thought he'd be made him uncomfortable. "We thought it would be simple. We'd buy a house, have lots of kids, and be a family."

"A baby doesn't make a family. You and Julie make the family. Babies come into the family you two establish." Grandma collected Grandpa's empty mug. Ethan's mug sat on the coffee table, untouched. "And if marriage were easy, there'd be no divorce."

"I never thought of it like that—the kid thing, I mean." Ethan mulled over Grandma's words. He liked the thought of Julie and him being a family, a real family. Not two people waiting.

"Go home. Call your wife. Get Lambert's Code in motion, but give it time, Ethan. You didn't get here in a day. You're not going to get out of it in a day." Grandpa stretched and reached for his book.

As Ethan stepped into the night, the moon high overhead lit a path for him in the darkness.

Chapter 14

Julie picked up the phone, tired, angry, weary of the upheaval. Discovering the Costa Rica trip revealed a surprise emotion—resentment.

Please be awake, she thought as she dialed.

"Hello?" The strong yet soft voice of Elle Adams answered.

"Hi, Elle. Can I come over?"

"Certainly."

Julie scurried to change into sweats and slip on her boots. She packed her overnight bag, not sure how to break the news to Elle that she wanted to stay for a few weeks.

Driving over to the Adamses' house, Julie poured out her heart to the Lord. "I'm not sure at all if I'm doing the right thing, but I need a break, God. I'm so tired, so *resentful.* How did I not know?"

Julie pulled into the driveway and the porch light clicked on. Elle opened the front door and stepped onto the porch.

"Oh, Elle, nothing is right." Julie fell into her arms.

Elle hugged her close. "I haven't seen you this upset since that time in high school when you thought Ethan was going to break up with you."

Inside, Julie flopped onto the couch. "I'm sorry to bother you so late. I'm sure Bobby's not thrilled."

Elle waved off the comment. "This time of night is his prayer time. I haven't seen him in over an hour."

Julie dropped her head against the back of the couch. "Maybe he can pray for me."

Elle curled up next to her. "What's troubling you?"

"What's *not* troubling me?" Julie rattled off the list of issues weighing down her heart, from being barren, to the arguments with Ethan, to the realization that she was resentful. "I told him I was going to stay with you guys until I left for Florida."

Elle was silent. Julie chewed her bottom lip while studying Elle's thoughtful yet serious expression.

"You and Ethan are looking to each other and children to meet needs only God can meet."

"What do you mean?" Julie slipped out of her coat, then shifted to see Elle better.

"You've always wanted children. That was going to be some life fulfillment."

Julie nodded. They wanted children, and deep down, that desire filled a void

201

in her heart. Growing up as an only child. . .

"Then you miscarried, so you decided to focus on school and careers."

"We thought we should be doing something instead of waiting around for the next baby. Get financially prepared."

"Right, but you still had the expectation. You expect Ethan to meet all your needs. When he doesn't, you withdraw. Even more so these past few years while you tried to get pregnant."

Julie clenched one of the throw pillows. Did Elle's assessment have merit? "What about Ethan?"

"He withdraws but does big-kid things like play basketball three nights a week."

"Or plan golf trips to Costa Rica."

Elle nodded. "And you get resentful of his actions."

"I never realized it before, but I resent his ability to accept our situation and move on, while I carry this guilt and burden of barrenness. It's not fair."

"Life is not fair. You can't blame Ethan."

"But I do." Julie sat forward, chin in her hand.

"Remember, Jesus tells us to abide in Him," Elle began. "Apart from Him, we can't do anything. Jesus is the only one who can meet your needs and heal your disappointments, Julie. No one person can satisfy like He can."

Abide in Him. She'd love to be confident in her relationship with Jesus. She imagined that submitting to one another, submitting to God's plans, and giving up resentment would come easy if she was sure of Jesus' love.

Footfalls echoed down the hallway. Bobby entered the room. "Julie, nice surprise." He bent down to give her a hug.

"Marriage troubles, Bob," Elle said.

"Will and I thought Ethan seemed preoccupied lately. This about the baby issue?"

Julie sighed. "And cars, and clothes on the floor, dishes in the sink, trips to Costa Rica."

Bobby sat in the chair adjacent to the couch. "Did he tell you about Costa Rica?"

"Only after I found the tickets."

Bobby exhaled with a whistle. "We warned him."

Hearing that Ethan ignored wise counsel recharged her resentment. "So should I go to Florida with the quartet? Take a break?"

"Pray about it, Julie," Elle advised, then explained the situation to her husband.

"Bobby, what do you think?" Julie glanced at the Lambert cousin.

"Just be sure you do it with a right heart. Let Ethan know how you feel. Don't go out of spite, Jules. Most relationships go through adjustments."

"May I stay here for a while?"

Elle looked at Bobby. Finally he said, "Call him. Don't hide from him, Julie.

I won't promise how long you can stay. I don't want to make it easy for you to avoid working out your problems with Ethan."

"I understand. Thank you."

❧❧

Sitting at his desk, creating a project schedule to reflect recent orders, Ethan could not concentrate. Today, Julie left for Florida in a van with Kit, Cassie, and Mike.

The past few weeks she'd spent at Bobby and Elle's wore on him. They'd met and talked, but the conversation usually ended in a gridlock.

The night he came home from Grandma and Grandpa's, all ready with his Lambert's Code speech, submitting one to another, he was sure she would surrender her trip to Florida. He never thought she'd really leave for Elle and Bobby's.

Will knocked on Ethan's office door, pulling his thoughts into the present. "Are you going down to say good-bye to her?"

"I said all I'm going to say."

"Come on, Ethan." Will looked his watch. "If you go now, you can kiss her good-bye. Kit's place is only about fifteen minutes away."

"If I go now, we'll argue, and I don't want her to leave upset. We've done enough of that."

"Then don't argue with her," Will said.

Ethan met Will's gaze. "Lately it happens whether I want it to or not."

❧❧

Julie fiddled with her watch, hoping to see Ethan's Honda zip around the corner any second.

The last six days had gone by in a blur as she prepared to leave for Florida, arranging for a substitute teacher next Monday and Tuesday, preparing lesson plans, and driving to Kit's most evenings for practice.

"Hey, Julie, hand me your suitcase." Mike stretched his hand toward her.

Julie lugged the large leather case over to the van where Mike and Kit loaded up a small trailer. As soon as they closed the trailer doors, Julie knew Kit would clap her hands and declare, "Wagon ho!"

South. Sun. Warmth. Julie tipped her head back to see the gathering New Hampshire clouds, gray and ominous. A sharp wind blew across her face, and she knew there'd be snowfall by midday.

It was hard to imagine that behind the heavy clouds the sun blazed against a blue sky. It'd been weeks since the sun broke over White Birch.

Ethan, please come. Julie fingered her cell phone, debating whether to call him. She wanted to hear his voice but didn't want to argue.

Their curt conversation from last night echoed in her head.

"Julie," he'd told her, "we have to live by Lambert's Code."

"So you've said. But just what is that, Ethan?"

Arms akimbo, he'd answered, "Submitting to one another. Yielding what we want for the good of both of us."

"Both of us?" Julie sat on the couch in the formal living room, head in her hands. She'd struggled with resentment each time he visited.

"Both, I guess." He leaned against the pass-through to the dining room, his eyes intent on a painting that hung on the south wall.

"So how do we do that?" she'd asked.

"Don't go to Florida." He must have said that a dozen times in the last week.

She would always respond the same. "Don't go to Costa Rica."

"I've paid money, promised Steve."

"And I've made a commitment to Kit. I'm the cellist."

The vicious cycle started all over, and Julie's resentment remained. She prayed their time apart would help her see things more clearly. *Oh Lord, help us.*

Kit came around the back of the van, slipped her long, slender arm around Julie's shoulders, and brought her back into the present.

"Ready to go?" She smiled. "It's going to be fun. Maybe even remove that dark cloud hanging over your head."

Julie widened her eyes. "What dark cloud?" She thought she'd done a fair job of hiding her soul from Kit and the rest of the quartet.

"The one that's been raining on you since the day I met you." Kit placed her hand under Julie's chin. "Whatever it is, the Lord is your umbrella, my dear."

Tears smarted in her eyes, and the knot in her throat prevented her from answering.

"All right. Let's go." Kit motioned to Mike and Cassie. "Wagon ho!"

Wagon ho. Julie climbed into the van and took a seat in the back, her cell phone in hand. She autodialed Ethan's office number, and a nervous energy coursed through her as his phone rang over and over. She hated the feeling of timidity that held her. *I'm calling my husband, not my enemy.*

When his voice mail picked up, she pressed END and slipped her phone into her coat pocket.

Situated in the driver's seat, Kit glanced in the rearview mirror, smiling at Julie. "Florida, here we come."

❧

Ethan honked his car's horn. The light had turned green at least five seconds ago. He sat behind Jasper O'Donnell, whose '78 Plymouth sputtered and choked when the old man pressed on the gas.

"Come on, Jasper. I'll miss her." Ethan clenched his jaw and the wheel. Honking at the senior White Birch citizen wouldn't change the situation. It wasn't Jasper's fault Ethan waited until the eleventh hour to see Julie off.

Finally Jasper cleared the lane, and Ethan whipped around him with a left turn. A speed limit sign caught his attention. He touched the brake to slow the car, but his heart raced forward.

A ten-minute drive down I-85, followed by a right turn and a left, and Kit's house came into view. Instantly Ethan knew. He'd missed her. He drove around the corner just to make sure that the van wasn't parked on the other side. It wasn't.

Julie's car sat alone in the driveway.

Ethan parked in the street. Stepping out, he stared down the road before him, straining to catch sight of the van in the distance.

Nothing.

He unhooked his cell phone from his belt to check for missed calls. There were none. *Why didn't she call me?*

He peered down the road again, and heaviness settled over him. "Why didn't you see her off, Ethan?" he muttered.

He wanted to be mad at his wife, but he couldn't. They were both playing this game and losing.

With a heavy sigh, he got in his car as large white snowflakes fluttered from the heavens.

Back in the office, Ethan called Steve Tripleton. "How's Costa Rica looking?"

"Fine, just fine. Arrangements are all made."

Ethan picked a piece of lint from his light wool gray slacks. "Nonrefundable deposits, right?"

"That's right."

Ethan could hear the question in Steve's tone. *Are you reconsidering?*

"We're looking forward to this trip. Weather's great down there this time of year."

Ethan sighed. "I'm sure it is."

Chapter 15

Dinner stop."

Julie roused from the backseat where she dozed.

"Hungry?" Kit reached through the middle seat and smoothed her hand over Julie's arm.

"Uh-huh." Julie stepped out of the van and brushed her hair with her fingers, her eyes squinting. "Where are we?" She stretched. From the chill in the air, she knew they hadn't reached the Mason-Dixon Line.

"Virginia," Kit said.

With Cassie, Julie shuffled into the restaurant, her stomach rumbling.

A day's drive away from home and she missed Ethan, already starting to see things in a different light. She felt guilty and disappointed that she'd stiff-armed him out of her life by living at Bobby and Elle's the past few weeks. Subtly they'd tried to urge her to return home and work things out, but she stubbornly resisted.

Maybe I shouldn't have taken this trip. What if I've caused a permanent rift in my marriage?

Her stomach twisted with the thought. *Lord, I shouldn't have surrendered to my resentment. I should have surrendered to You. Elle's right. I can't blame Ethan.*

Cassie nudged her. "What do you want to eat? Kit's buying."

Julie studied the value meals over the counter, hungrier than she realized. "I'll take a number three."

With a nod, Cassie completed the order. Julie grabbed some napkins, straws, and ketchup packets and found a relatively clean table.

Waiting for the others, Julie checked her cell phone for messages or missed calls. There were none.

Oh, Ethan, what are we doing? Without hesitation, she dialed home.

"Here we go." Cassie came to the table with a loaded tray. Kit and Mike followed with large sodas.

Julie pressed END. She didn't want to have her first away conversation in front of an audience. She barely knew Cassie and Mike, though Kit seemed to perceive things about Julie she didn't intend to reveal.

"Are you awake, love?" Kit asked, sitting next to her, passing her a wrapped burger.

"Getting there." The grilled food teased her senses and stirred her appetite.

Kit gave her a motherly hug, one arm around her shoulders. "These things have a way of working themselves out."

Julie bit off the end of her fry. "What things?"

Kit shrugged. "Oh, life things." She smiled at Julie before regaling the group about her cousin and the upcoming wedding.

Kit's cousin, marrying for the third time at fifty, had planned an extravaganza.

"So why'd the other quartet back out?" Julie asked.

Kit winked. "If I know Tina Marie, she backed them out to give us a chance to play. I'll bet my viola that she convinced them it was their idea to quit, too."

The quartet members laughed.

"Remind me to look out for Tina Marie," Cassie said, attitude accenting her words.

Kit waved off the woman's concern. "No need. She'll be looking out for *you*."

Finished with her burger, Julie excused herself for the ladies' room. There, she retrieved her cell and dialed home. The answering machine picked up on the fourth ring. "You've reached Ethan and Julie. We can't come to the phone. Leave a message." *Beep!*

Julie hesitated. *Do I leave a message?* Suddenly the words tumbled out.

"Hi, Ethan. It's me. We stopped for dinner, and I thought I'd call. Guess you're not home. Call me later if you want. Bye."

She hung up before she said what she really wanted to say. She hadn't uttered those three simple words in weeks: *I love you.*

Julie returned to the van where Cassie took a turn behind the wheel. Mike and Kit prattled on about a new sci-fi show airing in the fall. Julie half listened, sure Ethan knew about this show's debut.

She wanted to call him again. So in the dim lights of the highway, she dialed his cell. After several rings, his voice mail answered.

Ethan, where are you? What are you doing? She didn't leave a message this time. *He's probably at the rec center.*

"So, Julie, do you have children?" Mike suddenly turned his attention to her.

A recent college grad, the young man was in his early twenties, Julie figured, but his angular face and grandiose brown eyes made him appear younger.

Julie cleared her throat. "I wouldn't be here if I did." She faked a smile.

Mike matched her smile with a wide, toothy grin. "Guess not. One last hurrah before the kids come, eh?"

A prickly sensation traveled down her arms, and she counted her heartbeats, wanting to scream at Mike for being so nosy, but how could she? He didn't know.

"My husband and I can't have children." *I can't have children.*

At this, Kit and Cassie twisted around to see her. Mike tightened his lips and looked forward.

Kit deftly changed the subject. "Anyone want to charge their cell phones?" She held a cable over her head. "My cell is all charged."

Julie lurched forward. "Oh, me, please." She wanted to keep her phone on and charged in case Ethan called.

"Okay, Julie." Kit took her phone. After a moment, she said, "My charger doesn't fit your phone, love. Did you bring your charger along?" Kit arched around in the passenger seat.

In the blue and red lights of the dashboard, Julie could see the concern etched on her face. "No, I didn't." *Ethan always remembered those things. Wonderful, organized Ethan.*

Moisture clouded her vision as Kit handed back her phone. *I won't cry; I won't.*

❧❧

Ethan banged around in the kitchen, not sure what to do with himself. Home didn't feel like home. How many times in the past ten years had he rattled around their big apartment by himself? Hundreds. But he'd never felt alone—and lonely.

He went into the living room and upped the volume on the television; the noise of the game provided some kind of company.

Wandering back to the kitchen, he opened and closed cupboards, yanked open the refrigerator, then the freezer. Sparse. Not much in the way of eats. He found a frozen dinner on the bottom shelf and decided to nuke it.

Four minutes later, he dumped the contents of the package onto a plate, steam rising from a small pile of meat and rice. Ethan took a sniff and wrinkled his nose.

"Good eating." He dug a fork from the silverware drawer and sat on the couch.

He ate but didn't taste, mostly swirling his food around on the plate. He scraped the remains in the trash, rinsed his plate, dropped it in the dishwasher, and made himself a peanut butter and jelly sandwich. Emptying the last of the milk into his glass, Ethan returned to the living room.

He flipped through the channels and fidgeted in his chair like an antsy five-year-old.

This is ridiculous. With a sigh, he clicked off the TV.

He missed Julie. A lot. He didn't mind her evenings out or her busy schedule, because she always came home to him. Since he was eighteen, he'd never known home without her melodic presence. The weeks she stayed at Bobby and Elle's he'd missed her, too, but she was in town, just a short drive away.

Now she was hours and hours away.

He rinsed the milk glass and tucked it away in the dishwasher. He checked the time. Three hours before a reasonable bedtime.

Ethan wandered to the den and fetched a pad of paper and pen. Returning to his chair in the living room, he doodled between the thin lines, feeling melancholy, forming his thoughts and emotions into words. Time ticked away while he wrote.

Missing Julie

I cannot sleep, longing to be away
 And wandering a forest trail I know

On a clear night, and cool, when there is snow
As fine as powder, deep, and some would stay
Balanced on all the branches as they sway
Against the icy breezes that would blow
Great drifts into the valley far below
Where in the summertime a stream would lay
But it is winter now, when all is still
Across a great expanse of starry sky
The lonely moon rides pale into the dawn
And I would sit alone upon a hill
Bundled against the night, and wonder why
I am this way whenever you are gone.

Ethan read the poem aloud. "Eth, man, you miss your wife." He tossed the poem into an end table drawer and banged it shut.

He unclipped his cell phone from his belt with an idea that she might have called and just left a message. With a quick glance, he saw his phone was turned off. "Ah, I forgot to turn it on after the town council meeting. . . ." He'd gone with Will and Bobby to get approval to build their new warehouse since it butted up against city property.

Ethan powered on the phone and checked for messages. Nothing.

Restless, he wandered back to her music room. It felt empty and abandoned. He thought how accustomed he'd become to her playing. He hardly heard her anymore.

Now that she wasn't here, the silence was deafening. Wasn't he normally busier than this? He'd brought work home two or three evenings a week for over a year now. But tonight, he didn't even pack up his laptop. No games to play, no company business, no wife.

"Julie, what's happening to us?" Ethan considered the last few years, the strain and stress, the pain of waiting and wondering, the sadness of Dr. Patterson's news, her confession of resentment.

"Lord, I lean on You. Submit to You." Suddenly he sensed the Holy Spirit whisper, "Ephesians 5."

Lambert's Code. Ethan jogged upstairs for his Bible. He found it on the nightstand under a slight covering of dust. Propping against the pillows, he opened the Good Book.

After reading chapter 5 from Ephesians, he understood he didn't always encourage Julie as a husband should. He certainly didn't submit any of his decisions to her. Most of the time, he told her what he planned without consideration of her wants or needs. And as for loving her as Christ loved the church. . .

Not even close. No wonder she resents me.

"Lord, teach me. I want to walk in unity and submission with Julie. We need our lives to be submitted to You—and each other."

He didn't need another tap on his heart to know he had to honor her or his prayers would be hindered. After all, she was a coheir in the same grace of the Lord he walked in.

Meditating on this notion, he prayed for wisdom, prayed for Julie, and nearly jumped out of his skin when the house phone rang.

He answered the portable on the bedside table, his heart resounding. *Julie!* "Hello?"

"Ethan, what's up?" Will's question bounced over the line.

He grinned. "Not much. Sitting around praying. Thinking."

"Oh, man, sorry to interrupt. I'll catch you later."

"No, it's okay. I'm almost done."

"I had a taste for some of Sam's pie. You interested?"

"If you'd seen my dinner, you wouldn't even ask. I'll meet you there."

Ethan hopped off the bed, grateful for the company. He slipped on his boots and started downstairs when he remembered the diner's cold temperature. Sam walked around sweating while the patrons shivered. So unless he wanted to eat with his coat on, he'd need a pullover.

Stepping into the closet, Ethan hunted for his navy merino wool sweater, a Christmas present from his mom the year he turned sixteen. It had always been a favorite garment, but even more so in recent years. *I can still wear a sweater from my high school days. Got to be a favorite.*

"Weird." He flipped through the sweaters on the hangers, then the ones folded in his bureau drawer. The sweater was missing.

One last time, he checked the closet. Then a light dawned. *Julie.* She loved that sweater more than he did. They'd actually tossed a coin to determine who had rights to it one cold winter day.

With a warm heart, he reached for his university sweatshirt. Tonight his sweater kept Julie warm. So in some small way, so did he.

He hurried downstairs, retrieved his keys, and autodialed Julie's cell on his way out the door.

By the time he arrived at the diner, he'd left her two voice mails. Why she didn't answer her phone mystified him, and he wondered if their relationship would ever recover.

Chapter 16

The sun's golden hues kissed the dawning sky over the north Florida beach. Julie faced the ocean, Ethan's navy sweater guarding her from the chilly, salty air.

"Did you think Florida would be so cold at the end of March?"

Julie turned to see Kit walking toward her, barefoot and smiling. The breeze whipped her long flowered skirt around her ankles and wisps of her gray hair about her face.

"It's marvelous. Imagine being in New Hampshire right now. Cold, gray, depressing." Julie lifted her face to the morning light.

For the first time in weeks, her head felt clear. The ruins of her mind were swept away with the dawn of a new day.

"Do you miss Ethan?"

Julie faced her, noting that Kit didn't bother to cloak her question with formalities. "Yes, I do."

"What's troubling you two?" Kit linked her arm with Julie's and started walking.

"Things." Cold, soggy sand squished between Julie's toes.

"I could tell something darkened your soul from the moment I met you. Is it the having children issue?"

Staring straight ahead, Julie shared her burdens, not surprised by the older woman's insight. "Yes, we just found out about it. And we quarrel a lot, each wanting our own way. I'm resentful I can't have children and how easily he seems to move on with life." The words bounced around the walls of her soul like the crashing of the waves on the shore.

"Lars and I couldn't have children." Kit tightened her grip on Julie, stumbling a little on the uneven sand. "Of course, in those days we didn't have all the medical wonderment people have today."

"It didn't help. Just drained us and made me emotionally wacky at times."

"So what's next for you two?" Kit tugged on her arm.

Julie looked over at her. Light emanated from her hazel eyes. "You don't give up, do you?"

"The Lord's had me praying for you."

Julie blinked away her first batch of tears in over a week. "Someone had to be praying for me."

"Will you adopt?"

"We don't know. I always pictured myself with little Ethans and little Julies."

"We were going to adopt a baby. The ladies at church hosted a baby shower for me. We bought baby furniture; I knitted booties and a sweater. Lars painted the nursery, built shelves."

Julie's heart swelled with emotion at Kit's story.

"There we were, a couple of expectant parents, batting around names. Leslie if we had a daughter. John for a son, named after Lars's father. Oh, we were like a young couple in love again."

"What happened?" Suddenly Julie could feel their anticipation, waiting for a newborn to fill their arms.

"The mother went into labor, and by the time the little tike made his appearance, the girl's father refused to let her give him up. So she changed her mind."

Julie pressed her hand over her heart. "Oh, Kit."

"After that, a little piece of me died. Lars wanted to try again, but I just couldn't."

"That's how I felt the day I left the doctor's office. I even questioned why I married Ethan in the first place."

"Oh, love, don't start questioning. Marriage is for more than children. I can see God made you two for each other."

"I hope so. Lately I've begun to wonder." Julie wiped the tears from her cheeks.

"Marriage takes work. And you have to communicate about your plans and desires."

Julie laughed softly. "Lambert's Code."

"Lambert's Code?" Kit asked.

"It's Ethan's grandparents' code: Submit to one another."

"Sounds like a good blueprint for success, if you ask me."

They walked in quiet harmony for the next five minutes, the day breaking over them, the sun warming the frost from the air.

"Where's Lars now?" Julie ventured.

"He passed away ten years ago at the tender age of sixty. One minute, he was standing at the kitchen sink, and the next, he had collapsed on the floor. A heart attack took him instantly." A longing for her husband reverberated in her voice.

"I'm sorry, Kit. That had to be hard. I know you must miss him."

Kit nodded. "Yes, but I'm so busy with the symphony, the quartet, and my friends that if I had a husband and children, they'd accuse me of neglecting them."

"Were you ever resentful? Of not having children, I mean?" Julie asked, still searching for understanding of her own feelings.

"For a while. Being barren comes with certain harsh emotions. But God healed me. He will heal you, too, if you let Him."

"I want Him to, Kit. I do."

Kit pressed her fingers to Julie's cheeks and pushed her lips into a smile. "Your life is just beginning. God has wonderful plans for you. He's not forgotten you."

"I wish I had your confidence."

"Just one word of advice."

"Yes, please."

"If you ever are widowed and alone, don't buy a bunch of cats. Too cliché."

Julie laughed, deep and full. "My sentiments exactly."

It was snowing again. Big flakes landed on the office windowsill and piled against the pane. Ethan stared out, hands in his pockets. He had work to do but didn't feel much like doing it.

Three days without his wife and he thought he'd go crazy. They'd been apart before, like the time he went on a mission trip to Guatemala. But this separation came on the heels of discord.

He wanted to see her, hold her, kiss her, and tell her everything was going to be all right. Tell her he loved her.

Right now, life seemed to be a jumbled mess. The strain between them grew obvious to their family. Sunday, his mother pulled him aside and reminded him they were there for him if he needed to talk.

He thought about Dr. Patterson's diagnosis and how they had yet to tell their parents. *We can't put it off much longer.*

Ethan turned at the light rap outside his door.

"Bobby, come in."

Bobby perched on the edge of Ethan's desk and picked up his handgrip. "Do you have dinner plans?"

"No. I thought I'd hit the diner again."

"Elle said to ask you for dinner. She feels bad about giving Julie opposite advice from Grandpa and Grandma's."

Ethan rubbed the back of his neck. "Not really opposite, just not what I wanted."

"I suppose that's the lesson you're learning these days. Can't always get what you want."

"You're telling me." Ethan shoved his desk chair around and sat down.

"What's God saying to you in all of this?" Bobby squeezed the handgrip, making the tiny apparatus squeak.

"Get over myself. Love my wife. Submit to one another."

"You finally figured out Lambert's Code?" Bobby winked at him, grinning.

"Well, I understand it. Not sure I know exactly how to enact it."

They talked a bit more before Bobby left for a sales meeting. On the way out the door, he paused. "Elle's niece is staying with us for a few days. Just wanted you to know."

Ethan squinted at him. "Okay, Bob, thanks for the warning. Is she a shrew or something?"

"No, no, she's just going through a hard time."

"Ah, so I'll have some commiseration," Ethan said.

Bobby fanned his hands. "Maybe. I'll see you at the house, six o'clock."

Ethan stared after his cousin. *Lord, what is he up to?*

Nevertheless, he liked the idea of company. Not spending the evening at home alone, missing his wife. He'd found Julie's cell phone charger, so he understood why she never answered his calls. But he wanted to hear her voice, not the recorded one on her voice mail.

He paused to pray for her. Instantly the Lord's peace settled his anxious heart. Now if only this week would end and she would come home.

"Ethan," Grant Hansen called over the intercom.

Ethan pressed the TALK button. "What's up?"

"Need you down on the floor."

"I'll be right there." He'd barely stepped out the door when he heard his office phone ring. He hesitated. *Ignore it. They can leave a message.* But on the second ring, he scurried to answer.

"Ethan Lambert." *If this is a vendor, I'm going to be mad.*

"Hi, Ethan."

Ethan sank to his chair, a cacophony of emotion rising within him. "Babe, I miss you so much."

"I miss you, too," Julie said, a ripple in her words.

Ethan pressed his fingers against his eyes and breathed deeply. "How's Florida?" He hoped he sounded chipper and casual, but his voice wobbled.

"The sun shines every day." She sighed. "At least the two we've been here."

Ethan swiveled his chair around to peer out the window. Still snowing. "How are Kit and the rest of the quartet?"

"Fine. We slept the first day and went to the beach. But we've been practicing today. Kit's cousin set us up with an event for tonight. A retirement party."

"Do you have enough money?"

"I took a hundred dollars out of our account before I left. And tonight's performance is a paying gig, so I'm actually earning money."

Ethan sighed. "Okay, good to know."

"How's everything there?"

"Everything is fine here, besides missing you." Over the phone, Ethan heard the rhythm of the shore. "I tried to call you."

"My cell battery is dead. I didn't bring the charger."

"I know. I found it in the bedroom."

"I left you a message," Julie said.

"When? On my cell?"

"No, on the answering machine."

"Oh, Jules, I never check that thing."

The office intercom interrupted. "Ethan, we need you down here."

He wrenched around to answer. "Be right there, Grant."

"Do you need to go?" she asked.

214

"Well, in a minute. I went down to Kit's to see you off, but I got there too late."

"Kit likes to leave on time."

"I wanted to say good-bye. And—"

The intercom called again. "Ethan, really, we need you down here now."

"Grant, I'm on a call," he sighed.

"You have to go. I'll call you later," Julie said.

"No, it can wait."

She laughed. "That's a first."

"I'm working on it."

He sensed her hesitation. "It still bothers me that you lied to me."

"I didn't lie. I didn't tell you something."

"Same difference." Her soft voice sharpened.

"No, it's not." *Here we go, arguing again.*

The intercom clicked. "Ethan, we're going to miss production deadlines if you don't get down here."

Ethan pressed the TALK button, his lips pressed in a thin line. "What's the problem?"

"The CNC machine is down. We can't get it back online."

The words weighed on Ethan. He'd have to investigate. Last time this happened, production backed up a week.

"Listen, you have to go," Julie said. "I'll call you later."

"Julie, wait." Ethan stood. "I don't want to hang up arguing."

"Me neither."

"I love you, Julie. I do."

"I know. I love you, too."

Chapter 17

Kit, Cassie, Mike, and Julie arrived at an exclusive resort on Amelia Island a little after five, dressed in black tie and ready to regale the guests with their light classical repertoire.

"What's this gig for again?" Mike asked, tucking his violin securely under his arm. The beach breeze lifted the ends of his tux jacket.

"Big hospital executive's retirement party," Kit said.

"Then we have your cousin's rehearsal dinner and wedding for the next two nights."

Kit nodded. "After that, we head home."

Julie followed them inside, thinking of the night ahead, hearing her cello parts in her head.

Kit let Cassie and Mike go ahead and fell into step with Julie. "While praying for you and Ethan, the Lord reminded me of biblical heroines such as Sarah, Rachel, and Hannah. He heard their prayers; He hears yours, too."

Julie smiled. "Thank you." She stopped walking and faced her mentor. "I'm usually not this serious. I'm sorry we're becoming friends when my life is so difficult."

Kit pressed her hand gently on Julie's cheek. "We will be great friends. You and Ethan will take me to Paris for my seventieth birthday."

Julie laughed. "Will we now? When will that be?"

"Next year." Kit winked, and Julie suspected she would never really understand the hidden depths of Kit Merewether.

❧❧

The Merewether Quartet wowed the doctors, nurses, accountants, and executive administrators of North Shore Hospital.

"I'd forgotten the thrill of a live performance," Julie said, sitting in the back of the van, reveling in the moment.

Mike looked at her. "It pays to play."

Julie laughed. "I'd do it for free."

Kit held up a check. "Payment for the night is here, ladies and gentleman."

Since it was late, Kit promised to buy them all a luxurious breakfast in the morning. "I'll consolidate all the money from the trip and divide it up when we get home."

Back at their hotel, they said good night and went into their own rooms. Kit had arranged to share with Cassie, and Julie was grateful for the privacy. *Lord, thank you for Kit.*

The elation of the night waning, Julie changed from her performance clothes, remembering to hang them up. *Ethan would be proud.* She pulled her hair into a ponytail before washing her face and brushing her teeth.

Around 11:00 p.m., she curled onto her bed and opened her Bible. She read about Sarah, Rachel, and Hannah, searching for wisdom in the trials of her ancient sisters.

When she closed her Bible, Julie slumped against the pillow, praying, remembering Kit's reminder that God heard her prayers. *Oh Lord, have I made an idol of having children?*

Wanting children was honorable. God ordained. Making an idol of it was another matter altogether, and becoming resentful toward her husband was even worse.

While she didn't have a handmaid to give to Ethan like Sarah offered Abraham and Rachel offered Jacob, she had thrown a sports car into the works. Julie considered Hannah. She petitioned God for the desire of her heart. She trusted in the Father. Slipping off the bed and onto her knees, Julie surrendered to the Father. "I feel like I've been singled out, and I resent it. Yet I've made an idol out of having children. My dream became more important than You or Ethan. Father, please forgive me."

She cried as she talked to God. Being disappointed, even devastated, is one thing, but questioning her life, her marriage spoke of a deeper issue. Out of her meditation and prayer, Julie suddenly became aware of a new truth.

Sitting back on her heels, she pressed the palm of her hand against her forehead. "I never realized. . . All my life. . . Oh wow." An invisible burden lifted, and she laughed the laughter of freedom.

Julie glanced at the clock. It was after midnight. She hesitated, then dove for the room's phone.

❧

Around 10:00 p.m., Ethan unlocked the apartment, the day's mail in his hand. He hung his coat in the hall closet and checked the answering machine in the den. A single red digit blinked in the darkness. Hitting PLAY, he listened to Julie's message from three days ago.

Wandering to the kitchen, he muttered, "Julie, call me." He flipped on a light and glanced at the mail. The bank sent notice that the new car's first payment would automatically be deducted from their checking on the fifteenth.

"Let the good times begin." Ethan grabbed a bottle of water from the fridge and went to the den. He clicked on the little lamp Julie had given him for studying the first year they were married.

He smiled. In those days, she liked to go to bed early. He preferred to stay up late, studying.

Yet they wanted to be together. The little lamp was their compromise. She curled up next to him and went to sleep while he studied by the lamp's thin light.

"Lambert's Code in action, and we didn't even know it."

Dinner at Bobby and Elle's earlier in the evening came with an interesting twist. Elle's niece, seventeen-year-old Abby, was pregnant and contemplating adoption.

When Ethan realized the intent of Elle's evening, he got Bobby off to the side. "What are you thinking?"

Bobby gestured with one arm toward the kitchen where Abby was making brownies with their kids. "She's a sweet girl who made a mistake. If she finds a nice couple, she'll give the baby up for adoption. Elle and I thought—"

"Julie's in Florida after the three toughest weeks of our marriage, and you're talking to me about adoption?"

"Well, I know the timing is off, but we thought if you met her, you might talk to Julie—"

Ethan sighed and peered around Bobby at Abby. "I don't suppose I can sneak this past her like the golf trip."

Bobby shook his head with a chuckle. "Not likely."

"We talked today. It went well."

Bobby slapped his hand on Ethan's shoulder. "Elle and I've said nothing to Abby. But now that she knows you, she has a frame of reference if you decide to adopt."

Ethan grinned. "We recently adopted a car, Bob."

The older cousin chuckled. "Yeah, well, I hear you, but parenting is way more rewarding."

Ethan glanced toward the kitchen. Slender and petite, Abby barely looked pregnant. Her long blond hair reminded him of Julie, and she had the same guarded disposition. Julie would like her, he knew.

With his hands in his pockets, his body tense against the cold, Ethan stepped to the back of the porch. "I'm not sure we're ready to adopt, emotionally or financially."

"I understand, but Abby has four months left, so—"

Four months. At first, Ethan imagined he and Julie only needed a few weeks to fix their marriage problems. Now he knew they had a few months, or more.

Bringing his thoughts into the present, Ethan found the remote and clicked on the sports news. He dozed in his chair, waking long enough to channel surf, then dozed again. Around midnight, he shut off the TV and headed upstairs.

Lying awake in the dark, his mind churned with the day's events. The conversation with Julie, meeting Abby, the possibility of adoption. Were they supposed to adopt? Was that God's plan for them?

"Lord, I want Your will." He closed his eyes, slowly drifting away. The phone's shrill ring jolted him awake.

He grappled for the portable. "Hello?"

"Babe, it's me."

❧❧

"A little late for you, isn't it?" His voice was buoyant and reminded her of white summer clouds.

Julie giggled and propped herself against the pillows. "Our concert was amazing. I'd forgotten the thrill of a live performance."

"I'm glad."

"Ethan, you've got to spend more time with Kit. She's fantastic. And, oh, guess what?"

"What?"

"We're taking her to Paris next year for her seventieth birthday."

"Oh? *We* are?"

"Well, that is, if you want to go to Paris."

"I could do Paris," Ethan said.

"They don't have basketball or football, but you can survive a week without them, can't you?"

He laughed. "I'll manage."

"Good. Paris it is." She twirled the phone cord with her fingers and, for the first time in a long time, felt love for her husband.

"You sound happy."

She laughed. "I am. Oh, Ethan, I never saw it before. I knew, I think, deep, deep down, you know?" Her words flew at him.

"Babe, slow down. What are you talking about?"

"Me, my parents, babies."

Ethan scratched his head. "What do you mean?"

"Ever since I can remember, Mom and Dad always wanted more children. But alas, I was their one and only. Yet every holiday, every family reunion, they commented one way or another how sad it was they never had more children."

"Go on."

"Well, then it turned into grandchildren. 'Waiting for Julie to give us grandchildren.'"

"I think I know where you're going with this."

She gushed. "Ethan, having children became my obsession, my sole reason for existence. My idol."

"Strong words, Julie. Obsession. Idol."

"But it's true. I took my eyes off the Lord and did crazy things like buying an expensive car without talking to you."

"It makes sense." He answered low, as if contemplating her conclusion.

"God's plans for me didn't matter. Your plans didn't matter. Only mine, and giving grandchildren to my parents."

"So your issue is more than just a natural desire for children; it's the burden of fulfilling your parents' desires."

Julie shouted, "Yes!" She jumped up, standing in the middle of the bed.

"How did you figure this out?"

Julie explained her Bible study of Old Testament heroines. "I started praying, and all of a sudden, I knew."

"He's faithful to us, Julie."

"For the first time, I'm okay with this, Ethan," Julie said.

"Jules, I'm sorry I've been a jerk."

"Me, too." She laughed. "I mean—"

He laughed with her. "I know what you mean."

"Just making sure."

"I'm sorry I resented you," Julie confessed.

"You resented me?"

"Well, yes. I resented the fact you seemed to move on with life while I lived with the burden of being barren."

"I'm sorry I didn't see—"

She interrupted. "I didn't see it myself until I stayed with Bobby and Elle. Ethan, I want to move on with life, too, and you."

"I love you, Julie. More than I can say."

The words washed over her, warm and cleansing. "I love you, too, Ethan."

"I'm sorry you're a thousand miles away right now."

"Me, too."

Chapter 18

Ethan whistled a light tune as he reviewed the production crew's schedule and approved overtime pay.

Will popped into his office. "Did you buy a canary?"

Ethan shook his head and lifted one brow at his cousin.

"What's gotten into you?"

Ethan stopped whistling and motioned outside his window. "Did you see the bulldozer in the south parking lot? The contractor brought it out this morning, ready and waiting to clear the land for the warehouse."

Will crossed his arms and leaned against the door frame. "I did."

"If we can ever get past this snow, we'll break ground by May."

"God willing," Will replied. "So tell me. Why the whistling?"

Ethan rocked back in his chair, locked his hands behind his head, and gave Will the short version of his conversation with Julie.

"Sounds like you two are breaking some ground of your own," Will said.

Ethan grinned. "Yeah, we are."

"Good for you two. Listen, I'm meeting Grandpa for lunch. Want to come?"

Ethan checked the time. Two o'clock. "As a matter of fact, yes. I'm starved."

He rode with Will to Peri's Perk. Grandpa waited for them at one of the high, round tables, his hands around a large cup of whipped-cream-topped coffee.

"Does Grandma know you drink those things?"

Grandpa winked at him. "Lambert's Code."

Ethan laughed. "So you had to tell her?"

"Of course."

Will and Ethan shook their heads. Grandpa was a man of his word. They loved him for it.

They ordered sandwiches, and while they waited for their names to be called, they chatted about the new warehouse and the upcoming Spring Festival.

"How's Julie?" Grandpa asked without warning.

"Matt!" Peri called.

Grandpa got up for his order.

"Ethan!"

"She's fine," Ethan told his grandpa as they picked up their sandwiches.

"Will!"

"Talk to her recently?" Grandpa eyed Ethan as he took his seat.

"As a matter of fact, last night."

"Did it go well?"

Will dropped his platter onto the table. "He's smiling, isn't he?"

For a few moments, the conversation around the table stopped while the three men bit into their sandwiches. Grandpa broke the quiet. "Are you still going to Costa Rica?"

Ethan eyed Will, then his grandpa. "I'm not sure. I mean, yes, as far as Steve is concerned, but. . ." He held his sandwich between his hands.

"Something wrong with your sandwich?" Grandpa asked.

"Um, no." Ethan took a bite. A simple phrase echoed in his mind. *"Submit to one another."*

Grandpa leaned toward him. "What's on your mind?"

Ethan reared back. "Do you have X-ray eyes?"

"Only when the Lord allows."

Will and Ethan chuckled.

"I don't know," Ethan started. "You mentioned Costa Rica, and suddenly, I felt bugged."

"What do you make of it?"

Ethan stared at a point beyond Grandpa's head. *I don't want to go to Costa Rica.* But he'd spent the money. How could he throw it away?

Grandpa patted him on the shoulder. "I think you should go to Florida. Surprise your wife."

"I'd love to, but what about Costa Rica?"

Grandpa reached for his coffee. "Still stuck on that, are you?"

Ethan fiddled with his napkin. If he showed up in Florida, Julie would be shocked. Surprised. Over-the-top happy. "Will, do you think Bobby would go to Costa Rica in my place? Buy me out?"

"Now you're thinking," Grandpa said.

"I'm a little slow sometimes, but I get there eventually." Ethan sat up straight and jutted out his chin. "Will, what do you think?"

"Can't hurt to ask. Let me call him." Will dialed his cell phone while Grandpa continued talking to Ethan.

"You've cracked Lambert's Code, son. Yielding your will for the good of your marriage."

Confidence gripped him. "I'm going to Florida."

Will clicked his flip phone shut. "Bobby's calling Elle, but it looks like he's in."

Ethan rested against the high-back chair. For the first time in weeks, his soul felt right within him. "There's only one problem: I don't know how to find her."

Grandpa pulled a slip of paper from his shirt pocket. "Here, this might help."

❧❧

Julie reclined in a beach chair, her face toward the sun. The quartet practiced in the morning, but Kit gave them the afternoon off.

"Just be ready to go to the wedding rehearsal by five," she'd said.

Like the breeze, Julie let her thoughts go wherever they willed. She smiled when a picture of Ethan blew past her mind's eye. Last night's breakthrough changed her world.

Her thoughts drifted to this morning when the quartet met Kit's cousin for the first time. She chuckled out loud when she remembered Mike's impression.

"I feel like I just got hit by a bulldozer." Mike's oversized eyes, wider than normal, watched as Tina exited, Kit in tow.

"And when were you ever actually hit by a bulldozer?" Cassie clicked her tongue in disapproval.

"You know what I mean." Mike curled his lip.

Julie watched, amused, covering her lips with her fingers to keep from laughing. They were like brother and sister. Never mind the twenty-year gap between them.

When Kit returned to their table, she looked like she'd collided with a wind tunnel. "I forgot how bossy that woman can be." She smoothed her hair into place with her hands.

"Well, when you're getting married for the third time, I guess you want everything to be perfect," Julie had commented as she speared a piece of cantaloupe from her fruit plate.

Her thoughts returned to the present when she heard Kit call from down the beach.

"Here you are."

Julie rose to see her approach. "I thought I'd catch a little bit of sun. Otherwise, no one will believe I actually went to Florida."

Kit stopped by Julie's chair, hands on her hips, watching the waves. "What happened to you?"

"Excuse me?" Julie squinted up at her, shielding her eyes with her hand.

Kit looked down at her. "I knew the minute I saw you this morning. Your eyes. . .they have a different light in them."

Julie tried to squelch her smile but lost. "God is good, Kit."

"That He is."

"Last night I went to my room and read about Sarah, Rachel, and Hannah."

Kit listened, the hem of her skirt snapping in the salty breeze.

"I realized some things about me that needed to change." Julie explained what happened. "I feel like I lost a hundred pounds."

"Good for you." Kit patted her shoulder.

Julie dropped her head against the top of the beach chair and drew a deep, peaceful breath. At the core of her being, she still didn't understand the Lord's purpose in her barrenness. But she was weary of chasing her will. She wanted to surrender to God's will, submit to Him. For now, if children were not a part of her life's tapestry, then so be it.

One thing she did understand in the dawn of this new day. God loved her, and His plans for her were far better than any dream she could ever conceive.

❧❧

Ethan caught a flight out of Boston. His dad drove him down and shook his hand good-bye when they called for his row to board.

"You're doing the right thing," Dad said, giving his hand an extra shake.

Ethan looked down to find a folded bill. "No, Dad, I can't." He handed back the money.

"A gift from your mother and me." Dad waved away the return of the money.

Ethan thanked him. "You know we can't have children, Julie and me." His candidness surprised him, but the moment felt right.

Dad jutted out his chin with a slight nod. "Yes. Grandpa told us."

"I'm sorry you didn't hear it from us. Life hasn't been very smooth lately."

"We understand."

"Now boarding all rows for flight 1210."

Ethan held up his ticket. "Guess I'd better go." He lunged at his father, wrapping him in a son's hug.

When they separated, Dad reminded him, "Your mom and I are here for you two. Let us know what you need."

"Thank you. You've always been there for us." Ethan waved good-bye and jogged down the jetway.

When the plane rolled away from the terminal, Ethan checked the time. *Four–and–a–half-hour trip, with a plane change in Philly. . .taxi over to the island. . . find Julie. . . I'll get there just before she leaves for the wedding. Barely.*

Grandpa's little slip of information that day in Peri's contained Kit's cell number. Ethan had forgotten that Grandma and Kit had friendship roots reaching back into the '60s and their ladies' Bible study. They kept in touch even after Kit moved closer to Manchester.

"I'm thrilled to hear you are coming, Ethan," Kit told him.

"Keep it from Julie, will you?"

"Would I dare spoil such a romantic surprise?"

Ethan grinned at the notion. A romantic surprise? Julie just might faint away. "I hear we're taking you to Paris next year."

"Yes, darling. In the spring."

He liked the lilt in her voice. "I'm looking forward to it."

Sitting on the runway, waiting to take off, he shifted in his seat, rubbed his hands together, and peered out the plane's oval window. *Surprising Julie. . .this ought to be fun.*

Ethan whispered a prayer. "Let this be the first step to a deeper, more mature marriage."

"Ladies and gentlemen, we are experiencing a small technical difficulty," the captain's voice reported from the cockpit. "We're returning to the gate to let the mechanics check it out. We apologize for any inconvenience. We'll get it fixed as soon as possible."

Ethan moaned and snapped up his cell phone to dial Kit. This was not the romantic surprise he had in mind.

Chapter 19

"Is this seat taken?"

Julie lifted her eyes to see a handsome man, dressed in black tie, bending over the chair opposite her. For a brief moment, he took her breath away. "Um, no."

With his flawless smile fixed on her, he extended his hand. "Alexander Crawford."

Julie hesitated but took his hand. "Julie Lambert."

"Nice to meet you." His eyes were the bluest she'd ever seen, and his features were perfect and even as if sculptured by a master.

She tugged her hand away from his. *Where's the rest of the quartet?* They'd taken a break midreception for the cake cutting and bouquet toss. With cake and punch in hand, Julie picked an empty table in the back of the room. Mike and Cassie promised to join her, but she had yet to see them. Kit, she knew, was visiting with the family.

"How long has the Merewether Quartet been together?" Alexander asked, tipping his head to one side. His question did not reflect the expression on his face.

Julie held her hands in her lap as if to shrink away from him. "About a month."

His brow rose. "Really? You're quite polished."

"We've worked hard." His presence made her skin prickle.

"I'm having a little get-together at my home on the beach tomorrow night. I know it's late notice, but—"

Oh, that's it. Julie exhaled. "You need to ask that lady over there. She's the boss." She pointed across the room to Kit.

He followed the line and frowned. "Maybe you could come if the quartet is busy." He scooted his chair closer to hers.

She laughed. "I'm only prepared to play with the quartet." She fiddled with her fork and plate, pressing leftover cake icing into miniature pancakes. She didn't like the way he watched her.

"Forget the cello. What about you and me?" His tone said way more than those simple words. "You're a beautiful woman, Julie." He leaned forward and slithered his fingers across her arm.

His touch burned. She rocketed to her feet, fear creeping down her spine. "I'm married, Mr. Crawford."

He shrugged and pulled on her arm so she sat down again. "I'm not." He moved closer. "Is your husband here?"

"No, he's in New Hampshire." She regretted the words as soon as they left her mouth.

"Good for me then." He inched his chair toward her again.

Julie tried to push back her chair, but one of the legs was tangled with another chair. His warm, sticky breath made her nauseous. He'd been drinking. His smile, which first appeared flawless, now appeared evil.

Where does he get the right? She looked directly into his eyes. "Please leave."

"Only if you come with me?" He sat so close his leg touched hers.

She rose to her feet. "Excuse me." As she walked away, Alexander Crawford's sardonic laugh followed.

Oh Lord, oh Lord, help. Julie found Kit with her mother and aunt. She waited for a break in their conversation before whispering, "I need to see you."

Kit finished up and walked with Julie to the outside deck. The horizon, dark and ominous, harbored the sounds of the surf.

Kit propped her arms on the railing and lifted her face to the wind. "Hard to imagine being alone at sea when it's so dark, isn't it?"

The lump in Julie's throat kept her from speaking. "Mm-hmm," she muttered. She shivered and rubbed her arms with her hands.

Kit faced her. "What's troubling you?"

"I want to go home." Her teeth chattered, but she bit her lower lip to keep it from quivering.

"Now?"

"I don't belong here, Kit. I belong at home with Ethan, working on our marriage." She batted away tears. If she cried, her mascara would smudge, and they had another set to play before the evening ended.

Kit smiled and drew her into a hug. "We leave in a few days; can you wait?"

"A man came on to me in there." Julie wrenched her arm around, motioning to some obscure point behind her. "He mocked me when I told him I was married."

"A guest?"

Julie shivered. "Yes, a guest." She squeezed her eyes shut. "Kit, he was evil."

Kit put her arms around her. "I'm sorry, Julie. Tina Marie and Marco have unusual friends."

"Unusual?" Julie shook in the cold. "I've always known Ethan was special, but this week, I've realized how special. He is an amazing man, flaws and all."

"Being apart awakens love, doesn't it?"

"Too bad it took a personal crisis and one slimeball to make me realize it."

"Here, let me pray for you." Kit put her hand on Julie's back and asked the Lord for peace and protection.

Julie wiped the tears from her face as Kit said amen. "How much time do I have before the next set?"

Kit held up her watch, catching light from the reception hall. "Ten minutes. She's about to toss the bouquet."

"I want to freshen up in the ladies' room."

Julie found her purse shoved into a corner by the bandstand. She dusted it off and thanked the Lord for His peace. Kit motioned for her to hurry, so Julie darted down a long hall toward the door marked LADIES.

She stopped short when Alexander Crawford came into view. "I knew you'd come down this hall sooner or later."

⋙⋘

The plane touched down with a bounce and slowed with such force that Ethan lurched forward. But he didn't care. He was on Florida soil.

Eight o'clock. The delay in Boston caused him to miss his connection in Philadelphia. They shuffled him over to another flight that was full, then listed him on standby for a third flight.

He got the last seat on that flight, but they sat on the runway for thirty minutes. Still, the journey stirred a yearning in him. He couldn't wait to see Julie.

Once he deplaned, he ran through the terminal, his garment bag slung over his shoulder, anticipation mingling with adrenaline. Hailing a taxi, he climbed in the back and told the driver the reception hall address.

Amelia Island seemed like light-years from the airport. "Here you go." The cab driver glanced over his shoulder. "That'll be twenty-six eighty-nine."

Ethan dropped a couple of twenties over the seat. "Keep the change."

Standing outside the Plantation Resort, he ignored his rapid heartbeat and headed inside just as the bride tossed her bouquet. A gaggle of single ladies vied for the prize. Ethan couldn't suppress his smile when a lanky, pink-clad bridesmaid nearly toppled a flower girl to catch the cluster of roses.

Roses. Ah, he meant to buy Julie a rose at the airport but in his haste forgot. He spied a bouquet of carnations on an empty reception table and asked a passing waiter if he could take one.

"Help yourself."

Ethan selected one white carnation for Julie and surveyed the candlelit room. *Where are you, babe?*

"Ethan, darling, you've arrived. I was worried." Kit floated his way, dressed in a black evening gown, her arms extended.

"Finally." Ethan returned her hug, the edge of his nerves softening. "Where's Julie?"

Kit winked. "She's gone to powder her nose." She pointed across the room toward a narrow hall. "Why don't you go wait for her? When she comes out. . . Oh, a white carnation. Won't she be surprised."

Ethan gripped Kit's elbow lightly. "Will she?"

"How can you ask? Yes, more than you know. More than you know." She patted his cheek, then took his garment bag. "I'll set this with our things."

Walking between the tables, adorned with linen cloths and golden hurricane lamps, Ethan dug his hands in his jeans pockets. He'd planned to change into a suit, but that was before the delay.

Entering the hallway, he heard voices. "Let me go."

"Oh, come on. You and me." An eerie laugh reverberated off the block walls. "I said, let me go."

Ethan squinted in the dim light. Through the shadows he saw a large man pressed against. . .Julie!

❧

If this was terror, Julie never wanted to taste it again. She shook so hard she could barely catch her breath. "I don't understand what you want with me." She thought to run but couldn't command her feet.

"What does any man want with a beautiful woman?" He sauntered her way, hands in his tuxedo pants pockets, his shirt collar open, his bow tie dangling around his neck.

Julie's heart whispered prayers her lips could not utter. She felt frozen by Alexander Crawford's visual embrace.

Well, she would not be prey. "Step away."

He reached for her, but she fumbled backward, out of his grasp. "What, you don't want a little Florida fling?"

"Absolutely not!" She tightened her jaw. "Let me go."

The hallway reverberated with his laugh. "Perhaps the lady protests too much?"

"I said, let me go!"

Julie heard footfalls at the other end of the hall. "You heard her; let her go." She watched Ethan travel the hallway with long, purposeful strides.

She ran to him. "Ethan! What are you doing here?" She couldn't stop trembling.

Ethan wrapped her in his arms, smoothed her hair with his right hand, and cradled her head on his shoulder. His left hand encircled her waist. "Shh, babe, it's going to be all right."

"He. . .followed. . .me." Her words came between wobbly sobs.

"He's gone now. I'm here."

She locked her arms around him as if to crawl inside his skin. With an easy sway, Ethan rocked her from side to side until she'd cried every tear. Finally, she drew a deep, steadying breath. Ethan's fragrance, musty like the scent of the beach at the end of the day, filled her senses.

She wondered if she could love him any more than she did at this very moment. At last, she lifted her face to his. "I'm never leaving home without you again."

He laughed, then lowered his lips to hers. "Never?" he asked after their first kiss in weeks.

"Never." She tiptoed to kiss him again. He tasted sweet.

"For you." He handed her a white carnation. "I wanted it to be a rose, but. . . long story. I'll tell you later."

She took the flower and kissed him again. "Any flower from you is as precious as a rose. Thank you."

Kit appeared around the corner. "Hurry, Julie. Two minutes."

"Oh, Kit, my face."

Ethan kissed her forehead. "It's beautiful."

"No, it's not. Let me touch up my makeup." Julie handed him her carnation and dashed for the ladies' room. Her hands trembled slightly as she touched up her foundation and eye makeup.

Ethan stood guard outside the door. When she emerged, he slipped his arm around her waist as they walked toward the bandstand. "Who was that man?"

"Some man named Alex Crawford. He approached me when I was sitting alone, eating cake."

"Alex Crawford. The football player?" Ethan glanced around the room.

"I don't know about football, but he's a first-class stalker."

"Is he still here?"

Julie set her carnation and purse by the bandstand. Mike and Cassie had already taken their seats. "Don't tell me you want his autograph, Ethan."

He held her close. "Autograph? I want to ask him to step outside to discuss his rude behavior."

"No fighting, Ethan." Sixty seconds with Alexander Crawford terrified her, but she didn't want Ethan drawing attention to the situation by confronting him. She felt a deep compassion for women who had no one to rescue them from the Alexander Crawfords of the world.

But she had Ethan. Suddenly he was there to rescue her. "Ethan."

He stopped scanning the room and gazed down at her. "Yeah, babe."

"What are you doing here?"

"Chasing my wife to the ends of the earth to let her know how much I love her and how important she is to me."

Julie smiled. "Did your grandpa give you that line?"

He chuckled. "No, but he did teach me about Lambert's Code."

"We both have a lot to learn about Lambert's Code." She laced her fingers through his. "I'm glad you're here."

"I'm not going to Costa Rica."

She stiffened. "Really?"

"Not if it means driving a deeper wedge between us."

"But I put a wedge between us. I came here when you asked me not to, and I bought a car without your knowledge."

He kissed her hand. "We both made mistakes. I'm here because I want to start new. We're not teenaged newlyweds anymore, Julie, playing house with dreams of babies."

"It's real life—with hard decisions." Tears dropped from the edges of her cheeks.

He wiped them away. "With disappointments. We can't let every unexpected turn challenge our love and commitment."

She pulled him toward her and kissed him. "I'm sorry about everything. Forgive me?"

"Absolutely. Forgive me?"

"Yes." She sealed her promise with another kiss.

"It's behind us."

Kit floated toward the bandstand, waving a piece of paper.

"Tina had the presence of mind to pay me." Kit flashed the check for the group to see.

Ethan whistled low. "Where do I sign up?"

Julie laughed. "You can't play a note." She stepped onto the bandstand, still marveling at the dramatic events of the evening and the miracle of her rescue by Ethan.

Chapter 20

From the kitchen, Julie called up to Ethan, "There's nothing to eat!"

"Peanut butter and jelly."

She laughed. "Didn't you shop while I was gone?"

"Naw, what for?" He descended the stairs two at a time.

Walking into the kitchen, Ethan thanked God for His mercy and the lesson of Lambert's Code. He'd never forget it.

"I feel like pizza," he said, hugging Julie. The day and a half they'd spent in Florida revived their relationship.

"You want to go out?" She wrapped her arms around him and kissed him.

"No, let's order in." He kissed her cheek. "I'll build a fire in the fireplace."

Julie gave him a quick squeeze before letting go. "I'll call Giuseppe."

The fire crackled as they dove into the large pepperoni pie. Julie twisted the cap off a two-liter bottle of diet soda and poured.

"Bobby and Elle introduced me to someone the other night," Ethan said, bringing up Abby for the first time.

Julie paused from pouring to look at him. "Introduced you to someone?" She tipped her head.

He took a bite of his pizza. "Yeah, a woman." He couldn't hide his grin.

"What?" She set down the soda bottle. "Ethan, don't mess with me. I'm fragile."

He coughed. "Please. You're a rock."

"What woman?"

"Elle's niece, Abby."

Julie tore a slice of pizza off for herself. "I met her once. She was the prettiest ten-year-old I'd ever seen."

"She's seventeen now. And pregnant."

She swallowed her pizza with one gulp. "You're kidding."

"If she finds a family she likes, she'll give the baby up for adoption." Ethan studied her expression.

"When is she due?"

"About four months. Bobby and Elle asked us to consider adopting the baby."

"You didn't say anything to Abby, did you?"

Ethan held up his hand. "Not on your life. I learned my lesson."

Julie arched over the pizza box to give him a kiss. Wiping her hands with a napkin, she asked, "What do you want to do?"

Ethan shrugged, his emotions rising to the surface. "When I pictured children, they were ours. A daughter who could dunk a basketball while humming Beethoven, and a son who loved the arts as much as he loved scoring touchdowns."

Julie nodded. "And children who love the Lord with all their heart, mind, soul, and strength?"

He regarded her, his gaze intent on her oval face. "Yes. In fact, I'd like to work on that aspect of my own life."

"Me, too." Moving the pizza box, Julie sat cross-legged in front of her husband. "You know, almost every girl wants to be a mom."

Ethan nodded and took her hand in his.

"But trying to bear my parents' load made my desire more intense."

"Right."

"For the first time in years, I feel like I have choices. I'm pretty sure it will include adoption, but not right now. God has something for me to do; I just need to discover what. Is that all right?"

He pressed her hand against his chest. "Yes, that's all right. I want to discover God's plan for us as much as you do."

"Well, hold on to your hat—"

"I don't have a hat." He chuckled low and pulled her to him.

"Ha-ha. Ethan, we're on an adventure. . . ."

He nuzzled her neck. "Mm-hmm."

She responded to his tenderness with a kiss, then asked, "Are you paying any attention to me at all?"

He cleared his throat. "Yes, adventure." He brushed a strand of hair away from her face.

"I feel released, Ethan. Like I can stop trying to fit my life into this perfect picture box."

"I know what you mean. I feel like I can stop holding my breath." He picked up another piece of pizza.

"When it's quiet in my soul, I stop thinking how unfair all this is, and you know what I want the most?"

"What?"

"To be with you. Just you and me in a new adventure with the Lord."

"Me, too. So what about Abby?"

Julie's eyes glistened. "I want to wait." She laughed softly. "I can't believe I just heard myself say that, but it's all my heart can do at the moment."

"Actually, I feel the same way." Ethan stared at her for an intense second, then closed the pizza box and said, "Put on your coat; we're going for a ride."

❧❧

The moon reminded Julie of a rare pearl set against black velvet with diamonds scattered around. The celestial body's white halo lit the winter sky, and moonbeams danced over the tiny town of White Birch.

Ethan escorted her to the convertible, blankets tucked under his arm.

"Where are we going?" She waited by her door, shivering.

"It's a surprise." Ethan opened her door, then reached inside to pop the top.

Julie took the blankets he handed her, laughing. "What are you doing? It's freezing."

With the top tucked away, Ethan motioned to the passenger seat. "Your chariot awaits."

Enjoying the impromptu moment, Julie dropped into her seat with a giggle. Ethan spread the blankets over her legs and lap. Last, he plopped a wool beanie on her head.

Content and happy, Julie situated the beanie on her head while Ethan scooted around to the driver's side. He started the engine, cranked the heater, and tuned the radio station to something soft.

Shifting into gear, he tapped on the dash. "It's a modern sleigh ride. We've got two hundred and forty horses."

Julie dropped her head against the seat rest and sang, "Just hear those sleigh bells jingling—"

Ethan joined the song as he took the back roads across town.

"You still haven't told me where we are going," Julie said, her eyes on the night sky.

"You'll see."

In a moment or two, she knew, when the old bridge came into view.

"Perfect," she whispered as Ethan escorted her down the riverbank in the light of the moon.

The night was beautiful and serene, and the lullaby of the river serenaded them. With their arms around each other, they stood on the bank without speaking. For the first time in a very long time, Julie felt like she was running on the right track.

"Come to the bridge." Ethan guided her to the cover of the town landmark. He pulled a flashlight from his pocket and clicked on the small lamp.

"What's wrong? You look so serious." Julie lightly touched his cheek.

Ethan grinned and stuck the flashlight under his chin. "How 'bout now?"

She laughed and batted the light away. "Scary."

Ethan wrapped her in his arms. "My beautiful wife." He bent down on one knee.

"What are you doing?" She dropped to her knees, too, and faced him.

Eye to eye, Ethan said, "Julie, I asked you to marry me almost eleven years ago. We were barely eighteen, young and immature, but in love."

She let out a nervous giggle. "Ethan—"

"Shh, just listen. A lot of things have changed since I asked you to marry me."

"Yes," she said with an easy shake of her head.

Ethan grabbed her hands. "But life has taken a different turn. We have a new tapestry to create for our marriage. So"—he paused for a kiss—"with that in mind, Julie Hanover Lambert, will you be my wife? No expectations except to love and serve each other, and love God with our whole hearts?"

She smiled, her head cocked to one side. "I am your wife, now and forever."

Ethan looked at her, drawing a deep breath. "We've spent the past ten years trying to execute the life we thought we wanted at sixteen. Now, here we are adults, mature—"

Her laugh billowed around him. "Don't throw that word around too loosely, bud. Mature?" She pressed the tip of her nose to his.

He chuckled. "Given, I have my moments. But we know more what I'm about, what you're about, what curveballs life has pitched to us."

"We know the melody of our song."

"We know the rules of the game."

Tears slipped down her cold cheeks. "The last few weeks seem like a nightmare. I don't want to ever do that again."

He brushed away her tears with the tips of his fingers. "So tonight let's declare a fresh start. You and me. We might adopt ten kids, or move to Florida, maybe live to be a hundred and die side by side, holding hands. The possibilities are endless."

Throwing her arms around him, she shouted to the rafters. "And I'll be your wife. For the next decade and every decade after."

With a hoot, Ethan hopped to his feet and whipped out his pocketknife. "I carved our initials the first time I asked you. Guess a second proposal deserves a second carving."

"Don't fall this time." Julie laughed as she watched her husband scale the side of the bridge and, hanging from the rafters, carve their initials into the strong bridge beam.

❧❧

Monday morning, Ethan tossed his sports bag in the foyer by the front door. The aroma of coffee filled the apartment. Walking into the kitchen, he kissed his wife.

"Mom called. She wants us to come to dinner tomorrow night. Is that okay?" Julie handed him a plate of eggs and toast. She smoothed his cheek with the palm of her hand.

"Fine with me. I was thinking of playing some hoops after work tonight. Is that okay with you?"

They stared at each other for a second, then laughed in unison. Ethan held up his hands. "Are we taking this code thing too far?"

Julie sat down at the nook with him. "Well, maybe just a little. Besides, we have dinner with Elizabeth and Kavan tonight."

"Oh, right. I'll play another night." He bit into his egg. "I suppose we'd better break the news to your mom and dad tomorrow."

Julie reached for the butter. "We should have told them this weekend when we had lunch with them after church."

"You're right. I just know it will hit your mom hard." He sipped his coffee.

Julie nodded, spreading a thin layer of butter on her toast. "It will, but she's a strong woman. If we wait too long, they'll hear it from someone else, and that's not right. They need to hear it from us."

"Do you know why they never adopted?"

"Dad didn't have the inclination. At least that's what sticks out in my mind."

Ethan finished his breakfast and took his plate to the kitchen sink. He checked his watch. "It's getting late. We'd better hurry."

One last bite and Julie finished her breakfast. She passed her plate to Ethan, who stood by the dishwasher waiting, and said with a wink, "One of these days, I'm going to learn how to use that thing."

"Warn me first so I don't have a heart attack."

"Ha-ha, what a funny man for a Monday morning."

In a few minutes, Ethan met her at the door. "Should we meet here before going over to Elizabeth and Kavan's? I might just go over from work."

She tiptoed to kiss him. "Okay, be there by six."

Outside, a chilly breeze cut through the parking lot. Ethan stopped Julie before she went to her car. "I want to pray for you before you go. I liked what Pastor Marlow said in church yesterday about speaking blessings over our families."

"I'd love a blessing." Julie leaned her head against his chest.

Ethan set his laptop down and encircled her with his arms. "Bless my wife, Lord, my good wife. I pray she would know how much You, and I, love her."

Julie looked up at him with moist eyes when he said amen. "Thank you, Ethan. I pray the same for you."

Ethan watched Julie drive away, wincing as the car jerked and sputtered out of the apartment complex. He made a mental note to work with her on shifting gears in a high-performance car. Her old jalopy drove like a tired mare compared to the horsepower of the S2000.

When the car vanished from his view, he walked toward his car and called his grandpa. "Can you meet downtown at three o'clock?"

"I'll be there."

Chapter 21

Julie swerved into the school parking lot with zeal for the day—and an idea.

Walking through the front doors as the first bell rang, she dug her cell phone from her purse and dialed Grandma Lambert.

"Hi, Grandma." Julie walked the hall with dozens of kids scurrying to class.

"Julie, good morning. What can I do for you at this hour?"

"I need help planning a surprise."

"I'm your woman." Grandma suddenly sounded ten years younger. "Who are we surprising?"

"Ethan." Julie entered her classroom as the second bell tolled. "The night we got back from Florida, we took a ride to the bridge and Ethan asked me to marry him again."

Grandma chuckled. "I see. Florida must have gone well."

Julie smiled. "Yes, it did." She motioned for her class to come in and settle down.

"Good for you! So what do you have in mind?"

"Well, it occurred to me that when a man asks a woman to marry him, a wedding should follow."

Grandma caught her breath. "A second wedding."

"Well, there *was* a second proposal."

"A grand idea, my dear."

Sophia popped into the classroom as Julie made final arrangements to meet Grandma at Peri's Perk after school.

"How was your weekend?" Sophia whispered as Julie pressed the END button on her cell.

"Wonderful."

Sophia cocked her head to one side. "So I see. You're glowing. By the way, you never told me about Florida."

"I'll talk to you about it later." Julie tapped her watch.

Sophia left after making Julie promise to have lunch with her and give her all the details.

Julie's thoughts were all over the place when she finally called her first class of the day to order. Where to have the ceremony? When? How to get Ethan there? Would she get any teaching done today? She was too excited to focus. Until Miles Stanford raised his hand.

"What are we playing for the spring recital, Mrs. Lambert?"

"You mean you haven't been practicing? Oh, Miles." With a chuckle, Julie went to the blackboard and scribbled out the recital program, again.

Ethan waited outside Earth-n-Treasures, slumping down in the driver's seat, hoping no one would see him. When Grandpa tapped on his window, he jerked forward.

"Why are you ducking down like a teenager skipping school?" Grandpa asked as Ethan stepped into the street.

"I don't want any of Julie's friends to see me."

"Well, let's get going then."

A red velvet strip with silver bells rang out when Ethan pushed open Earth-n-Treasures' front door. Some of the letters on the glass had been scraped away with the swishing of the bells back and forth.

Cindy Mae, the store's owner, came around the counter to greet him. "How's my favorite Lambert?"

Ethan gave her a slight hug. "I bet you say that to all the Lamberts."

"I was talking to your grandpa." Cindy Mae tossed her thick blond braid over her shoulder with a sly grin and hugged the Lambert patriarch.

Grandpa chuckled. "How are you, Cindy Mae?"

"Meaner than a bear in winter."

Ethan laughed. "Spring's around the corner, Cindy Mae." He leaned over the jewelry case.

Cindy Mae walked around. "What can I help you gentlemen with today?"

"Something for Julie. A ring. Not expensive, but not cheap. I can't spend too much right now." Ethan pointed over his shoulder at his grandpa. "I brought him along to help me choose."

Cindy Mae pulled a few items out of the case. "I saw her driving around in a fancy sports car."

"Right." Ethan focused on the pieces Cindy Mae passed under his gaze, not willing to rehash the car ordeal with her. He loved her like a neighbor, but she was one of the strongest links in the town's gossip chain.

"Are you looking for an anniversary band, a new diamond, what?" Cindy Mae placed several more pieces in front of him.

Ethan examined each one, soliciting Grandpa's opinion. They were all pretty but too ordinary. He wanted something unique and extraordinary, like Julie.

After fifteen minutes of telling Cindy Mae no and asking to see something else, she said, "I suppose I could design you a piece."

He hesitated. "Well—"

"Oh, wait." Cindy Mae clapped her hands. She dashed into a back room, hollering over her shoulder, "Brill and I just returned from an estate sale."

With a grimace, Ethan confessed to Grandpa, "A few months from now, I could afford this better, but since I asked her to marry me again, I was hoping—"

"Let's wait and see what Cindy Mae brings out. You never know, son. The

Lord just might surprise you." Grandpa rocked back and forth on his heels, hands in his pockets.

"Here we go." Cindy Mae emerged from the back room. She set a cardboard box on the counter with a thump. Dust billowed.

Ethan's heart wilted. *What in the world could be in that box for Julie—a Cracker Jack prize?*

He couldn't look. Instead, he let Grandpa peer into the junk box while he studied more rings under the glass counter.

I have about two grand to spend. Maybe if I talk to Will about next quarter's bonus... He sighed. They really needed to concentrate on paying off the last of their medical bills and replenishing their savings. He didn't want to live in that apartment forever. What if they decided to adopt? Should they start saving for that right now?

Besides all that, he felt a little guilty spending the money without consulting Julie. But surely surprises didn't fall under Lambert's Code, did they?

"Ah, here it is." Cindy Mae's voice echoed across the small shop as she pulled out a velvet ring box. She popped open the lid and showed it to Grandpa.

Ethan leaned on the counter and watched his grandpa's expression. One snarl and he'd know. But the older man smiled. Big.

"I think we've found a winner."

Ethan hurried over. He saw a dingy band with delicate vines winding between two diamond and two emerald stones. *What? It's hideous.* He didn't know what to say, so he asked, "How much?"

Cindy Mae twisted up her face like she was about to announce he'd won a million dollars. "How much do you want to spend?"

"As little as possible." He sounded cheap, but he had to be honest.

Cindy Mae's grand master expression fell. "How much is that?"

Ethan gestured to the ring. "Cindy Mae, I wouldn't pay a hundred dollars for the ring.

She huffed. "Amateurs." She waved the ring under his nose. "This is real platinum, Ethan, with real diamonds and real emeralds."

Grandpa laughed and motioned toward Cindy Mae. "This is why he brought me along. Shine it up."

❦

Julie waited at Peri's Perk for Grandma. Late afternoon, the coffee and sandwich café was quiet. Peri and her employees sat together at a table in the back, talking and drinking coffee.

Sipping her latte, Julie reviewed the yellow legal paper in front of her.

New dress
Get nails and hair done
Cake by Ramona (if she has time)
New shoes (definitely)

Fresh flowers
Invitations
Buffet food (Grandma and Mom)
Mom's linen, silver/china

A few minutes later, Grandma came through the door, her cheeks a rosy red, her eyes sparkling. "Sorry I'm late."

Peri approached their table. "Hello, Mrs. Lambert. Can I get you anything?"

Grandma patted Peri's hand. "Yes, Matt raves about your chocolate toffee coffee. Let me try one of those."

Peri nodded. "Hot or cold?"

"Hot, please. There's a chill in the air today."

Julie moaned. "The weatherman says we're warming up starting tomorrow."

"Let's hope," Peri said. "Can I refresh your cup, Julie? On the house."

"Yes, thank you."

Peri hurried away. Julie slid her list across the table. "Can you think of anything else?"

Grandma perched her reading glasses on her nose and read. "Well, this is lovely, but I had a different thought in mind." She smiled widely.

Julie pulled the paper back across the table, an excitement stirring in her. "What?"

"Well, your first wedding was a big to-do. How about something simple but romantic and cozy this time."

Julie chewed on her bottom lip. *Hmm. . .* "Like what?"

"We could decorate our back deck and yard with white lights and build a big bonfire."

"Oh, we could wear jeans and sweaters."

"Matt could grill out. I could serve hot cider."

"Perfect, Grandma. I love it."

"Shall you enlist the Merewether Quartet?"

Scribbling on the paper, Julie agreed. "Yes, outdoor music. Kit can find someone to take my place, or just have the violins and viola play."

"We can hold the ceremony at twilight. I have plenty of white lights and candles from Christmas."

"Oh, candles." Julie added candles to the list. "I wanted a candlelight ceremony the first time, but Ethan said he would go crazy waiting until evening."

Grandma laughed. "He was ready to get married."

Julie leaned toward Grandma. "We loved each other, Grandma, but this ceremony is about a deeper commitment; it's about enduring love."

Grandma pressed her hand on Julie's. "I'm proud of you kids. You've endured difficulty and came out shining on the other side. I know many couples wouldn't have weathered such storms."

Julie tapped the corners of her eyes with her fingertips. "Only by God's grace."

She blew her nose, then fired the do-or-die question at Grandma. "So how do we pull this off?"

Grandma flashed a sly smile. "I'm glad you asked. We haven't had a family gathering at our house since Christmas. I'll tell him we're having one of our barbecues. He can help your grandpa dig the fire pit."

She burst out laughing. "Then show up later for his own wedding."

"What a grand surprise."

Peri came with their coffee specialties as they discussed the ceremony details, divvying up the to-do list.

"When shall we do this?" Grandma asked as she jotted notes in her notepad.

Julie tapped the calendar on her electronic planner. "Let me phone Mom and see what their plans are for the next few weeks."

"Remember, your dad, Bobby, and Will leave for Costa Rica on a Sunday, mid-April, I think."

"Right. We could have the ceremony the Saturday before they go."

Grandma waved her hand at Julie. "Perfect."

Autodialing her parents' home phone, Julie mentioned to Grandma, "I can't spend a lot of money. Eth would kill me, but I do want this to be a surprise."

"Don't worry. I'm queen of the shoestring budget."

"Mom, hi, it's Julie." In one breath, she detailed the wedding plans with her mother.

"What a marvelous idea."

"How about a week from Saturday?" Julie chewed on her bottom lip and glanced out the window. *Oh no, Ethan and Grandpa.*

"No," her mom said. "Not the night before your father leaves for his golf trip. You know him."

Julie chewed her lower lip. "Yeah, right. I forgot about his travel neurosis."

Her mom laughed. "Yes, he'll want to pack, worry if he got everything, then pack some more and go to bed early. Why not have the ceremony Saturday?"

That's six days away. Julie looked at Grandma. "Think we can pull it off this Saturday?"

"Certainly." She sat up straight, ready for the challenge.

"This Saturday it is, Mom. I'll talk to you later. I've got to go; Ethan is coming."

"What?" Grandma glanced over her shoulder just as Ethan and Grandpa pushed through Peri's front door.

Chapter 22

What are you two doing here?" Ethan slipped his arm around Julie and kissed her forehead. He fought the sense of guilt over spending the money on the ring without telling her. He'd better give it to her soon or bust.

"Chatting." Julie smiled up at him, but he caught her tucking a yellow piece of paper into her satchel.

"Chatting?" He shifted his gaze to Grandma. She never could mask her feelings well. They were up to something.

"What are you boys up to, hmm?" Grandma asked.

"Yes," Julie echoed. "Why aren't you at work, Ethan?"

He grabbed her hand and held on. "Running errands."

"Yes, running errands," Grandpa parroted. "Lambert's Furniture stuff." He pulled up a stool and waved at Peri.

"Be right there, Mr. Lambert. The usual?"

"Yes, the usual."

"What about you, Ethan?" Peri called.

"Bring me what Julie's having." He sat next to Julie.

Covertly, he glanced at her hand and the small engagement ring he'd slipped on her ring finger a decade ago. He'd promised her a new one, but they could never afford it; then life got in the way. But today he changed all that.

Cindy Mae had polished the ring like Grandpa asked and showed it to Ethan. He'd never seen anything more beautiful. If a piece of jewelry could embody his wife, that piece did.

Cindy Mae wanted three thousand for it. Ethan shook his head, deflated. "Can't go that high."

Grandpa pulled out his wallet. "You put up what you got, Ethan. I'll cover the rest."

"Grandpa, I can't let you do that. No." But his protest fell on deaf ears.

"I'll deduct it from your inheritance."

"What? Lambert's Furniture is my inheritance. I can't let you buy my wife a new ring."

"Then consider it a loan, interest free. You pay me back when you can, ten dollars at a time for all I care."

Just what I need, more debt. But he wanted the ring. "I don't know—"

Cindy Mae sighed and gazed toward the ceiling. "You two kill me. All right, twenty-five hundred."

So the deal was made. Cindy Mae agreed to redo the ring's shank and size it for free. Ethan could pick it up Friday. He couldn't wait to give it to her.

The sooner he gave Julie the ring, the better. He didn't think he could hide this expenditure too long. *Boy, it's hot in Peri's today. Am I sweating?*

"Here you go." Peri set a steaming, frothy coffee in front of him.

He handed it back to her. "Make it an iced coffee, please."

Julie regarded him. "Are you all right?"

He inhaled. "Sure. I'm fine."

"You're sweating." She pressed her hand on his forehead.

"I'm fine. Listen, how about dinner at the Italian Hills Saturday night? You and me?" The idea popped out of his mouth before his brain had time to meter his words. But he liked what he heard.

"Oh no, Ethan, we can't."

"Why not?"

"We're having a spring family barbecue." Grandma jumped into the discussion. "You'll need to help Grandpa dig the fire pit, get set up."

"When did this happen?" Grandpa asked.

"Just now, Matt." Grandma's firm tone surprised Ethan.

He faced Julie. "Then we can go on Friday."

"Um, no, I have quartet rehearsal. Let's go next week."

Ethan shrugged off his disappointment. He wanted to surprise Julie with the ring, but he didn't want to force it. *Lord, I'll submit to Your timing.*

"It's okay; next week is fine."

⊰⊱

On her way home, Julie stopped by Bella's Cards & Gifts to pick up invitations. She and Grandma planned to hand deliver most of them, knowing some friends wouldn't be able to attend on such short notice, but this ceremony was not about a plethora of people or a mountain of gifts. It was about her and Ethan's renewed commitment.

She sat in bed pretending to read, filling out invitations instead. *I hope no one slips up in front of Ethan.*

Grandma called to say Ramona would make the cake, and she'd already enlisted several ladies from the women's Bible study to help make food.

"I told them to plan for fifty to sixty people. What do you think?" Grandma asked.

"That's a good estimate," Julie confirmed. "Thank you so much, Grandma."

Her mom had also called, excited. She'd found Great-Grandma's linens and discovered a Sinclair's sales ad for tea lights while throwing away the newspaper. She would pick some up tomorrow.

"And guess what! Your father said the weather would be sunny and warm this weekend."

"Mom, I appreciate your help."

"Oh, this is marvelous. . . ."

Snuggled now in her bed, writing invitations, Julie felt content. "What a great day, God. Thank You so much for all Your blessings."

Ethan's dark, wavy head popped around the bedroom door. "What are you doing?"

Julie tucked the invitations between the back pages of her book. "Reading."

Flopping on the bed, he took the book from her hand and drew her to him. "I need to tell you something."

She brushed her hand over his hair, her emotions vibrating with a melody for her husband. "You seemed like something was bothering you tonight at Elizabeth and Kavan's."

"I spent some money, Julie."

She pushed herself upright. "On what?"

"You."

"Me?"

"I wanted to surprise you, but after my big money speech to you and hiding the Costa Rica trip, it didn't feel right."

Julie glanced around the room before looking Ethan in the eye. "What have you done with my husband? You look like him—"

"Come on, Jules. Help a guy out here."

She smoothed her hand over his chest and felt his heart beating. She knew it beat for her. "Do what you think is best. But don't spend too much money on me."

"Well, I won't buy a high-performance sports car, if that's what you mean."

She pinched his cheek. "Har, har. You love that car."

"I love you, Julie."

"I know you do. So what'd you buy me?"

He rolled off the bed and held up his hands. "It has to do with our conversation on the bridge the other night. That's all I'm saying."

"Really?" Her heart lurched, and she scrambled over to him. What did he do? Would it mess up her surprise? "Ethan, I need to tell you something."

He pulled off his sweater and disappeared into the closet. "Shoot."

"I spent some money, too. Well, I made plans to spend money."

He popped out of the closet. "On what?"

"On you."

"Me?"

"Well, not just you. You and me."

"How much?" He held his pajama bottoms in his hands.

"I don't know yet." She chewed her thumbnail.

"Less than a thousand?"

Julie gaped at him. "Did you spend a thousand dollars?"

"Did you?"

"No, I haven't spent anything yet, but I'll probably spend a couple hundred. I can keep it simple." Mentally, she ran down her checklist. She could pull off the ceremony without spending much, especially since she didn't need a fancy new dress or accessories. After all, it was a barbecue.

"What are you up to? Is that why you were with Grandma at Peri's? And what was on the yellow legal paper?"

She held up her hands. "Enough already. I'm not saying any more."

He grabbed her waist and tackled her to the bed.

"*Ack!* Ethan—" Her laugh filled the room.

"What are you up to, Mrs. Lambert?"

"Same as you, Mr. Lambert."

On Saturday night, Ethan showered after helping Grandpa dig a bonfire and barbecue pit. He splashed on cologne and dressed in jeans and a white oxford shirt. He looked for his favorite navy sweater. It was missing, again.

Julie. . . He grinned and found a burgundy pullover to wear.

Julie had left hours ago to help Grandma set up, or so she said. Did she mention the quartet might play, too? With her hair rolled in large curlers, she'd dashed out the door. Then dashed back in.

"Oh, Will's going to pick you up tonight."

"What? Why? I can drive my car."

She shrugged. "So we can ride home together."

Jogging down the stairs, Ethan chuckled, thinking of his wife with her big curlers wanting to ride home with him after the barbecue. Giving up the Costa Rica trip and going to her in Florida were the best decisions he'd ever made besides marrying Julie.

Deep down, he suspected tonight had to do with Julie's surprise for him, but he felt clueless as to what, or how.

The doorbell rang. "Come in."

Will opened the door. "Are you ready to go?"

"Yes." Ethan stood in the kitchen, holding the pantry door open. *We still need to clean this out.* "Have you eaten yet?"

"Are you kidding? I'm waiting for Grandma's barbecue."

Ethan regarded his cousin. "Do you know what tonight is about?"

"Family gathering. Nothing out of the ordinary."

"So you say." Ethan slapped him on the back. "Let's swing by the diner. Get a little preparty dessert."

"I like your thinking."

Will started out the door.

"Got your keys?" Will asked.

Ethan patted his pockets. "Check. Keys and wallet."

"Oh, hey—" Will pulled up short. "Grandpa said I should see that ring you bought Julie."

Ethan stopped on the porch step. "Now? You want to see it now?"

Will tipped his head and motioned over his shoulder with his thumb. "We're here, aren't we?"

Ethan furrowed his brow, shrugged, and ran upstairs to the bedroom with Will following. He'd hidden the ring in his sports bag, figuring Julie would never look there—for anything.

Will took the small red velvet box from him and lifted the top. He whistled low. "This set you back a bit. Do you need a raise?"

"No." Ethan reached for the box. Should he tell him about Grandpa's help?

Will examined the ring in the fading light of the window. "I'm definitely going to Cindy Mae if I ever need an engagement ring."

"She's got some beautiful stuff. Let's get going, or we won't have time for pie."

The phone rang as Ethan reached again for the ring box.

"You answer the phone; I'll put the ring away." Will stepped into the closet. "Hello?"

It was Grandpa. "What are you doing? I need some help here."

Ethan chuckled. "Okay, we're on our way." He turned to Will. "Grandpa beckons."

"Let's go." Will patted him on the back and started downstairs.

"Did you put it in the pocket of the bag? I don't want to lose it."

"Yes, I put it in the pocket. The ring is safe. Let's go, or we won't have time to stop for preparty dessert."

"I'm with you, Cousin. I'm with you." Ethan followed Will downstairs and out the front door.

Chapter 23

In Grandpa and Grandma's master bedroom, Julie slipped into a new pair of jeans and a blouse her mother had bought in Manchester.

"I couldn't resist." Her mother stood off to the side, hands folded together. "A woman has to have something new for her wedding. . .well, renewal ceremony."

Julie smiled at her. "Thank you, Mom. I love the clothes." She pulled on Ethan's navy merino wool sweater. "There, now I have something old, borrowed, and blue to go with the new."

Mom cried. Sniffling, she said, "I'll go check on how the ladies are progressing with the food." As she exited, Elizabeth came in.

"I've got red lipstick. But it's really red." She held up the wand for Julie to see.

She wrinkled her nose. "Not me."

"Didn't think so." Elizabeth closed that tube and opened another one. "This one is called blush. And it has sparklies in it."

Julie took the lipstick and striped it across her wrist. "Perfect."

Elizabeth raised her hands. "We have a winner. I'll take the red one down to Elle."

Julie made a face. "Elle? Bright red lipstick?"

"Yes, it's always the quiet ones, you know."

Julie laughed. "You're too funny, Beth." She watched her cousin-in-law exit, her middle slightly round with new life. Julie resolved to be the best "auntie" ever to the little Donovan.

Grandma bustled in after Elizabeth. "Oh, land sakes, I'm more nervous than at your first wedding. A barbecue wedding. What were we thinking?"

With a nervous giggle, Julie admitted, "It's going to be great. The surprise element alone will be worth it."

"Your hair. It's still in curlers," Grandma said.

"I know. Michele hasn't made it here yet."

Just then, a tall redhead stumbled into the room, breathless. "Sorry I'm late."

"Well, speaking of—" Grandma said as Michele's bag of beauty tricks toppled to the floor.

Elizabeth came in right after Michele, followed by Mom again. As Elizabeth helped Michele retrieve the contents of her bag, Elle entered.

"He's here."

Julie jumped. "He is?"

Elle nodded, her eyes wide with excitement.

"Oh no. Is Pastor Marlow here?" Julie jittered about, biting her bottom lip, while Michele took the curlers out of her hair.

"No, he's not."

Julie held up her hands. "Great. Don't let Ethan see him. He'll figure it out."

"I'm on it," Elle said.

"Oh, Elle." Julie darted after her.

"Julie!" Michele ripped the last roller out of the bride's head. "Stand still."

At the door, Julie reminded Elle, "Don't let the quartet play until I come out to the deck. That'll tip him off, too."

"Right."

"Have Grandpa or Dad put on a CD or something. The CD player is on the deck."

"Right again."

Elle went off on her mission, and Julie faced everyone in the room. "Am I a basket case? Yes, I'm a basket case."

All the voices rose to console her. Well, she had a right to be nervous. She was a bride after all. Even for a second time, it must go well. Especially the surprise part.

Michele jerked on her arm. "Sit down, or you're going down those stairs with a rat's nest for hair."

Julie sat in the chair and tried to relax. When she let herself exhale, she realized how fun it had been to plan the ceremony. She hoped Ethan liked his surprise.

What if he doesn't? She'd never considered that. She jumped to her feet and swerved around.

"Ow!" Michele dropped the hot flat iron to the floor.

"What if Ethan doesn't like his surprise?" She whipped around to Michele. "Sorry."

"Ethan will love his surprise," Mom reassured her.

Elizabeth added, "Didn't he ask you to marry him again?"

Julie fanned her face. "Okay, okay." She took a cleansing breath and sat down.

"Don't get up again." Michele came at her with the flat iron, her lips pressed into a narrow line.

In fifteen minutes, Michele worked her magic, and everyone agreed Julie looked radiant and beautiful. "I even like the jeans," Grandma said.

As if on cue, her father tapped on the door. "It's time, Julie. We've maneuvered Ethan to the center of the deck, away from the bonfire smoke." He smiled. "But I'm not sure he'll stay there. He's asking for you."

"Thanks, Dad. I'm ready." Julie's gaze lingered on his angular face for a moment, thinking how much she loved him. He and Mom had taken the baby news as well as expected. Mom cried, and Dad cleared his throat, even disappeared for five minutes without warning. Yet they offered their love and support for whatever decisions she and Ethan would make concerning future children.

"Okay, Julie?" Dad's gentle voice interrupted her thoughts.

She cleared her head with a slight shake. "I'm sorry. I missed what you were saying."

He grinned. "Go down the front stairs and out the front door. Wait at the edge of the house until you hear the quartet play 'Pachelbel's Canon.' Then walk toward the deck steps. We'll all be waiting for you."

Ethan leaned against the deck railing, arms folded over his chest. "Where's Julie?" he asked Grandpa. "I see Kit and the quartet setting up, but no Julie."

Grandpa glanced around with a shrug. "She's coming."

Ethan shook his head. *Something's not right here. Is that Mrs. Hayes from Grandma's Bible study?* Mark Benton passed by with Sophia. This was not a typical Lambert gathering. *Something's definitely up.*

From the opposite end of Grandpa and Grandma's wide deck, Ethan heard the quartet begin to play. The family started gathering around. They all smiled at him. *What?*

"Ethan, over here." Will motioned for him to come by the steps.

"What's going on?" he asked in Will's ear.

"Look." Will nudged him.

Julie emerged from the shadows wearing his navy sweater, a small bouquet of flowers in her hand. His heart flip-flopped. Every sound, every person faded away in the light of her beauty.

She stopped at the top of the steps. "Hi, Ethan."

He tried to speak but couldn't. Suddenly Pastor Marlow stood beside him. "Here's your surprise, Ethan."

Low chuckles rippled through the crowd.

Julie grabbed his hand. "You asked me to marry you again. So we're getting married, *again.*"

His smile burst wide, and he rubbed his forehead. "How'd you. . . ? I mean—I had no idea. All of you knew?"

"Surprise!"

Pastor Marlow settled the intimate gathering. "Let's get these two married before they change their minds."

The friends and family laughed.

Pastor Marlow prayed, then instructed Ethan, "Face your bride, please."

"Gladly." Ethan turned to Julie, his *bride* for all time. He winked. "Nice sweater."

"I think so."

Marlow started, "Do you covenant with God to love this woman as your wife, in laughter and sorrow, in disappointment and success, in poverty and riches, always remembering Lambert's Code?"

Ethan peered sideways at the pastor. The man was grinning. Shifting his gaze forward to Julie, he answered strong and sure, "Absolutely."

Pastor Marlow looked at Julie. "Do you covenant with God to love this man as your husband, in laughter and sorrow, in disappointment and success, in poverty and riches, always remembering Lambert's Code?"

Softly she said, "With my whole heart."

"Then I declare you husband and wife for a second time. Let no one separate what God has joined together."

While everyone cheered, Ethan snatched her into his arms and twirled her around. When he set her down, he heard Pastor Marlow ask for the ring.

Julie leaned toward him and said in a low voice, "There is no ring, Pastor."

Ethan winced. He had a ring—a perfect ring for a perfect occasion. But it wasn't here. It was at home, safe and sound in his smelly sports bag.

"How about this ring?" Will stepped forward and handed the pastor the red velvet box.

"I thought you put it back in the pocket." Ethan's eyes followed his cousin as he returned to his spot among the family.

"I did. My pocket." He tapped his jacket pocket and winked.

Ethan shook his head, grinning. *A conspiracy.*

Julie gasped when Ethan slipped the ring on her finger. "Ethan, it's beautiful. Oh my, I don't know what to say." Her hand trembled in his.

"Repeat after me," Pastor Marlow instructed. "Let this ring be a sign and seal of our covenant and pledge."

Ethan repeated the words with vigor. Then he added a vow of his own. "Babe, you are number one in my life: before sports, before work, before everything."

Her green eyes sparkled.

Pastor Marlow turned to Julie. "You don't have a ring, but repeat after me."

"Okay." Her gaze never shifted from Ethan's. He thought his heart might explode. Every ounce of heartache that led to this moment almost seemed worth it. Almost.

"Let this ring be a sign and seal of our covenant and pledge."

Softly Julie made her promise. Like Ethan, she added a few words of her own. "I promise to respect you by never keeping bad news from you and by consulting you on future car purchases." She squeezed his hand. "I love you, Ethan."

"I love you, Julie." He drew her to him.

"Ethan," Pastor Marlow said, "you may kiss your bride."

So he did.

Epilogue

Six months later

Julie cradled little Matthew Lambert Donovan in her arms, breathing in the scent of his newborn skin. With her fingers, she smoothed his soft, dark curls.

"He's beautiful, Elizabeth."

"I'm still amazed. He's a week old, and I can't imagine life without him."

Ethan marched into the nursery. "Where's my new cousin?" He sounded like a general looking for his troops.

"Shh, Ethan, he's right here." Julie settled Baby Matt in his arms.

Ethan stared down at him. His voice was husky when he said, "He's so little."

Kavan wrapped his arm around Elizabeth. "Listen, you two, please don't feel obligated, but we'd like you to be Matt's guardians. You know, in case something happens to Elizabeth and me."

Julie waved off the comment. "Come on, nothing's going to happen to you two. Please."

"Well, we hope not, but just in case, we'd want Matt to be raised by you guys."

Julie peered at Ethan. By reading his expression, she knew the answer without asking.

Elizabeth added, "Please, think and pray about it. We understand if you don't—"

"We'd love to," Ethan blurted, then gave Julie a sheepish grin. "If you agree."

"Of course I agree." She kissed Baby Matt tenderly.

Kavan smiled at Elizabeth. "Wonderful."

Later in the evening, sitting around the dining room table slicing pieces of chocolate cake, Kavan asked, "Have you two decided yet?"

Julie cut a piece of cake. "We're getting there."

Ethan picked up an empty plate when Elizabeth shoved the cake his way. "I've investigated several adoption agencies." He cut a large piece of cake.

"But we won't do anything until we get back from Paris with Kit in the spring," Julie said.

Ethan took a bite of cake, snickering. "Kit's at our apartment more than her own home. She said since she doesn't have children, she adopted us."

Julie sighed, feeling content and peaceful. While she and Ethan looked into having children, they'd found a *mom*. Instead of adopting, they were adopted.

Right now, Kit needed them as much as any woman needed a child. Only the Lord could have orchestrated such a union.

Elizabeth sat back, cake plate in her hands. "I'll be adopted for a trip to Paris."

They laughed and talked about Kit, babies, and adoption, and Elizabeth poured glasses of milk. "Let's eat all the cake," she said.

"Hear, hear!"

This is true family. This is right, Julie thought. In her heart, she thanked the Lord for His grace and for teaching her and Ethan the beauty of submitting to one another.

Lambert's Peace

Dedication

For Jesus, the Christ, the Prince of Peace.

Chapter 1

Taylor Hansen parked her new BMW in the shade of her childhood home, pressed her head against the steering wheel, and whispered a prayer.

Lord, what have I done?

After a moment, she drew a long breath, smoothed her hands down the front of her dark red linen suit, and popped the BMW's trunk. Stepping out of the car and into the afternoon light, she wondered how many times she'd driven the familiar roads from Manhattan to White Birch and back again.

Gold-tipped maple leaves rustled in the afternoon breeze as she yanked her suitcases from the car's trunk and slung the strap of her laptop case over her shoulder, then snapped the trunk shut.

Any other day, any other time, the beauty of the day would motivate her to change her clothes and go for a good, long run. But for now, in this moment, her heart remained locked in the dark places of disappointment, frustration, and anxiety.

As she walked toward the kitchen door, dragging her suitcases behind, Taylor pinched her lips together, determined not to cry.

She did this to herself. She'd calculated the cost and acted. Nevertheless, she never imagined *this* would happen to her.

Entering the two-story brick home she called, "Mom?"

No answer. The house was quiet and perfumed with the lingering scent of bread and cinnamon.

Taylor lugged her suitcases up the back stairs from the kitchen to her old bedroom. She dropped her designer purse and laptop case onto her worn oak desk, shoved her luggage and overnight bag against the wall, then fell face-first into the familiar comfort of her old bed.

Lord, please tell me I didn't ruin my life. She sat up with a jerk, pressing her fingers against her eyes.

"Get ahold of yourself, Taylor." She paced around her old room. "This is a minor setback."

She removed her laptop from its monogrammed leather case, booted it up, and hooked up to the phone line. While dialing out to the World Wide Web, Taylor made a note in her electronic data assistant: *Arrange for broadband Internet connection at Mom and Dad's.* She would need it.

For the rest of the morning and afternoon, Taylor surfed the Web, made calls, and e-mailed contacts. She barely noticed when the afternoon light faded to the muted colors of dusk and dark shadows fell across her room.

When a thin, familiar "Hello?" sounded down the hall, she glanced up from the computer.

"Mom, in here."

Trixie Hansen graced the doorway and flipped on the light. "Taylor, what are you doing here?"

Taylor gave her mom a hug. The petite, trim woman wore a navy suit with matching pumps. "How are you?"

"Fine; exhausted. I've been at a ladies' aid meeting for the church bazaar."

"Ladies' aid meeting? Can Mrs. Cramer still talk a mannequin to death?"

Mom smiled. "Of course. Some things never change; you know that. But never mind about Dot—what are you doing home? It's the middle of the week."

In the faint glow of the lamp's light, Taylor saw the concerned expression on her mother's delicate features.

"I just needed to come home." She sat on the edge of her bed, realizing she still wore her business suit and two-inch heels. Her makeup felt stale and congealed, and the idea of a shower reminded her of how good the community pool felt on a hot summer day.

Mom studied her for a moment. "Are you all right?"

Taylor kicked off her shoes and squished her toes into the carpet nap. "I'm fine. Is this carpet new?"

"Yes, it is." Mom studied her for a moment then added, "And it is highly unusual for you to show up unannounced, Taylor. Are you sure everything is all right?"

"Well, I'm not sick or hurt, if that's what you mean." Taylor opened one of her suitcases, looking for a pair of jeans and a T-shirt. She wanted to explain her sudden appearance in White Birch but still had trouble understanding the events of the last three days herself.

"Hello. . .anybody home? Trixie?"

Mom fluttered over to the doorway. "Grant. Up here in Taylor's room."

In few seconds, Dad's cheery face peered around the door. "My two favorite women." He kissed Trixie and wrapped his arms around Taylor.

"So," he started, holding her at arm's length, "what are you doing home?" His gray eyes sparkled with merriment.

Sadness washed over Taylor like a chilling waterfall. How could she tell her biggest fan—the man who had dubbed her the whiz kid—that she'd failed?

"Taylor, is everything all right?"

She said without rehearsal, "I left Blankenship & Burns."

Trixie leaned on Grant's arm. "What do you mean?"

"I quit." She hated the sound of that word—*quit*. It spelled failure.

Grant chuckled. "She's teasing us, Trixie."

Taylor peered into her father's eyes. "No, Daddy, I'm not. Movers are packing up my apartment as we speak. I'm putting my stuff in storage." She glanced around her room. "I'd like to stay here for a while if I could."

Mom gasped and covered her cheek with her hand. "Really, Taylor. You actually quit. Well, I never—"

Taylor snapped. "Yes, Mom, I quit."

Grant held up his hands. "Okay, you two, let's go down and have some hot tea and some of Mom's coffee cake. Then, Taylor, you can fill us in."

❧❧

Will Adams sat on the edge of the couch in his twin brother's spacious living room. A blind date. What was he thinking?

"I'm thirty-three," he muttered, running his hand along the back of his neck. "Going on a blind date like a desperate schoolboy."

"Come on, it's not that bad," Bobby said, laughing. Will stood to pace, jiggling the keys in his pocket. "I can't believe I let you and Elle set me up."

"Beats sitting at home on a Friday night with Harry."

Will turned to him. "Harry's great company. Man's best friend, you know."

"It's one night, Will. One night. Who knows? You just might fall in love."

They were to pick Mia Wilmington up on their way to dinner at Italian Hills, the town's most romantic restaurant. Not Will's idea for a first date. Wouldn't a casual night of eating pizza at Giuseppe's be much better?

"You know, you're making this way harder than it has to be," Bobby said, glancing over his shoulder at Will while clicking through the sports channels. "You run a multimillion-dollar furniture company."

"Furniture, I know. Mia Wilmington, I don't," Will said, laughing softly as he regarded the man whose features mirrored his own.

Elle entered the room. "The kids are settled in the family room with your mom, fried chicken, and cold sodas."

The men stood. "You look beautiful, Elle." Bobby kissed his willowy wife.

Will slipped on his tan sports coat. "Let's go before I change my mind."

Elle brushed her hand down his arm. "Give tonight a chance, Will. It's been so long since you—"

Bobby interrupted. "Don't go there, Elle. He'll bite your head off." He held his wife's coat for her.

Elle slipped her arms into the sleeves. "I know it's hard to meet new people, Will."

"People I can handle. Blind dates. . .different species."

Elle exhaled. "Honestly, if I'd known it would traumatize you this much I wouldn't have bothered."

Will squirmed. Elle deserved more from him. "I'm sorry."

She linked her arm with his. "Don't worry, it's going to be wonderful."

On the ride to Mia's apartment, Elle reminded Will that his date taught performing arts at White Birch High School, possessed a very gregarious and bubbly personality, and had the "most beautiful smile."

Her words did little ease to Will's disdain for the situation, but he only had himself to blame. He'd said yes. Never again. Bobby had made a good point earlier.

Will ran a multimillion-dollar company. He didn't need his sister-in-law to find him dates.

Walking alone to Mia's door, Will secretly hoped she wouldn't answer. But after one subtle knock, the door jerked open.

"You must be Will." A petite blond with deep-set green eyes stood in the doorway.

"I'm so happy to meet you."

"Nice to meet you, too."

She tossed her head back, flipping long, straight blond hair over her shoulders. "Elle was right; you are handsome." She flashed Will a sparkling smile.

He shifted from one foot to the next. "Ready to go?"

"Absolutely," she said like she owned the word.

At Bobby's Volvo, Mia glided into the backseat, greeting Bobby and Elle.

Will shut her door and hurried around to the other side. Though she'd overwhelmed him at first, he found her extremely beautiful. Maybe this evening wouldn't be so bad after all.

Fifteen minutes later they were seated in the glow of flickering candles at Italian Hills, listening to the stringed music of the Merewether Quartet. They waved hello to their cousin Ethan's wife, Julie, the quartet's cellist.

They ordered iced teas and appetizers, and Mia chatted endlessly. She went from describing the day's school lunch to a pair of shoes she wanted to wear tonight but couldn't find.

Will watched closely to see if she took a breath between sentences.

When their server arrived with the appetizers, Mia placed her hand on Elle's shoulder and said with a wink, "I should note Will's in the blue shirt so I don't accidentally try to get a good-night kiss from your husband. I never saw two faces that looked more alike."

Elle gave her a demure smile. "I'll make sure you don't get the wrong man."

"Oh, Elle," Mia said with an annoying cackle, "you're so bourgeois."

Will grimaced. *Bourgeois?*

Mia turned her attention to him. "How did you get to be the big cheese at Lambert's Furniture?" Mia reached out and gave his forearm a strong squeeze. "Wow," she said, raising a brow. "Do you work out?"

Will moved his arm and cleared his throat. "Bobby and our cousin Ethan carry a large part of the load. I merely oversee the big picture."

"Oh, modest." Mia looked at Elle. "Don't you just love a strong, modest man?"

"Yes, I do."

When Mia turned her attention to her appetizer plate, Elle cut a glance at Will and mouthed, "I'm sorry."

Will shook his head as if to say, "It's okay."

During dinner Mia continued to dominate the conversation with grand tales of her trips to Europe and the Orient—and not once, but twice more called Elle "bourgeois."

Will couldn't wait for the evening to end.

Around seven, they ordered coffee and dessert. Elle stood and said, "If you'll excuse me, I'm going to the ladies' room."

"I'll go, too." Mia picked up her purse, smoothing her hand along Will's shoulder as she went past, as if they were an intimate couple.

As soon as the women were out of earshot, Will draped his arm over the back of his chair and regarded Bobby. "Bourgeois? She called your elegant, socially astute wife *bourgeois*."

Bobby laughed. "I guess she is a little bit of a fruitcake."

"Cotton candy," Will said, his jaw set.

"Cotton candy?" Bobby crinkled his brow.

"Whipped sugar on a stick. All fluff and no substance. An evening with Mia is like consuming *verbal* cotton candy." Will made an *ick* face.

Bobby grinned. "She is beautiful, though. And well traveled."

Will reached for his water. "Look, she's a lovely lady. I don't want to be rude, but she's not for me."

"Maybe she's nervous, Will. Do the Giuseppe's thing, or take her to Sam's Diner. Just the two of you."

"No." Will shook his head and leaned to the side as the waiter placed cheesecake in front of him. "I can tell you now she's not for me. I don't want to waste her time or mine."

Bobby challenged, "You're that sure after one dinner."

His brother's perplexed expression made Will laugh.

"Look, I am at peace about being single. I'm content. I'll date when I meet the right one."

Bobby nodded, slicing off a corner of his dessert. "Fine, but I don't think one date is enough. Look at how many people start out hating each other and end up happily married."

"Trust me on this one, I—" A subtle motion across the room caught Will in midsentence. He dropped his linen napkin on the table and stood slowly. Across the room, the Italian Hills' maître d' escorted Grant and Trixie Hansen to a table nearby, and. . .

He couldn't believe it.

"I'm sorry I got you into this," Bobby said.

"Taylor," he said, his gaze following the lithe, exquisite brunette.

Chapter 2

The maître d' held Taylor's chair as she slid up to the table. "You really didn't have to do this," she said to her parents.

"It's nothing, kiddo. We've been planning to come here for several weeks now." Grant unrolled his silverware from his napkin.

Taylor smiled. "This would be nicer for you and Mom if you didn't have your daughter tagging along." She tapped her chest for emphasis.

"Nonsense," her mother said.

As she reached for her menu, Taylor surveyed the room, the chandelier-and-crystal atmosphere familiar to her. The last time she was here? She thought for a moment. Bobby and Elle's wedding reception. The night she and Will went wading. . .

Taylor shook away the image. *Too long ago to matter now.*

But it was the devastation of that night that made her flee White Birch for New York. In some ways she owed her career to heartbreak and Will Adams.

Her shoulders slumped. Her career. What career? She'd ended that two days ago. No thanks to Lisa Downey. She grabbed her water goblet and took a long drink.

Dad ordered a spinach and artichoke dip with focaccia bread, then turned to Taylor. "What's the plan?"

She put down her menu. "Excuse me?" Was it the lighting, or were her dad's cheeks pale?

"What's the plan? New job? Stay here in White Birch?"

Taylor laughed, reaching for her freshly poured iced tea. "Stay in White Birch? And do what?"

"Get married, give your mom and me more grandkids. Tim's children are practically grown."

"We're ten years apart, Dad." Taylor laughed.

Dad continued, "Claire's eighteen and already graduated. Jarred is sixteen and waiting tables at Sam's, and Quentin is fourteen going on thirty."

Taylor nodded. "He is a little precocious."

"He's very intelligent," Mom added in her best grandma voice.

"Much like you, Taylor. Another whiz kid in the making."

Taylor stared past her father, twisting her napkin with her fingers. "I don't feel like much of a whiz kid."

"Doesn't matter what you feel; it's what you know to be true."

Taylor focused her gaze on her father and smiled. He looked so frail. "Thank you, Dad. And yes," she said as she squared her shoulders, "I'm getting a new job. A better job."

"Taylor, don't you want to marry and have children? You're thirty-three."

"I'm aware of my age, Mom, but I can't leave my career and reputation flapping in the October breeze. I have to reestablish myself, or my career is over."

"Seems you've been all about your career for the last decade. Time for real life."

"She'll get there, Trixie. She'll get there. But she's right. She's worked hard. You don't become a principal CPA overnight. Quitting Blankenship & Burns shouldn't be the last line on her résumé."

The waiter brought the bread and sauce appetizer. Grant said a prayer, and Taylor mused over his wisdom. He'd never lived anywhere but White Birch; he'd never worked anywhere but Lambert's Furniture. Sixty-six years in one town, fifty years with one company.

Her parents amazed her.

The waiter came for their dinner order. Taylor ordered the baked ziti with a side salad. Her father ordered lasagna, and her mom ordered the chicken Alfredo.

"I'm splurging tonight." Mom smiled as she folded her menu.

Taylor smiled. "Good for you—" A sudden clatter interrupted Taylor. She looked across the table to see Dad mopping up his spilled water.

"Dad, are you okay?" Taylor picked up her napkin to help clean the mess, noticing again the pallor of his face.

"I'm all right. Just a little weak from hunger, I guess," Grant said.

"He's fine." Trixie gently pressed the back of her hand against his cheek. "He's fine. Just needs a good meal."

Taylor studied her father for a moment. He didn't look fine, and his wan complexion didn't come from hunger. "Dad, have you been to the doctor?"

"Not yet, no." He kept his gaze on the menu.

Taylor turned to her mom. "Get him to a doctor."

"He's fine, Taylor. He's fine."

"Dad, has this happened before?"

Grant held up his hand. "Taylor, I'll make an appointment."

❦

Will paid the check, and while Bobby helped the ladies with their coats, he whispered to his brother, "I'm going to say hello to Taylor."

Bobby shifted his gaze to the Hansens' table. "Don't make a big deal. You may not want to marry Mia, but she's your date for tonight."

Will held out his hands. "I'm going to say hello to an old friend."

"Then we'll come with you. Elle, Mia, let's go over and say hello to the Hansens."

"Who?" Mia asked, louder than Will thought necessary.

"Some friends of ours," Elle said, smiling, buttoning her top coat button.

"Taylor was my maid of honor."

The small blond smiled. "Really." She slipped her arm possessively around Will's.

He winced. If he moved his arm, it would be rude to Mia. But the last thing he wanted clinging to him when he greeted Taylor for the first time in ten years was another woman.

"Good evening, Grant, Trixie," Bobby said, shaking Grant's hand as the man stood. "Hello, Taylor."

"Elle! Bobby. Hello." Taylor rose from her chair.

Will stood back, watching. Her movements were sublime and controlled. He saw a confidence in her words and manner that must have come from living and working in New York.

"Where's her husband?" Mia asked, squeezing his arm.

Will looked down at her. "She's not married."

"Oh," Mia said sharply.

"You have to come over and see our youngest, Max. He's four already," Elle said to Taylor.

"Already? And I've never met him."

Will noticed her fingers tapping against the tabletop.

"Taylor's at the house; give her a call, Elle," Grant said, waving his cheese-covered bread in the air.

"Dad, please." Taylor faked a chuckle. "They don't want to know all about me."

Will recognized the look on her face. Apparently, New York hadn't removed all of her anxieties.

"Of course we do, Taylor. You've got to come over before going back to New York. Please."

"Well, all right." Taylor pressed her hand against the back of her neck, then glanced around at Will.

He waved and moved away from Mia's grip toward Taylor. "Good to see you."

"You're looking well," Taylor said, giving him a slight hug. The clean, subtle scent of her perfume lingered around him. Their eyes met for one brief moment.

"You look amazing," he said.

"Ahem." The blond dynamo sidled up next to Will.

He stepped aside. "Taylor Hansen, I'd like you to meet Mia Wilmington."

"Nice to meet you." Taylor offered her hand.

"Likewise." Mia slipped her arm through Will's.

Will smiled to cover his uneasiness. "Mia teaches at the high school."

Taylor grinned, revealing perfect, white teeth. Will thought she was beautiful. "Very nice." She shifted her gaze toward him.

He knew that look, too. Her "Adams, what are you doing?" look.

Grant brought up the topic of Lambert's Furniture, which took Will and Bobby off in conversation. Elle and Trixie were engaged in a discussion about the last ladies' Bible study, and Mia studied Taylor, arms folded.

Will kept one ear in the conversation with Grant, one listening to Mia and Taylor.

"What do you do?" Mia asked, her voice too sweet.

"I'm a principal CPA," Taylor said with control and grace.

When the waiter appeared with their salads, Will said, "Bobby, we'd better go." He smiled at Taylor. "Good to see you."

She tipped her head. "You, too. Nice to meet you, Mia."

Elle reached for a final hug. "It's been too long."

"I know," Taylor said.

Will was the last one through the door. Glancing over his shoulder, his eyes met hers as she watched him leave.

❦❧

Late Wednesday afternoon Taylor zipped her overnight bag shut and set it by the bedroom door. She slid a few extra résumés inside her leather portfolio. Tomorrow afternoon she would fly to Charlotte, North Carolina, for her first post-Blankenship & Burns interview.

It had been a week since she left the prestigious New York firm and the life she had built in New York. Mechanically, Taylor moved through the days, one goal in mind: Find a new job.

When Conrad & Associates called Monday morning, her hopes soared.

It had been a long time since she'd interviewed, so as Taylor changed from jeans to running sweats, she mentally rehearsed answers to possible questions.

Conrad: Where do you see yourself in five years?

Taylor: Contributing to the overall vision and goal of Conrad & Associates. Moving toward becoming a partner.

Conrad: What are your greatest strengths?

Taylor: Vision, determination, decisiveness, and ability to focus. Follow-through.

Conrad: Weaknesses?

Taylor: Don't know when to quit, sometimes. Stubborn.

She tied on her running shoes, laughing at herself. Perhaps she'd learned a lesson from the Blankenship experience after all. She was stubborn. More than she knew.

Conrad: How can our firm benefit from hiring you?

Taylor: I have more than ten years' experience in finance, accounting, and investments. I worked at one of the world's most popular financial magazines, Millennium. *I'm smart, quick, and an excellent team leader or player, whichever is needed.*

Taylor left her room and jogged down the back staircase into the kitchen.

Conrad: Tell us why you left Blankenship & Burns.

"Are you going for a run?" Trixie looked up from where she peeled potatoes, her housedress covered with a wide apron. "Dinner will be ready in an hour."

"Yes." Stretching her legs, Taylor regarded her mom. Trixie Hansen was more like a fifties housewife than a twenty-first-century woman.

Outside, Taylor scanned the orange and red horizon, colored by the setting sun. She drew a deep breath. Cold air, scented with the fragrance of fall leaves, filled her lungs.

Running down Main Street, she kept an even gait, gradually hitting a rhythm, and the anxiety over her life eased.

She would never admit it out loud, but being home—being in White Birch—was like coming home to her best friend. It rejuvenated her, made her focus and remember what's important in life. Odd to think that a town could be her friend. But in many ways, White Birch was just that.

With each step, Taylor reviewed the last few years. Rapid promotions—adding ten or more hours to each workweek. Almost engaged to Ryan Logan. She thanked the Lord many times for saving her from that relationship.

It had been two years since her last vacation. She and her girlfriend, Reneé, had spent a week in Paris. *Ugh, that was exhausting.* Reneé had refused to sleep. She had to see everything; the sunrise, the sunset, the Louvre, every mile along the Seine River. . .

She made a mental note to call Reneé with an update. When Taylor had decided to leave New York, she called the movers, then Reneé.

"Why are you leaving the city? Leave the firm, but stay here," Reneé had insisted with a girlfriend's whine.

"Girl, you know I love you, but it's time for me to move on. Crazy as it seems, quitting has freed me. Now I can see what the rest of the world has to offer."

The feeling of freedom and confidence lasted until Taylor ended the conversation with Reneé and drove out of the city limits. She had battled with anxiety ever since.

But her God was a God of peace. She had to trust in that.

Taylor let her thoughts wander over the past week—dinner with her parents at Italian Hills, her father's pale complexion, Pastor Marlow's Sunday sermon, seeing Bobby and Elle, and Will. . .

Will Adams. Handsome as ever, strong and quiet, speaking volumes with his blue eyes and rakish smile. . .

Taylor wondered about Mia. Though very beautiful, she didn't seem like Will's type. But what did she know after all these years?

Mia certainly seemed into him. Taylor remembered the woman's possessive hook on Will's arm.

As she headed down Main Street and rounded the corner toward Milo Park, she heard the echo of a bouncing ball then the rattle of a hoop.

She slowed her pace as she neared the courts, stopping to peer through the chain-link fence.

Catching her breath, she couldn't help but grin and challenge the lone player. "You still any good at one-on-one?"

Chapter 3

Will turned at the sound of her voice. In a million years, he couldn't have suppressed his smile.

He dribbled in place, regarding Taylor from midcourt. "I'm still better than you, if that's what you mean."

"You think so?" She rounded the fence, tall and angular in her baggy red sweats and faded university sweatshirt. It hung loose about her torso, and the ends of her short, chestnut-brown hair pointed in all directions.

Will laughed. "Any day of the week and twice on Sunday." Harry bounded across the court, his tongue dangling from the side of his mouth.

"And who is this?"

"Harry."

Taylor leaned forward and met him nose to nose. Harry surprised her with a sloppy kiss.

She wiped her nose with the edge of her sleeve and winked up at Will. "Harry, please. We just met." Harry nudged her again, and she buried her face in the fur around his neck. "He's beautiful."

Will watched with a grin. "He's an Old English sheepdog rescue. Some family in Maine couldn't care for him, so I adopted him a couple of years ago."

Taylor looked up. "He's a lucky dog."

"I believe you challenged me to a game of one-on-one."

She stood straight, her hands on her hips. "I believe I did."

Will motioned to the side of the court. "Harry, go lie down."

The big dog hesitated, looking between Taylor and Will as if he wasn't sure whether he wanted to obey his master or stay with his new friend. "Harry, lie down," Will repeated, pointing courtside.

This time, Harry obediently loped over to the grass.

Will tucked the ball under his arm. "Look at you. One face lick and you've captured the affection of my dog."

"Seems to be my only talent these days."

Will raised a brow, wondering what that was supposed to mean, but let the comment go. He bounce-passed the ball to her. "Ladies first."

"I haven't played in a while," Taylor said, dribbling, squaring off in front of Will.

"Whoa now, no excuses. You challenged me, remember?"

She laughed, and he remembered how much he loved the melody of her merriment.

With a mischievous glint in her eyes, she taunted him. "Is that a spare tire around your middle, Adams, or have you put on a few pounds?"

Will guffawed and patted his belly. "Nothing spare around here, Hansen. You worry about yourself. Having worked a desk job and all, I'm wondering if you have the stamina for this."

On the heels of his last word, Taylor drove the ball up the middle of the lane. Will moved into her path, but she shoved past him for an easy layup.

"I believe that's one for me and nothing for you." She tossed him the ball then turned in a circle, waving her index fingers in the air. "One to nothing, one to nothing."

Will shook his head, bouncing the ball. "You are so going to be humiliated, Hansen."

She made a funny face. "We'll see."

He'd forgotten how competitive she was. "First player to twenty-one wins," he said.

"What's the prize?" Taylor asked, leaning forward, her hands on her knees.

The word came without thought but from the depths of his heart. "Dinner."

Taylor stood upright, her jaw jutted forward. Will thought he saw a flicker of. . .what? Anger? Doubt? Resistance?

After a second, she said, "What about your girlfriend, Mia?"

Will squared his shoulders. "She's not my girlfriend. Just a dinner date."

"Does she know that?"

"I made no promises, if that's what you mean." Will bounced the ball once.

"All right, then, dinner," Taylor said.

Will smiled with a nod, then jumped into motion, running around the top of the basketball key. "Good. I hear your New York salary can afford to take me to a nice place."

Taylor tried to block, but he ran around her for an outside jump shot. An easy point.

Taylor took the ball, recounting the score. "One to one."

"Getting scared yet?"

"No, are you?" she asked with a sideways smirk.

Actually, yes—afraid of falling in love before the game is over.

Taylor made another basket, then he made two as daylight faded to dusk. Will played hard, but as always, Taylor proved to be a worthy competitor.

When the score reached fifteen to sixteen, Will called for a time-out. "I need a little water."

Taylor smiled. "I just ran five miles, and you don't see me begging for water."

"Overachiever."

"Jealous."

To Will, the whole scenario was like a picture out of their past. After high school, most of their friends married or moved away from White Birch, so Will and Taylor spent nearly every college summer break together, shooting hoops, taking long runs, or grabbing pizza at Giuseppe's. Then, during Bobby and Elle's wedding festivities, their relationship had spiked to a new level.

"Let's go." Taylor clapped her hands, the sound reverberating in the cold air.

Will took a last sip from the water fountain and dribbled the ball back to the court. He made an easy shot before Taylor was in place.

"Cheater," she protested with a laugh then took the ball and shot over Will's head.

"Sixteen to seventeen."

Will watched her, bemused. "Still think you can win?"

"Just make your shot, Adams. Stop stalling."

When the score tied at twenty, Will had the ball. "This is it. No backing out now. You're buying me dinner."

"Unless you lose." Taylor bounced side to side on the balls of her feet. Will chuckled at her energy. Sweaty and red-faced, yes, but she looked incredible anyway.

He drove up the lane, then stopped. Taylor rushed him, arms up, going for the block. Will aimed at the basket and released the ball right over her head.

Swish. The ball sank through the net.

Taylor flew past him, moaning as he scored the winning point. He retrieved the ball, tucked it under his arm, and slapped Taylor with a high five.

"Nice win, Will." She ran her hand through her hair, making it stand even more on end.

"Hey," he said softly, "you don't really owe me dinner."

"A deal's a deal."

Will walked over to the side of the court where his jacket lay. "Tell you what, dinner at my place. You bring the trimmings; I'll provide a couple of steaks."

Taylor hesitated. "I was thinking more like Giuseppe's."

"All right. Tomorrow?"

"I can't." She offered no more information.

"Friday night?"

She nodded. "Friday night. Six?"

He agreed, motioning for her to walk with him to his truck. "Harry, let's go, boy." Will whistled and the dog came running.

Taylor stopped short and squinted at her watch. "Dinner." She tapped the face of her timepiece. "Mom said it'd be ready in an hour." She looked up at Will. "I've been gone almost two hours." She turned to run home.

"Taylor, Taylor! My truck's right here." Will ran after her and grabbed her by the arm. "I'll give you a ride."

He opened the passenger door for her then climbed in behind the wheel. Thirty seconds later, they were cruising down Main Street toward the Hansen home.

He cleared his throat and glanced sideways at her, trying to think of something to say that wasn't sports related.

In the soft light of the dashboard, he could see the glow on her face from exercise and the cold.

How is it that it felt so right to be with her? After so many years. . . It astounded him.

"How long is the whiz kid in town?" he ventured in a casual tone.

She smiled but looked away, out the window. "Not long."

Will nodded once. With the energy of basketball fading, Taylor's bright countenance seemed to fade. "Does your dad still call you the whiz kid?"

She nodded, looking over at him. "He does."

"The whiz kid," Will repeated.

"Anyone good at computers, math, or numbers is a whiz kid to him."

"Oh no, but you're not just good at computers and math. You're the volleyball star, basketball MVP, debate team captain—I think you even won a spelling bee or two."

"Okay, okay." She held up her hand for him to stop.

"The whiz kid," he whispered with a light laugh.

She gave him a smirk. "And who, driving this truck, was Mr. Football and the baseball home run king? Hmm? I believe he also got *all* As, *all* four years of high school."

Will laughed. "Touché. I had a few Bs. Maybe."

Taylor said, "Right," with a snort. "Now you're Mr. President."

"How'd you know about me taking over Lambert's Furniture?"

"Dad. Who else?" She picked at the fuzz balls on her sweatpants. "Do you like it?"

He grinned. "I do. Bobby oversees sales. Ethan is over production."

"Guess you got what you wanted."

He sensed her gazing at him. "I guess so."

"You told me you wanted to run the family business the night of Bobby and Elle's wedding, remember?"

He remembered. The night he let her go. "When we were at the covered bridge."

Will slowed the truck as he turned into the Hansens' driveway. Taylor opened her door before he came to a complete stop.

"Thanks." She hopped out.

"Taylor, I—"

Taylor looked back at him. "I know, Will. Look, it's been a long time. Forgotten, forgiven. . .a distant memory."

"I'm sorry for the way it ended."

"Yeah, me, too." She shoved the door shut and disappeared in the darkness.

❧❧

As the jet taxied off the runway in Charlotte, Taylor settled in her seat, breathing a sigh of relief. She'd had an exceptional day. She loved the staff of Conrad & Associates. They were talented, enthusiastic, and reaching for the stars.

Taylor's interview with her potential boss, Katie Myers, Conrad's partner over investments and accounting, went exceptionally well.

Leaning her head against the side of the plane, she peered out the window. "Lord, this felt so right."

But was it right? Taylor drew a deep breath, twisted in her seat, and fought off a pang of anxiety. She needed this job. She needed to get her career back on track or fall by the wayside. Taylor exhaled, trying not to obsess.

As she tipped her head back against her seat, she thought of home. Her mother's cooking, her father's colorful tales from the workday, her brother Tim and his wife, Dana. . . Their children Claire, Jarred, and Quentin. . .

She'd missed a lot of family time over the years while chasing a corporate CPA career. She'd also missed a lot of time talking to Jesus. How easily the issues of life, busyness, and work overshadowed her desire to know Him more.

Suddenly, an image of Will bounced into her thoughts. She grinned, eyes still closed, remembering their basketball game. *That was fun.*

Jerky, faded images from her past rolled across her mind like an old-time picture show. A collage of all her times with Will, one scene playing after another until she wondered if she'd ever had a life without him.

She opened her eyes with a start and sat forward, shaking the images loose, pressing the palm of her hand against her forehead.

Chapter 4

On Friday morning Will sat with Bobby and Ethan in the main conference room with their laptops and the third quarter financial reports, discussing plans for next year's revenue.

Ethan sighed and slumped down in his chair. "I don't know. What's the initial investment, Will? For the new business system?"

"Eth, we've got to do this. Invest money to earn money," Bobby said, getting up for a cold soda. "Streamline our inventory and accounting."

"Would you grab me one, too?" Will said, holding out his hand. Across from him, Ethan stared at the ceiling. "What's your hesitation, Ethan?"

Ethan motioned to all the data on the table. "I convinced you guys to spend thousands of dollars to retool half the shop last year, and we still haven't gotten a return on that investment." He flicked at one of the reports. "At least not according to these records."

Bobby handed Will a cold soda. "The summer was slower than usual. But, Ethan, we've got to grow the business office or we can't launch our e-business. When I met with Web Warehouse last week to approve the new site they are designing, I was convinced we made the right decision to create a Web store."

Ethan shook his head. "I know, I know. But installing a new business system will take a ton of time. We'll have to train the financial staff and all the supervisors and team leads."

Will popped the soda top and stood. "We've got enough in the capital budget for overtime and training." Will looked at Bobby, then Ethan. "We have to do this."

"Will, we make furniture. Beautiful, fine furniture," Ethan said. "We know nothing about installing a new accounting system. It will overload Markie."

Will grinned. "Markie wants this more than I do. She tells me every day we're holding the accounting system together with twine."

Ethan moaned. "You're right."

"She's a good financial manager. If she says we need a new system, we need a new system."

Bobby agreed. "You're right. Let's do it."

Ethan sat forward, gathered his reports, and powered down his laptop. "We have the new warehouse only half to capacity. It wouldn't hurt to get the e-business running full steam."

Will nodded. "Now you're thinking like a CEO, Eth."

Ethan stuffed his bag with the production reports and his computer. "Yeah, that's what I was going for, Will." He laughed. "I'll see you. I've got a to-do list a mile long, and Julie and I are meeting her folks for dinner."

Bobby picked up his laptop. "Will, I'll call Hayes Business Systems and tell them we're ready to deal."

"Thanks, Bobby. I'll get with Markie and look over the schedule to see when would be the best time to do an installation." Will sat down, feeling the weight of the company's success on his shoulders for the first time in a long time. He sighed.

Bobby stopped in the doorway. "When we took over this company, we promised ourselves we'd be innovative and take risks."

"I know, and we're keeping that promise."

Will was deep in thought when the emergency buzzer resounded from the manufacturing floor. He jumped from his chair and ran into his office, Bobby coming in right behind. Together, they peered through the long production window.

Several workers huddled around a fallen man. Grant. Will stormed out and down the metal stairs to where Grant lay on the cold production floor.

Will shoved his way into the huddle where a crew member checked the vitals on an unconscious, pallid Grant.

"He just collapsed," someone said.

"We called 9-1-1," added another.

When the paramedics arrived, they took over. The flurry of activity never stopped, and as the paramedics loaded Grant into the ambulance, an oxygen mask on his face, Will snatched up his cell phone and dialed the Hansens'. "Trixie, it's Will Adams." He tried to sound cheerful, but his voice choked as the sirens wailed.

"Will?" Trixie's voice quivered.

"Grant collapsed."

❧

"He has to be all right. He has to be."

"Mom, he will be." Taylor guided her distraught mother through the ER doors where Will waited for them.

"Will, how is he?" Trixie pressed her hand on his arm.

"Better. I'll take you to him." Will glanced over his shoulder at Taylor. "The doctor said just one visitor at a time until he goes up to his room."

"Of course." Taylor watched her frightened mother disappear down the hall, Will's arm around her shoulders. *God, not Daddy. Don't take him home now.*

She sat in a worn waiting room chair, flipping absently through a celebrity magazine, feeling as if everything in her life teetered on the brink of disaster.

She tossed the magazine aside and looked up as Will walked toward her. He exuded such a confidence and peace; his presence was like a cool glass of water at the end of a long, hot day. When life buzzed with confusion, Will brought clarity.

"Your dad was glad to see your mom," Will said, his blue eyes steady on her as he sat in the adjacent chair.

She smiled though her bottom lip trembled. "How is he?"

"He's going to be fine, Taylor." Will pressed his hand on her back.

"He looked so pale at dinner the other night." Taylor covered her face with her hands. She didn't want to cry. She wanted to be strong for Mom.

"Hey, hey." Will cradled her head on his shoulder, stroking her hair. "Let's go sit someplace quiet."

Taylor followed him to the chapel, enjoying the sensation of being led. She spent so much of her time the last ten years out front, directing, leading.

The interior of the chapel was peaceful, but cool. Taylor shivered, rubbing her hands along her arms.

"We left in such a hurry I forgot my jacket."

"Guess they don't turn the heat up in here." Will shrugged out of his coat and draped it over Taylor's shoulders.

"Now you'll be cold," Taylor said, settling in the last of the red-cushioned pews.

"Don't worry about me." He sat in the pew in front of hers, angled sideways to see her.

Taylor regarded him for a moment. She loved the symmetry of his face. It was as if the Lord took extra care in aligning his features. And his skin. . . Most of her girlfriends paid top dollar for something he probably took for granted and washed with deodorant soap.

"What?" Will asked.

Taylor glanced away. "What?"

"You were staring at me."

Taylor bit her lower lip, her gaze downcast. "Now why would I stare at you, Will Adams?"

He chuckled. "You tell me. Do I have something on my face, in my teeth? Is my hair sticking up?"

Taylor smiled. "No, no. If you must know, I was thinking what great skin you have. It's downright wrong for a man to have such small pores."

Will laughed. "You're very strange, Taylor."

"I know, but that's why you love me." Taylor meant for the words to sound light and airy, like a joke, but they came with an echo from a deep, hidden place in her soul. She squirmed.

"I suppose you're right," Will said, his words weighty and real, as if emerging from a dark corridor of time.

When their eyes met, he coughed and twisted around. Taylor's heart thumped in her chest.

They sat in silence for the next few minutes. Taylor wondered what he was thinking but didn't want to ask. Not now, not here.

He got up and walked toward the front of the chapel. She could see his lips moving in prayer.

Taylor wanted to pray, but inner turmoil stifled her words.

"Did you call your brother?" Will asked as he turned to her.

Taylor made a face. "No, I completely forgot." She dug her cell phone from her purse and stepped into the hallway.

She paused for a moment, trembling, inhaling a cleansing breath. *It's been ten years, Will. Ten years and you still get to me. Still.*

With a press of a few buttons, she dialed her brother. "Tim, Dad's in the hospital."

Will watched Taylor through the narrow window in the chapel door. What was he thinking? He'd practically told her he loved her.

Did he love her? And what about her comment "that's why you love me"? Did she love him? They barely knew each other anymore.

Will paced up the chapel aisle, wondering how long she'd be in town. If she hung around too long, he felt confident he'd fall in love with her—if he'd ever stopped loving her in the first place.

"Tim's on his way," Taylor said when she reentered the chapel, dropping her cell phone in her bag.

Will nodded. "Good." He recognized her purse as a famous designer bag. Elle had bought one a few years ago. He remembered his brother and sister-in-law had waged war over the price of that bag for two days.

He guessed Taylor's New York City CPA salary afforded her those kinds of amenities.

Will grinned. She looked good in his jacket. Absently, he reached up and straightened the collar. "We were supposed to have pizza tonight."

Her eyes widened. "You're right." She motioned over her shoulder. "I hear the food here is terrible, but I'm buying if you're game."

Will made a face. "Are you kidding me? Our deal was for Giuseppe's. I'm not cashing in for hospital grub."

Taylor shrugged playfully. "Fine, then you can buy."

"Fine." Will bumped her as they walked toward the door, shoulder to shoulder.

She smiled at him, grabbed her purse from the pew, and bumped him back.

In the cafeteria, they ordered burgers and fries and large diet sodas.

Will bit into his hamburger. "Hmm. I thought you said the food here was terrible."

Taylor shook her head. "No, I said I *heard* the food was terrible."

He laughed. "Well, now we know you *heard* wrong."

"Yum, you could bring me on a date here." She glanced up quickly, as if catching her words.

"I will."

"I mean in general—*you*—as in. . ." She motioned with her hand, sitting with her back stiff. "People in general, could, um. . ." She coughed.

"Exit, stage left."

Her shoulders collapsed. "I think I will." She sipped her soda. "So, did you ever get your MBA?"

Will swallowed and wiped his mouth with his napkin, his heart thumping a little harder. Another pointer back to that night on the bridge. "Yes."

Taylor nodded, pulling the tomato from her burger. "Good for you. What else have you been doing besides taking over the family business?"

"I ran for town council. Beat old Walter Burnett out of his seat."

She grinned. "In general, ruling the world."

"Keeps me out of trouble." Will smiled. "What about Taylor Jo Hansen? How many worlds have you conquered?"

A sadness flicked across her eyes, and she concentrated too long on squirting ketchup over her fries. "Not many."

He coughed. "I find that hard to believe."

She jutted out her chin. "I quit." The words came out like a one-two punch. *I quit.*

He glanced up, confused. "Quit what?" He furrowed his brow.

"I quit my job."

"Really?" Will watched and waited, wondering if she would explain, but she didn't. "That doesn't sound like you. Quitting."

Taylor squared her shoulders. "No, but sometimes a girl has to do what a girl has to do."

"You're looking for a new job then?"

"I had an interview with a CPA firm in Charlotte a few days ago." She wiped her hands with her napkin. "It went really well."

The familiar "oh" of disappointment pinged in Will's heart. "Charlotte's a great city."

"Yes, I know." But Will knew in that instant he didn't want her to leave White Birch. He didn't have to think about it or ponder why. He just knew. "Taylor, do you think you might—"

"Taylor!" Tim Hansen rushed into the cafeteria. "I've been looking for you; we can see Dad now. Hi, Will."

Will shook his hand. "Tim."

Taylor stood, reaching for her handbag and slipping out of Will's coat. "Thanks for the burger." She smiled. "And the coat."

"Anytime." He watched her walk away, the words he wanted to say stuck in his throat, making it hard to breathe.

Chapter 5

Monday morning Taylor's cell phone woke her from a fitful sleep. Distorted dreams plagued her during the night, and she felt more tired now than she had before she went to bed.

Shouldn't have had that last cup of coffee.

She stumbled out of bed and padded across her room to her dresser where her phone sat, hooked to the charger. "Hello."

"Taylor Hansen, please."

"Speaking." Taylor rubbed her eyes with her fingers, squinting as a flood of morning light streamed through the opened blinds.

"Good morning. This is Gina Abernathy from Conrad & Associates."

Taylor's eyes popped open. "Good morning." She smoothed her hand on her pajama pants and looked out the window. It was a beautiful fall morning.

"You impressed our team, and we enjoyed meeting you."

"Thank you. Conrad is an excellent organization." The windowpane reflected Taylor's smile.

"We've filled the position you interviewed for, but we'll keep your résumé on file."

"I see." Taylor knew the routine from here. Thanks but no thanks. She'd done it to dozens of potential candidates at Blankenship & Burns.

She thanked Gina Abernathy, pressed END, and set the phone down. Shoving the window open, she welcomed the cold breeze against her face, cooling the heat of disappointment.

She thought she had that job. "Lord, now what?"

"Taylor?" Mom appeared in the doorway, her robe belted around her small frame. She looked tired. "You'll catch your death with that window open. Shut it. I can't have you collapsing on me, too."

"Sorry." She tugged on the window's frame. "The company in Charlotte called."

Mom clasped her hands together and sat on the edge of the bed. "Well, I suppose you'll be leaving soon, then."

"I didn't get the job." Taylor fell against the windowsill.

Mom straightened the edge of her robe. "The Lord has something better for you, angel."

Taylor sloughed over to the bed and fell back on her pillow. "I'm sure He does; I just wish I knew what." She hated being suspended between her past and her future.

Mom patted Taylor's leg. "He'll let you know."

"I have to believe He will; otherwise my stomach will stay knotted for the rest of my life."

"I'm going to the hospital to make your Dad's 10:00 a.m. doctor's appointment. He's going to recommend a procedure."

"I'll come later. I want to stay here. Pray. Call a few people. Look for leads." She hadn't done any job searching over the weekend; she'd worried over Dad.

Mom stood. "Taylor, you've always accomplished whatever you wanted. You're our whiz kid."

Some whiz kid. Besides, she hadn't gotten *everything* in life she wanted. Will came to mind. "Thank you, Mom. Kiss Dad for me."

As her mom exited, Taylor closed her bedroom door, grabbed her Bible, and curled up on her bed with her fretful thoughts.

"Okay, Lord, I surrender it all to You. The Bible says, 'be anxious for nothing,' but I need a job—the right job."

She thought of Will's strong and peaceful countenance. "And I need peace, Lord."

Will looked over his shoulder when a knock echoed outside his door. He smiled. "Grandpa, come in."

Somberly, the Lambert patriarch entered, his hands in his jacket pockets. "Just came from seeing Grant."

Harry trotted over to Grandpa, his tail wagging.

"I e-mailed the staff this morning to let them know what's going on."

Grandpa jutted out his chin and began petting Harry's head, absently. "The doctor is recommending angioplasty."

Will leaned back in his chair. "Angioplasty is less intrusive than open-heart surgery."

"Trixie's relieved about it. She came in this morning with her hair and make-up done, wearing a suit with matching shoes and hat, all smiles for Grant."

"I wouldn't expect anything less from her."

"She's a rock on the outside, but I'm afraid she's putty on the inside. Your grandma took her for coffee to make sure she's doing well."

"I grabbed a bite with Taylor Friday night at the hospital. She seemed to be taking it well."

Grandpa raised a brow. "Old Taylor—"

Will sat forward. "Don't get any ideas."

"Me?" Grandpa pointed to himself. "I'm already married. You are the one who needs to be getting some ideas."

"Not so sure Taylor wants me having ideas about her."

"Aha, is she the one?"

"The one what?"

Grandpa chuckled. "The one you've been waiting for all this time."

Will focused on his computer. "Don't you have someplace to go?" he asked, glancing back at his grandfather.

Grandpa rubbed his chin then said, "No, I've got all morning to hang around here."

Will waved toward the door. "Then go bug Ethan or something."

His grandfather chuckled again.

"What about me?" Ethan walked into the office and plopped into the chair across from Will's desk. Harry left Grandpa and plopped his chin on Ethan's knee.

Grandpa spoke first. "We were just talking about—"

"Nothing." Will eyed Grandpa.

"Good," Ethan said, scratching Harry behind the ears. "We need to talk about Grant's replacement until he's back on his feet."

"Hire me."

Will and Ethan stared at their grandfather.

"I'm available and could fill in for a few weeks. I did start this company, after all. I know most of the crew and the procedures."

Ethan looked at Will. "He's got a point."

Will regarded his grandfather. "I don't know."

Ethan stood. Harry retreated to his corner and curled up on his bed. "He's perfect, Will. Grandpa, you're hired."

Will grinned. "Fine." He pointed at the older Lambert. "But don't be bugging me about. . .stuff."

"Taylor?" Grandpa asked.

"What's this?" Ethan prodded, leaning on the edge of Will's desk.

"Taylor's back in town," Grandpa said.

"I know. Julie said she saw her the other night at Italian Hills. Will, is there something starting up again with—"

Will leapt to his feet. "Stop." He looked at Ethan. "Taylor quit her job in New York. But she interviewed in Charlotte and will probably be moving there soon."

"She didn't get the job," Grandpa said like a seasoned anchorman.

Will stared at him, his hands on his hips. "How do you know?"

Grandpa walked toward the door and motioned to Ethan. "Better show me around the production floor, refresh my memory."

Will shook his head as he watched them leave. Grandpa stepped back and stuck his head in the doorway. "Why don't you call her and find out?"

Will sat down, hard. Grandpa had a way of pushing his buttons. All the right ones. For a few minutes he pondered calling Taylor, and just as he reached for the phone, it rang.

"Will Adams."

"Hi, it's Taylor." Her voice reminded him of velvet.

He cleared his throat. "How are you?"

"Fine, all things considered." She chuckled.

"Tough week?"

"Tough couple of weeks."

Will leaned back in his chair. "I'm sorry."

She laughed. "It's not your fault."

"No, I guess not." He loved Taylor's forthrightness.

"Daddy is scheduled for angioplasty tomorrow. He's going down to Manchester tonight."

"Grandpa told me," he said, wondering if she'd tell him about Charlotte.

She sighed. "Dad's in good spirits and other than his arteries, he's in good health."

Will prodded her more. "Everything else going okay?"

"If I said, I might give in and cry."

"A good cry never hurt anyone."

She laughed. "Moving on. . . Thanks for being there Friday for Mom and me."

"Not a problem. Tell your dad Grandpa's filling in for him."

"He was already telling the doctor he needed to be back to work next week."

Will grinned. "Sounds like your pop."

"Yeah, well, Trixie the Terrible is on the scene, and Dad won't be back to work until she says so. She's insisting he use up some vacation."

Will laughed. "He has a lot of time banked. Tell him to relax, burn up some vacation, and heal."

"I will."

Then, as suddenly as the conversation started, it ended. Will wanted to ask about her job but hesitated. Too personal. If she wanted him to know about Charlotte, she would tell him.

Then he had an idea. "You still owe me pizza."

"Right, I do."

"You'll be with your dad tonight and tomorrow. So—"

"I'll be home tomorrow night by eight." Her tone sounded promising.

"Say eight thirty? Meet you at Giuseppe's."

"See you then."

❧❧

Taylor ladled soup into bowls and flipped the grilled cheese sandwiches on the griddle. Mom dropped ice into the glasses on the table with a *clink-clink* and filled them with iced tea.

"Tim, you want one or two sandwiches?" Taylor called.

"Two," Tim answered from the living room, where he was arranging kindling in the fireplace. "Mom, where'd Dad put the matches?"

"Oh, he uses one of those long lighter things. Look in the end table drawer." Trixie motioned in the air with her slender hand.

"Dad looked good tonight," Taylor said, reflecting on their trip to the hospital in Manchester where Grant had been transported. He had a nice private room.

Tim came around the corner. "It's still hard to imagine Dad in that hospital bed."

Mom fluttered around the kitchen, opening and closing doors without retrieving anything. "Well now, he'll be just fine. Just fine."

Taylor handed Tim a plate and a bowl. "Dr. Elliot said the surgeon in Manchester is one of the best." She touched her mother's arm. "Dad will come through with flying colors."

Trixie's lips quivered when she smiled. "He is in good health otherwise, isn't he?"

"Remember that health food kick he went on about twenty-five, thirty years ago?" Tim laughed, biting into his sandwich. A string of melted cheese stuck to his chin.

Taylor passed him a napkin, grinning. "Barely. I was what, six? You were sixteen?"

Trixie smiled. "He was so determined to get this family healthy."

"Were we sick?" Taylor asked.

"Oh, no, but your dad wanted to ensure long, happy lives for all of us."

Still laughing, Tim reminisced, pointing at Taylor. "Remember when old Smokey dug up the bread you buried in the backyard?"

She pounded the table. "Dad was so mad. But I thought the bread was made of twigs or something." She made a face, remembering.

"Oh, it was horrible bread," Trixie said, spooning a bite of soup.

"It made the worst peanut butter and jelly sandwiches," Taylor added.

"And that was the only thing you would eat that year," Tim reminded her.

"I remember."

"Speaking of eating." Tim popped open a bag of baked chips. "That was a cozy scene I walked into the other night with you and Will in the hospital cafeteria."

Taylor choked. "Cozy? A burger in the hospital cafeteria?"

"Maybe your old crush isn't so old."

"Have you gone crazy?"

"Taylor, lower your voice," Mom said. "Ladies don't shout."

She gaped at her mom. "And gentlemen don't make assumptions." She whispered toward Tim. "Have you gone crazy?"

Laughing, Tim scooted away from the table for more soup. "He's a great catch, Tay."

He didn't have to remind her. "I'm not looking for a man; I'm looking for a job, Tim."

"You could stay in White Birch and work for me. Dana's busy hauling Jarred and Quentin all over town. Claire's eighteen and doesn't want to admit she knows us."

"You actually want me to come down there and work in your office? You're an architect, Tim. I know nothing about building buildings."

"You don't fool me, Taylor. I could teach you CAD in a week."

She shook her head. "I'm a CPA, Tim, not a CAD operator."

"Well, I offered."

After Tim left for home and Mom readied for bed, Taylor decided to check her phone and e-mail for any messages. There were two job postings, but they were just above entry level and she wasn't sure she wanted to drop that far down the ladder. So far, Tim's offer was the best thing going.

Taylor shoved her laptop aside and dropped her head on her desk. She hated feeling anxious, but there it was, gripping her middle—gripping her heart and mind.

"Lord, I can't continue like this. I need Your peace. It's been so long."

Almost instantly, she thought of Will. It was his peaceful aura that attracted her to him as much as his blue eyes and broad, white smile.

Chapter 6

Will waited for Taylor in the back of Giuseppe's. The smell of garlic and baking dough stirred his appetite. He rapped his knuckles against the table in a steady beat, eager to see her. When she walked through the door, he smiled and stood to greet her. *Give her a hug,* he thought. But she stuck out her hand before he got close.

"Hi," she said, slipping her hand into his.

"Hi, back," he said, liking the feel of her palm against his. They slipped into the booth, sitting across from each other.

"Welcome to Giuseppe's." The proprietor's big voice bellowed toward them, all the consonants accented and rolling. "Will, who is this-a pretty lady?"

Will grinned. "You know Taylor Hansen, Giuseppe."

The big man's hands shot to his face and covered his jiggling cheeks. "Taylor, what is wrong? So thin. So thin."

She pinched her lips together, though a smile tugged at the corners of her mouth. "I lost a few pounds. Five years ago."

Giuseppe stuck his finger in the air. "I get extra garlic rolls with extra butter." He hurried away.

Taylor laughed, wrinkling her nose at Will. "Extra butter? That means an *extra* mile for me tomorrow." She unzipped her jacket.

"I love that about Giuseppe. In his eyes, no one can be too. . .endowed." Will reached for her coat and folded it on top of his.

Their waiter, Brandon, stopped by for their drink order, and Will asked Taylor, "Large pizza? The three cheese is excellent."

Her eyes sparkled when she looked at him. Or was he just imagining?

"Sounds good. I'm starved," she said.

Giuseppe swooped in with a large basket of bread and instructed Brandon to "keep it full."

"You're much-a too skinny, Taylor. Much-a."

"I'll work on it," Taylor promised with a wink.

When Giuseppe was gone, Will prayed over the food and the evening. After he said amen, he handed Taylor a plate with two garlic rolls. "You're not, you know."

She reached for her napkin. "Not what?"

Brandon set their drinks on the table. "Your pizza will be right up."

Will nodded to Brandon then answered Taylor. "Too skinny."

"Are you suggesting I'm overweight?"

Will laughed heartily. "I guess I'm treading on dangerous ground, aren't I?" She grinned and nodded as he sipped his soda and decided to change the subject. "How's your dad?"

"The angioplasty went very well. He looks a hundred percent better already. He's probably coming home tomorrow."

Will nodded. "We prayed for him this morning in our staff meeting."

Taylor tore a bite off her garlic roll. "You guys pray every morning?"

"Yes."

"I could've used prayer at the firm in New York," Taylor said in a soft, thoughtful tone.

"You want to tell me what happened?"

"Not really."

He reached for another roll. "Okay."

"I'd had enough," she said without preamble. "I had an egotistical boss—one of the partners—who drove me crazy. I worked seventy, eighty hours a week, and finally, I'd had enough."

"Good for you."

Taylor slapped her hands against the table. "Good for me? I'm unemployed. I own a brand-new imported car, my furniture is in storage, and a marvelous job opportunity in North Carolina passed me by."

"So what? You have a mountain of experience, and you're excellent at what you do, whiz kid. The Lord has something for you." Will suddenly had an idea. He'd have to run it by Bobby for a sanity check, but it just might be brilliant.

Taylor lowered her gaze, her slender hands around the small white plate holding her uneaten roll. "You make it sound so easy, so not-a-big-deal."

"I know it is a big deal, but, Taylor, you're so much more than your career. You know, when I want to carve something special, I hunt for the right piece of wood. At first, it's just a block with nice grain and maybe a fragrance like cedar. Then I start cutting, shaping, sanding. . . The wood becomes something beautiful. That's you in God's hands."

She regarded him. "What an amazing image. Thank you." With that, she sat back, dropping her arms to her sides, and stared out the window. "I just am so mad at myself for quitting. There had to be a better solution."

"Sometimes *resigning* is the solution. To act when you know it's time to move on."

"Pizza." Brandon cleared room for a large, round tray with a hot, thin-crust pizza oozing with cheese.

"I wish I had your confidence. . .and peace."

"Well," Will said, shoveling a cheesy slice onto Taylor's plate, "hang around me for a while, and I might let you have some for free."

❦❦

On a crisp, cold Sunday afternoon, Taylor donned her sweats and jogged to Milo Park.

Dad was home now, and Mom flitted around the house like a hen with a coop full of chicks. Taylor grinned, pressing her hand to her stomach as she remembered the four-course lunch Mom served after church.

As for Taylor, she spent an hour surfing for job openings, submitting her résumé online, and trying to get her foot in the door, any door. Last week it seemed every contact she called was either out of the office or "no longer with us."

When Will had called an hour earlier with a flag football invitation, she had jumped at the chance to move her cramped muscles.

As she ran toward the field, she could see a dozen or so guys gathering.

Five minutes later, the blue flag and white flag teams were chosen, then Will reviewed the rules. Last, he said, "Taylor, as our only woman player, is wearing orange flags. She's a wide receiver. Anyone grab anything but a flag, you're out of the game." Will jerked his thumb over his shoulder and shot each guy an intense glance. When his gaze fell on Taylor, she nodded her thanks.

"Since there's only eleven of us, we'll play half field. Huddle up."

Jordan West, the star quarterback at White Birch High when Will played running back, led the white flag team. Will quarterbacked the blue flag team.

"Hi, Taylor," Jordan said, tapping her on the arm. "I didn't know you were in town."

She smiled. "Yes, briefly." Jordan looked so much the same. Broad-shouldered and slender. . . Sparkling brown eyes. . . His blond hair was thinner than she remembered, though.

"I heard about your dad. I hope he's doing well."

"He's doing very well, thank you. He's home, and Mom is in her element taking care of him."

🙢🙠

"Hansen, let's go," Will bellowed, motioning for her to join the huddle.

"Better go," she said to Jordan, moving backward.

"Talk to you later. After the game maybe."

She nodded. "Maybe."

"What was that all about?" Will whispered when she joined the huddle.

"Nunya," she said with a smirk.

"Nunya?" He furrowed his brow. "What?"

"Nunya business." She laughed and clapped him on the shoulder. "None of your business."

"Har, har," he said. In the huddle, Will instructed his team. "They have one more player than we do, but we have Speedy Gonzales here." He pointed to Taylor. "On two, Cimowsky, you sweep around behind me. I'll fake a handoff." Will pointed to Taylor. "Run up the middle ten yards, turn, and I'll pass it to you."

"Do you want me to count one Mississippi, two Mississippi, three—"

Will bumped her with his hip. "No. I want you to run ten yards, turn, and catch."

She snickered. "Testy."

Will ignored her. "Everyone else, block. On three."

The team of five moved to the line of scrimmage.

Taylor lined up on the right, her adrenaline pumping. *This is going to be a blast.* She could already feel the week's subtle frustrations burning away.

Will walked behind her and touched her back. "Go for the touchdown," he said in a low voice.

She nodded. She knew what to do. Jordan lined up across from her. He smiled. She smiled. Will shouted "Two!" and Taylor went into motion.

As Taylor cut up the middle, Jordan backpedaled, calling to his scattered team, "He's passing to Taylor!" *Ten yards, turn, and look at Will.* Her gaze connected with his as he released the ball. It spiraled through the air and into her arms.

She ran for the goal, marked by two red cones, the sound of her heart beating in her ears. *Touchdown. Make the touchdown.*

Taylor hurdled over a defender who lunged for the flag flying from her waist and sailed past the cones.

"Touchdown!"

Her teammates raced to meet her, congratulating her with high fives.

Will busted through the group with a "Whoo hoo!" picked her up, and swung her around. "Taylor's *my* lady." He motioned to the rest of the guys. "My lady. Making touchdowns. Blowing past Jordan West."

Jordan protested with a deep huff, trying to catch his breath. "Taylor, next time, you play for me."

"Finders, keepers." Will wrapped his arm around her waist and pulled her to him.

Taylor stepped away from him. "Hello, I'm not a kept woman."

Jordan laughed and took the football from her. "Let's go, or we won't be able to finish before dark." He jogged over to his team.

Will caught Taylor's arm. "Sorry. I know that—"

"It's okay."

After the game, Will convinced Taylor to go for burgers and fries at Sam's. "Thanks for playing today. You made it fun. Bunch of smelly guys out on the field. . ." He winked at her. "Gets a little old."

"How often do you play?" she asked, taking a long sip from the straw in her water glass. She could see her red-faced reflection in Sam's shiny windows.

"Couple of times a month if the weather's good. Sometimes the guys have family stuff to do, or we're all at home taking naps."

She laughed then blurted, "Jordan asked me to dinner, Will."

He didn't flinch. "He's a nice guy."

"I have to be honest about something."

He picked up his soda glass. "There's more?" His expression remained friendly, but his tone was defensive.

"I'm not staying in White Birch; you know that. I can't let our relationship go beyond casual friendship. I don't want to end up where we did ten years ago."

"A lot of things have changed since then."

"Of course," she said, her voice elevated. "But at the root of it all, we are in the exact same place now as then. You are married to Lambert's Furniture, and I'm married to. . .out there, getting my career back on track."

She stopped, not meaning to toss the marriage word into the conversation. She didn't mean to imply. . . "Not that we would, you know, want to get married, to each other, but I'm just saying. . ." She gazed up at Will. "Help?"

"What do you want me to say?"

She shrugged, frustrated. *He's been flirting with me for three weeks, and now he's acting like he's the one being cornered. So typical. Exactly what he did ten years ago.* "Forget it."

"Look, Taylor, you can have dinner with whoever you want."

"I'm aware of that. I just thought you should know."

"I appreciate it," he said, his smile forced.

They were silent for a long time. Taylor excused herself to go to the ladies' room where she splashed cold water on her face. Glancing in the mirror, she muttered, "Nice move, Hansen."

By the time she got back to the table, Will had evidently rebounded from her awkward attempt to expose any romantic undercurrents in their relationship.

"Taylor," he said, "I know we have a history. I know things didn't go the way either of us planned. But being with you the past few weeks has reminded me of how much I love being with you. How much I treasure your friendship."

"I'm sorry, Will. I didn't mean to be so rude." She stretched her hand out to his. "I love our friendship. You're one of the most amazing men I know."

"You are the most amazing woman I know."

She laughed. "I take it you don't know very many women."

He grew serious. "Let's just take it one day at a time."

"Perfect. Now can we order? I'm starved."

On Monday morning Will entered his brother's office. "I have an idea."

Bobby glanced up from his computer. "I'm shocked and amazed."

"Funny man." Will sat in the adjacent leather chair. "Let's hire Taylor."

"Hire Taylor?" Bobby shot Will a quizzical look. "For what?"

"The new business system. She's worked at two major New York CPA firms and one financial magazine. I'm sure she's been through this kind of conversion before." Will propped his forearms on his knees.

Bobby regarded him, tapping an unsharpened pencil on his desk. "It's really a brilliant idea. She's available, she's experienced, and she's extremely intelligent."

"We'd be crazy not to contract her. If she's willing."

"What does Ethan think?"

"Let's get him in here and find out."

Bobby picked up his phone and dialed Ethan.

"I was just on my way to see you two," Ethan said as he entered Bobby's office, taking the vacant seat next to Will. "One of the new CNC machines is giving us trouble. I called the vendor and they are coming out to replace it, but that means we're behind in production for a day or two. Which means our schedule will get backed up a week or more. We're already behind three weeks because of that lemon of a machine."

Will hung his head and pressed his palm against the back of his neck. "See if you can get some of the crew to work overtime until we're caught up. Let's pay double time."

Ethan whistled. "It's fair, but really going to hit our payroll budget hard."

Will laughed sardonically. "With that machine down, we're already off budget. Let's do what we can to make it up. Might as well throw in a comp day for every weekend day worked."

Ethan grinned. "They are going to love you, Boss."

"Speaking of love," Bobby said.

"Hey, no fair," Will said.

"Will wants to hire Taylor to consult on the HBS system. What do you think?"

Ethan looked at Will, then Bobby, grinning like he'd discovered a secret. "Fine by me."

"All right." Will stood. "I'll go see what the going rate is for consultants."

"Did you kiss her?" Ethan asked, still grinning.

Will stopped at Bobby's door. "If I did, I wouldn't tell you."

Chapter 7

Taylor ate breakfast with Dad and Mom in the warm, cozy kitchen, then spent the morning researching job opportunities.

By noon she was frustrated and anxious. She trotted down to the kitchen for a glass of water.

"How's it going?" Dad asked, tucking his newspaper away as she strolled into the family room.

She sat on the ottoman, in the rays of the sun streaming through the windows. "Terrible."

"Nothing turning up?"

She sipped her water and shook her head. "It's like I'm searching in the dark with absolutely no light. I'm so, so. . ." She stood. "Frustrated."

"I can see."

Taylor regarded him, thinking how well he looked after only a week. His cheeks had color, and his eyes sparkled.

"You can't let this get to you," Dad said. "Anxiety leads to depression, then you make bad decisions." He patted his stomach. "Look for the peace of Jesus right here. The peace that resonates from your spirit—not your head."

Taylor collapsed against the couch cushions and flopped her arm over her eyes. "Easy for you to say."

"No, I've had to work at walking in peace, too. Just like you and every other human on the planet."

"Except Will Adams."

"What do you mean?"

Taylor lifted her head to see her dad. "He exudes peace like he drinks a cup of it every morning for breakfast."

Dad laughed. "He does, but I know he's worked hard at walking in peace. He didn't get there overnight."

"Well, whatever he's got, I want it."

"You can have it."

"Yeah, I know. Be like Mary of Bethany, sitting at Jesus' feet."

"That's right. Settle your heart and mind on Jesus. Stay in prayer, meditating on God's Word. Marry Will."

Taylor jumped up. "Dad!"

"You won't find a better man, Taylor."

She drank from her water glass. "Maybe not, Dad, but he isn't asking." She hopped up and went to the kitchen.

The phone rang as she rounded the kitchen corner. She snatched up the receiver. "Hello?" She glanced at her dad, shaking her head. *Marry Will. Ha!*

"Taylor, Indiana Godwin."

She raised a brow. Indiana was the former head of human resources at Blankenship & Burns. "Indy, hello. How are you?"

"Doing well," he said. "Loving my life in Boston."

"Good for you. How did you know I was here?" Taylor asked.

"Reneé Ludwig sent me your résumé."

Taylor smiled, going to the refrigerator for more water. "She did?" She made a mental note to call Reneé and thank her.

"It's a stellar résumé."

Taylor leaned against the counter. "Thank you."

"I didn't know if you'd be interested in working for the Print First Newspaper Group."

Taylor raised a brow. Print First was one of the largest newspaper chains in the country. "I might be."

"It's a little different than what you're used to at a CPA firm, but you could handle a CFO or financial director position with no problem."

"Absolutely." Excitement bubbled in her middle.

"Unfortunately, we're going through a corporate restructure."

"I see." She filtered out a resonating disappointment. "You and every other company on the eastern seaboard."

"If you can hang on, I'm sure I can get you in for an interview by the New Year."

"Indy, that's three months away."

"I know, Taylor. Tell you what—let me talk to a few people and see what I can find. Maybe one of the smaller chains has a CFO position."

"Indiana, I appreciate it."

"You don't care where you live, do you?"

"No, but, Indy, the pay has to be right."

"I understand. Taylor, one more thing. This is kind of a delicate matter. . ."

She felt the blood drain from her face. "What? Tell me."

"Let me close my door."

Taylor heard the *kerplunk* of Indiana's office door. "I could get in big trouble for this, but as a friend, I need to tell you."

A prickly feeling ran over her scalp. Dread anchored her feet to the kitchen floor. "This doesn't sound good."

"We post all applications and résumés on the intranet. One of our VPs saw your résumé. Impressed, he decided to call Blankenship & Burns. He's one of those corporate big shots who thinks he can call up the White House and talk to the president if he wants."

Dread. Definitely dread. "Oh, no."

"He talked to your boss, Lisa Downey."

Taylor felt sick to her stomach. "Lisa and I clashed."

"No kidding. She told the VP all about it."

Taylor inhaled sharply. "Indy, she can't do that."

"I know that and you know that, but she did. I thought you should know. If any other companies call, she may vent to them, also."

Taylor sank to the floor, her head in her hands. "What am I going to do?"

"If I were you, I'd shoot her an e-mail or give her a call. Clear the air, if you know what I mean. But, Taylor, if you mention me, I'll deny it." He chuckled.

"I understand. Thank you."

"No problem. I talked to the vice president who called Lisa. I told him I knew you personally and surmised Lisa Downey was getting revenge."

Taylor laughed sardonically. "I can't believe this."

"What did happen up there, Taylor?"

Taylor sighed. "She is one of those women executives who don't like other women in management. She came down pretty hard on me, demanded a lot. In return, I subtly undermined her initiatives and authority."

"Welcome to corporate life."

"Yeah, but I don't want to play that way."

Taylor hung up. Angry and disappointed—more with herself than Lisa Downey—she went upstairs, put on her sneakers, and grabbed her sweatshirt. She needed to get out. Fresh air. Run. Think. Pray.

❦❦

Will slowed his truck, driving down Main Street after the town council meeting. In the bright afternoon light, farmers lined their produce carts along the south side of the city's center. Fresh apples, corn, squash, tomatoes, and crates of other fresh vegetables glistened in the sun.

Will glanced at his watch. Two o'clock and he was hungry for lunch. He spotted a fellow church deacon, Hank Burgraf, and waved. Next to him was a cousin on the Adams side, Lyle.

At the far end of the line, a vendor whipped cotton candy onto sticks for the moms out with their toddlers. Will shook his head, remembering the night with Mia. Verbal cotton candy.

He wanted to linger in town and grab a sandwich at Peri's, but he needed to get back to Lambert's Furniture. A pile of work waited on his desk.

Yet, when he cruised past Milo Park, Will parked. There wouldn't be many more days like today—sunny, blue skies with a gentle breeze—and he wanted to enjoy it while he could.

The walk to the park benches cleared his head, still stuffy from the council meeting. To build a skateboard park or not had been the big debate. Will saw the merits on both sides—for and against. However, when the discussion ran well past lunchtime, he motioned to table it until the next meeting.

Half the room shouted, "Second."

Now, taking long strides across the grounds, the mental cobwebs blew away, and Will caught sight of a familiar dark, burnished head. Taylor.

She sat with her face tipped to the sun, her sweatshirt balled between her hands in her lap. She'd been running.

"Beautiful day, isn't it?" Will said as he plopped down next to Taylor.

She screamed. He laughed. She popped him lightly on the arm.

"Ouch." He rubbed the spot.

"You scared the wits out of me."

He laughed. "I doubt that."

"What are you doing in the park in the middle of the afternoon?"

Will stretched out and crossed his legs at the ankles. He locked his hands behind his head and closed his eyes. "Town council meeting every Monday."

"Ah."

"What are you doing?" Will asked.

"Praying. Well, trying to pray, but I'm sulking more than anything else."

He tipped his face upward. "What's going on?"

"Stuff."

He opened one eye. "Like what?"

Starting with a sigh, Taylor told him about the call from Indiana Godwin, the wonderful job possibility, and how her track record with Lisa Downey followed her.

Will thought for a moment. "I've learned there are always two sides to every story. This Lisa person must feel justified in some way."

"Whose side are you on?" Taylor jumped to her feet and walked back and forth in front of the bench.

"Yours, of course. But you're not going to get Lisa Dowling—"

"Downey."

"Downey—to admit any wrongs."

"So I'm helpless? At the mercy of her opinion?"

Will squinted up at her, catching the ire in her eyes. "No. But sulking over her isn't going to change anything. You've got to take the higher road. Don't let some woman hundreds of miles away in New York control your emotions."

She lifted her arms in surrender. "You're right; you're right."

Will patted the park bench. "Sit."

"No, I'm too antsy."

"Sit!"

Taylor sat. "I feel like your dog, Harry."

"No," Will said with a shake of his head, "he sits the first time I tell him."

"Ha, ha."

Will grabbed her hand. "Can I pray with you?"

Taylor bowed her head, her lips moving in silent prayer. Will noticed her grip grew tighter and tighter.

"Father, Taylor wants Your best. Give her wisdom and peace. Let her know the plans You have for her. I know You delight in her."

A drop of moisture hit his hand. Taylor sniffled then covered her face with her free hand. Will wrapped her in his arms. When her tears subsided, he gave her his handkerchief.

"Better?"

She laughed and blew her nose. "Much. Thanks." She faced him, her eyes and nose red. "I've been mad at Lisa for being an ogre when all along I should have been asking for forgiveness for my own selfish actions."

"Now it's forgotten. Over."

"Well, I probably need to e-mail or call Lisa, but yes, the Lord's forgiven me." Taylor carefully folded the handkerchief and tucked it in her pocket. "I'll wash it for you."

Will grinned and smoothed his hand over her hair. "It's going to be all right, Taylor Jo."

She leaned against him, and his hand cradled her shoulder. "Sure, but my career is still stopped at the red light of life. I need a green go."

"In that case, I have a proposal for you."

Chapter 8

To her surprise, the word *proposal* made her skin tingle. In an instant, time rolled back and she stood with Will on the White Birch covered bridge, serenaded by the water and surrendering her heart to love.

"...installing a new business system. We can't go forward with our e-business until we can handle the revenue and reporting."

Taylor tuned in to Will. "Um, what? Business system?"

He grinned, making her feel like they were the only two people in existence. He had a way about him that made her feel special. "Right. We're looking at HBS—"

She perked up at the familiar initials. "Hayes Business Systems?"

"Yes."

"Very classy. Kind of high-end for Lambert's Furniture, don't you think?"

"For now, but we've developed a line of furniture to sell online. HBS has a great solution for e-businesses including a module to work with online and distributor inventories."

"They do. But, Will, a lot of their standard modules are very expensive and over the top for the streamlined business you run. Even with adding the e-business, you'll—"

He held up his hand. "Taylor, this is exactly why I—we—want to hire you. Work for us as a consultant. Help us pick the right solution and installation process."

"Work for Lambert's Furniture?"

"Yes." He stood, arms out to the side, his expression like he'd discovered genius.

"I don't know, Will." She regarded him, wondering how it would feel to work every day with him. Her goal was to fix her career debacle, not lose herself in White Birch and fall in love, again, with Will Adams. "My career is important to me."

Will tipped his head to one side. "Consulting for a multimillion-dollar furniture company would look nice on a résumé."

She glanced up at him, squinting in the sunlight. "Can I pray about it?"

He knelt in front of her, forearms propped on his knees. "Absolutely."

❧❧

Taylor wandered upstairs to her room, her thoughts a million miles away.

"Taylor, is that you?" Mom knocked lightly on the bedroom door and peeked inside.

"It's me." Taylor kissed her on the cheek. "You look happy."

"Your dad just beat me at Scrabble." Her delicate smile fanned the tiny lines of her cheeks and around her eyes. "Dinner will be ready in an hour."

"Need help?" Taylor grabbed clothes to wear after her shower.

Mom waved both hands. "No. Go visit with your dad. He's in the library." She started down the stairs. "Tim, Dana, and the kids are coming tonight."

"That'll liven things up."

After her shower, Taylor knocked on the library door, her hair still wet.

"Come in," Dad called. "Did you have a nice run?" He closed his Bible.

"I did." Taylor sat on the window seat. She loved the library. It was bright from the southern exposure and cozy with its overstuffed Lambert's Furniture chair, ottoman, and a rocker. This was Tim's old room, but after he married Dana, Dad knocked out a wall to make a library.

"Will offered me a job," she said.

Dad stood and stretched. "Really?"

Taylor stared out the window. "He wants me to consult on the purchase of a new business system."

Dad joined her on the window seat. "They've been wanting to upgrade for a long time."

Taylor looked at him. His cheeks were pink again, his eyes bright. "Should I do it?"

"If you want," Dad said, his words even, not hinting of a yes or a no.

"What about my career?"

"What about it?"

Taylor stood, feet apart, arms folded. "If I work for Lambert's, I'll get caught up in the job, give a hundred and ten percent, and forget to keep looking *out there*." She motioned toward the window. She felt like a stuck record, repeating the same mantra, but she felt driven to land a CPA position with a lucrative firm.

"It's a consulting job, Taylor. A good line for your résumé. Unaccounted-for time is a negative, you know." Dad regarded her for a moment. "Still hurts, does it?"

"What still hurts?" She walked over to the desk where faded black and white photographs lined the edges.

"Losing Will."

Remembering pressed her emotions to the surface. "Yes," she said quietly. "Which is crazy after ten years."

She picked up a gold-framed picture of her parents on their wedding day in 1960. They smiled in black and white, walking up the church aisle, holding hands. That's what she had wanted with Will. But he wasn't ready.

Dad stood behind her now. "I almost lost your mom." He chuckled as he remembered. "She was a feisty one."

Taylor whirled round, the picture still in her hands. "Who, pixie Trixie?"

Dad gave her a deep nod. "Your grandpa insisted she marry into money and culture. Bringing home a common laborer from the furniture mill didn't fit Raymond's idea of a suitable husband for his little girl."

Taylor sat against the desk. "I never heard this. What'd you do?"

"Never gave up. Prayed a lot, as I recall. Did what I had to do to convince her father she'd have a wonderful life with me. For a while she dated Lem Maher down in Boston. I almost lost her then."

"Lem Maher of Maher Stationary and Business Supplies?"

"That'd be the one."

"Wow, Dad. Pretty *rico* competition." She rolled the *r* in *rico*.

He winked. "Love conquers all. Even money."

She put the picture back and crossed her arms. "And the moral to this story is?" She furrowed her brow.

Dad returned to his chair. "Not sure. Maybe there's a reason you and Will aren't married—to each other or anyone else. Maybe there's a reason you quit your job and moved home. Maybe there's a reason you showed up just when Will needed help with a new business system. Maybe there's a reason he asked you to help him. Maybe there's a reason you should say yes."

Taylor looked at him, a wry twist on her lips. "Aren't you full of reason tonight?"

Mom called up the stairs. "Grant, the kids are here. Taylor. . ."

Dad walked toward the door. "I can see lots of reasons why you should work for Lambert's Furniture. Least of all, finding out if you still love Will."

Taylor stopped him before he walked out. "I don't want to fall in love with him, Dad. It's over, too late."

He kissed her cheek. "Then don't. But do the job. Don't cut off your nose to spite your face."

❧❧

For Will, matters of the heart confounded him. They were confusing and complicated. He liked specific processes and procedures, clear-cut goals with achievable results. Why couldn't falling in love be like earning his MBA, running a business, or making furniture?

Instead, he had to navigate the minefield of Taylor's emotions. He had no map of her heart or his, no blueprint, no how-to manual. No way to know if he trod on dangerous ground.

Loving Taylor fell into a completely different category than loving his family and friends—the category of *difficult and hard*. Because if she didn't love him back, he didn't know what he would do.

Will pondered his relationship with Taylor as he parked his truck at Lambert's Furniture and trekked to the office door.

Did he love Taylor? After ten years? It didn't make sense, but then matters of the heart never did.

Will checked Bobby's office as he walked by. "I saw Taylor. Made my proposal."

Bobby reclined in his chair. "And?"

"She's praying about it."

"Does she know you proposed a job, not marriage?" Bobby asked, walking around his desk to shut his office door. "Got a minute?"

Will took a chair. "I know what you're going to say, Bob."

"Then why don't you do something about it?"

Will gazed at the ceiling for a second, thinking. Slowly he shook his head. "I'm not sure."

"Do you know how unlikely it is for a beautiful, intelligent woman like Taylor to be available and in town just when you're finally ready to settle down?"

"She wants a career, Bob. She always has."

"She wants you. She always has."

Will regarded him. "Not anymore. She told me."

"Told you what?" Bobby asked.

"That I'm married to Lambert's Furniture and she's married to *out there*." He pointed at nothing. "Besides, she's going on a date with Jordan West." Will shook his head. How could he even consider the notion that he might be in love with her?

Bobby nudged him. "Since when did *no* ever stop you?"

Will rubbed his forehead. "You sound like Grandpa."

Bobby grinned. "Thanks."

Will thought for a moment, rubbing his chin, then said, "I guess I could tell you now. After all, it's been ten years."

"Tell me what?" Bobby waited.

"What happened after your wedding reception."

A light rap on the door interrupted the story before it began. Ethan stuck his head inside. "Will, Martin Leslie's on the phone again. He really wants to talk to you about his last shipment."

Will slapped his hands against his knees and stood. "I'm on my way."

Bobby patted his shoulder as he passed. "We can talk later. See you at the grandparents' tonight?"

Will paused in the doorway. "I'll be there."

❦

Taylor read her e-mail to Lisa Downey one last time. Short and to the point, she simply apologized for her attitude during her final days at Blankenship & Burns.

> *It was never my intent to hurt you or your department. My actions and attitude were unprofessional. Please forgive me.*
>
> Sincerely,
> Taylor Hansen

She moved the cursor to the SEND button. Praying, she hesitated a second.

She didn't expect Lisa Downey to change her mind—or respond with her own apology. Taylor merely wanted to close a door she'd left ajar.

"Lord, here goes." She clicked SEND.

Downstairs, laughter reverberated from the family room where her parents played a board game with Tim, Dana, and the boys, Quentin and Jarred.

As Taylor came down, feeling like a weight had been lifted, she winked at Claire who was ending a conversation on her cell phone.

"What's up, Aunt Taylor?" she asked, clicking her phone shut.

Taylor smiled. "Not much." She sat on the edge of the ottoman.

"Can I ask you a question?" Claire flopped against the couch cushions. "If you cared about someone but they didn't care for you, what would you do?"

Taylor squared her shoulders, thoughtful. "Boy or girl?"

Claire hesitated. "Boy."

"How long have you, or *someone*, cared about the guy?"

Claire pinched her lips together then muttered, "Awhile."

"Well, the new wisdom of today is if a guy is into you, he'll let you know."

Claire nodded. "That's true."

"Otherwise, move on. Don't waste your time on a guy who's not treating you like you're queen of the universe. Move to New York, get a job, work yourself to death."

Claire laughed. "Like you?"

Taylor winced. "Yes, like me."

"Dad said Will Adams broke your heart."

The words punched up old feelings. "Yeah, well, your dad says a lot of things."

Claire moved to the ottoman. "What should I do?"

"Who is he?"

She shrugged. "Some guy from White Birch Community College."

"Claire, if I were you, here's what I'd do. Go home and write down all the ways you think you should be treated. Be real and honest. Write down how the Lord would want you to be treated. Your parents. Your friends. And if the guy doesn't measure up, he's not for you."

"His loss?" Claire asked, her voice weak and unsure.

"Yes, his loss," Taylor repeated, strong and sure, then kissed Claire's forehead. "You're too beautiful and precious to me, your parents, Grandma, Grandpa, and especially the Lord. Don't let any guy treat you like you're not."

From the family room, Tim called for Claire to join the game.

"In a minute, Dad," she answered.

"Sounds like he's getting clobbered," Taylor said, smiling.

"Probably. Can I ask you something else, Aunt Taylor?"

"Shoot."

"Why'd you quit your job? Dad said you loved it and loved life in New York."

Taylor laughed. "See, I told you your dad says a lot of things."

Claire giggled. "He does."

"Claire, sometimes you have to let go of one dream to realize another."

"Claire, help," Tim called again.

"You'd better go." Taylor nudged her niece.

"What is your other dream?" Claire asked, standing.

Taylor regarded her. "I'll let you know when I wake up."

Claire smiled and hurried to partner with her father, and Taylor went to the kitchen for the cordless phone. Breathing deeply, she dialed.

On the other end, the answering machine picked up.

"Will, hi, it's Taylor. I guess you're not home 'cause I'm talking to your machine. Thank you for your job offer. I'd be honored to help Lambert's Furniture. I can start Wednesday."

Chapter 9

"Come on, help me." Grandpa tapped Will on the shoulder. "Need more wood for the fire."

Will pushed away from the dinner table. "Thanks for dinner, Grandma. It was delicious as usual."

"Pineapple upside-down cake coming up next."

Outside in the cold, Will helped Grandpa gather logs.

"I like the direction you're taking the business, Will." Grandpa huffed and puffed a little as he hoisted a large log.

"Glad you approve."

"Hiring Taylor was smart."

"It's only an offer right now. It would be a huge blessing to have her experience and expertise on this project."

"For more reasons than one," Grandpa said, grinning as he dusted off his hands. "We've got enough wood. Let's go in."

"Grandpa, that's the only reason."

Grandpa opened the kitchen door. "If you say so." He shook his head.

"It's not that simple." Will dropped the wood by the fireplace, thinking how everyone oversimplified his relationship with Taylor. He tossed another large log onto the fire.

As he dusted bits of dirt and wood from his hands, Will's cousin Elizabeth approached. "Here, your arms look empty. I'm going to help Grandma." She handed him her one-year-old son, Matthew.

Will held the squirming child in the crook of his arm. When Matthew's father, Kavan, came around the corner, he laughed.

"Whoa, Will, he's not a football." Kavan set the boy upright.

Will grinned and glanced self-consciously around the room. "It's been a long time since I held a baby."

Ethan and Julie flopped onto the couch with plates of cake. "Looking good, Will. Thinking about getting one of those?" Ethan asked.

"He needs a wife first," Will's dad, Buddy, said.

Will held up his free hand. "Stop." He tried to jiggle little Matt to prove how good he was with children, but the little boy simply cried.

Julie stood, reaching her arms out. "Hand him over."

As more of the family gathered around the fire and talk of marriage and babies increased, Will stepped out. He needed to think.

The night was dark, but he knew his way down to the covered bridge without a light. The wind blew against his face, sharp and cold, until he reached the cover of the old bridge.

"Lord, all this pressure about Taylor. . ." He leaned against the weatherworn walls, hands in his pockets.

Suddenly, a small circle of light flashed across the bridge. "Grandma sent me down with this." Bobby held up a steaming mug of coffee.

Will grinned, reaching for the large cup. "It was getting crowded in there."

Bobby propped himself next to Will. "They just want you to be happy."

"Who says I'm not?"

"Well, they mean married happy."

"Naturally."

Bobby ran the flashlight's beam along the bridge's rafters. "I carved mine and Elle's initials right over there, I think, the night we got engaged."

Will's gaze followed the beam. "I don't think there's any room up there for more initials."

Bobby laughed. "You get engaged, I'll find room."

"Two miracles in one night. Don't know if the world could take it."

"What happened the night of my wedding?" Bobby asked.

Will sipped his coffee. He'd been expecting the question. How strange to share it now after so many years.

"Taylor and I came up here to the bridge. Maybe it was the romance of the moon, maybe it was your wedding, but love was in the air. Definitely in the air."

"I remember it was really warm that night. We had an outdoor reception and all I wanted was to leave with Elle and get into air-conditioning." Bobby laughed. "Seems so stupid now."

Will continued, the memory awakened. "Taylor wanted to go wading. We didn't have a flashlight. I had on my tux. She had on her bridesmaid's dress."

"Sounds like fun."

"We laughed so hard, I fell in. She tore the hem of her dress and stubbed her toe on a rock. When I tried to drive her home, my old orange Camaro wouldn't start, so we walked to Mom and Dad's."

"That's five miles, Will."

"I know. I carried her piggyback for half of it. She had on these funky shoes that were impossible to walk in." Recalling the picture made him laugh out loud.

"So what went wrong?"

Will picked up the story. "I knew I was in love with her. But I started grad school in the fall, and I wanted to be focused. Besides, all she ever talked about was living in Manhattan. I didn't think we were ready for the kind of love I was feeling."

"And you told her?"

Will looked out into the darkness, the coffee mug warm in his hand. "Are you kidding? I had the safe plan: Say nothing. Of course, I kissed her, which didn't help."

"What happened next?" Bob prodded.

"I got the keys to Dad's car and took her home. By then our feelings were so raw and out there, we didn't say anything. I've never, ever felt like that before or since. I knew I couldn't even kiss her again, 'cause if I did. . ." He stopped and drew a deep breath. "When I pulled into the Hansens' drive, she leaned over, told me she loved me, and. . ."

Will stopped. How could such an old memory provoke such a new love?

"Hey, don't leave me hanging."

"She asked me to marry her."

Bobby choked. "What?"

Will tossed out the last of his coffee and strolled down the length of the bridge. "She wanted to elope to New York—get married."

"Wow, I can't imagine Taylor laying her heart on the line like that."

Will shook his head. "I told you love was in the air."

"I take it your response wasn't 'Yeah, let's go!' "

Will laughed. "No. I didn't say anything for a long time. Too long. Finally, I babbled something about going to grad school. Never told her I loved her. Or that I would like to marry her someday. She jumped out of the car, ran inside, and the next day she was gone."

Bobby stood next to him on the edge of the bridge, shining the flashlight across the barren treetops. "And you didn't go after her?"

Will mumbled, "No," then added, "I thought I would, eventually. Eventually never came."

"You are one lucky man." Bobby shone the flashlight on Will's face. "Somehow, ten years later, *eventually* came to you."

❧❧

Taylor knocked on Will's office door. "Taylor Hansen reporting for work."

Will hopped up, sloshing coffee over the rim of his cup. "Good morning. Come in."

The heels of her designer pumps thudded against the hardwood floor.

Will regarded her for a moment. "You look nice," he said with a low whistle. "A little overkill, but very nice."

Taylor ran her hand down the front of her five-hundred-dollar suit. "This is a professional arrangement, is it not?"

Their eyes met, and she wondered if he could see right through her to her rapidly beating heart.

Will stuttered. "Of course, but you don't need an expensive suit to impress the bosses around here."

She cleared her throat and glanced at the floor. "I'll keep that in mind." Why did it seem as if they were talking about more than her job at Lambert's Furniture?

"Let me show you to your office."

Taylor followed Will. He introduced her to some of the administrative and financial staff, though she already knew most of them.

"Markie, good to see you." Taylor shook the hand of her old friend.

"Taylor, welcome home."

"Well, home for now." She felt shy about admitting her career failure. No matter how wonderful home might feel, it was a temporary stop.

"Here you go." Will opened the door, and Taylor stepped into a large, windowed office with a long, polished mahogany desk surrounded by old leather chairs. And in the corner, a stone fireplace beckoned.

"Will, it's beautiful."

"It's the old conference room. When we added the south wing we built a new one."

Taylor set her shoulder bag on the desk. "Are you sure you want me in here? This looks like a CEO's office."

Will perched on the desk's edge. "It's your office now. By the way, I didn't have time to get you any equipment." He motioned around the room. "No computer."

"I'm going to need one of those." Taylor winked at him, her hands on her hips. She liked being here, though the idea of being near Will both thrilled and terrified her. How he'd captivated her heart after all these years mystified her.

"We have about five thousand in the capital budget for a computer and software purchases, so—"

"That's a good start. But save that extra money for training. All I need is a fast computer and a connection to the Internet."

"We can handle that." Will pulled out a chair and sat, then brought Taylor up to speed on their business plan and how a new system fit into their strategy.

"I think HBS is a good choice, Will. I just want to make sure you don't get stuck with a bunch of modules you don't need," Taylor said when he finished.

She pulled her data assistant out of her case and made a note. "I know a few businesses who use HBS. I can give them a call."

Will nodded. "Bobby's been talking to an HBS sales rep, so you should get with him."

Taylor agreed, making more notes. "We should get them in here for a demo again and talk about your needs."

"Taylor, take the lead on this. Just tell us when and where."

Taylor tipped her head to one side. "I will. I'll get with Markie to see how things flow in the office and design a workflow and project plan. I can do that while I'm waiting for my computer to arrive."

Will was grinning at her.

"What?" she said.

"I like this side of you. Very in command."

She stared at him. If only he knew her insides were quivering like cold gelatin and if she weren't sitting in his place of business she'd want to kiss him. She cleared her throat and shook the image from her mind. "I'll need a computer to order my computer."

Will laughed. "My office."

Taylor scratched Harry's ears as she took Will's desk chair. He sniffed her shoes and wagged his tail.

Will gathered a stack of papers. "I'll be in the conference room."

She swallowed and smiled. "And I'll be here."

He paused at the door. "Markie is drawing up your contract. I researched the going consultant rates, but if it's too low, let me know."

Taylor waved off his remark. "I'm sure it's a fair wage." Besides, she wasn't really doing this for the money.

He nodded, grinned, and left. She slumped down in his chair, the aroma of clean soap floating around her. *I can't do this, Lord. I can't. I'm falling in love with him.*

Harry nudged her leg as if he understood her thoughts. Taylor stroked his head and sighed.

💨

For the tenth time in ten minutes, Will read the last line of their contract with Martin Leslie & Company. Thoughts of Taylor seemed way more intriguing than a distributor's contract.

He glanced at his watch. Ten o'clock. The coffeepot in the corner sat empty. Will shoved away from the conference table and dug in his pocket for change to get coffee from the production floor vending machine. No, no, what he needed was a cup of Peri's rich, special blend.

He headed to his office for his keys, suspecting he wanted an excuse to see Taylor more than he wanted a cup of Peri's best. But his chair was empty and disappointment twanged in his chest. He reached for his jacket and called to Harry. "Let's go for a ride."

Outside, early November snowflakes surprised him. It was too early for snow. But soft white flakes floated down over him. Then he heard screaming and. . .giggling?

He stepped to the side of the building, and there was Taylor, in her fancy periwinkle blue suit, catching snowflakes on her tongue with Markie.

Will guffawed. Harry barked.

"Laugh at us, will you?" Markie lobbed a tiny, powdery snowball at Will. It fell apart in midair.

Will laughed harder while Harry ran in circles, barking.

Out of nowhere, Taylor shouted, "Charge!" and ran for Will.

He tried to run, but his loafers provided no traction. Before he knew it, Taylor grabbed his collar and slipped an icy concoction down his back.

"Ahh! Cold. Cold." He whipped around, grasping at her.

She tried to escape, but running in heels proved impossible. She slipped, arms flailing. Will scooped her up in his arms just as his feet slipped out from under him. They went sprawling to the ground.

Unable to stop laughing, Markie stood over them, shivering, her hands grasping her waist. "I haven't done this since I was about ten, Taylor. Thanks, but I'm wet, freezing, and going inside."

Will helped Taylor to her feet.

"Ouch. I hurt," he said.

She laughed, adding, "I think I twisted my ankle."

He looked into her green eyes. "Are you okay?"

She nodded, dusting white powder from her suit. Her feet slipped again, and she fell against him. With her face inches from his, their eyes met.

He cleared his throat and stepped away, holding her steady with one hand on her elbow. "Can you stand?"

She jerked her suit jacket into place and smoothed her wet hair. "I think so." She hiccupped a giggle.

Will felt lost in time and space. He couldn't breathe. "You need help to the door?" he croaked. The moment was charged with emotion.

"I should change my clothes." She inched forward slowly. "So much for impressing the bosses."

"I can drive you home." He pulled his keys from his pocket and pushed the remote access button. The alarm chirped and the lights flashed.

"No, thanks. I'll take my car."

He started to protest, but one look told him her guard was up. "Would you like me to bring back coffee from Peri's?"

She paused at the door. "Yes, thank you. A large fat-free latte?"

He nodded, striking the air with keys in hand. "One fat-free latte."

Chapter 10

As the gray day faded to black, a fresh snow fell. Taylor glanced at her watch then massaged the back of her neck.

"Calling it a night?" Will stood in her doorway.

"I guess so. It's six thirty. I'm getting a little hungry."

"Can I buy you dinner?"

Taylor shook her head. It took her most of the afternoon to get rid of the image of him holding her, a dusting of snow on his head and shoulders. "Mom has lasagna waiting."

Will's eyes widened with a twinkle. "Trixie makes a mean lasagna."

Taylor shut down her laptop, which she'd brought from home to use for the afternoon. Her parents would love to see him. But she'd made it clear they were just friends. If they kept hanging around together, everything would get confused.

But when she looked up at him, she said, "I'm sure Mom wouldn't mind setting another plate."

Clicking off the office light, Taylor walked with Will to her car. She dropped her laptop into the passenger seat, then regarded him for a moment. "Thank you. For the job."

"You're welcome." He slipped his arm around her waist.

Her back stiffened, and she pressed her hands against his chest. Though, inside, she felt like a toasted marshmallow. "I guess we'd better get going."

"Taylor, I. . ." He looked into her eyes, tipped his head, then slowly touched his lips to hers, tenderly but with passion.

The kiss ended too soon. Caught up in the moment, Taylor couldn't speak. She cleared her throat and muttered, "Wow."

He laughed and kissed her forehead. "Is that a good wow?"

She stepped around him and slipped into her car. "See you at the house."

"Yeah, see you there," Will said, shutting her door and walked to his truck. In the side mirror, she watched him, tears stinging in her eyes. She couldn't love him again. She wouldn't.

She cried for several minutes; then she pulled herself together and drove home. But by the time she parked in the driveway, her tears had given way to ire.

Will parked his truck behind her. She jerked open the car door and stepped out.

"Don't you ever kiss me like that again," she said, pointing at Will as he walked toward her.

He didn't flinch. "I meant that kiss."

In the porch light, she could see the solid lines of his face. His warm breath smelled like mints. "I don't care what you meant, Will. Don't ever, ever kiss me like that again."

"I'm in love with you." He settled against her car.

In the cold, her voice rang out like bells. "In love with me? You're not in love with me; you're in love with a memory."

"No, I'm in love with you. Always have been."

She laughed, slapping her hand on her forehead. "Oh, right, I forgot. You wanted to marry me, but I said no. Then you chased me all over New York begging me to reconsider. But finally, you gave up and came home to run Lambert's Furniture."

He straightened away from the car. "Good night." He pulled his keys out of his pocket.

"Where are you going?"

"Home."

Taylor trembled, but not from the cold or the snow gathering on her hair and shoulders. His control irritated her. Deep down, she wanted him to fight this out—to fight for her.

"I loved you." She gestured at him with her arm.

He walked back toward her. "I was—am—in love with you, but I wasn't ready for marriage ten years ago. Neither were you."

"Then why didn't you say something?"

His jaw muscle tightened. "I thought it would be better left unsaid."

She growled and turned away, her hands balled into fists. "It took me three years to stop thinking of you night and day. Every man I dated I compared to you."

"I never stopped thinking about you."

She whirled around. "Then why are we here on the other side of a decade? Why didn't you call or write or stop by when I came home for a visit? It's not like I lived on the other side of the country or the other side of the world."

He reached for her. "I don't know. But, Taylor, you're here now, and I know what I want. Let's get it right in this decade."

"It's too late," she whispered.

The front door opened, and Mom stepped into a sliver of yellow light. "Will, Taylor, come in, dinner's waiting."

Will touched her cheek lightly with the back of his hand. "I'll go on home."

Taylor touched his hand. "Don't go." She rubbed her forehead with her cold fingers. "If you leave, Mom will ask a million questions."

Will chuckled wryly. "I suppose the tension between us won't make her suspicious at all."

"Trixie Hansen will be so glad to have you at her table she won't notice." Taylor reached into the BMW's backseat for her laptop case and handbag.

Will followed her up the walkway. "This conversation isn't over."

Taylor murmured, "No, I guess it isn't."

When the hallway clock cuckooed at nine, Will stood, declared Grant the king of chess, and said, "I need to go home while I still have some dignity."

Grant slapped his knee. "I was about to checkmate."

Will grinned. "I know."

Taylor watched from the chaise chair where she sat curled up with the *New York Times* and the *Boston Globe*.

"Anything interesting?" Will asked, stopping by her chair.

Grant walked past, calling to his wife, "Trixie, Will's leaving."

Taylor answered without looking up. "Lots of things. Mostly keeping up on the stock market."

Will moved the folded front page of the *Times* so he could sit on the arm of the chair. "I'm sorry—"

"It was lovely to have you tonight, Will." Trixie held out his coat, her perfect smile lighting her petite face.

"Thank you, Trixie. Dinner was delicious."

"Oh, let me wrap up some for you to take home." She handed Will's coat to her husband and bustled out of the family room toward the kitchen.

Grant gave Will his coat. "I think I'll get some ice cream," he said and left the room.

Will considered his next words to Taylor since he was sure he only had a few seconds before Grant and Trixie returned. "I didn't mean to upset you."

"I know you didn't."

He looked across the room. "So where does this leave us?"

"I don't know."

"Here you go, Will." Trixie handed him a square plastic container.

"You spoil me," he said, taking the lasagna and giving her a light hug. "Thank you."

"You've been so good to Grant." She stood perfectly straight, her hands clasped together.

"We like to take care of our *family*."

Grant hollered from the kitchen, "I can't find the ice cream scoop."

Trixie excused herself.

Taylor stared in the direction of the kitchen. "Dad's addicted to ice cream. It's his kryptonite."

Will pulled on his coat. "I probably fell in love with you over a scoop of chocolate in a sugar cone."

"I suppose so," she said.

He wondered when she fell in love with him but didn't ask. "Would you like to get some ice cream?"

She looked up. "Now?"

He shrugged. "Sure."

She shook her head. "It's late—and snowing. I'll pass."

He nodded. "See you tomorrow then?"

"Yes." Taylor flipped the edges of the newspaper.

"When are you. . ." He stopped.

"Going to dinner with Jordan?"

He nodded.

"Friday."

"Good night, Taylor," he said, turning to leave. "See you tomorrow."

She looked at him. "Yes, see you tomorrow."

Driving home, Will prayed, sorry his kiss caused such a quarrel. But he loved her. He knew that now, and he wouldn't give up until she loved him, too.

Jordan tried too hard, in Taylor's opinion. He reeked of cologne, his hair glistened with too much gel, and his normally graceful gait looked stiff and robotic.

He stared straight ahead the entire movie, and when they left the theater with hordes of other White Birch citizens, they walked to his car in silence.

Where was the fun, relaxed Jordan from the football game?

"Sorry about the mess," he said, moving more of his football gear to the backseat. A teacher, Jordan used his car as an office, or so it seemed to Taylor.

"What subjects do you teach?"

"I teach Phys Ed, of course, and I coach. I also teach a couple of history classes. I'm a little bit of a buff, as they say."

"What's your favorite historical time?" Taylor asked, settling in the passenger seat. The hinge moaned and squeaked as Jordan shoved the passenger door closed.

"World War I. It's an interesting time in world history," Jordan said when he got in his side of the car. "I've always loved the mystique behind Teddy Roosevelt."

"Yes, he's a fascinating man."

He placed his arm between the bucket seats, his right hand on the headrest behind her, and stared at her for a second. Taylor fidgeted with her hands and wished he'd start the engine.

She thought he might kiss her, so she moved back an inch.

He touched her shoulder and asked, "Where to now?"

She shrugged and quickly glanced at the dash clock. Nine thirty. "Where would you like to go?" She hated to suggest home already.

"Peri's Perk is a fun place on Friday nights. Lots of the town folks out, and there's usually a guitar player."

She smiled. "Sounds good."

It was late when Will left Lambert's Furniture. He didn't bother checking on Taylor. She'd worked late most nights this week, but he knew she had a date tonight.

He tried not to picture Jordan laughing and talking with her, looking into her green eyes. His cell phone chirped. "Hello."

"Hello, son, it's Grandpa."

Will unlocked his truck, hunching against the icy night wind. "What's up?"

"Grandma thought you might want some dinner."

Will laughed. "As a matter of fact, I do." He'd been planning to stop by anyway. He needed advice.

When Will entered the Lamberts' home on the hill, he hung his coat by the kitchen door. Next to the oven, Grandma stirred batter in a large bowl.

She smiled at him. "Let me get you a bowl of chili and a couple slices of warm bread."

Will kissed her on the cheek. "They don't make them like you anymore."

Her blue eyes sparkled. "I hear they're making them prettier and taller these days. Skinnier, too."

Will shook his head. "Just cheap imitations."

She laughed. "Scoot. Go see your grandpa."

In the living room, Grandpa swayed back and forth in his rocker. "How are things with your new consultant?"

"Worth every penny we've been paying her," Will said. "She's already saved us ten thousand dollars on the HBS deal."

Grandpa chuckled. "Not surprised to hear that."

"Here you go, Will." Grandma set a tray with steaming chili and hot, buttered bread on the coffee table. "What do you want to drink?"

Will shrugged. "Whatever you got. Water's fine."

"How about tea? Hot or iced?"

Will looked up at her. "Iced tea is good, but you don't have to wait on me, Grandma."

She fluttered out of the room. "Of course I do."

Grandpa regarded him. "What's on your mind?"

Will scooted to the edge of the couch, stirring the chili, letting it cool. "How did you win the heart of the prettiest lady in White Birch?"

Grandpa belly-laughed. "You're asking me?"

"Yes." Will slurped a spoonful of chili. Still too hot.

Leaning forward, Grandpa said, "I had the sympathy, man-in-uniform angle going for me."

Will laughed. "Are you telling me if it weren't for World War II, I might not be here?"

"There's a real possibility." Grandpa's smile seemed to make his dark eyes twinkle. "You'd better talk to your grandma about winning over a woman's heart."

"What's this?" Grandma came in with a tall glass of tea.

"Will needs our help, Betty."

She sat down and placed her hands in her lap. "You got ten minutes. Cookies are in the oven."

Will laughed. "Tell me how to win Taylor. She thinks our time has passed. Too late. Lost what we once had."

Grandma waved her hand. "Taylor's easy, Will. She already loves you. I can see it in her eyes. You just need to let her know that no matter what, you're going to be there for her. Never let her go. Prove whatever happened between you ten years ago won't happen again."

Will grinned. Simple. Wise. Brilliant. Hopefully, not impossible.

Chapter 11

"Well, well. Will Adams, we meet again." Mia Wilmington sashayed down the aisle toward him just as he tossed a forty-pound bag of dog food to his shoulder.

"Mia. Hello." He smiled but felt awkward seeing her again.

"What are you doing at Sinclair's alone on a Friday night? A man like you ought to have a pretty woman on his arm."

He agreed. But at the moment she was out with Jordan West. Pointing to the bag on his shoulder, he answered her question. "Dog needs food."

"How sweet. Is there anything more romantic than a man who loves animals?" Mia tapped his arm with her well-manicured hand and batted her thick eyelashes.

He took a step back. "I suppose there are lots of things."

She chortled. "Oh, you. Listen, let's go for a coffee or something."

"No, I'd better get home."

"Oh, come on now. Don't leave me hanging. You never did call after our date."

Will winced. He didn't mean to be rude to Mia, but he knew his affections belonged to Taylor.

"Well. . ."

"Come on, be a sport."

"I guess one cup of coffee with a friend would be all right." While he enjoyed Grandma's chili, a cup of Peri's coffee would top off his night.

"Sure, friend," she said coyly.

❧❧

Jordan held open the door to Peri's. "Can you believe this weather?" Jordan asked, picking the first available table.

"Cold for November, isn't it?" Taylor shivered and tucked her hands under her arms, breathing in the heady scent of blended coffees and teas and something that smelled like grilled bread.

Jordan offered to take her coat, but she declined. "Need to warm up for a second."

"Sorry that old beater of mine doesn't have better heat. I'd buy a new car, but I'm building a house, so all my money is tied up."

Taylor nodded and smiled. "How nice. A new house."

"Yeah, it's been a dream for a long time. Shall we order?" Jordan jumped to is feet. "What'll it be? Coffee, latte, tea?"

"Hot chocolate. Large. Extra hot," Taylor said.

"Coming up."

A chorus of "Hey, Coach" rose from Peri's patrons as Jordan made his way to the counter. He waved and clapped a couple of the younger men on the shoulder.

When he returned with steaming mugs and sat down across from Taylor, they smiled at each other, then stared in opposite directions, their conversation fading away.

"Well, isn't Peri's the place to be?" Mia bubbled, clasping the collar of her coat around her neck, beaming up at Will as he opened her car door for her.

"Maybe it's too crowded." He hoped Taylor wouldn't be inside.

"Come on, Will. Don't be a stick-in-the-mud."

Stick-in-the-mud? He followed her, wondering how he'd gotten himself into this situation. One weak moment at Sinclair's and his night changed from a cozy evening with Grandpa and Grandma, then Harry, to an evening with frilly, silly Mia.

Lord, help. He didn't want to lead her on. He planned to make it clear they were only going to be friends.

Inside, he saw a vacant table by the door and held out a chair for Mia. "I'll get us some coffee."

"Make mine a café mocha, please."

Taylor ran the recesses of her mind looking for a topic she thought would interest Jordan, but between the drive in the car to and from the movie, they'd exchanged all the what-are-you-up-to-now information.

Football, she thought. "The football team is doing well, I hear."

Jordan snapped to attention. "We are, so far. Eight and one."

Taylor tipped her head to the side, her eyes wide. "Good for you. Going to the play-offs then."

"Yes, then to state." Jordan made a praying gesture with his hands. "Lord willing."

"I hope you do. I know the boys on the team would be thrilled."

"You should know."

She sipped her cocoa. "Me?"

"State championship, girl's basketball. Power forward Taylor Jo Hansen."

"We lost."

"At state. Runners-up. Not too shabby. Weren't you MVP?"

"Long time ago, Jordan, in a land far, far away."

He scoffed. "You're a great athlete, Taylor. Last week's touch football game proved that."

"I love sports. Will and I used to. . ." She stopped, not meaning to mention his name.

"Is there anything between the two of you?" Jordan asked outright.

"No," Taylor said, reaching for a stir stick, swirling the whipped cream into the chocolate. "We're just friends. Well, business associates, really."

Jordan raised a brow. "Business associates?"

"I'm working with Lambert's Furniture as a consultant until I find a new job."

He nodded with an I-see look. "So you're not planning on staying in town long."

She motioned with her hand. "No, not at all. Temporary stop."

Will ordered then leaned against the counter, facing Peri's small stage as the guitar player took the stool and tuned up.

Glancing around, he recognized almost everyone in the place, then his gaze connected directly with Taylor Hansen's.

He squared his shoulders as his heartbeat picked up. He gave Taylor a half smile and waved.

She half smiled and waved.

Jordan sat on the other side, his back to Will. He seemed engaged in the conversation with Taylor, though from Will's point of view, it seemed rather one-sided.

Taylor looked uncomfortable, and Will grimaced, realizing it was probably his presence that did it, not Jordan's.

Mia, on the other hand, was engaged in a lively chat with the people at the table next to theirs. She gave Will a wild wave when she caught his attention.

"Here you go, Will." Sissy Larson tapped him on the shoulder. "Two large café mochas."

"Thanks, Sissy." Will picked up the mugs and worked his way back to his table. When he sat down, he realized he was directly in Taylor's line of sight.

He ducked his head and sipped his coffee, burning his lip.

Mia propped her chin in her hand and leaned toward Will. "So, what have you been up to these days?"

"Working, mostly." He nodded. "Working."

"Oh, I love a workingman. So romantic."

Will winced with an inward sigh. It was going to be a long night.

Taylor stared out the window. What was Will doing here with Mia? Were they on a date?

She picked up her hot chocolate and took a big sip, concealing most of her face with the bottom of the mug, and cut a glance across Peri's to where Will sat.

He watched the guitar player now, nodding his head to the rhythm of the song. Mia had her chin in her hand and seemed to be talking.

"More hot chocolate?" Jordan stood. "I could use another cup of coffee."

"Yes, please." *Anything for a distraction.* Jealousy tugged at her. But didn't Will have every right to be here with anyone he pleased? Especially after the speech she gave him.

While she was enjoying her time with Jordan, deep down, Taylor knew he wasn't the one. She glanced toward the counter where Jordan chatted with several men, waiting for their order. Reaching into her purse, she pulled out her electronic data assistant and jotted a note to e-mail or call Indiana Godwin again. Taylor slid the device back into her bag just as Jordan returned, with Mia clinging to his arm.

"Taylor, this is a fellow teacher and friend of mine, Mia Wilmington."

Taylor shook Mia's hand. "We've met."

"That's right. At Italian Hills. Good to see you again."

"Right." Taylor shifted her gaze beyond Mia to Will. He was looking right at her.

"Say, why don't you and Jordy join Will and me? We'd love it."

"Oh, I don't know. . ." Taylor shot Jordan what she hoped was a no-let's-not look.

"Taylor, what do you say?" Jordan asked excitedly.

Not only had he missed her visual petition, he seemed to like the idea. So the evening wasn't magical for Jordan, either.

"Okay, if you want to." She grabbed her things and stood.

"Oh, wonderful," Mia said, her arm still hooked to Jordan's as they went over to give Will the good news.

Was it possible for the night to go from bad to worse? Finding himself in the company of the woman he loved while on a coffee date with a woman he didn't?

He stood as Taylor approached. "Hello."

"Hello." She gave him a slow smile.

"Isn't this cozy?" Mia said as she sat down between the men. Taylor took an awkward seat off to the side, but the fragrance of her perfume invaded Will's senses. His coffee tasted even sweeter now.

He thought to focus on the guitar player's lovely tune, lovely words. *Focus.*

"Will," Jordan started, "Taylor and I were reminiscing about the 1990 championship basketball team."

"Were you now?" Will peered into her eyes.

"Just for a moment."

Jordan continued. "Taylor doesn't think it was any big deal to go to state or be named MVP."

She lifted her hands in defense. "We lost."

"But you went to state."

Mia fluttered in her chair like a disturbed hen. "What's all this sports talk? There are ladies present."

"Sports talk is fine with me," Taylor said.

Will bit his lip to keep from laughing. Her words weren't rude or snippy. They were honest—another reason why he loved her.

Their conversation quieted down during the last song of the singer's set, and when the young man finished, the patrons applauded cordially.

Will glanced between Jordan and Taylor. "What'd you guys do tonight?"

She answered. "Went to a movie."

"Good." He was so close he could have kissed her cheek.

Mia seemed to want the conversation to be about her—or at least things she liked—so she took over. Jordan engaged her, genuinely amused.

An hour later, the foursome stood to leave.

"Well look at that, snowing again," Mia said with a giggle as she slipped on her coat. "We'll be buried before Thanksgiving at this rate."

Will thought the scene looked beautiful, and if he had his way, he'd be holding Taylor close on a moonlit walk in the fresh snow.

He turned to Mia. "Good night." He shook her hand and purposefully added, "Good to run into you at Sinclair's."

"We must do this more often. The four of us," Mia said, unlocking her car.

Mia got into her car. Will watched as Taylor left with Jordan, a gnawing of jealousy in his middle.

Taylor stopped and gazed back at him. "Good night."

Chapter 12

The pews for the ten thirty service were almost full by the time Taylor arrived at White Birch Community Church with her mother and dad. Tim and Dana had saved seats for them near the front.

Taylor sat on the end, grateful to be near the front and away from any distractions. If Will or Jordan were in the back, she wouldn't even know. This morning she longed to focus on Jesus and His peace.

She'd awakened this morning with the familiar feeling of hopelessness, wondering if her life would never be right again. Would she find the right job? Would she ever surrender to love? Ribbons of sunlight filtered through the sanctuary windows. Taylor closed her eyes and exhaled, the presence of the Lord already touching her heart.

Someone patted her shoulder. "Move over."

Taylor refused to open her eyes, but she recognized Will's voice. "No."

"Taylor." He gently pressed his hand on her arm.

"Good morning, Will," Grant said. "Here, sit." Taylor peeked at her dad, who was moving over to make room for Will.

"Thank you, Grant. Good morning, Trixie."

Taylor watched Will through narrowed eyes as he hugged her mom, shook hands with Tim and Dana, then shared a man-slapping hug with Pastor Marlow.

Will looked amazing in his black suit, white shirt, and sage and gold tie. Her heartbeat faltered a little when he sat down next to her and said softly, "Taylor."

"Will," she echoed.

"Have a nice Friday night?"

"Lovely," she said with a smirk. "And you?"

"Swell."

His intonation made her laugh. She covered her mouth with the tips of her fingers. She wanted to ask him how he ended up at Peri's with Mia, but the worship leader took the stage and Taylor rose to her feet with the rest of the congregation.

Jeremiah strummed his guitar. "Let's worship the Lord this morning in Spirit and truth."

A chorus of "amens" echoed around the room.

"I'm here to focus on Jesus, so don't bother me," Taylor said to Will, leaning close so only he could hear.

"I was about to say the same to you."

Grinning, she joined in the song. *Oh, Will. . . You do have a way of getting under my skin.*

Will could have stayed in the sanctuary all day with Taylor. Hanging out with Jesus and Taylor. Did it get any better?

He listened closely to Pastor Marlow's sermon, making a mental note not to let Taylor's reaction to him push him toward anxiety.

Shifting his gaze for a quick second, he looked over at her. Without pondering, he knew he could love her for the rest of his life. He wanted to love her. Not only was she beautiful with her sleek nose, long eyelashes, and stubborn chin, she challenged him to be better, to look at life as an adventure, and to see people, not a list of to-dos.

Will needed Taylor. And with God's grace, he'd woo her heart.

Jesus wooed his heart every day, teaching him to respond in love. And in some small way, Will understood that the Lord loved him the way he loved Taylor.

"Let peace guard your heart and mind," Marlow concluded. "Pursue peace."

Will nodded and almost uttered amen. From the other side of the church, he heard Grandpa Matt vocalize his agreement with the message.

"Let's stand and pray." Marlow stepped from behind the pulpit.

Will stood. Next to him, Taylor rose to her feet, her expression serious.

"Everything okay?" he whispered.

She put on a bright smile. "Yes. I needed that message today."

"Words I live by." When the service ended, Will was about to ask her to lunch when Tim popped up between them.

"Do you two want to go to lunch?"

Taylor shook her head. "I had a big breakfast. I'm not really that hungry."

There went Will's idea to invite her to lunch.

"Suit yourself. Dana and I are taking Mom and Dad to the new steak place out by the theaters."

"Okay, but Dad needs to drop me home first."

Tim winced. "He already left. Mom wanted to stop by the drugstore to pick up his medication."

"Then you'll have to take me, big brother." Taylor popped him on the arm.

Will blurted, "I'll take you."

Tim grinned. "Thanks, Will. See you later, Taylor." And he was gone.

Will jerked his thumb over his shoulder. "My truck is on this side."

Taylor picked up her Bible and journal. "How convenient for you. If I didn't know better, I'd say you fixed this." She walked toward the foyer. "I need my coat."

"I'll drive around front to pick you up."

She started down the aisle. Will turned toward the side door as Grandma came up behind him. "Remember my advice now—from the other night."

Will smiled down at her. "I will."

Taylor talked to herself. "Just be cool. Don't agree to anything. No dinners or walks in the park. Just thank Will for the ride home and say, 'See you tomorrow.'"

Taylor hopped inside the warm cab of Will's truck. She chuckled softly as she thought of Jordan's heat-deprived car Friday night.

"Did I miss something?" Will asked, waving to Bobby, Elle, and the kids as they passed in front of the truck.

Taylor waved, too, then said, "Jordan's car doesn't have heat. We were so cold that night."

"He's a good guy."

"He's sweet." But he wasn't Will.

Will turned south out of the church parking lot, the afternoon sun burning bright and warm through the windshield. Patches of grass showed along the road as the warm sun melted the snow.

"Beautiful day," she said without really thinking. The words simply flowed from her heart.

"You're beautiful."

She looked at him. "Stop—"

He turned onto Main. "I mean it, Taylor."

She stared ahead, letting his words sink in, allowing herself to enjoy the compliment—for a moment. Then she asked, "What about Mia?"

"I told you we're friends." Will looked over. "I ran into her at Sinclair's Friday night. She insisted I go with her to Peri's for coffee. I couldn't say no without being rude."

Taylor nodded. "I see."

As he neared the Hansens', he asked, "Are you sure you aren't hungry?"

"Well, maybe a little. I told Tim I wasn't hungry partly because I am watching my spending. I didn't want to splurge on a big lunch I don't really need."

Taylor knew when she left New York it would be tight, but she'd planned to have a job long before now. The offer from Will to work at Lambert's Furniture came just in time. She might not have to sell her new BMW.

Will pulled into the Hansens' driveway. He shifted the transmission into PARK and turned to Taylor. "How about a little basketball?"

"What? No."

"It's a beautiful day, the snow's melting, and I need a little exercise."

Taylor reached for the door handle. "No thanks."

"Win or lose, I buy lunch." Will regarded her with his deep-set blue eyes, his arm propped on the steering wheel.

"No."

He touched her arm. "One-on-one. Milo Park. Burgers at Sam's afterward."

Taylor's lips formed the word no, but her stomach lurched when she pictured one of Sam's burgers. "I don't know. . ."

"Stick-in-the-mud." He winked and laughed.

"Stick-in-the-mud?" She jerked the door open and stepped out.

"Heard it from Mia. She called me a stick-in-the-mud when I hesitated about going for coffee with her."

"I always thought more of you, Will. A little name-calling never seemed to move you before."

His gaze intent on her, he asked one more time, "Milo Park in a half hour? I need to change."

"You're on." Taylor stepped the rest of the way out of the truck and slammed the door shut.

Walking up to the house, she muttered to herself, "Right, Taylor. Say no. Just tell him thanks for the ride and see you tomorrow."

❧❧

Sam's was quiet on Sunday night, so when Taylor and Will entered, they had their pick of booth or table.

"Any one you want, Will," Sam called to him. "How are you, Taylor?"

"Fine, thank you, Sam."

Will led the way to a table by the fireplace. "I never get to sit here; these tables are always taken or reserved."

Janet came up behind them. "Evening. What would you two like to drink?"

"Diet soda and a large water for me," Taylor said, draping her coat over the back of a chair.

"Same for me, Janet."

Taylor sat down and regarded him. His cheeks were red from playing ball, and his hair stood on end where he'd combed it with his fingers. "You were one terrible basketball player today."

He laughed. "I had lead feet this afternoon."

"Thanks for talking me into it. It was fun."

Janet set their drinks down and pulled out her order pad. "Do you know what you want?"

Will looked at Taylor and ordered for both of them. "Cheeseburgers—"

"With the works," Taylor added.

Will nodded. "And fries."

"Extra fries."

Janet lowered her pen and pad. "Are you starving, Taylor?"

"Yes."

"Anything else?" Will asked.

"Side salad for me. Light dressing on the side. No croutons."

Janet snickered as she walked away.

"Have to watch my calories," Taylor said to Will.

He shook his head, laughing with an echo of pleasure. "You amaze me, Taylor."

She fiddled with her straw wrapper. "How so?"

"You have your own way of living life. You go for your dreams. You understand God's grace—"

"But you understand His peace."

"I do. But it's been a lot of years pursing peace to be able to abide in it."

"I can't remember the last time I abided in peace."

"This morning, at church."

Tears stung her eyes. "For a moment, yes."

"Life's been difficult the past month, Taylor. Give yourself a break."

"The past month? Will, my life has been one big anxiety attack for years. Fighting to advance my career, working eighty-hour weeks. . . Dating so-called Christian men whose morals are no different than most non-Christian men's. Worried about money. Worried about friends, worried about gray hairs and wrinkles and the world coming to an end."

Will sat back. "The world coming to an end?"

"Once I get into a worry cycle, it's hard to stop." She snickered.

"Memorizing and applying scripture changed life for me. Grandpa and Grandma taught me about living a life of peace—about being a man of peace."

"That's what I admire about you, Will. You are so peaceful."

"I've had to work at it—change my thinking."

Janet set down Taylor's salad. Sam tossed another log on the fire. "Temperature's dropping," he said.

Taylor picked up her silverware. "I could use a few lessons."

"I could teach you. Pray with you."

She smiled. "I'd rather not, Will."

"Why not?" He couldn't let her comment go.

She looked him square in the eye. "You know why."

"Tell me."

She sighed, her fork loose in her hand. "I'll fall in love with you."

"Then we're even."

Chapter 13

By Friday noon, Taylor and Markie had mapped out their work flow and created a project plan that started with the day they purchased the new system to "go live."

Happy with the plan and the demo HBS gave them earlier in the week, Taylor recommended Lambert's Furniture purchase HBS for their accounting, timekeeping, and inventory system.

"Knock, knock." Will smiled and held up the papers in his hand. Harry followed, his tail wagging.

"Come in." She returned his smile, remembering her Monday morning promise to lighten up with Will yet maintain a safe distance. She had concluded that playing the gruff, once-rejected woman didn't fit her character or God's.

But it took until Thursday evening to stop daydreaming about their Sunday afternoon basketball game and eating burgers afterward at Sam's in front of the fire.

They'd had a great time that day. Being in Will's company always felt like coming home at the end of a hard day: peaceful, warm, and sheltered.

She drew a deep breath. "Did you sign the HBS deal?"

Will walked over to the fireplace and turned on the gas. "It's always colder on this side of the building." Harry sniffed Taylor's leg then passed by to curl up near the stone hearth.

"That's why I wear a parka and drink ten cups of coffee."

He laughed and handed her a copy of the contract. "You are an excellent negotiator. The salesman couldn't stop telling us how amazing you were."

"Let's see if he put in my last request for changes to the terms and conditions." She skimmed the contract down to the fine print. "Yep, he did."

"If you wanted a job with HBS, Taylor, you could probably get one."

She snapped her head up. "What?"

"He asked about you. I told him that you were only consulting."

"Thank you, but I know some things about HBS internally. Not my cup of tea. They make a great product, but I wouldn't want to be on the inside."

He nodded.

"Thank you, anyway, again." She looked down when their eyes met.

"You're welcome," Will said then left.

Taking her desk chair, Taylor felt disappointed with the simple, straightforward business conversation she'd just had with Will. Was she crazy or did she really want him to pursue her? Never mind her continuous song of "I'm not available."

Her phone rang just as she reaffirmed, again, that falling in love with Will did not fit her agenda.

"Taylor, it's Indiana."

She smiled. "I was going to call you."

"I have a job lead for you."

She stood, shooting her chair across the hardwood floor. "Really? Where? What?"

"Boswell Global in Sacramento is looking for a CFO."

"You're kidding." Boswell Global was a hot new dot-com company.

"A friend, Alex Cranston, is their human resource director. We were talking, and he wanted to know if I knew any qualified financial officer candidates."

Taylor sank toward her seat, which she realized wasn't there, so she perched on the edge of the desk. "Did you tell him about me?"

"I did. They're looking for young, chic, savvy executives. You're perfect for the job."

"Indiana, that's incredible," Taylor said. She asked several questions about the position, jotted down Alex Cranston's e-mail address, and thanked Indiana one last time.

"I wouldn't recommend you if I didn't think you were qualified, Taylor."

They talked a few more minutes about old job acquaintances and then said good-bye. Taylor felt as if she were flying. She balled her fist and allowed herself one controlled squeal.

By the hearth, Harry lifted his head and whined.

"I'm fine, Harry," she said, her hand pressed to her forehead. "Lord, I can't believe You answered my prayer with Boswell Global."

Without wasting any more time, Taylor launched her e-mail program and composed a warm, but brief letter to Alex Cranston and attached her résumé.

California, get ready to meet Taylor Hansen.

❧

At Peri's, Will ordered and took a stool at one of the high, round tables. He waved when his grandparents came in holding hands. "What are you young people doing?"

Grandma laughed. "Having lunch. Your grandpa is addicted to Peri's sweet coffees."

Grandpa shook Will's hand. "Hardly fair to call it coffee with so much whipped cream floating on top."

Will nodded in agreement. "How are things down in the shop?"

"Good. But I'm looking forward to Grant's return. I retired for a reason, you know."

Will shook his head. "You volunteered."

"I did. And I've enjoyed it." Grandpa held Grandma's chair for her. "But I'm ready to be home with your grandma again and puttering around the basement, working on my own projects."

"Ethan said Grant will be back after Thanksgiving."

Grandpa nodded. "He deserves some time off."

Grandma tapped Will on the hand. "What's going on with you?"

Will sat in the spare seat across from his grandparents. "We just signed a deal with Hayes Business Systems. Couldn't have done it without Taylor."

"What does that mean for the business?" Grandma asked.

Will grinned. "It's a major software upgrade. We launch our e-business as soon as the installation is done and live. Selling furniture over the Internet. . .did you ever imagine that, Grandpa?"

Grandpa shook his head. "No, but the Lord is really blessing the business, isn't He?"

Will nodded. "He amazes me every day. The fact Taylor was available with the talent and experience we needed is a miracle."

Grandma tapped his hand. "What is going on with you two? Elizabeth and Kavan drove by the park Sunday afternoon and saw you two playing basketball."

Will laughed. "My cousin, Elizabeth, the romance reporter. Remember when she met Kavan and practically despised falling in love?"

"She's a changed woman," Grandma said with a low laugh. "So, how goes the plan to win Taylor? Did you let her beat you in basketball?"

"I'm executing it one day at a time, just like you told me."

"Will, your order's up," Peri called.

Grandma pointed at him. "Don't let her go this time."

Will frowned as he stepped over to the counter and picked up his grilled chicken sandwich. "I'll try not to, Grandma. But she has her own plans."

"What's next on the wooing Taylor agenda?" Grandma asked as he took his seat.

Will shrugged. "What should it be?"

Grandma's expression told him it should be obvious. "Flowers."

❧❧

At four o'clock Will walked into Taylor's office. He gently grabbed her arm and lifted her from her chair.

"Come on," he said, guiding her toward the door.

"Will, wait. I'm in the middle of something. Where are we going?"

"It's Friday afternoon. Time to cut out for some fun."

"I'm having fun working. Markie and I came up with a great plan to move the data from the old system."

"Good. But it's quitting time." He tugged on her arm again.

"You want to tell me what's up?"

He grinned. "Football."

She headed back to her desk. "Oh no. Not me."

"Lambert's Furniture needs you." He bent over her, hands pressed on the arms of her chair. "Ethan challenged Creager Technologies in a touch game, and we can't lose."

"Will, I have work to do." She'd calculated the time it would take to get the office ready for a new system, then change over from the old one, and she needed several more weeks of intense effort. If Boswell hired her, she didn't want to leave Lambert's in a bind.

Besides, spending her free time with Will was dangerous to her heart.

"It's Friday at four, Taylor. Stop and smell the roses."

"I, um, just don't want to"—he moved a little closer. She cleared her throat and looked away—"to fall behind."

"Next week you can work to your heart's content. But for now, play football with us. The company needs you."

Grrr. He was hard to resist. "I thought Sunday was football day."

"This is a special game. We have a little friendly sporting rivalry going with the engineering firm." He reached for her purse and took her hand. "Come on, Taylor. Think of your Lambert's Furniture coworkers." He furrowed his brow, apparently attempting to look pitiful.

She broke. "Fine, but that's the worst pity face I've ever seen."

"I'm new at this."

She slipped her hand from his and walked with him to the door. "But this is the last time, Will."

He stopped and faced her. "Why does this have to be the last time?"

She gathered her fortitude, stepped into his personal space, and said, "Because you are dangerous, and I'm not putting my heart on the line."

He didn't hesitate. "Well, I am."

Her heart stopped beating for a second. What? She gathered herself and quipped, "I wouldn't if I were you. The lifeguard isn't on duty."

"I can swim."

Will was dead serious, and it petrified her. She took her purse from him and headed down the hall. "Give me twenty minutes to go home and change."

"See you at the park."

❦

Taylor hurried through the kitchen and up the back staircase to her room.

"Taylor?" her mother called up the stairs. "It's been a busy day around here for you."

"Me?" she asked, poking her head around the door.

"Yes, you. Come down."

"I'm playing football in the park. I need to change and get over there."

"Oh, Taylor, again? You're thirty-three. When are you going to start acting like a lady?"

Taylor laughed and looked down the stairs at her mother. "When it becomes as much fun to be a *lady* as it is to play football."

Mom's willowy hand muffled her dainty chortle. "Come down."

"In a minute." Taylor changed quickly for football, leaving her jeans and oxford shirt on the floor, her thoughts fractured between a job opportunity thousands of miles away and a handsome quarterback in a little flag football game two miles away.

Taylor bounded down the stairs. "Okay, what's up?"

"Didn't you see?" Mom asked.

"See what?" Taylor glanced at her mother's piquant face.

"Flowers." Mom motioned to the dining room table.

Taylor walked to the adjoining room where she found the most beautiful bouquet of red roses she'd ever seen. She reached for the card.

> *Taylor, for the night I should have said yes.*
>
> > *Love,*
> > *Will*

She trembled as a geyser of emotions erupted from deep within. What? Will, no!

Her eyes burned and her jaw tightened. Deep breaths held back the tears. She wouldn't let go.

"Who are they from, Taylor?" Mom called from the family room.

"Will."

"Will?"

"Yes, Mom." She cleared the emotion from her voice. "Didn't you say something about it being the day of Taylor? Did something else come for me?"

Mom came around the corner. "You had a phone call from an Alex Cranston. I believe he said he was calling from California." She handed Taylor a piece of paper.

Taylor read Alex Cranston's name and number written carefully in her mother's perfect handwriting. Her heart raced. "Did he say anything else?"

"He asked if you could call as soon as possible."

Taylor forced a smile as she folded the note in her hand. "I'll call him on my cell." She snatched up her car keys, the vase of roses, and the note with Alex Cranston's number. "I'll be back later."

Chapter 14

Will watched her stride across the field. It didn't seem right to him that a woman should look so beautiful and graceful wearing dingy old sweats.

She stopped when she got to him. "Can I see you? Over here?" She motioned toward the cars.

"Hello, Taylor." Jordan jogged up to her private huddle with Will.

"Hi, Jordan." She gave him a slight hug. "Are you playing today?"

He grinned. "Drafted by Creager."

She lifted her chin. "I see." Looking around him, she scanned the opposing team. "Will, isn't that your cousin Jeff?"

Will nodded. "My cousin Elizabeth used to work at Creager. She drafted Jeff and her husband, Kavan, for their teams." He pointed to a redheaded man standing next to Jeff.

"Family against family? Should be interesting." Then she turned to Jordan. "Will you excuse us?"

"Sure."

She smiled and patted him on the arm. "Thanks." Taylor turned to Will and motioned for him to follow her.

"What's up?" he asked, leaning in close when they stopped beside her car. His heart was smiling. Surely she saw the roses when she went home.

She opened the passenger door, reached in, and pulled out the flowers. "I can't accept these." She shoved the vase at Will.

His heart sank, but he kept his expression the same. "Why not?"

"Because I can't. We can't undo the last ten years."

"No, but we can start over."

She shoved the flowers at him again. "My actions that night were a foolish romantic notion. Let's not revisit it, shall we?"

"I'm not taking the roses back, Taylor." He stood with his feet apart, his arms crossed over his chest, one hand gripping the football.

"I'm not accepting them." She set the flowers on the ground and met his gaze, then placed her hands on her hips.

He reacted. He pulled Taylor to him and kissed her. She pushed away at first then melted into his embrace.

When he lifted his head, she muttered, "I wish you'd stop doing that."

He pressed his forehead to hers. "I guess it's not the best way to communicate."

"What are you trying to say?"

"I love you."

She drew a shaky breath. "Then you definitely have to stop."

He hooked his finger under her chin and lifted her head. Looking into her eyes, he said, "Give us a chance."

She gripped his forearms. "Now is not the time, Will."

"It's the perfect time."

Someone called from the field. "Hey, are you two going to play ball or kiss? We're losing daylight."

"The timing isn't perfect," she said as she walked backward toward the field and away from him.

He ducked his head, pressing his hand on the back of his neck, thinking. How should he respond to her determination? With more determination?

As he jogged back to the field, he clung to the peace he harbored in his heart and Grandma's advice. *Let her know I love her. Don't give up.*

❧❧

"If you move to California, I don't know what we'll do without you, Taylor," Mom said Saturday. She sat on the edge of the ottoman in the family room, her back straight, sewing squares together for a quilt.

"Same as you always did, Mom," Taylor said, waiting for Dad to move a rook or pawn. "Dad, are you going to make a move?"

He glanced up from the chessboard. "You cannot rush genius."

Taylor laughed and relaxed against the back of her chair. "I've been wanting a job like this one for a long time. I can't believe I'm even getting a shot at Boswell Global."

"California is so far away," Mom lamented.

"I'll come home on vacations. You all can visit me in California. It'll be great."

The phone rang. Taylor volunteered to answer since her dad was still contemplating his move and Mom had blocks of material on her lap.

"Taylor, it's Jordan."

"Hey." She moved to the living room with the cordless. The fragrance of Will's roses wafted in from the dining room. He'd refused to take them back, so Taylor brought them home with her.

"I enjoyed our date the other night."

"It was a nice night. But, Jordan, I—"

"I ran into Mia again," he interrupted, "and we started talking, and well, we've had dinner together every night this week."

Taylor bit her lips, trying not to laugh. Jordan and Mia? They were perfect for each other. "That's great."

"It looks like you and Will still have a thing for each other anyway."

"No," she protested. "No, we are just friends."

Jordan snorted. "I saw that kiss, Taylor. Will's mind is made up."

"It doesn't matter what Will wants."

Jordan chuckled. "Did you tell him that?"

Taylor sat on the sofa, a Lambert's Furniture classic piece. "As a matter of fact, I did. Besides, I have a job opportunity in California."

"Really? Then go for it, if that's what you want."

Taylor pressed her hand over her eyes. "It's what I want."

"Keep me posted."

"I will. Good luck with Mia."

"I'll send you a wedding invitation."

She made a face at the phone. "You think it will come to that?"

"I think so." They talked for a few more minutes and exchanged e-mail addresses.

When she hung up and replaced the phone on the cradle, Tim, Dana, and the kids walked through the door.

"The boys thought Grandpa needed an ice cream sundae," Tim said, unloading ice cream, whipped cream, several sauces, peanuts, chocolate, and cherries.

"Wow," Taylor said, hugging her nephews, praising them for their choice of desserts. Mom hurried about the kitchen, setting bowls and spoons on the counter.

Claire put on a CD, and the quiet house came alive with the melodies of a family.

Dad, however, remained poised over his chess pieces, calculating his next move. Laughing, Taylor coaxed him from his chair.

"You can't keep company with the chessboard when your grandsons were kind enough to bring over ice cream."

He stretched and patted his belly. "I guess ice cream would hit the spot." He high-fived his grandsons. "You boys always did know how to treat your old pop."

Taylor watched, her heart beating to the rhythm of the family's voices and laughter. *This*, she thought, *this I will miss.*

A half hour later, Tim sat in Taylor's chair opposing Dad in chess, who had yet to make his genius move.

Quentin and Jarred watched a movie in the living room, and Taylor sat at the dining table with Mom, Dana, and Claire.

Taylor realized for the first time in a long time, anxiety wasn't wheedling her into worrying. She felt the Lord's assurance. He would work out the details of her life.

"Okay, I can't take it anymore," Dana said. "Where did you get these roses, Mom? They are beautiful." She stood and leaned toward the bouquet, sniffing. "So fragrant."

"Will sent them to Taylor."

Claire's mouth dropped open. She grabbed Taylor's arm. "Oh, wow. Are you in love or what?"

"No, I'm not in love."

"Taylor, please," Dana said. "You and Will Adams are meant for each other."

"What? How so?"

The women talked at once. "You're perfect for each other."

"He's quiet, you're loud."

"I am not loud," Taylor protested.

"You both love sports. You both love the Lord."

"You're best friends."

Finally, Taylor stopped them. "Fine," Taylor said with a slap of her hand on the table. "But we are not getting together. Period."

Dana laughed and pointed at her sister-in-law. "I'll be singing at your wedding before this time next year."

Taylor spread her arms and chimed, "Wonderful. I'd love that, but Will won't be the groom."

"We'll see," said Dana. "We'll see."

❧❧

Wednesday afternoon Will sat in the conference room with Bobby, Markie, and Taylor reviewing the HBS installation schedule.

"It's tight. We have a lot to get done in eight weeks." Will looked up from Taylor's project plan.

"With year-end coming up," Taylor started, "I recommend converting over to HBS in January. Start the new fiscal year on the new system. Only transfer the data you need and keep the old system in maintenance mode."

"We still have to move account and billing records forward," Markie said. "But I'm eager to get the staff trained."

"I need to get the sales team in here for training on the contact management system," Bobby said.

Taylor smiled. "They'll love it. It will increase their sales."

"That's what I want to hear." Bobby slapped his hands on the table.

Taylor motioned to Markie. "You need to get a data dump from the old system so HBS can get to work on the conversion program. We can't do anything without the account records and inventory data."

Markie nodded, typing on her computer. "Will, I might need your help with that," she said.

"No problem."

After the meeting, Taylor stopped Will outside his office door. "Can I talk to you?"

"Sure." He stepped aside for her to enter his office. Things had been distant and cool between them since his impetuous kiss on the football field. He apologized Sunday after church and kept his distance in the office.

While he hated the strain between them, Will planned to relentlessly pursue her.

"What can I do for you?" He motioned to the chair by his desk, but she remained standing.

Hands clasped in front of her, she looked at him, her gaze seeming unfocused. "I have a job interview next week in California. I leave Monday, fly back Wednesday."

Will kicked out his chair and sat. "I see." This news definitely put a kink in his plan.

"It's an amazing company, Boswell Global. They are an emerging dot-com. They need a new CFO."

"You don't have to convince me." He picked up a short blue pen lying on his desk and began clicking it, on and off, on and off.

She bristled. "I'm not convincing you. I just wanted to let you know."

"Taylor, if this opportunity means so much to you, then—" He jammed the pen into a holder.

"It does. But I wanted you to know I will finish what I started here."

"If you have to go, then you have to go. We didn't contract you for any length of time." His hands gripped the arms of his chair.

She narrowed her gaze. "I don't want to abandon the job."

"Look, we got a great deal on the business system, thanks to you. Markie has the project plan. I run a multimillion dollar company; I think I can manage the installation."

She bristled. "Of course, I didn't meant to imply you couldn't handle the install, Will. But you contracted me for my expertise and. . ."

She was fishing, Will decided. If she chose not to go to California, she'd have to come up with a better reason than the new business system.

She stared down into the manufacturing plant. "I'll probably wait until after Christmas to move."

"If you get the job."

She snapped her head around. "Yes, if I get the job."

He walked over to her. "It'd be great to have you around for the holidays."

She stared again at the crew below. "I haven't been around for many holidays lately. Claire and the boys are getting older. Daddy's scare made me think how much family time I've missed. I'd really like to be home for this Christmas."

"You don't have to convince me."

She whipped around. "I'm not trying to convince you. I'm just saying. . ." She sat in the vacant chair. "What do you think?"

"About what?"

She stared at her hands and asked softly, "About the job. About me moving to California."

He slipped his hands in his pockets and peered into her face. "You always get what you want."

She stared straight into his eyes. "Not always."

"Now's your chance."

Chapter 15

Sunday evening Taylor packed an overnight tote and zipped her best suit into a garment bag.

"What do you think, Mom, taupe or black pumps?" Taylor walked into her parents' room with a sample of each pair.

Mom didn't look up from the chaise lounge where she sat with her sewing. "What color is your suit?"

"Dark red."

"Pants or skirt?"

"Skirt."

Mom set her sewing aside and motioned to see the shoes. "Black," she said after a short inspection.

"Really? I like the taupe." Taylor examined the shoes under the light. Who was she to question the impeccable Trixie Hansen? She'd wear the black.

"Are you sure this move is right for you, Taylor?" Mom asked, picking up her quilting pieces again.

"Y–yes." Her answer didn't sound as confident as she wanted. "How can I turn such an opportunity down?"

From the library, Taylor heard the rustle of her father's newspaper. He came through the door a second later.

"How much does the opportunity cost?" He settled on the chaise with Mom.

Taylor sat on the edge of the bed, dropping the shoes to the floor. "What do you mean?"

Dad examined a square of gingham. "If you want this position, you go to California and win it. Let Boswell see the excellent abilities of Taylor Jo Hansen. But think about what it will cost you in time and relationships."

She regarded him, half of her bare foot in the taupe pump. "I've calculated the cost, Dad." She slipped her foot the rest of the way into the shoe. She did like them better.

"Mom, I'm going with the taupe." She shoved her other foot into the black pump and stood.

"Your choice, Taylor."

"I don't think you have, Taylor," Dad said, firm and low. "Don't go to California if there is the remotest chance that you are in love with Will."

Taylor whirled around. "In love with him? He's a friend, period."

She walked toward the floor-length mirror to check out the shoes.

Oh, pain. She kicked off both shoes, remembering now why the soles were barely worn on the taupe pair. They pinched her toes.

"I'm wearing the black." She picked up her shoes, grimacing at the taupe.

Trixie laughed softly. "I had a pair of taupe shoes that hurt my feet, too. But I loved them."

"Taylor," Dad said as she started to leave.

"What, Daddy?" She held up the black pump. "Maybe I should wear my beige suit."

Mom glanced up. "No, it will make you look too pale. Let me look at your wardrobe."

Trixie went past Taylor into her bedroom.

Dad finished his thought. "You won't get another chance at Will. So pray about it long and hard."

Heat picked its way across her cheeks and down her neck. "I hear you, but I don't think it changes anything."

He came over to her and rested his hand on her arm. "I've watched you over the years, Taylor. There's more to the story than you're telling your mom and me."

She stared at the floor. "It's over. Forgotten."

"You left town like your hair was on fire. And if I remember right, you were in love with him."

"Correct. Were—was."

"You're a grown woman, Taylor, and I've seen you make some excellent decisions. Make sure this California job is the Lord's leading, not you running away from the ghost of summers past."

She lifted her head and jutted out her chin. "I am praying, Dad."

"All right. Just know that if you move to California, Will won't be single and waiting when you come home again."

She jutted out her chin. "So you've said."

Dad embraced her. "I love you, and I would like nothing more than for the Lord to bless you with a godly husband."

Taylor batted away tears. "Me, too. Better see what Mom's picking out."

In her room, Mom coordinated the perfect suit and shoes. Taylor stood back, shaking her head. "Perfect. How come you didn't pass your gift of style to me, Mom?"

"I did."

"Right. I wouldn't have thought to put that rose-colored jacket with those chocolate slacks."

"You have style, Taylor. It shows in the way you wear your hair and the way you carry yourself. It shows in the way you do your job and live life. I wish I had your gusto."

"Gusto?" Taylor repeated. That was not a Trixie Hansen word.

She tossed the black and taupe pumps in the closet and pulled out a brown pair of Mary Janes.

"Yes, gusto." Mom smiled at her. "Oh, those shoes will go nicely."

"They're comfortable, too."

"When I was your age," Mom reminisced, sitting on the edge of Taylor's bed, "I sewed and crocheted and decorated cakes for church auctions. I wore hats and white gloves to social events."

Taylor sat on the edge of her desk. "Times have changed."

"Yes, they have." Mom stood, smiling. "I don't know if I'd do as well in your generation, Taylor. But I'm very proud of you."

"Don't sell yourself short, Mom. Dad told me how you stood up to Grandpa when you and Dad wanted to get married."

"That was so long ago. I was young and in love."

Taylor regarded her. "There's no force in the world more powerful than a loved woman."

Mom stood. "No, I imagine there isn't."

After Mom went back to quilting, Taylor puttered around her room, reorganizing her overnight tote, selecting toiletries, and wondering if she should bother with her laptop.

By eight o'clock, she'd wandered restlessly through the house. She picked at the last piece of cake, split an apple with her dad, and flipped through the TV channels.

Something bugged her, deep down. She glanced at her dad. It was his words reverberating in her heart. *"You won't get another chance."*

She grabbed her car keys and called upstairs, "I'm going for a drive." She drove slowly down Main Street, passing Sam's and Earth-n-Treasures, the library, and Golda's Golden Beauty Parlor. She ran her fingers through her hair, thinking she should have gotten it cut before flying to California. But she'd doubted Golda could match the color and style of her favorite New York salon.

"If I get this job, I'm treating myself to a spa day."

On impulse she reached for her phone and autodialed Reneé but got her voice mail. "Hey, it's me. I'm leaving tomorrow for the California interview. Pray. Call you later."

She pressed END and tossed the phone into the passenger seat as the White Birch covered bridge came into view. Slowly, Taylor pulled alongside the road and parked.

There was no moon. The only light came from a street lamp and the distant glow from Grandma Betty and Grandpa Matt's home up on the hill.

Taylor pulled on her coat, zipped it all the way up, and tucked her hands into her pockets.

Walking toward the middle of the bridge, she remembered the last time she was here with Will. With love.

"Lord, is Dad right? Am I fooling myself about Will?"

She prayed, listening to the gurgle of the river and waiting on the Lord.

❧

In the basement, Will helped Grandpa put the finishing touches on a chest of drawers he was making for baby Matt.

"I'm going to want this design for the business, you know," Will said, running his hand along the polished cherrywood.

"Can't. It's special for little Matt."

"We can name it after him." Will stood back to take in the whole piece. Grandpa's designs amazed him.

The elder Lambert stood next to his grandson, his shoulders squared. "Well, maybe we can make a few changes so it's not an exact replica."

Will laughed. "Done."

He stepped over to the sink to wash up just as Grandma called down the stairs, "Hot chocolate and hot cookies in the kitchen."

Will dried his hands and said to Grandpa, "See you. I'm going up."

Grandpa waved. "I see you've got your priorities straight. I'll be up as soon as I put the tools away."

In the warm kitchen, Will sat at the breakfast nook. Harry left his warm spot by the oven to rest his chin on Will's knee.

"Only one cookie, boy, and don't tell Grandma."

"Too late; she already heard." Grandma came in with a fresh batch of dish towels. "I gave him one, too."

Will scratched Harry's ears. "He's hard to resist."

Grandma brought over two mugs of cocoa and joined Will at the table. "How goes the war of love with Taylor?"

Will set down the cookie he was about to bite into and shook his head. "She's going to California for a big job interview."

"I guess you have your work cut out for you."

"You know she tried to give me back the roses, but I refused to take them."

"You broke her heart, Will. She's not going to let you back in easily."

"What about my heart? It could get broken in this process."

"Then you'll know you gave love a chance."

"And bleed all over the place?"

"If necessary."

Grandpa came into the kitchen, shutting the basement door behind him. He sat next to Grandma and reached for a cookie.

"People today," Grandma said, getting up to pour Grandpa a mug of hot chocolate, "want love to be easy—to be fair. Fifty-fifty. But love requires you to give one hundred percent. It's not always easy, and it's not always fair."

"I'm willing to give it one hundred percent if she is."

"What if she's not? Are you going to give up? Sometimes love is about one giving a hundred percent and the other giving nothing." Grandma returned to the nook with a big, steaming mug and set it before Grandpa.

"Thank you, Betty."

Will shrugged. "I'm not sure I want to give myself to something that may end up causing pain."

"Jesus did," Grandma said.

Grandpa added, "He went to the cross, rejected by His own people, abandoned by His friends, and knowing that many more generations would also reject Him. He gave one hundred percent while we gave zero."

Will pondered that truth for a moment. What kind of love moved God to send His Son to pay the price for man's sins? What kind of love endured the brutality and rejection of the cross?

Just the thought made Will tremble inside. That same God knew and loved him.

"It moves me to humility," he said.

"If God did not spare His own Son, how will He not freely give us all things? We can trust Him," Grandpa said.

Will shook his head. "I'm amazed every time I think about what He did for us, for me."

"Will," Grandma said gently, "if you pursue Taylor and she moves away, then you'll know it wasn't meant to be. But don't give up too soon. If you ask me, whatever happened between the two of you all those years ago is still happening."

"It is, Grandma. Only we've switched places this time." Harry scratched at the door. Will stood, picking up his hot chocolate. "I'll let him out." Will reached for the knob. "There ya go, boy." Harry woofed and darted down the hill toward the bridge. Laughing, Will decided to follow. "Heeellloooo," Will shouted, running onto the bridge after Harry. Harry's bark echoed in the rafters. A shrill scream answered him from the other end of the bridge. "Who's there?" someone asked.

"Will Adams. Who are you?"

"You scared me, Will."

He grinned as Taylor stepped toward him. He could barely see her face in the slivers of light that reflected off the river and up through the bridge's beams. But her voice and her fragrance were undeniable.

He recognized love. "What are you doing here?" he asked as she drew closer.

She shrugged. "I went for a drive. Sitting around the house waiting for tomorrow morning was making me crazy."

"I can imagine."

She sniffed. "Hot chocolate. Hmm. . ."

"Would you like some? Grandma made a huge pot."

She stepped back, waving her hands. "No, no, I don't want to trouble Grandma Betty."

"Are you kidding me? She lives for moments like this."

"It does smell good."

He had an idea. "Don't go anywhere. I'll be right back." He set his mug down on the bridge floor and darted away. "Harry, stay here with Taylor."

"Will, wait. Will?"

He ran up the hill and into the Lambert kitchen.

Opening and closing cabinets, he searched until he found Grandpa's old fishing thermos then filled it with hot chocolate. He found a paper bag, snapped it open, and stuffed it with warm cookies.

"Should I ask what you're doing running around my kitchen like a crazed man or just not worry about it?" Grandma asked.

Will grabbed a mug. "Be at peace, Grandma." With that, he disappeared out the door.

His grandparents' muted laughter followed.

On the bridge, Taylor stood exactly where he'd left her. "Hot chocolate and cookies." He held up the bag and mug.

"Oh, wow, they smell so good."

"Where should we sit?" Will strode to the edge of the bridge. "The ground is wet."

"My car," Taylor suggested. "We can put the top down."

"Can Harry join us?"

Taylor reached to scratch the sheepdog's ears. "Of course."

With a click of a few buttons, Taylor tucked the BMW's top away. They climbed in and settled on top of the backseat. Will poured her a mug of hot chocolate and refreshed his.

"Have a cookie." He held out the bag for Taylor.

She took a bite. "Yum. These are so good."

Harry set his chin on her knee, his tail swishing against the leather seat.

"I think Harry likes you," Will said, reaching for a cookie.

Taylor giggled. "Only because I have cookies."

Will grinned. This was good, right. Only the Lord could have arranged this. "No, Harry just knows a loving woman when he meets one."

Taylor broke off a piece of her cookie and gave it to Harry. "Mom and I were talking tonight about how different women are today than when she was growing up and how different her world was from mine."

"It is amazing, isn't it?"

"She gave birth to me at thirty-three. I'm a single career woman, possibly about to land the job of a lifetime."

Will sipped from his mug. "It's what you want?"

She looked up at his face. "Yes, it's what I want."

Chapter 16

Taylor refilled her hot chocolate from the thermos and cupped her hands around the ceramic mug for warmth.

As much as she determined she wouldn't fall in love with Will again, she loved being in his presence. But his countenance challenged the walls around her heart, and she wondered if she would ever find another man like him.

"Favorite color?" he asked suddenly.

She laughed. "Okay. That came out of nowhere."

"Fess up; it's black isn't it?"

"Black? Not a color, my friend. Actually, I like blue."

"Favorite gem?"

"Diamonds are a girl's best friend."

"Guess I walked into that one."

"Yep." Taylor sipped her hot chocolate.

"Favorite song?"

"Now that's a hard one." Taylor thought for a moment. "I know this is corny, but I really love 'The Old Rugged Cross.'"

"I like 'Just As I Am.'"

Taylor smiled. "Both of those songs make me cry."

Harry shifted in the seat between them, curling up against the cold leather, his snout on Taylor's foot.

"You just might have to take Harry home with you," Will said, reaching down to smooth the fur on Harry's back.

"Right. That would go over real well with Trixie No-More-Pets Hansen."

Will laughed softly. "Remember when you wanted to keep that stray cat?"

Taylor nodded then sipped the last of her hot chocolate. "Talk about a cat fight."

"Okay, favorite memory?"

The question struck a chord in the resonant places of her heart. The answer was easy: Will. But she wouldn't confess it out loud. Her time with him eclipsed all the fun days of high school and college, her first apartment, and her first career job and move to New York City. It was as if life without Will had never existed.

But she had to answer with something. "Hmm, let's see." She thought about the night on the bridge. Funny, her best memory was also her worst. She decided to bail. "You go first. What's your favorite memory?"

He looked over at her then down at his empty mug. She couldn't see his face, only the outline of his symmetrical nose and chin.

"You."

A prickly sensation ran over her skin. "Me? What do you—"

"You're my favorite memory." He lifted his head, looking out into the darkness. "Playing basketball, football; eating ice cream; movie night in Franklin Murphy's basement with those of us who came home from college; driving down Old Town Road in my Camaro. . ."

Will had held her hand for the first time while driving down Old Town Road. A tingle ran across her hand as she remembered, just like it did that night.

They certainly had a strange relationship. One or two hand-holdings. One kiss. One marriage proposal. Ten years of silence.

She knew he was looking at her. "The job in California means a lot to me, Will."

"I know. I guess I wish I mattered as much."

"I'm sorry. But I've invested ten years in my career."

"Ten years that should've been with me," Will said.

"But they weren't, were they?" she answered without malice.

They were silent for a few moments. Taylor imagined it was getting late, but she didn't want to leave just yet. Tonight may be her last with Will.

"You never told me your favorite memory," Will said, reaching down for the thermos.

"I don't know if I can pick one. Maybe my first job. Oh, my first big paycheck. The year I made the cheerleader squad."

Will tipped up the thermos. A few drops flowed out into his cup. "Didn't you try out as a joke?"

Taylor laughed. "Yes, I did."

"You beat out Tammy Carter her senior year."

"Oh, that's right. Okay, that's not a favorite memory, then. I hated that I took Tammy's spot."

For a long while, they talked about high school and college, comparing experiences and tales. For a man who had lived most of his life in White Birch, Will understood a lot about the world.

Finally, he said, "I hear it never rains in California."

She laughed and bumped him with her shoulder.

Will bumped her back and scooted a little closer. Harry growled softly when Will's foot moved him into a different position.

Taylor clicked her nails against the side of her mug. "It will be a change, for sure." Why did she feel like he was going to kiss her? Did she want him to kiss her? One last kiss. . .a kiss good-bye?

Will reached down for the empty bag of cookies. "It's late. I should get going." He pressed the backlight on his wristwatch. "Wow, it's ten thirty."

He hopped out the side of the car, and Taylor felt oddly alone.

"Do you want to put the top up?" Will asked.

She slid out of the car on the opposite side. "I'll freeze if I don't."

Will opened the passenger door and called for Harry. Taylor leaned over the wheel, turned the key in the ignition, and powered up the top.

Will walked around to the driver's side. "Have a good trip. I'll pray for you." He took her hand and pulled her into his embrace.

A shiver ran over her scalp and down her spine. She closed her eyes, waiting for his lips to touch hers.

He wrapped her in his arms, and with a light squeeze he said, "See you in a few days. Come on, Harry."

She swallowed and muttered, her heat beating with the force of eagles' wings, "Um, yes, a few days."

~~

Boswell Global rolled out the red carpet for Taylor. Alex Cranston personally met her at the airport then escorted her around the plant as if she were the queen of England.

The early morning interviews went well, and by the time Alex met her for lunch, she wondered if she glowed.

"I see you've had a good morning," Alex said, leading her toward the parking lot and his car. "I thought we'd eat at a great little pizza place in Redwood City."

Taylor lifted her face to the warm California sun. Yesterday, New Hampshire's gray sky threatened snow. "Perfect."

Soon they were sitting on the patio under the pizza parlor's pavilion. When the waiter left with their order, Alex said, "The VP of marketing wanted to know which rainbow I followed to find you."

"Really?" Taylor sat back, lifting her chin a little. In light of her recent failure at Blankenship & Burns, it felt good to hear she'd impressed the Boswell executives.

"We have a few more candidates to interview, but my guess is you're their choice."

A spark of excitement ignited in Taylor. "I would be honored to join the Boswell Global team."

Alex asked a few typical interview questions, such as how she saw herself fitting in at the company, and, just as she expected, to describe her greatest strength and weakness.

She smiled and answered with honesty. "Ambition. Both my strength and my weakness."

Alex motioned to the waiter to refill their water glasses. "I thought so. Best weakness to have if you learn to manage it."

"Believe me, after two years on my old job, and by the grace of God, I learned to manage my ambition."

Alex regarded her after that comment but didn't probe further. "Tell me your career plans. What's up with Taylor Hansen in five years?"

"Well," she started, prepared for this answer. In Charlotte, she'd gone over the top with her response. A month later, her perspective on life was more realistic.

"I want to contribute to Boswell's vision, be a part of the decision-making process that leads us into the next generation. I'm thirty-three, so I have a lot of years ahead of me. I'm not married, so I can be devoted to the company."

"Good to hear," Alex said, smiling and reaching for his water. "Off the record, it's a plus that you're not married for now."

"How so?"

"The last CFO left us in a little bit of a mess. You're going to have your job cut out for you."

"I see." Taylor absorbed the reality of what Alex communicated.

He set his water down. "Don't worry; the pay is worth it."

She smiled. "Good to know."

Their pizza arrived, and the conversation went to more casual topics, such as the surrounding communities and life in northern California.

Yet thoughts of Will interrupted her concentration. She shifted in her chair and focused on eating a slice of pizza, shoving images of Will back to New Hampshire.

"Boswell seems to have a strong team environment," Taylor finally said. "I like that."

A lot like Lambert's Furniture, she thought. She answered that with an internal *grrr. Stop thinking about home.*

Alex nodded. "It's one of the company's strengths."

He went on to describe the benefits of living in northern California, but when lunch ended, Taylor felt she'd lost some of her enthusiastic glow while trying to fight the rising tide of love for Will.

❧❧

How could he miss her so much? He'd lived the past ten years without her; now her sudden presence in his life drilled into the very core of his being, and he felt lost without her.

The matters of the heart confounded him. Anxiety threatened. What if she took the California job?

Will took a deep breath. "Be anxious for nothing," he prayed. "Let the peace of Jesus guard your heart and mind."

Feeling restless, he wandered from his living room to the kitchen to the back porch. Harry sat watching, his head tipped in wonder.

"We need Taylor, don't we, boy?"

Harry whined, wagging his tail. When the phone rang, Will answered on the second ring with a deep hope that Taylor would be on the other end.

"I'm hungry for some of Sam's pie." It was Ethan.

"Pie?" Will echoed. "I could go for a big salad and soup."

"Eat whatever you want. I'm having pie."

Will laughed. "Don't worry, I'm having pie, too, but I haven't eaten dinner yet."

"It's eight o'clock."

"I know. Meet you there."

At Sam's, Will found his cousin in a booth by the door. Sam greeted him while Taylor's nephew set water glasses on the table.

"Have you heard from your aunt?" Will asked Jarred.

"Nope," the young man said with a quick, shy smile.

After they ordered, Ethan asked, "Speaking of Taylor, how's it going?"

Will shrugged as he unwrapped his silverware from the napkin. "It's not."

"She's still determined to move to California?"

"Yes, and still determined not to fall in love with me."

Ethan laughed. "And how do you know that?"

"She told me."

Chapter 17

From the balcony of her hotel, Taylor looked out over Coastal Highway 1, awed by the blazing colors of the Pacific sunset.

"Oh, Lord," she whispered reverently, "what a beautiful day." During her end-of-day wrap-up with Alex, he asked Taylor about her earliest possible start date while informing her of their generous relocation package.

"What's your minimum salary?" he asked, a smug sort of look on his face.

Taylor exhaled. She took his pen and jotted down a fat figure—ten percent more than she'd earned in New York.

Alex didn't even flinch. "Not a problem."

Now, on the balcony at her hotel with a cool breeze carrying the scent of the ocean brushing her face, Taylor pondered her options.

"Lord, do I say yes if they offer?" She loved what she heard and saw at Boswell Global. She loved the idea of living in sunshine and making a six-figure salary. Before she turned thirty-four, she would have accomplished more than she'd hoped.

She was envisioning Saturdays on the beach just as her room phone rang. "Hello?"

"Taylor, it's Alex Cranston."

She sank onto the bed. A nervous knot tightened in her middle. "I didn't expect to hear from you so soon."

Were they turning her down already?

"I just called to see how you like your room."

"It's very nice." She chewed on her bottom lip.

"Well, you're our front-runner. They loved you."

"That's good to hear." She sat against the hotel bed's plump pillows.

"As far as the president is concerned, you're the one. I had to remind her we'd already scheduled interviews with the other candidates."

Taylor smiled. "Pamela and I had a lot of common experiences and thoughts on how the finances should be run."

"That's what she said. She can't imagine anyone fitting the bill as well as you do. But we still—"

"I know. Interview the other candidates."

"Right. Have a good night. Order room service, watch a movie, and have a safe trip home. We'll send a car for you in the morning to take you to the airport."

"Thank you, Alex, for all you've done for me." When Taylor hung up, she thought she should jump for joy over Pamela's favor. Instead, she wandered back to the balcony feeling melancholy.

In the last few months, she'd gotten used to the safe comfort of being home. In the early morning, she would lie in bed praying and listening to her parents' morning routine.

"Grant, do you want coffee?"

Her mother's intonations were like Taylor's down comforter—soft and warm.

"Yes, Trixie. No cream this morning."

Her father always answered from the top of the stairs while dressing for the day. Taylor knew because the clean scent of his aftershave perfumed the hall and seeped into her room under the door.

California—three thousand miles away and a six-hour plane ride.

She leaned on the balcony rail, longing to talk to someone. She thought of her friends in New York. Strange, how she'd lost touch with them so quickly. Except Reneé. Taylor sighed. This wasn't about Reneé or her friends in the city. It was about calling Will.

Whether she liked it or not, he'd taken up residence in her heart as her closest friend. She couldn't deny it any longer. He simply was her best friend.

With a decisive step across the room, she dug her cell phone from her purse and dialed. She shivered when he answered the phone.

"Hi, it's Taylor."

❦

Will was cutting the end of his apple pie a la mode when his cell phone jingled. "Will Adams."

He did not expect to hear her voice on the other end. He dropped his fork and cut a glance at Ethan.

"So you got the job?" he asked, running his hand through his hair.

"They liked me a lot."

"I believe it." He ignored the stab of disappointment. He was happy for her but sad for himself. "How's California?"

"Beautiful. The sunset is amazing. You'd love it here."

"I bet I would." Because she was there.

Taylor talked about her day with enthusiasm—the wonderful staff at Boswell Global, the funny story the president told during their interview, lunch at the cutest pizza place, and her hotel balcony overlooking the Coastal Highway.

"Sounds wonderful."

"I don't think I can say no." Taylor blurted the amount of her possible salary. Will whistled.

"What? What's she saying?" Ethan whispered, poking Will's arm with his fork.

Will jerked away and swerved in the booth so Ethan couldn't hear. He felt vulnerable, as if his emotions might explode and spew all over the place.

"Hard to turn that down."

"R—right."

The conversation lulled. Will choked back a mountain of words, but how could he say again what he'd already said? Taylor had turned him down cold. "When will you know?"

"Week or so, I guess."

Will managed one word. "Good."

"They have more candidates to interview, but the president really wants to hire me."

"He knows excellence when he sees it."

Taylor laughed. "She. The president is a she. Pamela Carlton."

"Ah, forgive me." He faced forward again and reached for his fork.

"Oh, Will, I can see some kids playing on a basketball court." Excitement buoyed her voice.

He cut a bite of pie. "Who's winning?"

"Hard to tell. There's a couple of kids playing. One is dribbling. Stops to shoot a three pointer. He makes it." Taylor cheered the unknown player, her voice vibrant.

"Well, maybe if I visit you in California, we can play one-on-one on that court."

She didn't answer for a moment, then said, "I'd like that."

"We'll miss you." He had to say it. He wanted her to know. So he masked his *I* with a *we*, but she knew.

"We? You and Harry."

He grinned. "Yes."

"Well, I'll let you go. Thanks for listening."

Will pressed END and placed the phone into the holster clipped to his belt. "That was Taylor," he said.

Ethan eyed him. "I gathered."

Will shoved his plate aside, missing Taylor more each minute.

❧

Thanksgiving Eve, Taylor tossed and turned, trying to sleep, her mind troubled by a myriad of anxious thoughts.

She prayed intermittently, meditating on the peace of Jesus. Her interview in California seemed like years ago.

Since she'd returned to White Birch and Lambert's Furniture, she'd been working fourteen hours a day. The data conversion to the HBS system aggravated her, and today had been especially trying.

In the morning, she'd battled technical problems with the test database. In the afternoon, she and Markie ran a test conversion, and all the fields were populated with the wrong information. Then, just before leaving for the night, she and Markie ran into a snag with the accounts receivable modules, and she feared they didn't work the way HBS promised.

Taylor sat up in bed and glanced at the clock. Nearly midnight. She reached for her bedside lamp.

The crash course she'd gotten from the installation team generated more questions than answers. And when they flew through the instructions on how to connect to the test and live databases, Taylor's notes began to look like ancient Chinese.

If I wasn't connected to the right database, then the system settings would be wrong. She sat with her arms on her knees. She felt lost on this one and feared she was letting Will down.

She slipped out of bed and changed into a pair of jeans and a university sweatshirt. She had to fix the problem. She tied on her running shoes.

The office was closed Thursday and Friday for the holiday, so she'd have the place to herself all weekend if she wanted to work.

Maybe Will didn't count on her long-term, but she wanted to complete the job with excellence. She'd dealt with new installations before, and the amount of overlooked details could be staggering.

Tiptoeing downstairs, Taylor picked up her purse and grabbed her coat.

Under a blanket of night, White Birch slept.

Maintenance crews had hung Christmas decorations yesterday afternoon and the front windows of Main Street shops twinkled with tiny white lights.

Suspending her thoughts for a moment, Taylor imagined she lived in a land far, far away where love conquered all and hearts were never broken.

She decided she must be longing for heaven. The idea touched her soul with peace as she passed White Birch Community Church and steered toward Lambert's Furniture.

She parked by the side office door, punched in her security code on the keypad, and dashed upstairs to her office.

Within fifteen minutes, she'd found the problem with her settings and had successfully run a partial test of the data conversion.

She clapped her hands and did a little jig around her desk. Still wide-awake, she thought she might as well work on modifying reports before going home.

Footfalls echoed from the hallway. Taylor rose slowly from her chair, angling to see beyond her door, a cold feeling washing over her.

⋙⋘

Will couldn't sleep. He checked his bedside clock for the tenth time in the last half hour. After midnight. With a sigh, he stepped out of bed and wandered past the sleeping dog to the window.

In the moon's pale light, he surveyed his yard, half in the moon's glow, half falling into shadow.

"It's Thanksgiving and I'm fretting." He clicked on a light and reached for his Bible.

The words from Philippians 4:6 reminded him that the Lord watched over him.

He repeated the verse out loud. "Be anxious for nothing, but in everything by prayer and supplication, with thanksgiving, let your requests be made known to God."

Will paced the width of his bedroom. His day had been so fragmented by meetings, phone calls, interviews for a new administrator in accounting, plus a production meeting with Grandpa and Grant, that he felt burdened by the unattended details on his desk.

He stopped pacing and muttered to no one, "Might as well get dressed and go to the office."

As he pulled up to Lambert's Furniture, he expected to see a dark building, but the corner office glowed with a low, white light. Will smiled. Taylor.

"Wonder what she's doing here." He punched in his security code and bounded up the stairs.

Taylor's heart beat so fast she had to draw hard to breathe. She looked around for something to use as a weapon.

"Settle down, Taylor Jo, the building is secure," she muttered.

The steps drew closer. She blurted, "Hello?"

Will's handsome form came through her doorway. "What are you doing here?"

Taylor slapped her hand over her heart. "Oh, it's you."

Will grinned. "I've got to stop scaring you."

"Yes, you do." Taylor sat down in her desk chair. "What are *you* doing here?"

Will crossed his arms and leaned against the door frame. "I asked you first."

The collar of his leather jacket was flipped up on one side, and his bangs flopped over his forehead. Taylor thought he looked like an eighties pop star—and very handsome.

He caught her staring. She blushed and turned away. "I, um, couldn't sleep. Problem with the conversion setup kept me awake. I finally figured it out."

Will walked over. "Funny how brilliance comes at midnight."

She laughed. "Yes." Their eyes met, and Taylor felt warm all the way down to her toes.

He stepped closer, his gaze never leaving her face. She couldn't breathe for a second.

"Taylor," he said, lightly grasping her arm and pulling her to him. He lowered his face to hers.

"Will." She pressed her hand against his chest.

He chuckled. "You drive me crazy, you know that?"

"I'm sorry."

Releasing her, he backed away. "Don't be. It's my problem. But, Taylor," he said as he walked toward the door, "when a man finds a woman who drives him crazy, he doesn't easily forget."

Chapter 18

Taylor bolted upright when her cell phone rang. She fumbled through her purse, squinting in the bright morning light. Sun rays streamed through the frosty windowpanes like ethereal ribbons and fell across the wide wood floor.

"Hello," Taylor croaked, rubbing the sleep from her eyes.

"Taylor, where are you?"

"Tim? I'm at the office," she said, her voice raspy and weak. She stood to stretch. Her back ached.

"Mom called this morning."

"What happened?"

"It's Dad. He woke up with severe abdominal pain, chills, and vomiting, so Mom took him to the hospital. She looked for you, but thought you went for a run."

"I'm on my way." Awake now, she grabbed her coat and purse but stopped outside her office door, suddenly overwhelmed. Her eyes burned, and she trembled all over.

"It's Thanksgiving. Oh, Father, please. Be with Dad."

Shaking off the sense of despair, she started down the hall.

❧❧

Will looked up when he heard footsteps. *Is Taylor still here?* He glanced at his watch. Seven a.m. He'd fallen asleep a few times, brewed and drank two pots of coffee, then continued working. A lot of things were going to change with the new business system and work flow, even timekeeping and payroll.

"Taylor?"

She peered around the door bleary-eyed, her hair in disarray. "Mom took Dad to the hospital." Taylor explained his symptoms.

Will grabbed his coat. "Let's go." He unclipped his cell phone and dialed as he led Taylor downstairs and out the door.

"Bobby, I'm on my way to the hospital with Taylor. It's Grant. Call Grandpa and let the family know. And, oh, will you go let Harry out, then take him to Grandpa's?"

He opened the passenger door and helped Taylor in. Then, getting in behind the wheel, he said, "It's going to be okay."

She nodded, her lips pressed together, the tip of her sleek nose red.

Will scooted across the seat and cradled her in his arms. He didn't know if she would resist and pull away, but he didn't care. She was trying too hard to endure this alone.

After a few moments, he reluctantly released her and moved back to his side of the truck. "Not a great way to start Thanksgiving Day, is it?"

"No, it isn't."

By midmorning, Dad had been admitted and several tests ordered.

Taylor paced the waiting room with Tim and Mom. Dr. Griswold promised an update within the hour. Will went to the cafeteria in search of coffee and donuts.

"I can't lose him. I'm not ready. He's only sixty-six," Mom said, her voice weak like a lost child's.

Tim stood off on his own, his hands on his hips. "He'll be fine, Mom."

Taylor glared at him. He sounded like a coach telling a player to get up and shake it off.

"Mom," she said softly, putting her hand on her shoulder. "Tim's right. Dad is going to be just fine. We just have to trust in the Lord."

Mom pressed her hand on Taylor's. "Be brave for me, okay?"

Taylor rested her cheek on her mother's head. "I'll try."

Will returned with the coffee and donuts, followed by Bobby, Ethan, and their grandparents, Matt and Betty.

"Looks like the Lord sent in the cavalry," Will said, motioning to his family.

"Yes, He has," Mom said, welcoming Grandma Betty's embrace.

"Thank you," Taylor whispered to him as he handed her a cup of coffee and a donut. "Your family is amazing."

She didn't resist when he slipped his arm around her and kissed her tenderly on the forehead.

Grandma Betty took over comforting Mom, reminding Trixie Hansen that the Lord would not forsake her. Taylor loved the older woman's wise, soothing ways.

Grandpa motioned for everyone to huddle up. "Let's take this matter to the Father."

Will took Taylor's hand when Grandpa started to pray. "Lord, Your Word says You give us peace. Not as the world does, but the kind that transcends understanding. You said we must not let our hearts be troubled or fearful. So I ask for Your peace to guard Trixie and the Hansen family. Especially Grant."

Dr. Griswold approached as Grandpa said amen. "Well, Trixie, we know what's going on."

She wiped her eyes with the edge of her handkerchief. "Oh?"

Taylor felt a release in her middle, as if she'd been carrying a weight around all morning. Her hand remained in Will's, but she didn't care.

"Looks like food poisoning," the doctor said. "We're going to treat him overnight, but he's going to be fine. Do you know where he ate last night?"

"We had seafood," Trixie said, giving Dr. Griswold the name of the restaurant.

The doctor smiled. "Well, we'll make sure he's feeling better soon, but keep those prayers coming."

"Thank you, Doctor, we will," Grandpa said, his arm around Trixie's shoulders. Doctor Griswold offered to take Trixie to see Grant while the rest of the Hansens figured out how to celebrate Thanksgiving.

"Dad would want us to celebrate," Tim decided.

"We have a big spread at our house," Grandma said. "The girls are basting the turkey as we speak."

So it was agreed. The Hansens would join the Lamberts for a Thanksgiving feast.

Luscious smells wafted from Grandma's kitchen as Will tussled on the living room floor with Bobby's boys, Jack and Max. From Grandpa's easy chair, Will's dad, Buddy, coached the boys.

"Get your arm around Will's neck, Jack. Yeah, that's it."

When the six-year-old almost pinned his uncle, Will raised his head and asked his dad, "Whose side are you on, anyway?"

"My grandson's, of course."

"All right, all right." Will grabbed Jack by the ankles and dangled him upside down. "Say 'Uncle Will's the best.'"

Jack giggled. "No."

Will shook him. "Say it?"

Still giggling, Jack refused.

"Well, I have no alternative but to tickle you." A slight move of Will's hand and Jack caved.

"Uncle Will's the best. Uncle Will's the best."

Will lowered him to the floor. "Go bug your dad and Ethan."

Laughing, Jack scurried off to the family room where Bobby, Ethan, and Kavan watched football.

Four-year-old Max trailed after him, calling out, "Uncle Will's the best!"

Will sat on the floor and propped himself against the sofa. "That wore me out."

His dad chuckled. "I remember when you and Bobby used to jump on me. Two of you. Same size. Same weight."

Will took a deep breath, grinning. "My apologies, Dad."

Buddy shook his head. "Wouldn't trade those days for all the gold in Fort Knox."

Grandpa peered around the corner. "Buddy, you up for carving a turkey?" Grandpa held up his carving knife.

Buddy slapped his hands on his knees. "If it gets us closer to dinner, I'm your man."

Will waved. "Call me when it's time to eat."

As Buddy went off with Grandpa, Claire and Taylor walked by with Jack's eight-year-old sister, Eva.

Will waved at Taylor, and she answered with a smile. Her presence messed with him. Loving her came easy, like she was a part of him. If he thought about it long enough, his desire turned into a steady ache.

But she set up invisible boundaries, and he had no choice but to respect them.

He winced every time he thought about the night she asked him to marry her. It changed their relationship forever. If he knew then what he knew now, he wondered if he would have agreed.

But he doubted it. He'd needed the years to mature and discover who he was in this life and in Christ.

He would have made a lousy husband at twenty-three. Suddenly, Taylor dropped down next to him.

"Having fun?"

"Yes, are you?" He loved the cool fragrance that surrounded her.

She stared at her hands. "As long as I don't think too much about Dad."

He reached for her hand. "Grant is going to be fine."

"I know, I know." She looked over at him. "It's wonderful being here. So peaceful. Mom's busy in the kitchen with Grandma, your mom, Elizabeth, and Julie. Dana's playing with baby Matt—and I think trying to talk Tim into one last child."

Will laughed. "How's he taking it?"

Taylor shook her head and made a face. "Not well. Not well at all." She laughed.

"Taylor, I want you to know that—"

"Dinner! Let's go," Grandpa bellowed from the hall.

Taylor drew her hand from Will's and stood. "Let's eat."

He grabbed her and whispered, "You're determined to drive me crazy, aren't you?"

❧❧

"All right, who's up for a little flag football?" Ethan pushed back his chair and surveyed the table.

Bobby's boys shouted, "Me!" and scrambled from the table.

"Easy, boys," Elle called after them.

Taylor grinned. "They're good kids, Elle."

She nodded. "Thank you. They're trying at times, but I can't imagine life without them."

"Come on, who else?" Ethan cajoled the others. "You can't leave me with a four- and six-year-old."

Julie laughed. "Please, somebody play with him. He's been dreaming of this all week."

Bobby sighed and slapped his napkin on the table. "I'll regret this tomorrow, but I'm in."

Tim, Jarred, and Quentin agreed to play.

Will downed the last of his tea. "I'll get the football and organize the little guys." He looked at Taylor. "You playing?"

She glanced at the long table loaded with dirty dishes. "No, I'll help in here."

Grandma held up her hands. "Now, Taylor, I've got a room full of women who couldn't care less about playing flag football. You go ahead. We can handle this."

Elizabeth and Julie egged her on. "Yeah, Taylor, give those boys a run for their money."

"Well." She stood, unable to hide her grin. "I guess I can play."

Eight-year-old Eva piped up. "I want to play." Her big, blue-eyed gaze shifted to Claire. "Are you playing?"

Claire cut a glance at Taylor. "Should I?"

Laughing, Taylor slipped her arm around her niece and smoothed her hand over Eva's dark hair. "Absolutely."

"This game needs a referee," Buddy said. "Besides, I need to work off some of this turkey so I have room for pie."

"Everyone who's playing, go on," Grandma commanded. "We'll clean up and have pie later."

❧❧

"Down! Set! Hut, hut, hut!"

Jarred snapped the ball to Will. He dropped back to pass, his sights on his brother.

But the opposition rushed hard, mainly Taylor, and he had to scramble to keep from losing the blue flags tucked into his waist.

"You're mine, Adams," she shouted, running after him.

On the run, he cut to the right. "Don't tease me, Hansen. Bobby, get open!"

Ethan ran circles around Bobby, waving his arms in his face.

"Bob, come on! Shake him!" Will shouted, laughing. Just as he drew his arm back to pass, he stumbled, with Taylor on his heels and lunging for his flag.

Thud!

"Ouch!"

Will looked behind him as he released the ball.

"Taylor, what happened?" He looked down at the svelte, athletic brunette lying on the ground, her hand over one eye.

"You elbowed me."

He pinched his lips together to keep from guffawing and knelt on one knee. "Let me see." He pulled her hand away. A dark, reddish ring circled her eye.

"Oh, baby, I'm so sorry."

"No, it's not your fault. All's fair in war and football. Is it a shiner?"

He smiled, cupping her chin in his hand. "A beaut." Gently, he touched the bruised area. "Does that hurt?"

She swallowed. "No." Her fingers gripped his hand.

"Liar." Will tipped his head and gently kissed her eye. Then her cheek. Then her lips.

Chapter 19

Sunday morning Taylor dressed for church, her mind made up. No more Will Adams kisses. No more romantic interludes. No more football. No more walks down memory lane. The past is in the past and should be left there. They couldn't recapture ten-year-old emotions. It was ridiculous to try. Life moved on, and so should they.

Her face felt hot when she thought of his Thanksgiving Day kiss in the Lamberts' backyard. Everyone saw them.

"A weak moment," she muttered, brushing mascara on her lashes. "I let the man who gave me a black eye kiss me."

In spite of herself, she laughed. "It *was* funny." She leaned in to get a closer look at her eye. The swelling had gone down and now, with makeup, she could barely see the dark circle.

"Taylor, I'm going on ahead. I have to set up for Sunday school refreshments," Mom called up the stairs.

Taylor stuck her head out the door. "Okay."

Mom said to Dad, "We'll be home right after church, Grant."

Grant answered, "The weatherman said it's going to snow, so don't dally after services."

Taylor smiled. She would miss these exchanges when she moved to California. "Come on, Alex Cranston, call with the offer."

Peace and warmth filled the church sanctuary. Taylor took an aisle seat as the pastor opened the service with a prayer.

"Scoot over."

She looked up at Will's handsome face. With a grimace, she made room.

"How are you?" he whispered, turning her face to his with a touch on her chin. "Your eye looks good."

"I'm fine." She pulled away from him. His two-second presence melted all her resolve to move on without him.

One whisper, one touch, and she found herself remembering his kiss and longing for another.

She squeezed her eyes shut and bowed her head. *Lord, take this away.*

Up front, Jeremiah strummed his guitar, opening the worship service by exalting the name of Jesus. Will's smooth baritone washed over her.

Oh, Will! There were too many wonderful things about him. Why couldn't he have said yes ten years ago?

Taylor tried to focus, tried to worship the One who loved her and deserved all her adoration. But Will's presence almost overwhelmed her.

She had to get out of there. Picking up her purse, she pressed her hand on Will's arm. "Excuse me."

Surprised, he asked, "Where are you going?"

"California."

By late afternoon, snow had covered the town in a blanket of white.

Will lit the gas logs in his fireplace and settled in his recliner to read, but he couldn't focus. He read a whole chapter without comprehending one word.

With a sigh, he closed the book, walked over to the window, and watched the snow gently falling.

Harry nudged Will's leg. "This is your kind of weather, isn't it?"

The dog barked once, loudly.

Will laughed. "Guess we could go out for a walk."

Harry yipped at the word "walk" and wagged his tail. Once outside, the huge sheepdog romped in the snow like a puppy. Snow fell steadily, and with every step, Will plowed a new path.

After an hour, he beckoned Harry with a whistle. "Come on, boy, let's go home."

As he turned toward home, the path he'd plowed to this point was already covered in snow.

A reflection of my life with Taylor, he mused. Just when he thought he'd made headway with her, he found he'd left no imprint on her heart at all.

"Lord, am I like that with You? So calloused at times that Your touch on my life is buried and hidden?"

Will stood in the moment, praying, yearning to yield more of his heart to the Lord's touch. Taylor or no Taylor, he was nothing without the love of Jesus.

In the quiet, with Harry panting softly next to him, the familiar peace of Jesus fell on him. He understood the Lord commanded his life—even his relationship with Taylor.

"You can have all of me. Even my love for Taylor." The words stung for a moment, but Will determined to make Jesus Lord over every area of his life.

From the twilight horizon, Will heard the music of sleigh bells. He turned to greet Jamis Willaby.

"Nice day for a sleigh ride, don't you think?" Jamis called out. "Whoa, boy."

Will slipped off his gloves and touched the horse's velvety nose. "Is this Polo?"

"Yep," Jamis said with a nod, his breath billowing about his head. "Son of Marco."

The horse tossed his head with a snort as if he understood, the bells ringing.

Will laughed. "Beautiful sleigh." He walked back toward Jamis. "The craftsmanship is excellent."

"My granddaddy made it. Don't get to use it much, but I couldn't resist today. The salt trucks will be out soon and by tomorrow the sleigh won't be able to go the roads."

"You're right. Nothing like a romantic—" Will stopped abruptly. "Say, Jamis, how much to rent the sleigh?"

The older man laughed. "Nothing. You need to borrow it?"

"Just for tonight."

Jamis moved over and motioned for Will to hop in. "I'll give you the two-second lesson."

❧❧

Taylor stood back, her hands on her hips. "A little more to the right, Tim."

He pushed on the tree.

"No, now that's too much," Mom said. "Back to the left."

Tim peered at them through the blue spruce tree's branches. "Would you two make up your minds?"

Taylor spread her arms. "We are. You're moving it too much. Just a half inch to *your* left."

The spruce moved slightly.

"Perfect," the ladies said in unison.

"Okay, Taylor, hold it in place while I tighten the bolts," Tim said.

Taylor hurried over. "This is fun. I haven't decorated a Christmas tree in ages."

"Really, Taylor, you should slow down and enjoy life a little," Mom said.

"One day, Mom, one day."

"Hot chocolate." Dana carried a tray from the kitchen. "Jarred, Quentin, Claire, hot chocolate."

The boys shut down the video game, but Claire remained at the kitchen counter, cell phone pressed to her ear.

"How about some Christmas music?" Taylor suggested.

"Got it, Aunt Taylor." Quentin moved to the stereo.

Taylor picked up two mugs and handed one to her father as she sat next to him on the family room sofa.

"You think Boswell Global is going to make you an offer?" Tim asked, perched on the edge of the love seat with a steaming mug in his hand. "Claire, hang up and join the family."

"She's in love," Dana said, sitting down next to her husband.

"With whom?" Taylor asked, her eyes wide.

"Zach Maybrey. Nice boy—very cute."

"Is that the boy she asked me about several weeks ago?"

"Probably," Dana said.

Tim called to his daughter again. "Claire, come on, off the phone."

"Shh, Tim, she's eighteen."

Tim sat back. "Don't remind me."

Dad laughed. "Never had to worry much about Taylor and boys. Only one she ever hung around with was Will, and I'd trust him any day."

Tim laughed. "Yeah, did you hear about the Thanksgiving Day kiss?"

Taylor jumped in. "All right, change the subject. Yes, Tim, I do think Boswell will offer me the job."

Mom entered from down the hall, her arms loaded with ornaments. She set them on the coffee table with a sigh. "Jarred, please do your old grandma a favor and bring the rest out."

"Help him, Quent," Dana said.

The boys scurried away. Claire walked past her dad, kissing him on the cheek. "I'm off the phone. You happy?" She plopped down next to Taylor.

"Yes," Tim said.

"So, are we talking about Will and Taylor's kiss?"

Taylor leapt to her feet. "No, we are not. Time to decorate the tree. Claire, help me with the lights."

"Taylor," Dad said, moving slowly off the couch. "Can I talk to you?" He motioned to the living room.

"See what you've done now?" she said over her shoulder to Tim then whispered to Claire, "If he grounds me, I'm running away from home."

Claire laughed.

In the living room, Dad clicked on a low light. "What's this kiss business? I thought you two were just friends."

She blushed. "He kissed me." Taylor fell to the couch and hugged a throw pillow, flipping the fringe between her fingers.

"He loves you."

She hopped up. "That's his problem." Her tone was deep and solid. "I've made my position clear. I'm not grabbing some romantic thread left dangling in the corridor of time. If I pull on it, my whole life unravels."

"Or your whole life is finally sewn up, neatly pieced together."

"Har, har. Very funny." Taylor tried to frown, but a smile tugged at her lips. "I'm pressing forward to what lies ahead, Dad. I'm thirty-three, at the crux of my career. If I don't get going soon, I'll be left behind. Technology changes so fast, companies reorganize on a whim. Dot-coms die overnight. Boswell Global is on the rise, and I want a California job with a big fat salary."

Dad tipped his head in understanding. "You're at the crux of love, too, Taylor. True love and men like Will are hard to find. I know you're determined to get this California job, but I'm warning you, as your father and friend, make sure. Look deep."

Tears burned in her eyes. "I'm sure, Dad. I'm sure."

He regarded her. "For some reason, I don't think you are."

"Taylor!" Claire ran into the room. "You have to come see this."

"See what?" Taylor followed her back into the family room and looked out the open side door.

There, standing in an old sleigh, was Will.

"Would you like to go for a ride?"

She pressed her hand over her mouth, hiding a big grin. He looked amazingly cute with his dark bangs flopping over a skier's headband.

The sleigh bells rang out as the horse shook his head. Harry answered with a sharp bark.

Will grinned. "I brought Harry along to chaperone."

Say no. No, Taylor. No. "Well, the family is here. We're decorating the tree—ouch," she said, rubbing the spot where Claire's sharp fingernail had jabbed her in the side.

"She'll be right out, Will."

Claire pulled her away from the door. "Get your coat. You may be moving to California, but you never pass up a romantic sleigh ride with a man as incredibly wonderful and good-looking as Will Adams."

"Claire, please. You're a young fool in love." Taylor stomped up the steps, Claire's hand pressing against her back.

"Say what you will, but if I were seven or eight years older, I'd be making goo-goo eyes at Will myself."

"Whatever. And I never make goo-goo eyes." Taylor yanked her coat from the hanger.

"Well, maybe you should."

Taylor zipped up her coat and sighed. "How do I look?"

"Beautiful. Now get going."

"Okay, okay. But, Claire, I'm not falling in love with Will. Been there, done that—not doing it again. In fact, this is the last time I'm hanging out with him."

"Yeah, you're like Dad. You say a lot of things."

✦✦

"It is beautiful," Taylor said, settling next to him with a deep sigh.

"You sound content." Will switched the reins from his right hand to his left, and despite the pump of adrenaline, he gingerly slipped his arm around her shoulders. She squared her shoulders, bumping his hand away, but he dropped it back into place, and after a few moments, she relaxed and leaned against him. Sort of.

"What a great way to start the Christmas season," she said. "Decorating the tree with the family and a sleigh ride with a friend."

"Sorry to interrupt your tree decorating."

Taylor nestled closer to him. "Are you kidding? The family practically kicked me out the door when you showed up."

He grinned. "So I noticed."

Taylor rested her head against his shoulder, and he wondered if she could hear his heartbeat beneath his coat.

"They think I'm in love with you."

"Are you?"

"No," she said with a *hmm* in her voice. "But you smell nice."

355

Chapter 20

Polo held his head high as he followed a moonlit path down Main Street. Will held the reins loosely in his left hand, guiding Polo out of town, but wrapped his right arm tighter around Taylor.

"It's cold," she said, snuggling closer. For once, she didn't stop to check the wall surrounding her heart, guarding against the charms of Will Adams. It felt good to be near him, locked in his embrace. Just for tonight.

"Do you want to go home?" He pulled her closer.

She shook her head. "No. I'm having fun."

"Be careful; you might fall in love with me."

She peered up into his face. "I'll let you have your dream."

He laughed. "My dream? Oh no, Taylor. My destiny. You are my destiny."

"That sounds like a line from a movie."

"It's from my heart." He brushed her cheek with his gloved hand, the leather reins dangling. "You *are* so beautiful."

Taylor's heart beat like thundering horses. She closed her eyes and buried her face in his shoulder. Dreamy, romantic notions threatened her resolve. "I can't—"

"Or you won't?"

"Please," she muttered.

"I won't stop telling you how I feel."

She sat up. "Neither will I."

"Then I guess we're at a stalemate."

She looked down. "We want different things."

"I used to think about you living up in New York. I wondered what you were doing and how you were doing," he said.

"I wondered about you, too."

"But I didn't call."

Taylor shook her head. "Neither did I."

"We chose career over love, I guess," he said.

"So you have to understand why this job in California is so important."

"So you have to understand why having you here is so important to me."

She shoved him slightly. "Don't make fun of me."

He pulled her close. "Never. I'm using your words to get you to understand."

Suddenly Polo stopped. Taylor glanced up. "Where are we?"

Will laughed as he wrapped both arms around her. "The covered bridge."

❧❧

They left Polo standing on the shoulder of the road and walked onto the bridge.

356

"When do you think you'll hear from Boswell Global?" Will asked. He had to leave the subject of *them* before Taylor's stubborn streak made her refuse to even spend time with him.

Her breath billowed in the cold as she said, "This week, I think. It's been two weeks already."

He leaned against the railing. "You've been a big help to Lambert's Furniture."

"Markie is catching on very quickly. She's going to be key to the new system's success."

The cold prevented them from staying too long on the bridge. As they walked back to the sleigh, they talked about their favorite Christmases. "I think this is my favorite Christmas," Taylor admitted, as Will gathered the reins and chirruped to Polo. "I'm actually baking cookies with Mom tomorrow night."

Will smiled. "I think this is my favorite, too."

They rode in a comfortable silence with only the sound of Polo's bells jingling and jangling, until Taylor asked out of the blue, "Do you think a Yankee like me can survive in California?"

His laugh rang out. "You can survive anywhere. The Californians won't know what hit them."

Taylor punched him lightly, giggling. "Stop."

"I'm serious. When you're around, Taylor, the atmosphere changes."

She settled against him. "It must be Jesus in me, 'cause I'm not that special."

"You are very special, but you let Him shine. A lot of people don't."

"You do."

He snuggled closer to her. "I try."

"I wanted to tell you, you're a very good boss."

He smirked. "You're excellent at what you do, too. We'd make a great team, Taylor."

To Will's delight and surprise, she leaned into him and purposefully, softly kissed him while Polo drew the sleigh over mounds of fresh snow toward the moonlit horizon.

❧

Early Monday morning, Taylor sat under twinkling Christmas lights at Peri's Perk, picking at a cinnamon muffin, clicking her fingernails against the sides of her latte cup and reliving her kiss with Will for the hundredth time.

Not his kiss. *Her* kiss. She caved, weakened by a romantic setting, and kissed him. She felt like a walking contradiction, and her actions weren't fair to Will.

"Hello, Taylor."

She shifted to see Julie Lambert walking toward her, smiling.

"Julie, good morning." Taylor rose and gave the pretty blond a hug.

"Mind if I join you? I have a few minutes to sit before school starts."

Taylor smiled. "Please do."

She watched as Julie picked a Danish and ordered coffee from Peri. Despite her feelings about her relationship with Will, Taylor loved the Lambert family.

She'd spent many summer nights eating Grandma Betty's barbecue, roasting marshmallows over an open pit, watching movies with the cousins, and playing basketball, football, and baseball.

"So, what is up with Taylor Hansen these days? By the way, you look fabulous." Julie settled on the high, round stool with her breakfast.

Taylor smiled. "Thank you, but I exercise too little and eat too much. Work too much."

Julie smiled. "Exercise? I see you running around town all the time. I have a treadmill that moonlights as a clothes hanger."

Taylor laughed. "It gets harder the older I get."

"Tell me about it," she said. "Between teaching at the elementary school, conducting private music lessons, and playing in a quartet, I never seem to find time to exercise."

"I'm surprised you and Ethan don't have a houseful of kids," Taylor said. "I hear they keep you running."

Julie's expression darkened, and she broke off the edge of her Danish without taking a bite. "Ethan and I can't have children."

"Oh, Julie, I'm sorry." Taylor's cheeks flushed.

With a small smile, Julie said, "No, it's okay. We are going to adopt next year."

Taylor rested her hand over her heart. "Wow, that's wonderful."

Julie leaned forward, placing her elbows on the table. "It was hard at first. . . when we found out. But life comes with unexpected curves and dead ends. The Lord has blessed us in so many other ways."

"Life does come with ups and downs, doesn't it?"

Julie paused for a moment, then said, "Ethan tells me you have a job opportunity in California."

Taylor sipped her coffee then bobbed her head yes.

"What about Will?" Julie asked, her expression pure and earnest.

"What about him?" Taylor retorted, gently setting her cup down.

"Honestly, Taylor. I mean, well, he's in love with you."

Taylor crossed her legs then uncrossed them. "What makes you say that?"

Julie laughed. "It's written all over his face. It was the talk of the kitchen cleanup crew Thanksgiving Day."

"We're keeping our relationship as friends."

Julie cocked one eyebrow. "Really? You know it's written all over your face."

Indignant, Taylor scoffed, "What's written on my face?"

"That you, my friend, are in love with Will Adams."

❧❧

Will headed to Ethan's office with a cursory glance down the hall toward Taylor's office. Her light was on, but he had yet to see her.

He'd been unable to sleep, so he'd taken an early run along the freshly salted White Birch streets, praying and asking for the Lord to intervene in his relationship with Taylor.

The memory of her kiss made his lips buzz, and he worried things would be uncomfortable when they saw each other.

When he knocked on Ethan's door, his cousin motioned for Will to come in.

"What's up?" Ethan reclined in his desk chair and locked his hands behind his head.

"Are those production reports right? We're up ten percent?"

Ethan nodded then said, "I just got off the phone with Julie."

Will crossed his arms and cocked his head to one side. "And she confirms our increased production?"

"She ran into Taylor at Peri's."

His heart thumped once. "That's nice."

"She asked Taylor about the two of you." Ethan's crooked, mischievous grin lit his face.

"Why would she do that?"

"Because the whole family can see that you two love each other."

Will rubbed his forehead with his fingers. "Can we forget about Taylor for a minute? About our production—"

"Can you forget about Taylor?" Ethan refused to let the topic fade.

"Can we get some *grown-up* work done?"

Ethan shook his head. "I'm telling you, Taylor—"

"Yes?" Taylor popped her head into Ethan's office. "Did you call me?" Her green eyes scanned the room.

Ethan laughed, slapping his knee.

"No," Will said, shooting a sharp glance at Ethan. "Sorry."

Taylor hesitated, looked Will in the eye for a lingering moment, then at Ethan. "What's so funny?"

"Nothing," Will said with a stifled smile when she looked back at him. Her gaze contained no emotion, as if her kiss never happened.

Taylor shrugged and continued down the hall.

Will leaned forward, placing his hands on Ethan's desk. "If you weren't my cousin, I'd fire you."

Ethan laughed. "Right. . ."

Will took a deep breath. "Can we get back to the business of Lambert's Furniture?"

Chapter 21

A little before eight p.m., Taylor's cell phone rang. Bleary-eyed from staring at the computer screen for almost thirteen hours, she batted her eyes to clear the fog from her contact lenses and answered with a raspy hello.

A low laugh sounded in her ear. "Did I wake you?"

Taylor straightened. "No."

"Good. This is Alex Cranston."

"Yes, I recognize your voice." She got up to pace, resting her hand on the small of her back.

"Welcome to Boswell Global."

"Thank you." She checked her cheer to maintain a professional tone. "That's wonderful."

"Corporate wants you right away, Taylor."

"Before Christmas?" Taylor understood Boswell Global would own her once she signed on the dotted line.

"By December 11, actually. That'll give you the rest of this week and next to make arrangements and drive out."

"Of course." She didn't sound confident. Not what Alex needed to hear.

Will's handsome face suddenly appeared in the doorway. He made an eating motion and whispered, "You want something to eat?"

Taylor held up one finger. To Alex she said, "Sounds good." For some reason, she didn't want Will to know. Not yet.

"I'll e-mail the formal offer. The salary is. . ."

Taylor gripped her middle when Alex said the amount—more than she'd asked for—and reminded her of their benefits package.

"Amazing," she said, tapping her fingers on the old polished desk. "Hard to turn down."

"They'll make you earn it."

"I can imagine."

A sharp memory of the corporate life stabbed at her. Long hours. Stress. Missed lunches. Fast-food dinners. Nonexistent personal life. She wondered if she was ready for the heavy commitment.

Will leaned against the door frame. He wore a navy button-down that matched his eyes. "Dinner?" he mouthed.

Taylor shrugged, listening to Alex, then shook her head no.

Will waited for a second, then left. For a brief, intense moment, she longed for him.

"So do I have a formal yes?" Alex prodded.

Taylor hesitated a fraction of a second. "Yes. You do. I accept."

"Excellent. Excellent. Listen, I've got a meeting, but why don't you give me a call tomorrow at your convenience, and we can talk start date and other details."

After saying good-bye to Alex, Taylor sat in front of the computer trying to remember what she was working on before his call.

But she couldn't. Unable to concentrate, she gave up, powered off her computer, and headed home, her emotions swirling with a mixture of exhilaration and anxiety.

Hands on his hips, Will looked at each face sitting at the boardroom table.

"What do you guys think?"

Bobby propped his elbows on the arms of his chair, his lips pursed. "I can't believe David Thomason called and offered us his business."

Ethan stood and walked around the long table. "This is amazing." He shook his head but smiled.

Grandpa agreed. "I've known David a long time. Thomason's produces quality furniture, but, Will, I'm sure his business practices are a mess."

Will nodded. "We'll perform a due diligence, of course. Ethan, I'd like you to do one on his environmental practices. Are they up to code, et cetera."

Ethan reached for his palm computer. "Will do."

Grandpa rapped on the table with his knuckles. "Wait, Will, are you boys saying you want to buy Thomason's?"

Bobby pushed away from the table then picked up his papers and laptop. "I need to meet with a new distributor down in Boston." He glanced around the room. "I'm for it. Let's buy Thomason's if the price is right and the due diligence report is good."

"I agree," Ethan said.

Will grinned. "I'll call Dave and set up a meeting."

Grandpa stood. "I think you boys are making the right decision." He walked to the door. "I'm going to see how Grant's doing down in production."

"Thanks for coming in for this meeting, Grandpa." Will waved at him as the elder Lambert exited. Grant Hansen had returned to work a few days ago, rested and healed. He'd taken over his supervisory duties without missing a beat.

"You know, Will," Ethan started, returning to his chair, "we could really use Taylor to help us with the due diligence and merging these two companies."

Will ran his hand over his hair. "We could."

"I mean, we can manage, but she'd be invaluable."

"Except for one thing. She's moving to California."

"Why don't you just ask her to marry you and stop this silly dance?"

"She doesn't want to marry me, Ethan. I've told you that."

"Have you formally asked her to marry you?"

"No, but she's made it clear she's moving on."

"Will, put it out there. Ask her to marry you. All she can do is say no." Ethan reached for his palm computer and stood.

"Whose side are you on?"

Ethan laughed as he walked toward the door. "Yours."

Will walked down to Taylor's office, pensive. "Knock, knock," he said outside her door.

She smiled and waved him in, finishing her conversation with Markie. "I think we're going to have to require this field, or we could lose the order information."

Markie sighed. "I agree, but it's just more for us to fill out."

"I'll try to find a shortcut or create a quick key or something. But we're going to have to use it."

"Let me go play around with it, too." Markie stood. "Hi, Will," she said as she left.

Will sat next to Taylor in Markie's vacant seat. "How's it going?"

"Good. Making headway."

"David Thomason called. He offered to sell us Thomason's Furniture."

Taylor's eyes widened. "Will, that's incredible. Are you going to take him up on it?"

"Probably." He hesitated. "I'm here to offer you the job as CFO."

"You're kidding."

❧❧

Awake most of the night, fighting anxiety, Taylor mentally designed a new inventory work flow for the production department to use once the new business system went online.

She tried not to think of moving three thousand miles away—tried not to think of Will's job offer or the ever-present memory of the sleigh ride kiss.

Around three a.m., she tiptoed downstairs and microwaved a cup of hot chocolate. She prayed in the family room then sat quietly, staring at the red, blue, green, and white lights of the Christmas tree.

Jesus came to bring peace, but all she felt was anxious, tired, frayed, and jittery. At six a.m., she woke again after dozing on the couch. From the kitchen, she heard the sounds of Mom making breakfast. "Hey, sweetie," Dad said, peering into the family room. "Sleep on the couch?"

She got up, straightening and plumping the couch pillows. "I came down for hot chocolate and the Christmas lights." She kissed him on the cheek as she passed, remembering how scared she was after his heart attack. What would life be without Grant Hansen? She didn't want to know.

From the stove, Mom offered to make Taylor a couple of eggs and toast.

"No thanks. I'm not hungry." Taylor went up to take a shower.

A little after lunchtime, in her Lambert's Furniture office, Taylor drew a deep breath and dialed Alex's number.

"Alex Cranston."

"Alex, hi, it's Taylor."

"Good morning."

She grinned. "Actually, it's afternoon here."

"Well, good afternoon then."

She rolled her eyes. He was far too chipper. "Yes, good afternoon."

He got right to business. "Here's the deal. We need you here by the eleventh." His words were firm, final.

"Is there any negotiation?" She bit her lower lip in anticipation.

"The January product launch is strategic to the company's financial goals, Taylor. I'm sure you understand the criticality of your involvement as CFO. You know—"

"Yes, I know." Taylor understood the meaning behind Alex's words. "I'll be there by the eleventh."

"Is there a critical reason why you need an alternate start date?"

"No." She sank to her chair. "Not really."

"Okay, good." His voice buoyed. "We'll put you up in a studio apartment until you find a place, and we'll take care of your initial food and other expenses."

"Of course." She forced a smile. "How's Christmas in California?"

"Beautiful."

"I'm sure it is." Maybe she could get her mom and dad to fly out so she wouldn't have to spend her first Christmas in California alone.

Wednesday night at church, the children's choir sang Christmas carols before the message. Little Susie Sharpton belted out "Away in a Manger" like a Broadway star.

Will applauded with the rest of the congregation, winking and waving at Jack and Max.

As Pastor Marlow blessed the children before they scurried away to children's church, Will felt a nudge on his arm.

"Move over."

He looked into Taylor's tired eyes. "You're working too hard," he whispered when she slid in next to him.

"Is that Max in the little suit?"

"Yes, and don't change the subject." He bumped her shoulder.

"I have a lot to do." Taylor bumped him back.

"Well, there's time. Don't kill yourself. Enjoy the holidays."

"Right."

Maybe it was his imagination, but Will thought he caught a flicker of sadness in her expression, just for a moment.

"There's a gathering at Grandma's after this."

"Thanks, but I think I'll go home."

He slipped his arm on the back of the pew and cradled her shoulders. "Cookies, eggnog, hot chocolate, warm fire, Christmas music, huge decorated tree. . ."

She shrugged away from his touch. "Shh, I'm listening to Pastor Marlow."

"Sorry." He pulled his arm back.

She propped her elbow on the pew's arm and rested her forehead in her hand.

Something had bothered her, Will could tell, for over a day now. He imagined it had something to do with the California job but didn't press her. He'd wait for her to open up in her way, in her time.

He whispered, "I'm here for you if you need me."

She nodded. "Thanks."

After the service, Will waited for Taylor outside the sanctuary doors. He felt awkward and a little like a desperate dog begging for a bone, but he'd decided to pursue Taylor until she married him. If she moved to California, he'd still pursue her, stopping only if she married someone else.

"It's cold tonight," he said, stepping in time with her.

He opened her car door for her after she pressed her remote access button. Taylor peered into his eyes. "Thank you for being my friend."

"You're welcome." He leaned toward her, wanting to kiss her, but Trixie suddenly appeared.

"Taylor, darling, there you are."

Will smiled. Taylor's mother looked so perfect in her matching coat and shoes and a sixties-style pillbox hat on her head, no less. Only Trixie.

"We're all going to Betty and Matt's for cookies and hot chocolate."

Will cocked his right eyebrow with an I-told-you-so smirk.

Taylor made a funny face. "I'm tired, Mom."

"Well, of course; you've been working unseemly hours. I haven't seen you for three days. You must join us at the Lamberts'."

Grant hammered the last nail. "Come, Taylor. It's a family night."

She agreed with a muffled okay. When Trixie and Grant walked away, Will stepped around the car door and drew her into his arms.

Taylor burst into tears. He ached to help her, to understand what storm brewed beneath her smooth-as-glass exterior. But he didn't ask questions. He just let her cry as he cradled her head with his hand.

Chapter 22

Every window of the Lamberts' home glowed with warm, golden light, and when Taylor turned into the driveway, she couldn't imagine being anywhere else right now.

Taking a moment to compose herself, she checked her face in the rearview mirror for mascara tracks and quieted her soul before the Lord.

"Father, You lead me. I'm not going to worry tonight."

Stepping out of the car, she saw Will walking her way, an oil lantern in his hand.

"What, out of flashlights?" She pointed to the lamp.

"No." He grabbed her hand. "It was on the porch. I grabbed the closest thing."

He led her to the house, his strong hand holding on to hers. If she could let her heart go for a moment, free to feel without consequence, Taylor would fall in love with him. She knew it.

He amazed her. His peace, his confidence, his unassuming manner. . .

Just beyond the front porch, he stopped. "It's a madhouse in there," he said, facing her.

She laughed. "I figured."

Two of the younger boys burst through the front door and thundered down the front steps, laughing and screaming.

"Oh, to be that carefree," Taylor said without preamble.

He chuckled. "Are you going to be okay?"

She nodded and dropped her head against his chest. "Sorry about earlier."

"Anytime. You've been working crazy hours."

"I want the installation to go well. Revenue is involved."

"Taylor, you've done a phenomenal job. Markie is begging me to find a way to keep you here."

She lifted her head to see his face. "I'm not sure you can afford me."

"I'm willing to try. The CFO job offer still stands." He brushed his cold hands along the sides of her face and hair.

"I know." She smiled and leaned into his touch.

"Can I kiss you?"

"Now you ask?"

He pulled her to him and gently pressed his lips to hers.

❦

The next morning, Taylor woke when her cell phone trilled. She looked at th clock on the nightstand. Nine o'clock!

She slapped her hand to her head. "I'm late." Scrambling out of bed, she reached for her phone. Probably Will.

"Is this Taylor Hansen?" a woman asked.

"Yes." Taylor hauled a pair of jeans and a sweater out of the dresser drawer.

"Wonderful," she said perkily. "This is Gretchen Levi from *Computing Today*."

Taylor jerked her head up. "*Computing Today*?"

"Yes, you're familiar with our magazine, right?"

Taylor swallowed. "Of course."

"Great. I'm doing a feature on women executives in dot-com companies. I'd love to feature the piece around you. Boswell Global's newest female exec and CFO."

They've sent out a press release already? "I haven't even started the job."

"Close enough in our book. This is a big coup for women in the dot-com world, Taylor. You're our icon." Gretchen's chipper voice grated on Taylor. Too early to be so cheerleader-like.

An hour later, Taylor hung up, finally finished talking with the gregarious Gretchen who'd asked a million questions. Thankfully, she didn't ask much about Blankenship & Burns.

While giggly, Gretchen proved to be a skilled reporter. Taylor felt a renewed excitement for her job.

❧❧

The story would run a week from Monday, hitting the streets on her first day at Boswell. What a nice way to start her career there—in the news.

Walking toward her office, Taylor heard Will and Bobby laughing, Ethan's deep voice weaving through their merriment.

She stopped, thinking no place would feel like Lambert's Furniture. Family. Comfortable. Peaceful.

She decided to tell Will that Friday was her last day. She had to leave on Sunday. Was it that soon?

Markie had made great progress in the HBS installation, and right after Christmas, training started. Taylor felt she was leaving them in capable hands.

"Taylor, good morning." Will met her in the hall and placed his arm around her shoulder. "Sleep in?"

She laughed and flipped on her office light. "Yes. Guess I was tired."

"It's ten thirty." Will gave an overexaggerated look at his watch. "Are you feeling okay?"

She set her purse on her desk and slipped out of her coat. "I need to talk to you."

"S—sure." He sat down.

A minute later, it was done. She told him. "Sunday, it's 'California, here I come.'"

He stared at her, his hands folded together in front of his face. "I can't believe you're going."

She couldn't look at him. Tracing her finger along the corner of her desk, she said, "It's an amazing opportunity. I never knew I could make so much money this soon in my career."

"I suppose it's especially sweet after New York." Will's words were strong, though his tone was low and soft.

Taylor nodded. "It is." Her gaze met his. "But thank you for the job here—and the CFO offer. I documented the procedures, setup, and work flows for the HBS system. They are stored out on the network." Taylor handed Will a single page of instructions.

He reached for it. "Thank you. I'll have Markie cut you a check." He started to say something but hesitated. "I'm not giving up on us." His voice was kind, but his words were sure.

Tears smarted in Taylor's eyes as Will walked out of her office. When her cell phone rang, she answered, grateful for the distraction. "Taylor Hansen."

"Congratulations! You got the job!"

She smiled, pressing on the edge of her eyes with her fingertips. "Indiana, hi. Yes, thanks to you."

"You're the industry buzz right now."

She set her hand on her waist. "What?"

"The word is you're the feature in *Computing Today*'s next issue."

"Word travels fast."

"Lisa Downey, eat your heart out, eh?"

"No, Indiana, I wish her well," Taylor said. "She taught me a lot."

"Well, you're on to bigger and greener pastures," Indiana said.

"Right. Bigger, greener." Taylor glanced down the hall toward Will's office.

❧❧

"Are you sure?"

Will leaned toward Matilda, White Birch Bank's senior teller. "I'm sure."

She shook her head, muttering, "Well, I never," under her breath.

"First time for everything, Tildy," Will said with a wink.

"I've never known you to withdraw so much as a penny, let alone. . ."

Will tucked his money away, waved to the bank president, Fred Moon, and walked out the door.

Fresh snow drifted from low, gray clouds. Will tucked his coat collar around his neck and walked to his truck. Opening his door, he beckoned to Harry. "Come on, boy."

When he passed Duke's Barber Shop, he stuck his head in the doorway. "Need a haircut. I'll be back in about a half hour."

Duke waved from where he worked on Tom Laribee's balding head. "I'll hold my breath."

Will laughed and continued down Main Street, past Sam's. When he got to

Earth-n-Treasures by Cindy Mae, he stopped and wiped his clammy hands down the sides of his khakis. He felt hot and nervous, yet peaceful and excited.

"Lord, here we go." Will was leaping out in faith, knowing the hand of the Lord would catch him. He had to take a chance; he had to risk it all.

"Will Adams." Cindy Mae looked up from her workbench on the far side of the shop. "I never thought I'd see you in here." She snorted.

He made a face. "You're seeing me now."

She hopped down from her large wooden stool, settling her hands on her wide, round waist. "What can I do for you? Something for your mom? Grandma Betty?" Harry nuzzled her leg, and she patted him on the head.

"No." Will pulled a printed Web page from his coat pocket. "I want this ring."

She whistled loud and long. "You're not going for cheap, are you?"

"I'd like to have it by Saturday."

"Saturday? What's this, an emergency engagement?"

He cleared his throat. "Can you have it by Saturday?"

"Let me do some checking. Be right back." She maneuvered her large frame toward the back office. "There are some dog treats over by the door if Harry wants one."

Will pulled a crunchy bone from a plastic container and gave it to his furry companion.

His blood pumped. He'd discovered the ring about a month ago while surfing the Web. If a man could fall in love with jewelry, he guessed he had with this ring. Elegant and modern, bold and beautiful, it was a platinum and diamond representation of Taylor Hansen.

This is crazy. But at the very core of his being, Will knew he had to ask Taylor to marry him. Ethan was right. He'd said everything but "Will you marry me?"

"I have two options for you," Cindy Mae said, coming toward him. "I can get this ring in by tomorrow afternoon." She held up the picture Will gave her. "Or, I have this piece here." Cindy Mae held up a black, felt-covered ring box.

Will took it from her and pulled the ring from the slit. It was beautiful.

"Same karat weight as the one in the picture. Brill and I picked it up at an estate sale last summer. Belonged to old Martin G. Snodgrass."

Will snapped his head up. "The old bachelor?"

Cindy Mae nodded. "One and the same. He fell in love with Carrie Waterhouse back in the sixties. But she was a wild child and ran off to California to make it in the movies."

Cindy Mae's words pelted him like hailstones. *"Ran off to California."* He put the ring in the box and thrust it at her.

"No thanks."

Cindy Mae gently closed the box's lid. "It's a beautiful ring, Will. Cheaper than the one you wanted."

"It's not the money," he said, looking her in the eye. He wanted something new. Something fresh. A ring that had never been slipped on a woman's finger with the words "Will you marry me?"

He didn't want a ring that signified a man's broken heart, a ring that signified a woman running off to California. He didn't want to be another Martin G. Snodgrass.

"Suit yourself," Cindy Mae said. "I'll have this ring for you by tomorrow." She tapped the printed paper.

"How much?" Will pulled the bundle of bills from his inside pocket, unable to suppress a buoyant smile.

"Cash?" Cindy Mae said, her brows raised. "Well, well. Will Adams is finally in love."

"No, Will Adams is finally putting his money where his heart is."

Chapter 23

Friday night, Taylor packed. She separated her clothes into piles: California clothes and Northeast United States clothes. Claire sat on her bed, cross-legged, reading a teen magazine.

"Okay, Claire, pick what you want from this pile." Taylor motioned to the Northeast pile.

Claire poked her pretty face from behind the magazine. "Are you kidding me?" She tossed the magazine onto Taylor's desk. "This is all designer stuff, isn't it?"

Taylor anchored her hands on her hips. "Yes."

"I don't believe it." Claire picked up a cashmere sweater. Her mouth dropped open when she looked at the label. "My friends are going to die."

"Well, just don't rub their noses in it." Taylor picked a pair of slacks from the California pile and put them in her suitcase.

"Did I tell you Dad agreed to pay for half of my plane ticket when I visit you over Christmas break?"

Tears burned in Taylor's eyes. "Great. I can't wait. We'll go shopping, and you can help me replenish my wardrobe."

"You won't have to work too much will you?" Claire asked, reaching for a dark wool suit.

Taylor sighed. "Probably. But we'll have some part of the evening and weekends."

The teenager shrugged. "Would you mind if Chelle came with me?"

Taylor shook her head. "The more the merrier."

Leaving the family so close to Christmas tore at her. For the first time in years, she'd hoped to spend the Christmas season with the family, not dashing down from the city late on Christmas Eve only to leave Christmas Day after dinner.

White Birch Community Church had a Christmas play this year, and Pastor Marlow would play Joseph. Taylor so wanted to see it.

She'd imagined staying up late after the Christmas Eve service to watch Christmas movies and drink hot chocolate with Mom.

She wanted to wake up Christmas morning and listen to her father read about the birth of Jesus from Luke's Gospel. She wanted to help Mom and Dana cook a turkey dinner and learn, finally, how to make homemade rolls.

"I'm trying this on," Claire said, dashing from the room with a red dress in her hands. "It's perfect for Christmas Eve."

Taylor answered without looking up. "Okay." She sat down on her bed, a silk blouse in her hands. Missing Christmas. It's the price she paid.

Boswell needed her, and she had a feeling *Computing Today*'s article hitting the newsstands the same day she started her job was not coincidental.

It bolstered her confidence to know Boswell invested so much in her—from her salary right down to a news article.

"Besides," she said, getting up to resume packing, thoughts of Will flickering across her mind. "Other than family, there's no reason for me to stay in White Birch. None. The first day of the rest of my life begins with Boswell Global."

❧❧

From his chair, Grandpa watched Will pace. "You've talked to Grant, I assume."

Pensively, Will said, "Today. After I picked up the ring."

"And?"

Will faced his grandfather. "He said it was between me and Taylor, and if I could get a yes out of her, he'd be amazed. But I have his blessing and prayers."

Grandpa grinned. "He's got a point."

"I don't care. I let her get away before; if I don't ask her to marry me now, I may never get another chance."

Grandpa looked proud. "Good. You don't want to go through life wondering."

"Not about this. Not about Taylor. She's amazing, isn't she?"

"Yes, she is. Tell me, what are you going to say to her?"

Will stopped and raised his hand to lean on the mantel. "I don't know. Give her the ring—ask her to marry me." He held out his hands in question.

Grandpa cocked a brow. "That's it?"

Will pondered a minute, his chin raised. "Yeah, that's it."

Grandpa rose to his feet, chuckling. "Now look, son, I'm not a great romantic, but I've learned over the years that women like the flowery words."

Will slapped his hand to his forehead. "Flowers. Should I get flowers?"

Grandpa laughed outright. "No, no, I said flowery *words*. Tell her how you feel. Tell her what's in your heart."

"She knows how I feel."

Grandpa shook his head. "Don't tell me you need me to be your Cyrano de Bergerac."

Will furrowed his brow. "No, I don't need you to whisper sweet nothings in my ear."

"Let me remind you that the beautiful, intelligent Taylor Jo Hansen is not waiting for you to come calling. If you want her to say yes, you're going to have to bare your soul. Lay it on the line."

Will clenched and released his fists, still pacing. "You're right." He looked at Grandpa. "I know what I want. I know how I feel, but saying it in a way to win Taylor. . .I'm going to need the help of angels."

"Well, you're in luck. I happen to know our Father in heaven commands the angels. Let's pray and ask Him for a little assistance."

"Thanks, Grandpa."

⌖

Around nine, Claire gathered up the clothes Taylor had given her and went downstairs to watch a Christmas special with Mom. Taylor promised to join them in a minute.

She was leafing through a stack of financial periodicals when a familiar, strong voice spoke to her from the door.

"Is someone in this room moving to California?"

She whipped around, her hand jerking to her hair and her heart beating like a runner taking off at the sound of the gun.

"Will." *I'm a mess.* "W–what are you doing here?"

"Came by to see my friend."

Her cheeks flushed when he winked at her.

"Sorry I'm such a—I mean—the room is such a mess."

His gaze never left her face. "The room is beautiful."

⌖

He held out his hand. "Come on."

She slipped her hand into his. Downstairs, the family sat way too quietly in the family room. Taylor wondered what was going on as she put on her boots and coat.

"I'm going out with Will for a while," she called.

"Okay," they answered in unison.

She made a face at Will. "That's odd. Usually when they're watching a movie the house could practically burn down around them and they'd never know it."

Will opened the front door. "Who knows? It's Christmas."

Outside, the night was cold and clear. Taylor bumped Will. "What, no horse and sleigh?"

He smiled and bumped her back. "No, just you and me."

His tone sent a tingle down to her toes. When he slipped his gloved hand into hers, she wrapped her fingers around his and suddenly wanted the moment to never end.

Our last night together, she thought. Out of nowhere, her heart was overwhelmed with love for him. She tightened her jaw and pressed her lips together to keep the tears at bay.

Tomorrow night was the family Christmas dinner—weeks before the actual day—but it was their only chance to celebrate. Sunday she planned to visit New York City to say good-bye to Reneé and several of her girlfriends. Monday, she began the journey of her life.

But for now, she decided to live in the moment. "White Birch is beautiful this time of year. All the lights and decorations. . ."

"It is," Will said.

They walked several blocks toward the town square where a giant Christmas tree, much like the one in New York's Rockefeller Center, twinkled in the night.

"I watched Markie run a complete trial data conversion today. It went really well. We also reviewed the installation checklist."

He let go of her hand to put his arm around her. "Thank you. But let's not talk about business systems right now."

He made her nervous.

Suddenly Taylor heard music and found Will leading her down a path lined with dozens of glowing sand bags. "Will, what are you up to?"

Will stopped at the tall, thick Christmas tree, his pulse thundering so loudly he wondered if he'd be able to hear himself propose.

He envied ninety percent of the other men in the world who popped the question to women willing to say yes.

No guts, no glory, he thought. For the first time, he understood the depth of Taylor's devastation when she leapt out on the wings of faith and asked him to marry her.

Now the tables were turned.

"Let's have a seat." He led Taylor to the back of his truck where a thermos of hot chocolate and a pile of blankets awaited them. He opened the tailgate and helped her up.

"Did you do all this?" she murmured.

"Yes, it's your going away present." He felt cautious, afraid to reveal his hand too soon. He propped himself against the side of the truck and swept Taylor into his arms.

"You're scaring me," she said with a shaky laugh.

Will kissed her hair then rested his chin on the top of her head.

Her body stiffened. "Will, I'm leaving in three days."

He nuzzled the back of her neck. "You smell good."

"Will—" She scooted around to face him. "Please."

He cupped her face in his hands. "I love you, Taylor." He kissed her lightly, tenderly.

When he released her, words flew out of her mouth. "Why, Will, why? Why now? Why not ten years ago? What do you want me to do with this information? Not go to California because you love me?"

"No." He resituated himself so he could retrieve the ring box from his pocket. "I don't want you to go to California because I can't live without you."

"You seem to have survived until now."

He pressed his finger over her lips. "Can I finish?"

She sucked in her bottom lip and nodded.

"You are the most incredible woman I've ever met." He looked into her green eyes. "You inspire me. You make me want to live my life better; achieve all I can achieve. Love the Lord more; love others more. I let you go ten years ago, but I can't let you leave without telling you how I feel now."

"I know how you feel." Her words landed hard, like bricks being added to a wall.

He laughed softly, the tension between them rising. "I've been praying all day about what I want to say to you."

"And?"

"I have peace. No words, just peace."

She leaned against the side of the truck and regarded him. "That's what I love most about you. The peace you exude. Not just any peace, but the peace of Jesus. I'm always so anxious."

"We'd make a good pair then."

She snarled. "Ten years ago, maybe."

"Taylor, I wouldn't have been a good husband ten years ago."

She adjusted the blanket around her legs. "Maybe I wouldn't have made a good wife."

He reached for her hand. "We loved each other. But I had grad school on my mind and wanted life to selfishly revolve around me."

"I wanted to move to New York and have a big-city career." She looked at him as a light, chilly breeze brushed through her hair. "But I like to think I would have given it up for you. I really loved you, Will."

"You would have resented me."

"Maybe." She shivered in the cold and fell against him.

"How about right now?" He wrapped her in his arms.

"What do you mean?"

He dug the ring box out of his pocket. "Would you give up California for love? For me?" He could feel her tremble. "Taylor, if you go to California, fine. But go knowing I'm yours and you are mine." He opened the box, and the ring sparkled in the glow of the candles and Christmas lights.

She gasped and covered her face with her hands.

"Taylor, marry me."

Chapter 24

It wasn't supposed to be like this. Will asking her to marry him with candles and music on their last night together.

"You're kidding, right?"

Will took the ring from the box. "Does it look like I'm kidding?"

Her hand shook as she reached for the ring. "It's beautiful."

But she pulled her hand back. If she touched the jeweled piece, if she let him slide it on her finger, she'd never move to California. Never.

"Taylor?" Will turned her face to his.

She jumped off the tailgate. "What are you doing, Will? I can't marry you." With long strides, she started down the sidewalk. She stopped and whipped around. "Marry you? I'm moving in three days, Will. *Computing Today* is doing a story on me and my new job. It comes out the day I start!"

He walked toward her. "You're going to base a major life decision on a magazine article?"

"No, Will, I'm making a major life decision based on years of hard work. Am I supposed to say no to a tremendous job opportunity because Will Adams finally got his act together and asked me to marry him?" She stepped his way, hating her words but unable to cap her anger. "Ten years *too late*."

Will grabbed her arms. "No, I'm asking you to say yes to the greatest love of your life. You may think it's ten years too late, Taylor, but our time is now."

She jerked herself free. "No, Will. No."

❧❧

On the west side of Kansas, weary and hungry, Taylor pulled into a small diner around seven o'clock. A light snow fell as she stepped out of the car, an empty soda cup and fast-food bag wadded up in her hands. She stretched, taking a deep breath, cleansing away the fog in her mind.

She felt dull and lifeless, and dazed from the endless stretch of prairie highway. The cold evening air refreshed her, but the gentle snow reminded her of home. Of Will.

She'd cried for two days after leaving Will standing alone in the flickering lights of the White Birch Christmas tree.

Her visit with Reneé in New York centered around sobs and tissues, and ping-pong dialogue about Will's last ditch proposal.

"Sounds incredibly romantic, Taylor, but you can't pass on Boswell because Will's trying to get what he can't have," Reneé had concluded over a large slice of New York–style pizza.

Taylor shook her head. "He's not like that. If he didn't mean it, he wouldn't have asked." Then the tears had surfaced again, and Reneé handed her another tissue. "But I made a commitment to Boswell Global."

On the roof of the Kansas diner, a red-nosed, blinking Rudolph reminded her she'd be spending Christmas away from home. Mom and Dad agreed to come for New Year's, right after Claire and Chelle's visit. Taylor tossed her trash in the garbage can and stepped inside the diner. It was cozy and quaint, and she was the only customer.

A slender, gray-haired woman behind the counter greeted her. "Be right with ya, hon."

Taylor reached for a menu, her mind numb, her thoughts wandering. For the first day and a half of her journey west, she'd cried. Tears of anger—tears of heartbreak.

She'd waited ten years to hear those words from Will. She'd waited ten years to get an offer like the one from Boswell Global. "Oh, Father, I need wisdom."

"What'll it be?" the woman asked, her order pad in her hand. Her name tag read LANA.

"Diet soda and a large garden salad."

"Would you like grilled chicken or steak on the salad?"

Taylor thought for a moment. "Grilled chicken."

"You okay, honey?" Lana asked.

Taylor glanced up into a warm, friendly face. "Tired."

"Long journey."

Taylor winced at the irony. "Yes, very long."

By the time Lana brought her dinner, snow fell in big, round flakes.

"Snow's coming down pretty hard," Lana said.

Taylor smiled with a nod and picked up her knife and fork. "I'd better hurry."

"There's a motel about a mile down the road. You should stop there for the night." Lana crossed her arms and leaned against the booth.

"Thank you." Taylor wondered why Lana hung around. She was hungry and wanted to eat, but not with an audience.

"Hard decision, wasn't it?"

Taylor had just cut into her chicken. "Excuse me?"

"Hard decision—to leave love for a job."

Taylor felt the blood drain from her face. "How do you know that?"

Lana smiled as she slipped her hands into the side pockets of her uniform skirt. "The Lord spoke to me as you came in the door."

Tears burned in Taylor's eyes. "Who are you?"

Lana tugged on her name tag. "Lana Carr. My husband, Ralph, and I own this place. Been here thirty-two years."

"How do you know about my decision?"

Lana motioned to the bench across from Taylor. "May I?"

"Please." She offered her hand. "My name's Taylor."

Lana slipped into the booth. "Pleased to meet you." She shook Taylor's hand then turned and hollered across the empty dining room. "Ralph, bring me a coffee, please."

"All righty." The answer came from somewhere in the kitchen along with the clanging of pots.

"How do you know about my decision?" Taylor asked again.

Lana smiled. "I'm just a friend of Jesus, same as you."

Taylor sat back. A friend of Jesus? The notion warmed her all over. "He told you about me?" She reached for her fork and speared a slice of chicken and tomato.

Lana rested her arms on the table. "This is our slow time of night. I pray when we hit these lulls, and I simply felt the Lord speaking to me about a woman who's torn between love and her career. I started interceding; then you walked in."

"You knew I was the one."

"I did."

Ralph came to the table with Lana's coffee. "This the young lady you've been praying for?"

"Yes. Taylor, this is my husband, Ralph."

Taylor reached up and shook his hand. "A pleasure to meet you."

"Same here," Ralph said then excused himself.

"Why did the Lord tell you about me?" Taylor asked, shoving the food around on her plate, her appetite waning.

"I wondered that myself," Lana said, holding her coffee cup and cooling the coffee with a quick puff. Taylor sipped her diet soda, studying Lana. She felt comfortable and at home with the genteel woman. She let the words flow from her heart.

"I am so torn. The job in California is an incredible opportunity. But Will Adams is an incredible man and probably the love of my life."

"And you can't have both?" Lana asked.

Taylor gave Lana a wry smile, shaking her head. "He runs a family business in New Hampshire. He can't leave."

"What about you? Do you have family in New Hampshire?"

With that question, Taylor's heart came alive. "Yes." She described her mom and dad, her brother and his family, and the beautiful pieces of fabric that made up the community quilt of White Birch.

"Sounds like a wonderful town."

"It is." Taylor took another bite of salad and washed it down with a sip of soda.

"What about this job?"

Taylor laughed, thinking of the comparison. "Work, work, work. Lots of money. Sunshine. More work."

"A new life, eh?" Lana said.

"Sort of more like a major career move."

Lana looked down and, from Taylor's angle, it looked like her lips moved in prayer.

After a few seconds, Lana said, "I had an opportunity many years ago to move to Hollywood and be in the movies."

Taylor's eyes widened in surprise. "Really?"

"Yes, I was one of those 'discovered' girls. Local beauty contest. You've heard the stories."

"That must have been exciting."

Lana shook her head. "I felt like the queen of the universe. Once the talent agent called me, I was knocking the dust of this little town off my feet and moving to Hollywood."

"What happened?" Taylor scooped up more salad then buttered a corner of her roll.

"That man in there happened. We were high school sweethearts. He wanted to marry me. But I refused. How could I turn down Hollywood?"

"I know," Taylor said. "That's how I feel."

Lana nodded with understanding. "Finally my wise mother pulled me aside. She said, 'Lana, it's okay to choose love.'"

Taylor sat back, her brow furrowed, the simple words *choose love* drilling into her heart. "What did that mean?"

"That if I chose to stay home and marry Ralph, that was just as wonderful as moving to Hollywood to be a star. Even more so."

"You chose love."

Lana smiled. "I did. Forty years, five children, and twelve grandchildren later, I can honestly say I've never doubted my decision."

Taylor leaned forward, wrinkling her nose. "Don't you wonder how Hollywood would have gone? Would you have become a famous star? Become rich? Lived a life of glamour?"

"Most of the girls rounded up by that agent ended up with nothing. Not one made it. A couple of them had flash fame and married rich men but wound up divorced, in custody battles—several of them were addicted to drugs and alcohol."

"Wow."

"Truth is, Taylor, I might have made it. But the Lord's will for me was right here in Kansas. Ralph built this diner, and we've led so many people to the Lord I can't count them all. It downright humbles me. Out here in the middle of nowhere, God sends us people who need His love."

"And I'm one of them."

"I suppose so."

"Oh, Lana, what do I do?"

"Tell me. Do you love him?"

Taylor lowered her head. Until now, she'd never allowed herself to ask that question. She had loved him. Past tense. But did she love him now? Present tense?

"Taylor?"

She looked up at Lana. "Yes, I love him. Very much." As soon as she said the words, peace fell over her. A sure, strong, steady peace.

"Then choose love, Taylor. Choose love."

❧

Will dialed her cell phone for the fifth time that night. Once again, her voice mail answered. Once again, he left a message.

"I'm coming to visit you over Christmas."

Taylor left six days ago, and he'd managed short, tense conversations with her the first two days. He hadn't spoken to her since.

She'd be in California by now, but he wasn't giving up. He was keeping to Grandma's plan. Pursue her until she married someone else—or he flat grew weary. But that would take awhile.

He missed her. Everywhere he went, he thought of her. Work, the park, Peri's, the diner, church. . . In the core of his being, he knew Taylor Hansen was his wife.

"Lord, how long do I have to wait?"

Harry listened from his bed by the fireplace as Will talked out loud. His home didn't feel like home anymore. It needed a woman's touch. It needed Taylor.

She's not even here and she's driving me crazy. He grabbed his coat and keys. "Be back later, Harry."

He drove downtown, not sure where he wanted to go or what he wanted to do. Unclipping his cell phone, he dialed Ethan.

"Are you in the mood for some of Sam's pie?"

"Not tonight. Julie's playing down in Manchester with the quartet. I'm on my way down there."

"Have a good time." Will slowed and pulled into a slot in front of the diner.

"Why don't you give Grandpa a call?"

"I just might." But there was no answer at Grandpa's, Dad's, or Bobby's, so Will decided to eat his pie alone.

Sam's was crowded. Will waved to the proprietor as he looked for a table by the fireplace. It was a cold night, and he doubted he'd find one. But as he walked toward the back, a couple vacated a table for two, and Will took their place.

A seat for me. A seat for Jesus, he thought.

Janet handed him a menu. "Eating alone tonight?"

Will grinned. "Not really."

Janet cocked a brow. "Oh, expecting someone?"

"No," Will said, trying not to laugh out loud.

Janet shook her head. "Whatever. What'll it be, Will?"

"Coffee and the biggest slice of. . ." He looked over the menu. "Apple pie a la mode."

"Coming up." She took the menu and hurried away.

Will's gaze roamed the diner. Jordan and Mia sat on the other side, deep in conversation. He was happy for them. He saw several families from church, and—oh, Grandpa and Grandma. He thought of joining them, but they looked like they were enjoying their time together.

The fire crackled behind him, and the diner's music consisted of clinking dishes and the steady murmur of voices in conversation.

He glanced toward the front door just as it opened and Taylor walked in.

His heart jumped to his throat and he couldn't breathe. Slowly, he rose to his feet.

Her eyes scanned the room as if searching for someone. When her gaze landed on him, she stormed across the diner.

"All right, all right," she said in a voice too loud.

Will moved toward her. "Taylor, what are you doing here?" He couldn't hold back a grin. Her dark hair stood on end, and her coat slipped off one shoulder and down her arm. Her designer handbag dangled from the tips of her fingers.

"There I am, halfway across the country, exhausted, crying every tear I could cry. . ."

"Do you want to sit down?" He reached for her, motioning to the other chair. Laughter bubbled from deep inside.

She jerked away from him. "No, no, I don't want to sit down."

"O–okay."

"I'm halfway across the country—I said that. Okay, I stop at this little diner to eat, out in the middle of nowhere. Nowhere, Will." Her green eyes locked on his face.

"Nowhere," he echoed.

"I finally stopped crying. I was over you. Over you."

"Over me," he said with a nod, suddenly aware of the quiet and that all eyes were on them.

"So this lady, Lana, is talking to Jesus. He tells her about me. Not me, but a woman who is choosing between love and career. Can you believe that? I never, I mean never—and she says to me, 'Choose love.' Choose love!"

Will's middle tightened with anticipation. Taylor made no sense, but he didn't care. "Love is good."

"Why did you do this to me? Why? Six days on the road and I'm still in White Birch!" She whacked his arm with her purse.

Will reached for her and pulled her to him. "What are you talking about?"

Tears streamed down her face. "I love you, Will. Always have. Always will."

He kissed her. At first tenderly then with every emotion in his heart.

The diner erupted with applause and cheers.

"All right!"

"Way to go, Will and Taylor!"

"About time!"

Taylor wrapped her arms around him and bored her head into his shoulder, weeping. "Marry me, Will. Marry me."

He stepped back and lifted her head. "No."

"What?" she asked, her expression twisted with confusion.

Slowly, Will dropped to one knee.

Taylor laughed through her tears, wiping her eyes with the back of her hand. Janet waved a napkin at Taylor with one hand, blowing her own nose with the other.

"Taylor," Will began, looking up at her, "I love you. Always have, always will. Will you marry me?"

She laughed and gripped his collar, pulling him off his knees. "Yes. Yes! I'll marry you."

He picked her up and whirled her around, laughing and hooting. When he set her down, he looked her in the eyes and kissed her with passion.

Epilogue

"Are you sure?" Will set a plate of spaghetti with his homemade sauce in front of Taylor. Behind him, the window framed a snowy January twilight evening. Miniature snowflakes swirled and floated toward the ground.

She smiled up at him, winkling her nose. "It's unusual, isn't it—getting married in the town square?"

He laughed softly, sitting in the chair across from her at his kitchen table. "Yes, but"—he nodded to one side—"with you, I should never count on life being *usual*."

Taylor slid her spaghetti aside and leaned toward him on her elbows. "And I can't imagine life without you—usual or not."

Will met her smiling face halfway across the table. "I want to marry you. I'd do it tomorrow, if you'd agree. So I don't care if we get married in a church, in the woods, or in White Birch's center square as long at the end of the ceremony, *you* are my wife."

She tapped her nose against his. "And you will be my husband."

He lowered his lips to hers, kissing her with longing. "May can't come soon enough."

❧❧

On the first Saturday in May, the sun drifted west across the late afternoon sky, blue with wispy white clouds. The spring breeze carried a hint of last winter's chill along with the balmy promise of summer.

A little before five o'clock, White Birch residents walked toward the white gazebo set up in the town square, swinging shiny tin lanterns from their fingers.

Taylor watched from inside Peri's Perk.

"Are you nervous?" Elle asked, slipping her arm around Taylor's shoulders. She wore a tea length garnet matte satin gown with a wide skirt and belle sleeves.

"My stomach feels like I'm on a rollercoaster." Taylor pressed her hand against her middle, smiling softly at her matron of honor. "The dresses are beautiful," she added glancing from Elle to her bridesmaids, Claire and Reneé, dressed in the same style dresses. "I hope it's not too cold."

Elle brushed her hand down Taylor's white satin sleeve. "We'll be fine. Relax, enjoy your day." She grinned with a giggle. "Will's eyes are going to pop out when he sees you. You're the most beautiful bride I've ever seen."

Taylor stepped closer to Peri's large, paned window where the stream of lantern light continued to flow toward the gazebo. "It is a lovely night, isn't it?"

Agreeing in soft intonation, her bridesmaids gathered around her. "Oh, there's Dad." Taylor pressed her hands over her middle again with a shaky laugh. "I'm really nervous now."

Elle picked up her rose trimmed lantern. "Claire, Renée, are you ready?" She walked toward the front door, then turned to Taylor. "Remember, relax, enjoy your day."

"Well, well," Dad said, his eyes glistening. "Don't you look like a picture."

Taylor tugged at the edges of the matching white jacket her mother made to go with the gown. "My day's finally here."

Dad stepped closer, drawing Taylor to him. "Will's pacing anxiously. You ready?"

"I'm ready." Despite the nervous twitter, Taylor's words ran true in her own heart.

Peri shoved open the door, grinning, her clipboard tucked under her arm. "Julie's quartet is playing Pacabel's, Taylor. It's time."

Dad held out his elbow and Taylor slipped her around through his. Walking the rose petaled path from Peri's, down Main Street, to the gazebo, she tried to take in all the smiling faces and whispers of congratulations.

But as she neared the gazebo, peace wrapped around her when her gaze met Will's. The guests and music faded into the background. Only Will mattered. The expression on his angular, handsome face caused a warm swirl in her middle.

When Dad stopped in front of Will, Pastor Marlow asked, "Who gives this woman to be married to this man?"

Dad started to speak, but his voice broke. He pressed his fist to his lips, then managed a whispered, "Her mother and I."

Tears flooded Taylor's eyes when Dad placed her hand in Will's. He leaned down to her ear, squeezing her hand with his. "You take my breath away."

She smiled, gazing at him through watery eyes. "You look amazing."

They took the gazebo steps and met Pastor Marlow under the glow of a thousand tiny white lights, and Taylor and Will were finally married.

A Letter to Our Readers

Dear Readers:

In order that we might better contribute to your reading enjoyment, we would appreciate your taking a few minutes to respond to the following questions. When completed, please return to the following: Fiction Editor, Barbour Publishing, Inc., P.O. Box 719, Uhrichsville, OH 44683.

1. Did you enjoy reading *New Hampshire Weddings* by Rachel Hauck?
   ❏ Very much—I would like to see more books like this.
   ❏ Moderately—I would have enjoyed it more if _____
   _____
   _____

2. What influenced your decision to purchase this book?
   (Check those that apply.)
   ❏ Cover   ❏ Back cover copy   ❏ Title   ❏ Price
   ❏ Friends   ❏ Publicity   ❏ Other

3. Which story was your favorite?
   ❏ *Lambert's Pride*   ❏ *Lambert's Peace*
   ❏ *Lambert's Code*

4. Please check your age range:
   ❏ Under 18   ❏ 18–24   ❏ 25–34
   ❏ 35–45   ❏ 46–55   ❏ Over 55

5. How many hours per week do you read? _____

Name _____

Occupation _____

Address _____

City_____ State_____ Zip_____

E-mail_____